A ROYAL MILE

RETURN TO DUBLIN STREET
BOOK TWO

SAMANTHA YOUNG

A Royal Mile
By Samantha Young

Copyright © 2025 Samantha Young

Cover Design By Emily Wittig
Edited by Jennifer Sommersby Young
Proofread by Julie Deaton

ABOUT THE AUTHOR

Samantha is a *New York Times*, *USA Today*, and *Wall Street Journal* bestselling author and a Goodreads Choice Awards Nominee. Samantha has written over 60 books and is published in 31 countries. She writes emotional and angsty romance, often set where she resides—in her beloved home country Scotland. Samantha splits her time between her family, writing and chasing after two very mischievous cavapoos.

ALSO BY SAMANTHA YOUNG

The Fragile Ordinary

To all the Nate and Liv fans.
I hope you love the beautiful future I gave them and the
beautiful Lily they gave to us.

CHAPTER ONE
LILY

Edinburgh, Scotland

Cars and black cabs continually moved up and down Leven Street. My gaze wandered from the street to the shops opposite the flat, to the Victorian apartments above them that mirrored the one I stood within. My fingers twitched on the curtains as I attempted to dispel the melancholy hovering over me.

Bruntsfield has been my home for two years. After a year in university accommodation, Madison, my freshman roommate and best friend, and I moved into this flat near the Meadows, a park close to the main campus. We were a quick walk to the library and the Dugald Stewart Building, which housed my psychology classes. The flat was old with a crappy heating system, several broken sash-and-case windows, and a stubborn mice problem. But it was airy and roomy, and it held within it two years of memories. Some extremely happy. Some not so much.

But it was home.

And it was my final year here with Maddie.

A soft object connected with the back of my head, bringing me out of my musings. A sharp glance over my shoulder informed me the object was a cushion and my attacker was Madison.

She grinned unrepentantly from her spot on the sofa next to Sierra. "Hey, daydream believer, I've been calling your name."

I turned, settling against the windowsill. "Sorry. What's up?"

"It's our first night back at uni. We need to celebrate," Sierra, our podcast cohost, piped up in her American accent. She was a full-time international student at the University of Edinburgh, originally from New Hampshire. We'd met in one of my English lit modules in freshman year before I made the switch to psychology. Sierra wanted to work her way up to becoming a developmental editor at a publisher when she moved back to the States.

"Teviot? For old times' sake," Madison suggested.

Sierra and I glanced at each other before immediately shooting our friend's idea down with a cacophony of increasingly emphatic nos.

Maddie raised her hands in surrender. "Jesus, it was only a suggestion."

Teviot was part of U of E's student union. It was housed in a beautiful, Gothic-style building on the main campus at Bristo Square. It had a nightclub inside and a couple different bars, including the Library Bar and Teviot Lounge Bar. Sierra and I considered Teviot primarily for freshmen. Also, a wee bit gross. There were much-needed plans in place to redevelop the entire building.

"I guess we're too cool for Teviot these days," Maddie continued sardonically in her Geordie accent.

I snorted because I'd never been cool a day in my life. "It's not that. It's freshers' week and it will be teeming with eighteen-year-olds. Let's go somewhere less freshmany."

"Somewhere less freshmany requires paying full price," she reminded us.

"We could go to BrewDog." Sierra shrugged. "Student discount."

A twenty-minute walk later, we were in the busy bar on Cowgate, a long way from our first-year uni accommodation. Lucky for us, a table of people were leaving as we came in and we grabbed their booth. The girls strode off to order drinks at the bar while I protected our spot. Indie rock music pumped through the room, loud enough to be heard but low enough you could still have a conversation. In fact, the loud hum of discussion and laughter overpowered the music. Because we'd nabbed the table before a server could clean it, it was sticky and the earthy smell of hops permeated the air.

"You're doing it. I can feel it," Maddie said as they returned, sliding a pint of pale ale toward me.

I frowned. "What am I doing?"

"You're missing this already." She gestured among us all. "You're being all sad and mopey when we have an entire year ahead of us."

Sierra nodded. "Don't you think I'm the saddest of us all? When I leave, I'm heading back over that great big ocean. Maddie's heading back to Newcastle, which is only a few hours away, so you guys can see each other whenever you want. I doubt *we'll* see each other more than every other year or so, maybe not even then."

My heart ached at the thought. "I'm going to miss you. So much."

"No!" Maddie yelled dramatically, causing heads to turn our way. She made a face at the onlookers and shooed them. "Back to your own business, people." Turning to us, she narrowed her pretty blue eyes. "We are not doing this. We are not spending our senior year missing one another before we even leave. We're going to enjoy the shit out of this year and each other." Maddie raised her glass. "Promise me."

Sierra and I shared one last melancholy smile before I made a concerted effort to shrug off the sadness. Maddie was right. We knew Maddie would be returning to Newcastle with her MA in architecture to work at her dad's firm. We knew Sierra would travel back to the States, hopefully to one of the publishers she'd already started querying. But that didn't mean we should waste the time we had together worrying about our impending separation. I raised my glass, along with Sierra, and we clinked it against Maddie's with an "I promise."

By the time we were on our second pints, we were deep in conversation about our plans for our podcast *Seek and You Shall Find*. We chatted about themes for the upcoming episodes and how we were going to introduce January and her friend Aiysha as the new hosts. Our podcast was primarily a dating advice show where we shared our experiences and dos and don'ts of dating.

My very outgoing and charismatic cousin, Beth, had started the podcast when she was studying at Edinburgh. She'd named it after the university motto because it began as a uni podcast but had grown exponentially in popularity over the years. We'd even won a national podcast award and been interviewed by the BBC and Radio Times. I didn't seem like the most obvious person to host, but I'd graduated high school with grand plans to push myself out of my comfort zone and so Beth turned the show over to me when she graduated.

Between Sierra's outgoing, confident, casual dating expertise, Maddie's perspective from the cool girl monogamist, and my perspective from the introvert attempting to date, the podcast grew ever more popular under our watch. Beth, who now ran a social media management company, had helped us with the marketing side of things and we'd made some good money from ad sponsorships. Money that had helped toward accommodation and expenses, super useful since we lived in one of the most expensive cities in the country.

Now I was slowly turning the podcast over to my younger sister, January, who was a freshman BA fashion student this year, along with her high school friend, Aiysha. While I'd still be attending Edinburgh for my postgrad next year, I knew I wouldn't have the same time to dedicate to the show. Introducing Jan and Aiysha now was smart. Plus, it meant freeing up some of our time this year so we could concentrate on our dissertations.

"I can't wait for Jan to start." Maddie had a mischievous glint in her eyes. "She's such a riot."

It was true. My wee sister could not be more opposite to me. While I was generally quiet and reserved, Jan was loud, brimming over with confidence, and she was a bit of a nutter, to be perfectly honest. I'd grown up with the girl and even I sometimes didn't know what she'd say or do next. Though I knew it would never be boring.

The audience was going to love her brash, no-filter fearlessness.

I opened my mouth to tell Maddie not to encourage my

little sister's crazy but was stopped when a shadow cast over our booth and a deep, familiar voice drawled, "Lily Sawyer, just the person I was hoping to see."

My heart skipped a beat.

Such a cliché, I know.

But it really did.

Clamping my mouth shut, I looked up at the owner of said shadow and drawl, and a crushing hurt squeezed my chest.

He was as beautiful as I remembered.

Sebastian Thorne.

His name was apt. Considering he was a thorn in my side.

My friends grew quiet. All I could hear was the drone of voices chatting over the music, glasses clinking, chairs scraping against the floor. Strangers' laughter was suddenly too shrill.

Sebastian stared openly at me, his dreamy blue-green gaze washing over my face as if he hadn't seen me in years. The tall, broad-shouldered Englishman was too good-looking to be true. He was Theo James, Max Irons, Lucas Bravo, and whatever other Adonis celebrity you could think of rolled into one. With his sun-bleached dark blond hair and a pouty mouth at odds with the sharp angles of his jaw and nose ... he was ... he was perfect.

Physically.

Internally, he was a lying arsehole.

Movement at his back thankfully unlocked our gazes. Two blokes stood behind him. Blokes I recognized. Harry and Zac. Zac met my stare with one of sympathy and remorse.

Sebastian flicked them a glance and turned back to me. He had a posh, plummy Etonian English accent that had once upon a time made my belly flutter uncontrollably. "How are you? How was your summer?"

Really?

He thought after what he'd done, we could pretend like we were friends? Like all was well and good?

My indignation and anger were unfamiliar but potent.

It surprised everyone at the table when I answered uncharacteristically, "Fuck off, Sebastian."

CHAPTER TWO
SEBASTIAN

I had never heard Lily Sawyer swear. Had never heard that cool but biting tone pass between her plump lips before. My eyes blurred, glazing over the computer screen as I heard her cutting *"Fuck off, Sebastian"* over and over in my mind. It was driving me to distraction.

What had I expected? For her to smile and announce all was forgiven and invite me and the lads to sit at her booth?

Okay, yes, a small part of me had hoped for that exact response.

Lily was good and kind, and I'd expected that with time she would have forgiven me.

I was so stunned by her response in the bar that I had, in fact, fucked off. Without another word. Zac lingered behind, saying something to Lily and her friends, but he caught up with me and Harry outside.

"I thought you were going to apologize?" Harry asked as he and Zac hurried to keep up with me. I strode quickly down the Cowgate and turned through the dark cluster of buildings, climbing my way up toward South Bridge, a straight shot to our apartment on the Royal Mile.

"Are you going to speak ever again?" Zac queried.

I glanced at them, not quite sure what to say.

The truth was, as soon as I saw Lily enter the bar, I'd known it was fate. All summer the woman had plagued me, because I genuinely liked her and wanted to be friends. And I didn't like that I'd hurt a friend. I'd told the guys I was going to apologize, smooth things over.

That had been my intention.

Instead, I'd stupidly spoken to Lily like nothing had ever happened.

The first words out of my mouth should have been sorry.

And when she told me to fuck off, I should have said sorry before I did.

Moron.

I startled in my computer chair at the sudden ring of my phone. With a groan, I got up and crossed the room, swiping the phone off my bedside table.

Juno calling.

With a sigh, I answered and flopped onto my bed, staring up at the ceiling. "What?"

"Well, that's a charming way to answer the phone, brother." My sister's familiar voice was nice to hear, contrary to what my greeting might have suggested.

"Sorry. Shit day."

"Why?"

"Didn't sleep much last night."

"Why?"

I huffed at her interrogative tone. Juno was two years older than me and still treated me like a younger brother she had to protect. "Why are you calling?"

"Have you heard from Mumsy? Or Pa?"

I lifted my phone to tap on the screen. There were two

unread messages. One from each of our parents. "Yes, but I haven't looked at what they want yet."

The thought of finding out filled my gut with dread.

"They're already arguing over Christmas. They're both demanding we spend Christmas Day with them. I think we might need to split up. Each take one of them."

I scrubbed my hand over my face. "Bloody hell." It was impossible that we'd gotten to this place as a family. Ever since my parents announced at the beginning of the summer that they were divorcing, I'd lived in a state of disbelief.

My entire life, my parents had been sickeningly in love. They used to joke how they couldn't quite fathom they'd raised two children who were so commitment-phobic, considering how happily married they were.

I'd honestly thought they were taking the utter piss when they'd sat Juno and me down and announced their separation. Neither would tell us what had caused this sudden devastation between them.

Whatever it was, they were angry. Bitter. And my sister and I were caught between them like Ping-Pong balls.

"I'm sick of this excrement," Juno huffed. "I swear I'm going to divorce both of them."

"You're an adult. You can't divorce them," I muttered tiredly.

"I can symbolically divorce them. It starts with blocking both their numbers and taking back their copy of my flat key."

"The flat they bought, you mean?"

"Oh right. Fuck. Does that mean I'm stuck with them?"

"Yes. Because you love them," I reminded her. "Even though you don't like them very much."

"Ha! Diplomatically said. When, in fact, I'd quite like to

shove both their heads up their respective arseholes, but I can't because their heads are already currently shoved thoroughly up their rectums."

My lips twitched. "It's always a delight talking to you, Junebug."

Her tone softened at the use of her childhood nickname. "You sound ... off. What's going on? Why didn't you sleep last night?"

Sitting up with a groan, I considered telling Juno about the situation. My sister was a straight talker and sometimes even gave good advice. "I ... I hurt a friend. And she won't let me near her to apologize."

"*She*?"

At her puerile tone, I growled, "Hanging up now."

"No, no. I'm sorry. Okay. Details. I need details."

So I told her. How I'd "infiltrated" Lily's life. Misled her. How it was all a stupid mistake that got out of control.

"Hmm," Juno mused after I finished speaking. "There is much I'd like to dissect about why you're so invested in this girl, but in fear of you hanging up on me, I will just say, find a way to apologize."

"Excellent advice. Don't know why I didn't think of it."

I could practically feel her rolling her eyes at my sarcasm. "I mean, bump into her somewhere she can't tell you to fuck off or run away from you. And lead with the apology this time, little brother. Your face can't get you out of this one, apparently. For that, I already like her a lot."

"I don't use my face to get out of anything," I grumbled. I used my charm. My face just helped people to be open to my charm.

"Right. Apologize first."

"Got it."

"Did you check your messages from Mumsy and Pa yet?"

With a sigh, I tapped the screen on Mum's text first.

> Spoke to Lady Sarah Shrewsbury. Her daughter Lady Amelia has started at Edinburgh. I promised you'd befriend her. Very pretty girl. Here's her number …

Irritation thrummed through me. "Mine isn't about Christmas. She's trying to set me up with Amelia Shrewsbury."

"I thought she was five."

"Almost. She's eighteen."

"Oh, listen to you, you old fart at twenty-two."

"This is the third text like this in a matter of weeks. What the bloody hell is happening?"

Juno sighed. "Mother has decided she's all about Granny and being a 'seen' member of the royal family. Prudent matches are now important to her. She tried to set me up with Foster Fairly last week. I told her if she gives him my number, I'm going to answer it as a fake escort service. A really dirty one."

I chuckled despite my indignation. My whole life, my parents had skirted the edges of the royal family. We'd attended important royal functions and I'd gotten on rather well with my late great-grandfather, King Henry. My grandmother was his youngest daughter, Princess Mary. Grandmother, being a bit of a black sheep party girl in her heyday, had never bothered that Mum and Pa weren't much for the pomp and circumstance of the crown. But she seemed happy to welcome Mum back into the fold. And apparently that meant foisting aristocratic men and women at me and Juno.

Why was beyond me. We were twenty-ninth and thirtieth in line to the throne. We provoked the bare minimum of interest from the public. Most people didn't know who Juno and I were. Society pages talked about us only sometimes. Now and then some magazine or newspaper would do a piece on the lesser-known members of the royal family, but that was as far as our fame or importance stretched.

Otherwise, we were merely the Thornes. Children of Paul Thorne and Lady Clarissa Hanover. Our father was from Leeds, a self-made millionaire out to prove himself. By the time I was born, my father was a billionaire hedge fund manager. By the time I was ten, he'd retired our family to a country estate in Norfolk where he and my mother lived happily like landed gentry of old, checking in on their vegetable patches each day and involving themselves heavily in village society. It was an idyllic life, one mostly free of the trappings of royalty, and one filled with so much love, I'd known from the abysmal state of my friends' family lives how lucky we were.

I still couldn't comprehend how our family had fallen apart.

"Where did you go?" Juno asked suddenly.

"Just wondering how we got here. Do you think one of them is having a midlife crisis?"

"I don't know. I don't know, Bastian. But I do know that I might never forgive them for doing this to us."

I squeezed my eyes closed. "Yeah."

"At least we've got each other, little brother."

"Yeah. At least we've got each other."

"So ... how are you planning to apologize to this mysterious girl who you only want to be friends with?"

I ignored her snort at the end. "I do just want to be friends with her. When have I ever wanted to be more?"

"Hmm ... well?"

"She's a psychology student. I think I might start there."

Juno cackled down the line.

I frowned. "What?"

Her laughter filled her words. "Trust you to pick ... a *friend* who is studying how to psychoanalyze people. Good luck with that."

"She's not like that." And Lily wasn't. Yes, I knew she planned on becoming a psychotherapist, but I never felt under a microscope with her. Which was probably why she'd make a damn good one.

"No need to get defensive," Juno teased.

"I'm not defensive."

"You really like this girl, don't you?"

"As a friend," I bit out between clenched teeth. "I'm hanging up now, *Mother*."

"Ugh, that was just rude." Juno hung up before I could.

CHAPTER THREE
LILY

Last Semester

When Beth first started the podcast *Seek and You Shall Find*, she ran it out of her student accommodation with very basic equipment. Now that it had gone from a uni podcast to a national show, the university provided us with the use of their recording studio at the campus radio station. The caveat was that we had to stick to a strict schedule.

It was a professional setup, much like you'd find in any professional radio station. A large booth for recording and all the recording equipment in a room separated by sound-proof glass. Kenny, one of the station producers, managed the sound and recording for us for a fee. We all took turns editing, but Sierra did the final production.

"Ready?" Kenny asked into his mic. We heard his question through our headsets and gave him our go-ahead to start recording.

I always got a wee case of butterflies before we started a show. While I did the outreach to listeners who wanted to call in for advice and had a general idea of what they were going to ask, listeners often went off on tangents. Sometimes we never knew where the discussion would take us. Today the butterflies were for something else entirely.

For weeks, a rival podcast, *Potterrow Blokes*, had been encroaching on our territory with a deliberate spitefulness that was driving us bonkers. After a lot of back-and-forth, we'd finally gotten them to agree to speak on the podcast. A laptop sat in the center of the table and Madison was getting ready to connect to the Zoom call with them. I didn't want it to turn into a national argument, but I also wanted to know who the arseholes were behind the denigration and mocking of a show I'd worked extremely hard on.

With a small smile at Sierra and Maddie, I leaned into the mic. "Welcome to *Seek and You Shall Find*."

Maddie hit the button on the Zoom call. It connected as I continued, "I'm Lily, and both Sierra *and* Maddie are joining me because we have a special episode today. After weeks of our podcast being used as fodder in the *Potterrow Blokes*' attempt to profit off our success, I called them out last week and dared them to come on the show. While it turns out they're too cowardly to come into the studio, *one* of them has agreed to chat with us via Zoom. And for the folks listening at home, we're not staring at one of the *Potterrow Blokes*' faces right now. We're staring at a screensaver of the Hulk taking Thor up the arse. If the expression on the Asgardian's face is anything to go by ... he's actually really into it."

Maddie and Sierra gave a bark of laughter. I could even hear Kenny chuckling in my ears.

Good. I wanted to set the exact right tone for this.

A deep, American accented male voice spoke from the laptop. "I'd like to say that the screensaver is not mine and I have no idea how to change it."

Right.

Cowards.

I should've known they wouldn't show their faces. My agitation got the better of me and I had a bite in my voice as I asked, "And to whom are we speaking?"

"I'm Elijah."

I narrowed my eyes. His accent seemed to slip on his name.

"Well, Elijah, thanks for being on the show today. I guess I wanted to chat about the stupid rivalry between us, instigated by yourselves. Why do you feel there's only space for one dating podcast at the university?"

"I don't think that at all."

The nape of my neck prickled. I felt like I'd heard that voice somewhere before. "That's surprising to me, considering how much you guys have gone out of your way to discredit our show. It certainly feels like you don't want to share this space with women. Are you misogynists?"

"Certainly not!" He sounded insulted.

I knew his voice from somewhere.

"Is it me, or is your voice familiar?"

"No. We've never met," Elijah responded hurriedly.

"He answered that a little too fast," Maddie said, giving me a look as if to say, *"You're on to something here."*

"I did not. Look, did you bring me on to interrogate me, or can we talk about putting this daft competitiveness to rest?"

Uh! The effrontery of him making it out like we'd started this moronic war.

"Daft?" Sierra butted in, expression gleeful. "I knew it! I thought I could hear a British accent coming through. He's putting on a fake American accent!"

"Aha!" I knew there was something fishy about his voice.

Elijah's twang got even more twangy. "I am not."

Sierra scoffed. "Oh, really? Where in America are you from?"

"California."

I watched Sierra as she rapid-fired questions at him. "Where?"

"Santa Barbara."

"How long did you live there?"

"Jesus, are we really doing this?"

"Definitely a fake accent," Sierra decided with certainty. She was right. I could hear the Britishness leaking through. "So fake! He's a fake!"

"I'm not listening to this childish rubbish."

"Rubbish? Daft? Only the Brits say *rubbish* and *daft*."

Maddie raised her hands to get our attention. "Uh, guys, he hung up."

"See? Totally faking it!"

I winced at Sierra's outrage. We'd completely lost the calm, rational, mature tone I'd been hoping to maintain throughout the interview so that we looked like the calm, rational, mature podcasters in this scenario. Wonderful.

"Okay, can we lower the volume, please?" I sighed heavily. "Well, there you have it, folks. Elijah from *Potterrow Blokes* is not only a thief, he's a coward and maybe even an impostor."

"It is now my mission in life to find out who these guys are," Sierra announced. "This feels personal. Like a vendetta against one of us."

"I'm voting you," Maddie cracked.

"Uh, why me? It could be Lily."

"No. Never. Lily is like the nicest person ever."

"Shucks, thanks." I grinned as I shoved my bestie affectionately.

While she chuckled, Sierra huffed. "And I'm not?"

"You're awesome," Maddie insisted. "But nice is not your moniker."

Sierra considered that. "Yeah, fair enough. It's probably me. But that gives me a starting point. I'm making a list of everyone I think might have a problem with me."

"Is that a very long list, then?" I teased.

"Hey, you're supposed to be the nice one."

Laughing, I turned to Kenny to see if we were ready for our first caller. He gave me the thumbs-up, and I glanced at the laptop to see who was first in line. "Let's get back to doing what we do best and actually help some people. Our first caller today is Hayley." As Hayley started to tell us about the problem she was having with a boyfriend who didn't want to have sex in any position but missionary, I tried not to let my mind wander to Elijah. To the rival podcast.

Our ratings had been down the last few weeks, and I knew it was because of them. If we weren't going to achieve a ceasefire, our next move was to ignore their existence and try to pull our listeners back in with good content.

CHAPTER FOUR
LILY

Present Day

"Just breathe," the redhead said, rubbing a soothing hand over her friend's back. I recognized her and the blond. We were in the same Human Personality course last year.

The blond wiped away tears. "I'm sorry. I just ... got overwhelmed. It's a lot."

"I know." Her friend patted. "But we've got this. We can do this."

Sympathy coursed through me as I turned away so they didn't catch me being nosy. The first week of fourth year was overwhelming.

We had an eight-thousand-word dissertation to write this year, advanced option courses, and two compulsory courses to take. I was the weirdo who wasn't, in fact, overwhelmed with the workload. I liked knowing what was expected of me, so I could schedule it all out. I might be a wee bit more stressed out if I didn't have it so cushy with my podcast job. The girls and I were able to cover for one another when things were too busy.

And honestly, I was relieved Jan and Aiysha were joining the podcast this year. I was weary of dating. So bloody weary. And yet I had to for the show. This year, however, maybe I'd get to take a break from the revolving door of zero-chemistry dates I'd found myself on for the past few years.

Thankfully, I'd quit my tutoring job at the library. However, I had promised Mum—the university's head librarian—I'd help her out whenever I could, and she'd pay me for hours worked rather than a set salary. It was nice to be able to see her whenever I wanted, and I was happy I'd still get some opportunity to this year.

I scanned the notice board in the main entrance of the psychology building, looking for the sign-up sheet I'd been told was pinned here. It had tickled me that the sign-up form wasn't digital until I discovered the psych experiment was being run by Arthur Banks, a teaching assistant who was a postgrad student. He'd been the teaching assistant in my Thinking and Reasoning course last year and he abhorred modern technology. I suspected his abhorrence was more about being thought of as eccentric than actual loathing for the digital world.

There was no information on what the experiment was, other than it was a social psychology experiment. Considering I was writing my dissertation on the impact of social media on self-esteem across genders, a social psych experiment was in my wheelhouse. Did I already have enough on my plate? Yes. But I'd most likely be running my own experiments in grad school and I considered this research for that. I was reaching into my bag for a pen when someone drew up beside me.

Lifting my head, I tensed.

Sebastian.

He stood far too close and peered at me like I was something in a petri dish.

"What?" I snapped.

"Give me five minutes." Sebastian leaned in, his cologne tickling my senses, a woodsy spice that just a few months ago made me want to rip off his clothes. Now I'd quite like to find the bottle of surely expensive fragrance and stick it where the sun didn't shine.

"Goodbye, Sebastian." I turned from him, reaching up to sign my name on the form.

"Lily, please. Just give me a chance to explain."

"Explain what exactly?" I capped the pen and dropped it in my bag, not meeting his eyes. "That you are a bully, a snake, a wee *turd*."

"Turd?" Laughter trembled in the word, and I glowered up at him.

"Do you think this is funny?"

His lips twitched. "*You* calling anyone a turd is extremely amusing."

"What does that mean? That *I'm* a turd so I shouldn't be throwing turd stones?"

"No!" He reached for me, and I flinched away from his touch. Exasperated, he snarled, "Goddamn it, Lily, don't put words in my mouth."

"Easy fix to that—don't talk to me. Ever again." I marched away, infuriated that my legs were shaking as they hurried me from this arsehole who had somehow managed to make me feel as small as the arseholes who had come before him.

"Lily!"

I stuck my middle finger up without looking back, even as my mind flashed me backward in time ...

Last Semester

With our busy lives, I hadn't seen much of my cousin Beth in real life. We'd texted and called, but it had been a while since we'd had a face-to-face. Therefore, I was delighted when she stopped by the library for a quick catch-up. Beth wasn't technically my real cousin. Our parents were best friends, so we'd grown up like cousins. She was more like a big sister I looked up to and admired. Confident, smart, kind. Beth walked into a room, and everyone stopped to stare.

I didn't mind she was an attention hog because it wasn't intentional. In fact, I was pretty sure Beth was oblivious to her effect on people.

We chatted about the podcast and the rivalry, and we talked a little about family and how much Beth worked. Mum told me Aunt Joss, Beth's mum, was worried Beth worked too hard. That she lived to work and not worked to live. When I diplomatically touched on the subject, Beth waved off my concerns. I worried about how driven she was. That one day she'd hit burnout and hit it so hard, it would incapacitate her. Ambitious people usually were the last to realize their minds and bodies needed a rest because they genuinely enjoyed the challenge of hard work.

While I prodded about her career, we were interrupted.

By the most gorgeous man I'd ever seen in my life. And

he was looking at me and not my stunning cousin with her tip-tilted blue eyes and leggy blond beauty.

"Are you Lily Sawyer?" he'd asked in an upper-class English accent that was not uncommon around the university campus, considering how many wealthy students from the south of England attended. We referred to upper-class students as *toffs*. Now that I thought about it, I wondered if that was an offensive word. I'd need to look up its origins.

This toff appeared to be around my age and towered over us in all his blond godlike gorgeousness, wearing a T-shirt with one of my favorite bands on it. Kaleo.

I gaped at him, confused why he'd said my name.

"Is she Lily Sawyer?" he asked Beth.

I was trying to catch up. One minute I'd been grilling Beth about how hard she was working and the next this ... this ... Dior model was interrupting us.

"Who's asking?" Beth inquired with a teasing smile on her beautiful face that would make most men fall to their knees in worship.

He shockingly turned to me instead. "The person paying for a tutoring session."

What a deeply erotic voice he had. All rumbly and plummy Etonian English. Bloody hell, a woman could come to that voice alone.

My cheeks burned at the thought, and I'd never been more grateful I wasn't a blusher. I licked my lips nervously as I realized this was the person who had signed up for today's tutoring session. "You're Sebastian Thorne?"

Please say no.

"At your service." He gave me a sardonic bow of his head while I contemplated what kind of *dirty* services he could provide.

Mentally swatting my filthy thoughts away, I embar-
rassingly tripped over my words. "A-and you n-need help?"

Great. I was fourteen again and unable to speak to a
cute boy without stuttering with anxiety.

"In more ways than one." Sebastian frowned at me.
Almost suspiciously. "Are you sure you're Lily Sawyer?"

"I'm Lily Sawyer. Lily Sawyer is me. I have ID if you
want."

What?

Oh, dear God, bury me six feet under now.

"I have ID if you want."

I was tragic. I was an actual tragedy.

His lips twitched like he found me amusing. Wonderful.
Just wonderful. "Not necessary." Then he stared at me.

At me.

Like ... I was interesting.

Or a specimen.

It could have been either.

"Well, I'll leave you to it. I'll talk to you later, Lily." Beth
abruptly stood and my heart sank at the thought of being
left alone with the Adonis.

"But—"

"Nice to meet you, Sebastian." She cut me off and sent
me a conspiratorial smile before walking away.

And Sebastian ... He didn't even look at her.

He was too busy studying me.

Lily Sawyer, get yourself together now! So, he's gorgeous.
You've met gorgeous men before. You've even dated one or two of
them.

Okay, so they weren't this level of hot, but they were
cute.

I could do this.

Be professional.

Reaching for my books, I snatched them up, using them to cover my stomach as I stood. Maddie had talked me into buying a cropped sweater and I'd paired it with jeans this morning. When I left the flat, I'd felt good about the outfit, but as the day wore on, I became increasingly self-conscious of the flashes of skin it revealed. I wasn't toned to the hilt like Maddie who worked out every other day or naturally skinny like Sierra. I was what January called *lush*. I rode my bike everywhere, which kept me physically fit, but I was soft and curvy.

I'd been called fat a few times in my life and, unfortunately, that crap stuck to the brain like a leech.

Why, oh why, did I have to be wearing this stupid cropped top the day I met Sebastian Thorne?

Like he'd ever be interested in you, the snotty voice of my low self-esteem taunted me as I led him through the library to the study room my mum had given me the key to.

Sebastian raised an eyebrow as I led him inside. "These are like gold around here. How did you manage to get one?" He dropped his books on the table of the small room.

"My mum is head librarian." I mentally patted myself on the back for losing the stutter as I took a seat and gestured for him to do the same.

Sebastian's brow furrowed as he sat adjacent to me. His masculine cologne hit my senses, making my belly flutter. "I think I know who you mean. You have her coloring."

I nodded because I did have Mum's dark hair, olive skin, and hazel eyes. My dad also had dark hair and olive skin, so it was a crapshoot which of them bestowed those on me. The hazel eyes were definitely from Mum, though.

"So ... you need help in Human Personality."

"Excuse me?" He sounded affronted.

I blinked, wondering what the hell I'd said wrong this

time. "Human Personality. The course you'd like tutoring in."

Sebastian let out a huff of laughter and rubbed his nape almost ... self-consciously. "Right. Right, of course."

Pulling on my professionalism, I gestured to my books. "Which part of the course is giving you bother?"

Those beautiful blue-green eyes of his washed over my face. As if searching for something. "Quite a bit, really."

I frowned because I didn't think the course was difficult to grasp. At all. Disappointment withered my attraction. Sebastian was apparently all beauty and no brains. As a sapiosexual, this was a big turnoff for me.

My disappointment turned to relief. I could relax now around him. "Okay. Is it the personality typing, theories, applications, data analysis ...?"

"I ... I had some personal stuff happen this year and I've missed nearly all the course. So, I thought you might be able to bring me up to speed since it doesn't seem terribly taxing."

Terribly taxing.

He smiled coaxingly, and the way his mouth curled more on one side made the butterflies in my belly go wild.

Speak, Lily!

I cleared my throat, dragging my attention off him since his face seemed to render me speechless. "It's not ... terribly taxing. But that's a lot to catch up on. Nearly a whole year. That's not really what I do with the tutoring sessions." In fact, I was surprised the university was letting him continue the course rather than redo the year over. The curious, sympathetic part of me wondered what personal stuff had happened to him.

"Please." Sebastian covered my hand with his and I blinked rapidly as goose bumps rose on my arm at the touch. His hand was huge over mine. Long fingered. Big knuckled. The kind of hands an artist might want to draw. Masculine but beautiful.

Every inch of him was.

"Please don't let me be the first *Homo sapiens* to fail Human Personality. It would be rather embarrassing for me."

Charmed, I couldn't help my grin.

His eyes widened ever so slightly. "You have dimples," he announced, as if it was some kind of miracle to have indents in your cheeks.

"I do."

"They are very disarming."

Was he flirting with me?

No.

He couldn't be.

Right?

I cleared my throat, my palms sweating as I flipped open the textbook. "Okay. Let's start at the beginning, then. Personality types."

"What personality type are you?"

His eyes roamed my face again, like he found me truly fascinating. His intensity up close was discombobulating. If I was going to make it through this session, I needed to get his focus off me. "The type that has another tutoring session in an hour, so I need you to pay attention."

Sebastian's lips twitched. He saluted me. "Yes, ma'am."

My own trembled with laughter. "Is that paying attention?"

"It's very difficult when you're this adorable."

My cheeks caught fire. I was so glad he couldn't tell. "Pay attention," I insisted, even though I was squirming inside with delight.

"Okay." He nodded, leaning into me to see the book. "I'm all ears." His deep voice rumbled in mine. "My thalamus is yours to stimulate."

He was not stupid. Not stupid at all. The laughter huffed out of me before I could stifle it, even as my heart raced at his proximity. It took every ounce of professionalism to ignore my attraction to his face and brain. "Are you going to make everything sound dirty?"

Sebastian grinned, like he was surprised by my response. "It only sounds dirty if you're receptive to it sounding dirty."

"I am not," I lied, tapping the iPad he'd placed on the table. "Now, start taking notes or fail Human Personality."

"I think we can both agree that I shall not fail." He winked at me.

Bloody hell. "Are you incapable of concentrating?"

"I am very capable of concentrating." He opened the note's app on his tablet. "I'm going to prove it by staring at your mouth for this entire session as you talk."

Deciding the most prudent way to move things forward was to ignore his flirting, I also ignored the way every part of me was hyperaware of every part of him. "Okay, so let's start with understanding what the mission of personality science is …"

To my surprise, Sebastian not only listened but he took notes and asked questions. I was a little taken aback by some of his questions because they were things he should have covered in second year of psychology. Something occurred to me as we finished up.

"Why have I never seen you in any of my courses?" I would have remembered him.

He looked down, not meeting my eyes as we rose from

the table. "I usually sit at the back of the lecture hall. I like to get out of there before everyone else."

Oh. Well, I usually sat nearer to the front, so I guess I wouldn't have noticed. "It's funny we've never had any tutorial classes together."

"Pity that." He finally looked at me as he opened the door to the study room. "Are you available for another session?"

Another session of feeling nuclear attraction to this guy?

Sebastian bowed his head toward me, searching my face. "I'd really like another session, Lily."

The way he said it ... like ... maybe it was more than a tutoring session for him. Could he ... might he ... Did he find me attractive in return?

"Okay," I replied softly. "You know where to sign up."

He grinned. "Great. I'll see you tomorrow."

"Great—wait." Tomorrow? I didn't have a session open tomorrow. "Tomorrow I'm—"

"Same time, same place. See you then." He was gone before I could say no.

A smile prodded my lips as I locked up the study room and headed toward my mum's office. I guess I needed to let her know I required the study room tomorrow too.

CHAPTER FIVE
SEBASTIAN

Present Day

With only a brief hesitation, I hurried after Lily, but as I burst out of the building, it was too late. I watched her gracefully plant her curvy arse on a bicycle and pedal away. It looked like one of those adorable old-fashioned bikes from the 1950s, light blue with a basket and brown leather seat and handlebars. It suited Lily to a tee.

However, the way she zoomed away from me suggested it was in fact an e-bike.

I rubbed my nape. "That went well."

The truth was if the lady didn't want to speak to me, I should back off.

Yet, I needed to explain myself. Just once. And if Lily decided she still didn't want to talk to me after that, then I would respect her wishes.

How the hell would I get her to stand still with me long enough to hear what I had to say, though?

I suddenly remembered she'd been signing something on the notice board in the main entrance of the psychology building. Curious, I marched back inside. I looked over the posts pinned to the board until I found her name written on a sign-up form for a social psych experiment. Grad students were looking for volunteers for an experiment they were doing in groups. Lily had signed up for the one taking place next Saturday.

Perfect.

She was going to kill me.

But hopefully, I'd get a chance to apologize first.

I called out to a girl passing by. "Excuse me."

The girl turned, eyeing me, her mouth curling into a smile. "Yes?"

"You wouldn't happen to have a pen on you, would you?"

"Sure." She rummaged in her bag and then strode over, holding out the pen. "Here you go."

"Lifesaver." I took it and signed my name under Lily's. "Thanks."

The girl took the pen back. "I'm Lindsay."

"Sebastian."

"Do you fancy grabbing a coffee, Sebastian?"

I considered it. I did like a woman who was bold enough to ask a bloke out and I had time until my next class. And it would give me an excuse to put off returning my mother's call from this morning. It would also distract me from my agitation. An agitation that had grown exponentially since returning to uni to a sullen, unforgiving Lily. "I'd love a coffee."

Last Semester

Guilt and anticipation mingled as I strode up the library steps. This whole situation had gotten out of hand. I promised myself this was the last time. Then I saw Lily sitting near the entrance, chewing on the end of her tablet pen as she studied something on the screen. If she were anyone else, I'd have already slept with her. In fact, the first time I saw her, I was pretty sure that's where our interaction would end up.

But six fake tutorial sessions and several weeks later and ... I liked her. A lot. So much I couldn't sleep with her because it would make things awkward and weird between us and I realized I didn't want that. I'd quite like to keep Lily in my life. Plus, I knew from her podcast that Lily didn't do casual sex.

That, unfortunately, was all I could give her. That or friendship.

So, friendship it was.

As if sensing me, Lily looked up, and her lush mouth widened into a gorgeous smile. Those dimples. Bloody hell, those dimples did something to me. She stood, tugging down her sweater self-consciously. "Hi."

"Hey." I studied her stunning face and felt the words, the truth dancing on my tongue. I should tell her now.

"Ready for more human personality tutoring?" she teased.

I smiled. "If you feel it's still necessary."

Lily laughed and gestured for me to follow her. I did, my eyes dropping to her arse with a mind of their own. Her narrow waist sloped dramatically into her curvy hips and round bottom. She had the kind of body I didn't think existed outside of sexist cartoons. The alarming thing was, Lily was not only completely unaware of how beautiful and sexy she was ... she clearly had confidence issues. She was forever fidgeting with her clothes or glancing away shyly when she revealed something personal.

I'd known this from listening to her on her podcast. But the skeptical bastard I was, I'd thought it was a schtick, the whole shy, reserved girl dating from an introvert's perspective. I thought it was to help sell the podcast. Especially when I saw her in real life because surely a girl that stunning *knew* she was that stunning.

But it wasn't a schtick.

Lily Sawyer had no idea how fucking gorgeous and likable she was.

She was everything she'd seemed on the podcast and more. Funny, kind, insightful, smart. "I've been listening to your podcast," I blurted out. Immediately, I wanted to pull the words back in.

It was one thing to try to dig myself out of a hole I'd made but another to perpetuate a lie. It was bordering into manipulative.

Damn it.

Lily wasn't leading me to the study room. She led me down some aisles of books instead. She glanced over her shoulder in surprise. "Really? You listened? Also, I need to grab a book for my Thinking and Reasoning paper."

I nodded, continuing to follow her, lowering my voice as we entered a quieter area of the library. "I listened to the episode when you talked to Carly. The young woman grieving her boyfriend." Carly's boyfriend had died of cancer, and they'd been together since they were thirteen years old. Truthfully, I'd listened to the episode weeks ago. It was my motivation for seeking out Lily. Carly had called into the podcast to explain how her boyfriend had been gone for two years, and she still couldn't bring herself to date. That she'd tried, gone out with a bloke a friend set her up with, and had thrown up as soon as she'd returned home. Lily had been so compassionate while she gently suggested the girl start counseling. But she'd also advised her not to be pressured by family and friends into doing anything she wasn't emotionally ready for. She explained grief was not linear and it wasn't a one-size-fits-all.

I couldn't stop thinking about Lily after that episode and I didn't understand why. I only knew that I had to know her.

"You were incredibly kind to her."

Lily stopped at a shelf, her expression sincere. "That was a difficult one. But I heard from Carly last week. She's been speaking to a counselor, and she thinks it's helping."

"That's amazing. You're amazing." Guilt swamped me.

I was a shithead. Truly. Because secretly, I was Elijah, a current host on *Potterrow Blokes*, a rival podcast started by Olly because he was pissed at Lily's friend and cohost Sierra for dumping him. The podcast seemed like a joke at first. Olly started it with Harry, one of my roommates. They'd invited me onto it, and I'd done it for a laugh, faking an American accent so no one would know it was me. No one knew it was Harry and Olly either.

But I soon discovered Olly started it as some kind of lighthearted vendetta against Sierra, and that didn't sit right with me. Especially as I began to suspect that Lily's podcast meant a hell of a lot to her and it actually did some good.

I'd wanted to find out for myself.

Of course, to do that I signed up for a (fake) tutorial session with her. As one does. Note the sarcasm. I am very much aware that one does not in fact fake signing up for tutorial sessions for a degree I'm not even working toward.

I was not a psychology student.

My degree was in civil engineering.

Truthfully, I hadn't thought much beyond assuaging this intense curiosity about Lily. I hadn't expected to like her so much that I'd want to be her friend in a more permanent way.

Something that would soon be impossible if I didn't get up the nerve to tell her the truth.

"What made you want to do the podcast?"

Lily grabbed the book she needed and then leaned against the bookcase. She shrugged. "Me and my roommate and our friend Sierra run it. Beth—you met her that first session—she started it when she studied here."

"You didn't start it?"

Her pretty hazel eyes searched my face. They really were the most extraordinary color. Golden mossy. "Beth did. Then she invited me on in my first year. I took it over when she graduated the following year. At first, I wanted to push myself. I don't know if you noticed, but I'm kind of an introvert and not the most confident person."

"Why? You're smart and gorgeous."

She swallowed hard, her gaze dropping to my mouth.

Bloody hell.

"Thanks," she muttered, seeming to have to wrench her attention off my lips.

Be her friend, be her friend, be her friend. Only her friend.

I cleared my throat against the heat building low in my gut. "You were saying?"

"Right. Aye, at first I was challenging myself. Then ..."

Lily shrugged sheepishly. "I realized how much I got out of helping people. I never realized how curious I was about what made people the way they were and how it was possible to help them onto a path that could alleviate certain emotional and mental health issues by understanding what was causing them in the first place. I switched my major from English lit to psychology after only a few weeks on the podcast. And I've applied to Edinburgh for my postgrad to become a psychotherapist."

Wow. She was really in it for life. This wasn't some college pastime for her. "It means a lot to you? The podcast?"

"Aye, it does. It's not ... I'm not trying to be famous. In fact, I never wanted any part of that. I ..." She lowered her eyes and shrugged. "It might be difficult for someone like you to understand."

I frowned, leaning into the shelving so our bodies were almost touching. "Someone like me?"

"Someone confident who knows he's good-looking." Lily shrugged again, staring at her feet. "Sierra's like you. Even Maddie, to an extent. But more people are like me. Uncertain of themselves. Awkward." She winced. "We don't find social interactions as easy as some people. It's an effort. And we kick ourselves for saying stupid things and get anxious about certain social situations, including dating. I represent everyone like me, and I think having someone like me talk openly and vulnerably about what it's like to be a shy dater helps people feel seen. Also, the girls have helped me, given me great advice, and it's wonderful to be able to share whether that advice works for my personality type or how I've tweaked it to suit me. Listeners have really responded to that. And when we get call-ins or emails thanking me for helping them find love or ask out their crush ... it makes being vulnerable worthwhile."

I swallowed hard, my heart pounding loudly in my ears for reasons I didn't quite understand. "You're a really good person, Lily."

Her dimples flashed as she shyly looked me in the eye. "You're full of compliments today."

For a moment, I forgot what I'd promised myself. That Lily was off-limits. Friend-zoned. It was easy to forget when she was the most beautiful woman I'd ever seen, and I suddenly found myself desperate to know what her moans of pleasure sounded like.

My skin flushed hot. All rational thought fled my mind and there was nothing more important than learning how soft Lily Sawyer's plush mouth really was.

I bent my head toward her and at the hitch of her breath, my balls tightened.

"If you aren't going to use the study room, should I give it to someone else?" A voice had Lily jerking away from me with a squeak of surprise.

Irritated, I blinked out of my sexual fog and turned to find a woman standing in the middle of the aisle.

A woman I recognized.

Bloody hell, it was Lily's mother.

I straightened and turned.

"Mum." Lily pushed off the bookshelves, her eyes wide with embarrassment. "I was just grabbing a book before we used the study room."

I'd never met Olivia Sawyer, the head librarian. I'd seen her around and heard some of the blokes making crass, sexist jokes about her being a MILF. She'd given Lily her coloring, including the hazel eyes. However, she was much curvier than Lily, a little taller, and if I was being honest, a little plainer in the face. She didn't look old enough to be Lily's mum.

"Sebastian Thorne." I held out a hand to her, feeling grateful she'd interrupted, even if Lily was embarrassed by it. For a moment, I'd let my cock do the thinking. Lily deserved better than a casual fling.

"Olivia." Lily's mum shook my hand with a mischievous grin. The woman had a glamorous smile that transformed her from merely pretty to stunning. "I'm Lily's mother as well as head librarian here. What are your intentions with my daughter?" She had a mixed accent. American with Scottish inflection.

I laughed at her forwardness as Lily squealed, "Mum!"

Olivia hushed her but was still smiling. "This is still a library, Lil." She held out her hand to her daughter. "I'm going to need that key back. I've kicked couples out of the study rooms too many times to count, and my kid is not going to be one of them."

"Kill me." Lily closed her eyes. "Please kill me now."

"After I get that key."

"I assure you nothing untoward was about to occur," I interjected.

"I'm still going to need that key."

Groaning with pure mortification, Lily handed it over. "Nothing happened."

"And now nothing will." Olivia thumbed over her shoulder. "You can use the cubicles on the second floor. The ones out in the open for everyone to see."

I snorted. Lily's mum was funny.

"You do realize I'm almost twenty-two," Lily hissed at her as we all turned to walk down the aisle.

"I do. But you do realize I'm the head librarian and I

can't condone sexual activity in the library ... even though it's an uphill battle."

"There was no—ugh, you're so embarrassing. Come on, Sebastian." Lily stomped away.

"Nice to meet you," I said to Olivia as I passed. Lily was out of earshot now. "Really, truly, nothing is happening. We're just friends."

"I remember a male friend of mine looking at me the way I caught you looking at my daughter."

"Oh?"

She grinned and waved her ring finger. "He married me." With a chuckle, she sauntered off in the opposite direction, her heels clicking on the hardwood floor.

Biting my lip, I turned back to search for Lily. Hurrying after her, a different kind of guilt clouded my mind. I didn't want to lead Lily on and that's exactly what I'd done. Shit.

I had to fix this.

All of it.

I knew I had to tell Harry and Olly we needed to back off the girls' podcast. Olly had started winding the girls up, trying to make it a competition between the shows to get a rise out of Sierra. He said it was only for fun, but I had a feeling Olly had really liked Sierra and his ego was badly bruised by her lack of interest in taking their relationship further. Sierra didn't know it was Olly behind *Potterrow Blokes*, which seemed to piss him off even more that she didn't recognize his voice.

But the joke had gone far enough.

Lily and her friends didn't find the interference funny.

And it wasn't.

It was immature.

I was done with it.

As for Lily ...

First, I had to quit the podcast. I'd promised Harry I'd do tomorrow's show, and I would. But after that, I quit.

And then next time ... next time Lily and I met, I'd tell her the truth. Everything. Hopefully, she'd forgive me long enough to want to stay in my life. As a friend. *Only* as a friend.

CHAPTER SIX
LILY

Present Day

I should have listened to my sister.

As I walked into the old student accommodation the next Saturday, my sister January texted me.

> Please tell me you're not going to that psych experiment after all.

I'd chuckled and replied:

> Arriving now.

My phone beeped immediately.

> Well, unarrive! It's a trap! IT'S A TRAP!!!

Snort-laughing, I texted back.

> So dramatic.

A stream of texts followed.

> My drama will keep you alive.

> This is the opening to a horror movie.

> Old disused building.

> Attractive but dim student lured there under false pretenses.

> What part of this doesn't scream Wes Craven to you?

I was impressed she knew who Wes Craven was. Still, rolling my eyes, I'd replied.

> Dim? You just talked yourself out of the cupcakes I baked last night.

> You're not returning to claim them.

> I'll comfort-hoover them down while I wait for the police to arrive to tell me my sister was unalived by a psycho psych grad.

Still smiling at her nonsense, I'd followed the signs directing me to where I needed to be, only to walk into the room and lock eyes with the last person I wanted to see.

For the five minutes we waited for everyone to arrive, I tensed against his approach.

But he just stood there, staring at me.

This wasn't happening.

No.

I was going to kill him.

Seething, I hoped Sebastian Thorne could feel the laser beam of my anger shooting from my eyes to where he stood across the room, smirking unremorsefully.

"It looks like we're all here," Arthur said, glancing around what had once been the kitchen of a student flat. The accommodation was much like what I'd lived in my first year. Five bedrooms off a narrow hallway, a shower room, and a kitchen/common room with uncomfortable chairs and no soft lounging area. I always suspected they didn't include a comfortable lounging area in the accommodation to deter students from socially gathering too often when they were supposed to be studying.

"Thanks again, everyone, for volunteering for our experiment. We've been running it for two weeks. You're group three, week three. We're running a six-week experiment over six groups to provide plenty of data to extrapolate from. What is our experiment, you ask? We seek to discover whether our reliance on technology is affecting the way we connect socially with one another."

That distracted me momentarily from the fact that Sebastian had signed up to the same psych experiment.

This experiment had some crossover with my dissertation. However, it was highly unoriginal. Disappointingly so. Perhaps it was part of some grander research Arthur was partaking in. Though, he did seem generally obsessed with our reliance on technology and his personal loathing for it.

Ultimately, however, I didn't care about originality. I was more interested in the structure, organization, and process of the experiment so I had some practical experience going into my grad degree. I'd already compiled data from the psych experiments I'd signed up to in second and third year.

"We're going to pair you up in twos and put you in different environments. Note, you will be under visual and audio surveillance while inside your rooms. We have a disclaimer for you to read and a waiver to sign." Arthur stared down at his list and started calling attendance to make sure we were in fact all here.

In the meantime, uncaring he was being rude by talking over Arthur, a stocky guy with short black hair stepped into my personal space. He had striking, pale blue eyes and a cocky swagger. "I'm more than happy to pair up with you," he said in a European accent I couldn't quite place. "Maybe they'll put us in a room with only a bed. A man can hope." Stocky cocky guy dragged his gaze over me lasciviously, before gluing his eyes to my breasts as if imagining all manner of dirty things.

It took everything not to throw up in my mouth.

I hadn't even been aware of Sebastian's approach until he drawled with quiet menace, "Look at her like that again, and I'll rip your fucking balls off."

My eyebrows rose. I'd never seen Sebastian look or sound so dangerous.

The creep blanched, holding up his palms as he backed away. "Sorry, I did not know she was taken."

"I'm not—" I stopped myself from continuing. The creep wasn't worth it.

Sebastian glared at the dark-haired guy as he called over his shoulder in Arthur's direction, "There is an odd number in the group."

Arthur frowned, midway through his attendance call. He quickly counted the people in the room. "You're right. Someone on the sign-up hasn't shown."

Sebastian gestured to the creep. "I wouldn't put this cretin alone in a room with anyone if I were you."

"What did I miss?"

"He was sexually suggestive to my friend." He placed a protective hand on my shoulder, and I glowered at said appendage.

Arthur scowled. "Well, we're having none of that. You may leave."

"But—"

"Leave," Sebastian commanded.

Stocky cocky shot Sebastian a foul look but left swiftly, his cheeks a ruddy red with embarrassment.

I was both relieved and irritated.

"Who are you?" Arthur asked the gorgeous liar before me.

"Sebastian Thorne."

"Okay." He eyed me. "Lily Sawyer, right? I remember you from a tutorial last year."

"That's me."

"You and Thorne are a pair." He turned away before I could naysay his plan.

Sebastian's lips twitched, his eyes gleaming. "Well, this worked out way better than I could have planned."

My urge to demand a new partner stuck in my throat because I didn't want to give Sebastian the satisfaction. After much thought about our previous interactions, I realized I was allowing him to believe he had some kind of power over me by giving him a reaction. Now I wanted him to believe me indifferent.

Which was difficult when every part of me was tense with quiet anger at Sebastian's side as Arthur paired people and his team started leading them out to their respective rooms.

Arthur sauntered over to me and Sebastian. "Last but not least. Each pairing will be placed in a different room under different circumstances. You two are the no-technology room. I'm going to need you to hand over any devices you have with you, including your beloved smartphones."

Wonderful.

My lips thinned as I nodded and proceeded to remove my phone from the back pocket of my jeans. Checking it was locked, I passed it over to Arthur who gave us a gloating, smug grin as he took both of our phones and placed them in a locked box. "Now follow me."

I could feel Sebastian's eyes on me as Arthur led us out of the flat and across the cool, dreary hallway to the flat next door. The sound of a TV blared from behind the door of bedroom one.

"They have a smart TV. But don't worry, you won't hear it because you're all the way down here in bedroom five." Arthur guided us to the opposite side of the flat and pushed open the heavy door. "Welcome to the no-technology room."

My stomach dropped.

The room was set up as it would be for a student. Single bed by the window. Desk opposite. One wardrobe.

The window was completely taped up, and they'd lit extra lamps to make up for it.

"Cameras." Arthur pointed to the upper corner above the door and the one near the window that had a straight shot of the bed. "We've also placed mics around the room so we can clearly hear your conversations. You're in here for three hours. If at any time you need to leave, press this." He pointed to a red button that had been attached to the wall near the door. "Someone will come to let you out."

He offered us the clipboards he'd carried under his arm, along with a pen. "We need you to read this disclaimer and sign the waiver. It pretty much states that you're happy for us to use our recordings for the experiment. It also states that none of the footage or sound recordings will be uploaded online for public consumption, but we may include excerpts of conversations or actions in our research paper, which *will* be available online."

Great.

Now I had to watch what I said unless I wanted everyone to know what Sebastian had done.

That compromised the integrity of the experiment because Arthur and his team were looking for authentic interactions.

As if he read my mind, Arthur continued, "Please try to be as honest and genuine with each other as possible. Guarding your words, your interactions, will compromise the experiment. Thank you."

Once we'd signed, he nodded, thanked us, and left.

The door locked behind him.

Reluctantly, I turned to Sebastian.

"I read that book. The one with the dragons. It was quite good."

Was he serious?

"Any more romance recommendations?" He gave me a coaxing smile I wanted to smack off his face.

He thought he could woo me with his "sexy man reading romance books" schtick? I cursed the day my copy of a romantasy book fell out of my bag during our session. Intrigued by the cover, Sebastian flipped through it and happened to land on a sex scene. His teasing led to me defending the romance genre and effusively explaining the benefits of reading it. I'd argued so passionately on behalf of my love of romance books—all subgenres!—that he'd promised to read it.

I hadn't actually thought he would, and I still wasn't sure he had. He was a known liar, after all.

I wanted to interrogate him about the plot details to catch him in his lie, but that would mean validating his decision to once again act cavalier about our estrangement.

Instead, I glared sullenly at him.

Sebastian's countenance turned serious. "I'm going to apologize now and if you still hate me when I'm done, I'll leave you alone."

Last Semester

"This is a mistake. We shouldn't be doing this," I whispered, feeling panic rise in my chest as I crouched behind a hedge with Sierra.

"That dickwart Olly is doing this because I dumped him, and I'm going to prove it," Sierra seethed, peering over the top of the hedge to the building across the busy street.

We'd jumped on a train to Haymarket with our bikes and ridden from the station to the student accommodation in Westfield. All because Sierra got a lead on who the *Potterrow Blokes* were. When I'd gotten back to the flat after my tutorial session with Sebastian yesterday, Sierra was there. She'd told us she'd bumped into a drunk friend of Oliver Abernathy's last night and he'd let the cat out of the bag.

Olly Abernathy was the son of a wealthy financier in London. He'd been brought up in Kent, attended boarding school, and was friends with lots of highfalutin people. Last year he and Sierra had engaged in casual dating. Sierra ended it when Olly started to get attached.

According to the drunk friend of Olly's, he'd decided to get a little revenge on Sierra for rejecting him by setting up a rival podcast to malign us.

If that was true, I honestly despaired at the immature toxicity of the male species.

Sierra had pumped drunk friend for a lot of information. According to drunk friend, Olly ran the podcast from a studio in his apartment. Sierra had slept over in his flat, so she knew exactly where that was.

"This is breaking and entering. We could be charged." I tried to dissuade my best friend because now that we were here, rationale was returning. Maddie had decided she quite rightly didn't want to be a part of unmasking the guys if it meant possible criminal charges. I'd gone along with Sierra because she'd been determined to do it with or without us. Her indignation knew no bounds.

"Plus, someone might steal our bikes."

"So." She glowered at me. "These assholes are trying to ruin something we worked our asses off to build just because one of them didn't like that he got dumped. Tell me you're an entitled toxic male without telling me!"

I absolutely agreed with her. But ... "My e-bike cost my parents, like, a grand. That's a lot of money for us."

Mum might have made good money as head librarian, but it wasn't epic money. And Dad ran his own successful photography business, made even more successful by some clever social media marketing. He mostly did weddings and big events, but he had a side business where he sold beautiful prints of scenes from Edinburgh and Scotland. He did well for an artist, but it wasn't like we were rolling in it like Beth's parents.

A grand on a bike was a lot.

And I treated that bike like my child.

Sierra sighed heavily. "We've secured the goddamn bikes." She gestured angrily to the bike rack at the end of the large car park behind us.

"I'm not familiar with the area." I sniffed haughtily. "Our bikes might not stay there very long if we leave them unattended."

"Enough with the bikes." Sierra abruptly stood and took off across the road.

Heart in my throat, I hurried after her, flattening myself against the wall of the apartment building. The guys could see us coming any second. Sierra had it on good authority the lads recorded the show Friday mornings. I was skipping a class for this ludicrousness!

Without another word, she pressed all the buttons except button 2A on the intercom system. Someone answered the intercom. "Yes?"

"Amazon package," Sierra lied.

The door clicked open two seconds later. Shaking my head at her deviousness, I followed her inside and up the stairs to flat 2A. The student accommodation was new and modern, but it didn't have the character of my flat on Leven Street. *It probably doesn't have the mouse problem or draftiness either*, I thought with momentary longing.

"Now what?" I hissed as we stopped outside the flat.

My pulse was deafening in my ears.

"I should have brought Jan." Sierra cut me a wry look. "She lives for this stuff."

My wee sister did live for misadventures and mischief. "She'd also give you away in two seconds."

Sierra let out a snort that was quickly replaced by determination. "I'm coming for you, you bastards." She reached for the door handle.

"What are you doing?"

"Well, I'm not knocking and giving Olly a chance to hide his dirty work." The handle twisted and she beamed triumphantly as she quietly pushed open the door.

Oh my goodness, we were going to prison.

We were so going to prison!

Legs trembling, I tiptoed in behind her as we entered an airy, modern hallway.

There was no sound from within.

Nothing.

Sierra placed a finger to her lips to ensure my silence before she tiptoed down the hall, glancing into doorways. The reception hall led into an open-plan living room and kitchen with lots of windows. It was empty.

There was only one closed door in the entire flat.

"I'm going to be sick," I muttered as Sierra crept toward it.

She shot me a sharp *shut up* look as she grasped the door handle.

Then she threw open the door, marching inside. "Aha!"

I followed her in and abruptly ran into her as she halted.

My eyes widened.

The room had been soundproofed with foam panels. It was small. A round table sat in the middle, recording equipment on it with two laptops open beside it.

And around the table were three guys with headsets. Mics hung on stands near their faces.

Olly gaped at Sierra from one seat.

A guy with light brown hair turned to us with an expression of moderate surprise.

My heart stuttered as I looked at *Potterrow Bloke* number three.

And then it felt like it crashed into my stomach as nausea rose.

Sebastian Thorne stared back at me, wide-eyed and panicked.

CHAPTER SEVEN
SEBASTIAN

Present Day

"Do you really want to do this here?" Lily defensively crossed her arms over her chest. She wouldn't meet my eyes. "I'm not sure I want our business aired publicly."

"As opposed to the hundreds of thousands of people who listen to your podcast?" I teased, trying to ease the tension between us.

"You're the one who kept your identity a secret."

"For reasons."

"That you're happy to share here?"

I shrugged. "It's not like what I'm about to tell you isn't already in the public domain."

With a sigh, she brushed past me. She smelled amazing. I'd thought at first it was her perfume, but it wasn't. It was her hair. It was floral, but not in a heady way. It was fresh and slightly intoxicating. I'd imagined burying my face in her hair more times than I could count.

I watched as she settled on the bed, her back against the wall. My eyes narrowed as she tugged down her sweater to cover her lower abdomen, crossing her arms to hide herself. I didn't want her to do that. I wanted her to know how gorgeous she was.

Anticipation agitating me, I had to force a look of patience.

"Fine." Lily finally let out a heavy sigh. "There's nothing else for us to do in here, is there?"

Relief surged through me. I gestured to the spot beside her on the bed. "May I?"

She considered the spot and then shrugged. "You may."

Attempting to mask how adorable I found her irritation with me (I was smart enough to recognize that would not go down as anything other than male condescension when, frankly, the truth was I found everything about her adorable), I sat down on the bed. Settling with my back against the wall, I was careful to maintain distance between us. I didn't want her to think I was pushing my luck.

My attention lingered briefly on her strong thighs. She wore distressed jeans and the tears in the denim revealed tantalizing glimpses of smooth, olive skin.

Ignoring the heat scoring through me, I looked away and tried to get comfortable. Sitting side by side was not the optimum positioning for this conversation. Finally, I gestured to the wall at the head of the bed. "Would you mind sitting there so I can look at you when I tell you this?"

Lily considered it, biting into her lush lower lip. With a small nod, she got up off the bed and then sat back down again with her back against the wall next to the window. I turned to face her.

This time, she met my stare as if to say *"Get on with it, then."*

"First, a little backstory," I began. "Olly isn't a particularly close friend. He's a friend of my roommate Harry. He went to boarding school with us but was in the year below. I didn't know him because they played rugby together. I played football." I internally rolled my eyes at that inane detail. "Anyway, Olly started the podcast as a way to get back at Sierra."

"I know about that," Lily said dully. "The part I don't understand is, number one, why you thought that was okay, and two, why you pretended to be a psychology student so I'd tutor you. Was it another way to infiltrate us? Get information you could use against us? Do you even realize how messed up and immature that is?"

I blanched. "Lily, I didn't know that was the reason Olly started the podcast until I was in it. They asked me to join them. I thought it would be a lark, but because of who my family is, I didn't just hide my identity like the lads, I decided to mask my accent, my voice."

She frowned. "Who your family is?"

That surprised me. I was so sure she would know by now. "You ... you don't know who I am? I thought you'd have investigated the hell out of me after you broke into Olly's flat."

Her eyes widened and she pointed at the camera. "Not break. I did not break into anyone's flat."

Laughter thrummed in my throat. "Of course not. I meant when you *visited* Olly's flat."

She nodded with a huff. "Aye, *visited*. And no. I didn't.

Maddie did, but I told her I didn't want to know anything about you."

I winced. "Right."

"So ... why is your family a ... thing?"

I didn't care about admitting this in front of the psych grads. It was public knowledge. "I'm a member of the royal family. Thirtieth in line to the throne, to be exact."

Her lips parted in comical shock. "Och, you're joking, right? This another prank?"

"Not at all. Once you get out of here, you can google it."

"You're a member of the royal family? You are. You." She pointed at me.

I nodded again. "My mother is the daughter of Princess Mary."

Lily sat forward. "Your grandmother is the sister of the current Queen of England?"

My great-grandfather King Henry passed away two years ago, and his eldest daughter Anne was now queen.

"Yes."

Her beautiful eyes darted over my face as if searching for my sincerity. Then she sat back against the wall. "I can see it. The resemblance. Especially to Alexander." She referred to my second cousin, Queen Anne's eldest son and heir to the throne. He was somewhat of a royal heartthrob.

"I'll take that as a compliment."

"Don't take anything I say as a compliment, Sebastian. Not yet, at least."

Ouch. "Fair enough."

Lily considered me. "So, you hid your identity to protect your family?"

"My immediate family couldn't give a rat's arse. The institution, however, might not have taken too kindly to me publicly giving dating advice and encouraging blokes to let their ladies massage their prostate. Maybe in private but not on a national level."

Lily snort-laughed and then clamped a hand over her mouth as if to take it back. Goodness, she was cute.

Trying to stifle my smile, I continued, "Anyway, that was the reason for that. Then as I got pulled into the show, I realized it was some kind of vendetta for Olly, which I thought was bollocks, but it wasn't until I started listening to your podcast that I attempted to talk him into giving up the revenge."

At her encouraging silence, I went on. "I could hear how much the show meant to you. How much real effort you put into helping people. It wasn't merely a comedy dating show. You did your research, you showed kindness and compassion, and I could hear you making a difference." I scrubbed a hand over my neck, not quite sure how to artic-ulate my desire to know her. "You might not believe it, but I really wanted to meet you. To know if you were really who you made yourself out to be. It didn't seem like such a bad thing signing up for the fake session until I met you. And I liked you."

Her expression was, for once, annoyingly unreadable.

Sighing, I continued. "I-I've ... my friends ... let's say we hang out, we have a laugh ... but it feels like it never goes much deeper than that. It sounds cheesy, but ... I wanted to be your friend. Like a ... real one."

CHAPTER EIGHT

LILY

S ebastian Thorne had just friend-zoned me.

That shouldn't have been my first (crushing) thought. My mind should be processing his explanation and whether I could trust him enough to forgive him.

But my brain stuck on *friend-zoned*. And then proceeded to tabulate all the reasons why.

Ugh, I hated that my first reason was superficial.

I wasn't thin enough, pretty enough.

He was a golden god who could date the most beautiful humans on the planet.

Then the "Maybe I'm not posh enough" filtered in almost immediately. Sebastian was a member of the royal family. He probably couldn't date a commoner like me.

I wrinkled my nose.

I was *not* common.

My parents raised January and I to believe in our importance to them and to the world, if we did our part to make a difference in it. My podcast might seem silly to some, but I felt like it was making a small impact. Moreover, I intended to become a psychotherapist. To help people identify problems with their mental and emotional well-being so we could put in place processes to help relieve those problems, i.e., improve people's lives.

Perhaps it was the commoner thing though, after all. The friend-zoning. Because ... there had been moments when Sebastian definitely seemed attracted to me. The almost-kiss in the library in front of my mum, for a start.

"Where did you go?" Sebastian asked, bringing me out of my tangent. "I quite literally saw you disappear somewhere inside your mind."

"Literally?" I teased.

He grimaced, eyes bright with amusement. "Forgive me for my imprecise use of the word. You know what I mean. Where did you go?"

Goodness, I did not want Sebastian to know that my first takeaway from his confession was that I was somehow not good enough to be girlfriend material, but I definitely made the cut as a friend. "Just ... processing. Your explanation is reasonable. That doesn't mean I can magically have a reasonable response to it. Emotions sometimes don't follow a logical process, as much as we'd like them to. I can't switch on the trust button. It would have to be earned again." I winced almost apologetically before I continued. "And I don't know if I want to give us the space to explore a friendship to build trust."

He blew out air between his lips and sank back against the wall. "Spoken like a psychology student."

Now I winced for a different reason.

Sebastian saw. "I meant that as a compliment, believe it or not."

"Okay."

"Lily ..." His expression turned pleading. "Please give me a chance."

Could I be friends with Sebastian when I was attracted to him?

Well, it wasn't like I hadn't done it before.

When I was fifteen, I'd had a massive crush on Euan, a guy in our friend group. My girlfriends knew about it, and I got along really well with him. I'd thought we were heading into girlfriend/boyfriend territory. Until one day, my friend Nikki approached me sheepishly to tell me Euan had asked her out and she'd said yes. I'd been hurt. However, I was a weirdly rational teenager and reasoned that there was no point in standing in the way of the happiness of two people I cared about, even if they'd shown little care for mine. Would I have appreciated an honest conversation with my friend before she agreed to date the boy I liked? Yes. And I wouldn't have stood in her way then either.

Anyway, long story short, I created a new place in my mind for Euan once he became my friend's boyfriend. Somehow, I'd emotionally managed to friend-zone him. In fact, eventually watching him be so clingy with Nikki, I began to find him annoying.

I could do that with Sebastian.

Couldn't I?

Not the annoying part. Hopefully. But the friend-zone part.

There was no point in pretending I wasn't drawn to him. He was obviously drawn to me, even if only platonically. Maybe I could get to that same place. I did like him. I liked being around him. Before I found out about the podcast.

My attention turned to the camera in the corner.

However, I couldn't authentically make strides toward

that in a room where our conversation was being recorded. If I'd been locked in the room with a stranger, we could have passed the three hours making idle chitchat or awkwardly ignoring each other.

Sebastian and I were definitely not in a place for idle chitchat. It would only confuse things more.

Which meant I'd spend the next three hours guarding my words and emotions because I didn't want them being recorded for use in a research paper.

Och, this could hurt my reputation with the grad students, but the decision had to be made.

Hopefully, they'd recognize my integrity and desire to not compromise their research rather than think me a flake and a waste of their time.

I got up off the bed to cross the room.

"Where are you going?" Sebastian asked. "What's happening?"

Pressing the button by the door, I glanced back at him. "I'll explain in a minute."

Thirty seconds later, the door opened. An irritated Arthur stood on the other side. "You two have a background and you can't interact authentically, and you don't want to compromise the integrity of our data," he supposed.

Grimacing, I nodded. "Sorry."

"My fault. As soon as he said you were his friend, I should have switched you with someone else. Rookie mistake. You may leave." He gestured, waving us out of the room.

"Sorry, again."

He shrugged off my apology as I walked out, motioning for Sebastian to follow me. Arthur handed over our smartphones and we left. He was irritated, but I got the impression he wouldn't hold it against me.

I didn't speak until we were out of the old student accommodation building. Sebastian followed me over to my bike. He watched me warily, curiously, as I unlocked it.

"We can try," I finally said. "To be friends."

His expression softened. "Really?"

"Sure."

"Friends have each other's phone numbers." He held out his smartphone, wearing a hopeful, boyish look on his gorgeous face.

With a shake of my head, I attempted to suppress a smile as I rhymed off my phone number. He immediately hit the call button, and it rang in my pocket.

"Didn't believe me?" I snorted, tugging out the phone.

"Of course. I wanted you to be able to add me as a contact." He pointed at my phone screen. "My name is spelled S-e-x-y F-r-i-e-n-d."

I did laugh now. "You're incorrigible."

"That's a word we don't hear enough these days. *Incorrigible*. Your beauty is incorrigible."

"That's not how you use that word. Also is flirting the way you 'friend'?"

"*Friend* is a verb now, is it?" he teased back. "And yes. It's a disease I was born with, I'm afraid. I even flirt with my granny's dog. Though I did have to stop because she took it as encouragement to hump my leg any bloody time she pleased."

"I can guarantee you I won't take your flirting as encouragement to hump your leg."

"How disappointing." He grinned wickedly.

I rolled my eyes. "Maybe I take it back. Maybe I don't want to be friends."

"Too late, I have your number. And you should know I was that annoying child in preschool who hugged everyone and refused to go away and play with someone else when told to."

Trying not to laugh at his silliness, and failing, I shook my head. "No, you weren't."

"No, really I was." He cocked his head, studying my face. "You aren't just placating me? You really mean you're going to give this a shot?"

"Why do you want to be my friend so badly?" I blurted out.

Sebastian shrugged. "Because I like you." He suddenly looked away, his expression grim. "People can be so disappointing, Lily." He turned back to me, seeming sincere. "It makes you want to hold on to the ones you feel you can really trust."

"And you think you can trust me? We don't really know each other."

"But my gut instincts are usually never wrong. I want to know you. I want you to know me. And if you decide you don't want to be friends, that's fine. I'd just like the chance to try."

Friends.

That hadn't stopped stinging quite yet.

Deciding I would leave the ball in his court, I got on my bike. "If you text, I promise I'll answer. Goodbye, Sebastian."

"See you soon, Lily," he called after me as I rode off.

I was barely a minute from him when my mobile beeped in my pocket.

It could have been anyone, but when I got back to the flat, I anxiously pulled out my phone. There were several texts. One of them was from Sebastian.

Meet me for coffee at Books 'n' Cup
Monday at 11 a.m.?

My belly fluttered, which meant this was a very bad idea. But the coffee house he referred to was only a two-minute walk from my flat and I didn't have a class then.

I replied before I could change my mind.

See you there.

Not a minute later, Sebastian replied:

Can't wait.

CHAPTER NINE
LILY

While the flat in Leven Street did feel like *our* place, stepping into the house I grew up in, in Kirkliston, was truly like coming home. I wondered if it always would or if one day I'd find some place new that made me feel like I was stepping into a warm hug and not merely a building. The village was on the outskirts of Edinburgh, not far from the airport.

Most of our extended family of friends lived in the city, but my parents had opted to move to Kirkliston because they could afford a bigger property farther out. Grandpa Mick, my mum's dad, moved to a bungalow a street over a few years after we moved. He lived there with Granny Dee, my mum's stepmother. My dad's parents, my nana and papa, still lived in Dad's childhood home in Longniddry. When we were kids, we'd go stay with Nana and Papa for a week during the summer holidays and Jan and I used to love it, not just because they spoiled us, but because they lived near the beach.

To January's delight, our parents' best friends, Aunty Jo and Uncle Cam, moved to Kirkliston before their youngest

Louis turned five. They wanted more space for their kids Louis and Belle, and since there was only a year between Jan and Belle, the cousins were delighted to be attending the same school. Despite Belle graduating a year before Jan, the two of them were best buddies.

Everyone else, however, lived in or around the city center. Beth and her brother Luke and sister Elle grew up in this amazing Georgian townhouse in New Town with my Aunt Joss and Uncle Braden. Once a month or so, they still invited us all round for Sunday lunch, and I never missed the opportunity if I could. Not just because I loved our big extended family but because I adored that house. That house was Edinburgh goals!

Our house, though, was *home*.

"It's me!" I called as I stepped inside. The smell of Mum's soup hit my nose, and my belly rumbled. No one made veggie soup like Mum.

"In here, Lily-Billy!"

I let out a beleaguered sigh. At least she refrained from calling me that at the university.

Following my nostrils, I walked down the hall and into the new extension Mum and Dad added a few years back. It made for a spectacular kitchen, dining, and living area.

"Aunty Jo!" Happiness lit through me to see Mum's best friend sitting on a stool at the island.

Jo hopped off said stool to envelop me in a hug. "Lily, it's been ages, sweetheart."

Squeezing her tight, I replied, "Too long. You haven't been to the Sunday dinners at Aunt Joss's for a while."

"Work has been crazy," she told me as I rounded the island to hug Mum. "Things are finally calming down a little."

Aunt Jo was a highly sought-after painter and decorator. She used to take on any job, but over the last decade she'd started working exclusively with the top interior designers in the country. Sometimes it meant traveling around Scotland.

I nodded as Mum and I hugged. "Where's everyone?"

"Dad and Uncle Cam are out in Dad's man cave with Louis watching the game."

Along with the extension, Dad had a garden pod put in that served as a gym/office/TV room.

"Jan and Belle?"

"Jan's on her way."

"Belle is out with her boyfriend," Jo said with a twist of her lips.

Slipping onto the stool next to her, I carefully asked, "How's that going?"

"I hate him. He's every creep I ever dated before I met your Uncle Cam." Jo shrugged unhappily. "But I know if I keep coming down on him, I'll only push her away."

"Jan hates him too," I told her, sure I wasn't telling her something Jan wouldn't happily share herself. Jan had told me he set off her arsehole radar and couldn't understand why Belle couldn't see past his pretty-boy face. "She's not afraid to let Belle know that. Hopefully it'll sink in soon."

"I wish Belle was at Edinburgh with Jan. Maybe Jan could knock some sense into her."

Belle attended Napier University because she wanted to study journalism and it was the top university in Scotland for it. She was in her second year there and had switched from journalism to advertising and public relations.

"Knock some sense into who?" January asked, sauntering into the kitchen. She snapped a huge chunk of the large carrot in her hand and waved it at us. She said something around a mouthful of orange vegetable.

Today she was dressed like Wednesday Addams, if Enid had gotten into her wardrobe. Her bright pink polka-dot dress had a big white Peter Pan collar with the pointed ends, large white cuffs, and straight lines. Black tights, pink patent boots, pink nails with white tips, and pigtails completed the look. January dressed however the hell she liked and always had, and I admired the heck out of her for it. She gave zero effs what anyone thought of her.

"Well, aren't you adorable with your carrot and pink dress?" Aunty Jo teased.

"Why are you eating a carrot like Bugs Bunny?" Mum queried lightly. "I'm making lunch."

"Mrs. Brown asked me if I wanted a carrot from her garden and I thought it would be rude if I said no." Jan referred to our neighbor down the street as she crossed the room to kiss Aunty Jo's cheek. "Also, is it Belle you want me to knock some sense into?"

"Only metaphorically."

January scowled as she rounded the island to hug Mum. "I'm going to have to do it literally, I'm afraid."

"Is this guy really that bad?" Mum asked.

"Worse." Jan sighed heavily. "This might be breaking the girl code, but a new friend at uni knows him. She said he's dating her friend too. So, the motherfu—fritter is cheating on Belle. My Belle! The audacity."

I felt sick for my younger cousin.

Aunty Jo looked murderous. "Are you kidding me?"

Jan shook her head. "Unfortunately not. I'm telling Belle today. And if she doesn't believe me, I'm going to have to make her face some harsh truths no matter what. I might even enlist Sara."

Sara was another pseudo-cousin of sorts. Growing up, my dad and Uncle Cam were best friends with Uncle Peetie.

However, tragically, Uncle Peetie and Aunt Lyn died in a car accident when I was eleven and Sara was nine. Sara's paternal grandparents adopted her, but Dad and Uncle Cam and our whole extended family had gone out of our way to make sure Sara was looked after and loved. Sara, Jan, and Belle were particularly close because Sara was only a year older than them. However, Sara was in Illinois, on a semester abroad program at Northwestern University, and probably couldn't be of much help thousands of miles away. Not that I thought Jan's plan was a solid one.

"Is that wise?" I worried anything too forceful would only humiliate our cousin in an already painful situation.

"Tough love." Jan shrugged unapologetically. "She'll thank me for it one day, even if she hates me today. And Sara is the ying to my yang. Together we can make Belle see sense. She's calm and reasonable like you. While I'm blunt, like a tire iron to the face."

I snorted in my glass of soda.

"Despite the tire iron reference, I'm so grateful she has you." Aunty Jo's eyes were suspiciously wet before she looked away. "She doesn't seem to want to talk to me much these days."

"It's just a phase," Mum promised. "Lily wouldn't talk to me for the last two years of high school."

"That's not true."

"It's so true. I had to get everything out of January."

"Uh!" I glowered at my sister. "Traitor."

"Tough—"

"If you say tough love, I'll stick the rest of that carrot up your nose."

My wee sister cackled, completely unthreatened. "Drinks, anyone? I fancy Sunday mojitos!"

———

"Before the men return from the cave, any exciting dating news, Lily?" Aunty Jo asked. "I had to stop listening to your podcast, sweetie. Too many details for your aunt. You're still Lily-Billy to me, you know."

"Me too," Mum agreed.

Thank goodness for small favors. I'd die if my family listened to the podcast.

"Jan's done an episode." I attempted to turn the limelight off me.

"Oh? How did that go?" Aunty Jo inquired with laughter in her eyes.

January sipped loudly through her mojito straw. I was nursing mine slowly.

"It was just introductory. But I've got a date this Friday, so I'll have something more to talk about next time."

"Date?" Mum and I asked in the same overprotective tone.

It was an ingrained reaction, not a necessary one. If there was one person I didn't need to worry about when it came to dating, it was January. She was confident, assertive, and took no prisoners. Which was probably why she was more of a casual dater. She'd never had a long-term boyfriend, and I thought it might be because the boys she'd met so far were a little intimidated by her.

January nodded. "He's a second year. I met him at Teviot. He knew of the Shambolics, so I said yes to a date. We're going to a gig together."

"Who are the Shambolics?" Mum asked.

"An indie rock band from Glasgow. They're amazing." Jan reached for her phone. "Here, listen."

"Or not." I cut her off. "I need advice on something I can't ask about on the podcast."

After reviewing my response to Sebastian's text and how much I couldn't stop thinking about him yesterday, I was beginning to suspect being friends with him was a terrible idea.

Mum looked so happy she might cry. "You want my advice?"

"Aye. And Aunty Jo's."

"And mine!" Jan piped up.

"No, you're merely here."

"You're getting spicier in your old age." Jan narrowed her eyes at me. "I like it."

Shaking my head at her nonsense, I turned back to Mum. "Do I not ask you for advice?"

"You haven't in a while."

Guilt suffused me. "I don't mean not to." I made a mental note to make more time for Mum and to confide in her more. After all, if there was one person in the world I was most like, it was Mum.

Realizing we didn't have much time before Dad, Uncle Cam, and Louis appeared, I rattled off the story about Sebastian, finishing up with yesterday's promise to be his friend.

"Is this the guy who almost kissed you in the library?" Mum asked.

"He did?" Jan looked gleeful at the prospect, the dimples we both inherited from our father appearing. "You almost got kissed by a member of the royal family?"

"A lesser-known member of the royal family. And I don't think that's what was happening then, Mum. Not after talking with him."

Mum raised an eyebrow. "Lily, whatever he says about his intentions now, his intention then was to kiss you."

"What does he look like?" Aunty Jo asked Mum.

Mum grimaced. "It's weird for me to comment on a student's appearance."

"Think of him less as a student and more as Lily's friend who almost kissed her."

"He's beautiful," Mum responded promptly, her lips pursing. "And a charmer, like her father."

I wrinkled my nose. "Don't compare him to Dad."

"He had that glint of mischief in his eyes like your dad."

Jo grinned. "I am very intrigued."

"Here." Jan stuck her phone in Aunty Jo's face. "That's him there."

I almost fell off my stool. "Where did you get a photo?" I peered over Aunty Jo's shoulder.

"I googled him. And after seeing him, I'd quite like to *google* him, if you know what I mean?" My sister winked with exaggeration, making Mum snort.

Scowling at her for a long second, I then looked back at the phone. Sebastian was googleable! There were actual shots of him at royal events. When he told me he was a lesser-known member of the royal family, I hadn't really understood what that meant.

"Oh, Lily, Liv is right. He is beautiful. Go, you." Aunty Jo nudged me playfully.

"No," I grumbled, sitting back up on my stool. "Not *go, me*. Didn't you hear what I said? He friend-zoned me. So, I have two questions for you. Do you think I'm being stupid forgiving him and giving him a chance? And is it silly to agree to be friends with a guy I'm very attracted to?"

Jan snorted. "Just say it. You want to google him, and no one blames you."

"Would you stop using that as a verb for sex?"

"Fine. You want to fu—"

"Finish that sentence never, young lady." Mum pointed a wooden spoon at my sister.

January gave her an unremorseful smile before she pretended to zip her mouth shut.

"Unlike you, I don't do casual sex," I said evilly.

"What?" Mum gaped at January. "Lily better be joking."

My sister peered at me with a mixture of admiration and irritation. "It seems I've taught you too well, young Padawan."

Aunty Jo smothered a laugh with her hand while I tried to swallow my own.

Jan turned calmly to Mum and said with mock seriousness, "I won't lie to you, Mother. I'm afraid I have engaged in casual sex acts."

"B-but ... but you're only nineteen!"

"Oh, they started when I was fifteen."

Mum's eyes bugged out of her head.

"Not *sex* sex," January tried to reassure her. "I lost my virginity when I was sixteen. It was Michael Williams. Do you remember him?"

"Jan, I don't think that's helping." Aunty Jo grimaced.

"Lily was sixteen too."

Mum's head whipped around to me.

"Thanks for throwing me under the bus with you. At least mine was with a steady boyfriend."

"Who was a spectacular arsehole."

"I'd like to rewind this moment. Or deafen myself with that carrot of yours." Mum glowered at January.

"You did want Lily to confide in you more. I thought that meant you'd want me to too." My sister shrugged unrepentantly.

"Look ... I'm not stupid. I had my suspicions, but you could have left me with just the suspicions. I'm going to kill Michael Williams if I ever see him again."

"You should. He was a rubbish lay."

"Nope! No!" Mum stepped back from the stove. "New rule. Confide in me, yes, but spare me the details."

"I think," Aunty Jo spoke up calmly, "we should return to the topic at hand. Lily wants our advice."

"Only if Mum isn't too traumatized to continue?" I winced at her shell-shocked expression.

"Well, hold on a minute." January leaned across the island. "Be honest, Mum. When did you lose your virginity? And don't lie and say it was to Dad."

Mum shared a look with Aunty Jo who shrugged. "Belle asked me, and I told her."

"Fine." Mum stirred the soup without looking at us. "I was twenty and in my sophomore year of college. I was very shy and inexperienced, and I wanted to get it over with. It was a huge mistake. Then I wasn't with anyone until I met your dad and that isn't a lie."

"Oh, tell them everything, Liv. January, in particular, deserves the truth." Aunty Jo wore a wicked smile.

"Jo ..." Mum snorted. "Don't."

Intrigued, I pushed. "Now I want to know."

"You do?" Jo smirked. "Okay, your mum asked your dad to give her flirting and sex lessons and that's how they ended up together."

Despite the ick factor of it being my parents, I kind of loved that. It was like a romance novel. "Really?"

"Don't." January glared. "Don't encourage this line of discussion. It's yucky."

"What a mature descriptor."

She stuck out her tongue at me.

"I think it's romantic." I smiled.

"You would."

"It was and it wasn't." Mum gave me an understanding look. "I was attracted to your dad before all of that started. He only saw me as a friend. It could have destroyed our friendship."

"Except I didn't only see her as a friend." Dad's voice had us turning to look toward the sliding doors. He stepped inside with Uncle Cam and Louis at his back, his eyes on Mum. "I was lying to myself. But you can only lie to yourself for so long before you risk losing the best person you've ever known."

Mum smiled sweetly as Dad reached her and pulled her in for a kiss. He nuzzled her neck, wrapping his arms around her waist before he looked at me. "What prompted the trip down memory lane?"

"Your daughters were trying to traumatize Liv, so I thought I'd try to traumatize them back. Didn't work out with Lily. January looked faintly green, so that's a win, I suppose." Aunty Jo shrugged.

"Traumatize your mum how?" Dad narrowed his eyes behind his glasses.

Jan answered while I smiled up at Uncle Cam as he cuddled into Aunty Jo's back. September was proving mild this year, so he wore only a T-shirt, showing off his tattoos. Jo's younger brother, Cole, had a full sleeve (fair, considering he was an award-winning tattoo artist), but Uncle Cam was catching up to him, having added to his collection over the years.

"Hey, Uncle Cam. How are you?"

"I'm good, sweetheart. How are you?"

"Same."

"Final year. Dissertation?"

I nodded, thinking about the workload awaiting me back at the flat. "I have a ton of interviews to conduct for mine, so I've spent the last few nights sending out a bunch of inquiries."

"You've decided on a topic, then?" Dad asked, having overheard.

"I'm starving," Louis grumbled as he rounded Mum's side. "Is it ready, Aunt Liv?"

"Louis," Uncle Cam warned. "That's rude."

"I'm getting ready to serve, sweetie. Soup first and then the roast. Sound good?"

"I could eat the entire fridge, so, aye, that'll do."

"Where do you put it?" January eyed the thirteen-year-old. He was tall like his dad but thin and wiry.

"In my gob." Louis shrugged as if to say *duh*.

"Lily?"

I looked back at Dad. "Oh, sorry. I have." I told him my plans for the dissertation.

"I'll be interested to read it," he said honestly.

"Me too." Mum smiled proudly at me.

As we all settled down at the kitchen table, Aunty Jo leaned into me. "We'll get a minute before the end of the day to talk about your royalty problem."

Sure enough, after a boisterous lunch (any lunch with January was boisterous), Uncle Cam, Dad, and Louis were on cleanup duty, so we shuffled into the front room to pick up where we left off.

"I say yes to giving him another shot," Mum said. "Just as long as you know where you stand with him."

"Even though I'm attracted to him?"

"I've scrolled through his Instagram—do you know he has thirty-nine thousand followers—and there are photos of him with groups of people that include girls, but no solo one-on-one pics with him with girls. I'm going to ask around. See if he's a player." January nodded decidedly.

Thirty-nine thousand followers? He couldn't be *that* lesser known, then.

Then what she said registered. "No. No, you're not. The last thing I need is my wee sister asking around after Sebastian like I'm some kind of lovesick idiot."

"But—"

"No." I put my foot down. "I mean it, Jan. I'll be really pissed off if you do."

She blinked rapidly. "Okay, I won't. I promise."

Aunty Jo caught my eye. "I agree with your mum. Be his friend. You might stay friends, you might not. But you clearly like him. I think it's worth giving him a shot."

"And if I get hurt?"

"It's better to get hurt trying than to ache with regret because you didn't."

I let that sink in, feeling better about my decision to meet Sebastian for coffee tomorrow after all.

"That was profound, Aunty Jo," January said, ruining the moment. "I'm writing it down and using it on the podcast. Do you mind if I take the credit? Great, thanks. Love you."

CHAPTER TEN
SEBASTIAN

L ily had told me during one of our fake tutorial sessions that she lived on Leven Street, so I'd chosen the coffee shop not just for the good coffee but because I knew it was only a two-minute walk from her flat. I didn't want to give her any reason not to show. For me, it was a twenty-minute walk from the three-bedroom penthouse on the Royal Mile where Harry, Zac, and I had lived since second year. Harry's father had insisted his son live somewhere that represented his status and had bought the apartment. But Harry didn't want to live there alone, so Zac and I moved in with him.

Harry continually mocked his dad because he seemed to forget where the family started. Harry's grandfather was Baron Grimstone of Kensington and a member of the House of Lords. However, he was born outside of Glasgow, never attended university, and worked his way up in life. He'd been in television in the eighties, as in he owned a UK studio. He'd then gone on to become a director of a massive telecommunications company, before snowballing more businesses under his billionaire wings. While Harry's father had grown up in Kent, attended Eton, and St. Andrews University, Harry's grandfather had never forgotten he was a working-class boy who did well for himself. He'd dedicated a lot of time and money to charities and was knighted for his philanthropy. From there, he'd ascended to the House of Lords.

Harry got on better with his grandfather than his dad who really was the most pretentious arsehole I'd ever met. I could have lived anywhere. I wasn't fussed about accommodation. Neither was Zac, whose mother was an Academy Award-winning actor who had him through artificial insemination with donor sperm. She'd sent Zac to a posh prep school and then Harrow. Unlike Harry, whom I'd known since boarding school, we'd met Zac in our first year. To give Harry some peace from his old man, we'd moved into the posh flat on the Royal Mile.

We should have been the party pad, but many of the other residents were not students and didn't put up with that shit. We'd tried holding parties in second year and they were constantly broken up by building security. In third year, we held our annual Hogmanay party and nobody stopped us, so we tried to push for a second event and once again, building security were called.

"If we'd rented some shithole, we could have a party every week," Harry had grumbled last night. "We'll have to settle for Hogmanay again this year."

The three of us had chatted a little about it over beers and burgers on our large roof terrace.

I stepped out into the welcome sunshine of a mild September, wondering if Lily would be in my life long enough to invite her to the New Year's Eve party. Music blared from my phone via my earbuds. My playlist mostly consisted of indie rock music, and I wondered what kind of music Lily liked. We hadn't talked about that stuff yet.

I winced as what I soon realized was my new ringtone cut through a Hozier track as I headed down Victoria Street. "Bugger," I muttered, pulling my phone out of my pocket to see it was my mum. Not wanting her to interrupt my coffee with Liv later, I answered. I also made a mental note to kill Harry who'd switched my Stereophonics ringtone to the retro Crazy Frog. Immature arsehole. "Mum," I answered a little snappily.

"What's wrong? What's happened?" she asked tartly.

"Nothing, sorry. Harry just being an idiot."

"That boy." She sighed heavily. "Are you at the flat?"

"Just heading to meet a friend for coffee." I braced myself. "What's up?"

"Well, your father is being imperious about the use of the villa next spring."

"The villa?" Our family owned a villa—a large farmhouse—in the south of France. We usually spent a few weeks there together in the summer, but, of course, it didn't happen last summer, and it wouldn't happen next.

"Yes, the villa. He has it for Christmas and three weeks in the summer. I want it for spring and September. But he's arguing that he should have it in spring since I don't like the mild rainy weather then, which is utter nonsense. Anyway, Juno has claimed a few weeks in the summer for herself, so I thought to spite your father, you could claim it for your spring holiday. You could invite some friends with you."

Frowning as the steep descent of Victoria Street came to an end on the Grassmarket, I clarified, "You want me to have the villa for a week in spring? All to myself? To spite Dad?"

"Yes."

"Fine." Who was I to argue with that? "Is that all?"

"You're rather abrupt this morning. Did you get my texts about Amelia? Have you seen her yet?"

"Mother, I have no interest in an eighteen-year-old fresher, whether she's Lady Amelia or a pop bloody princess."

"You're saying she's too young?"

"Yes, she's too young. Also, I have no interest in a serious relationship, so please stop foisting women on me."

"Would you prefer me to foist young men on you because you know I love you no matter your sexual orientation?"

Affection softened my tone. "I know you do. And I appreciate it. Though my interest does only lie with females. My interest also only lies with females who aren't looking for monogamy or love."

"That's because you haven't met the right one."

I groaned.

"And I met the Viscount Wellmount's daughter, Margaret, and she was quite lovely. Perhaps when you're next at home, I can—"

"No," I cut her off. "Mum, I'm really not interested."

"Fine." She sniffed haughtily. "Who is this friend you're meeting? A loose woman?"

"Oh, for God's sake. When you and Dad decided to separate, did you stumble into a time machine and travel back to the nineteenth century?" Indignation filled me. Lily was far from a loose woman, whatever that meant.

"Bastian—"

"Mum, I love you, I do. But please don't become one of those women who judges other women. You never have before, and I'd really like it if you didn't start now."

"You sound like your sister." She was silent a moment. "I don't mean to come across as judgy. I merely want you both to end up with the right sort of person."

"I happen to think the right sort of person is the one you're in love with regardless of their background. Not because they have a page in *Debrett's*. I used to think that's who you were too, or you wouldn't have married my father."

"Maybe I shouldn't have. Maybe I should have married the man my mother wanted me to marry."

At her sad tone, I dared to ask, "What really happened between you and Dad?"

"Nothing for you to worry yourself over, my darling. I'll let your father know the villa is yours next spring. I must go. I'm meeting Mummy for afternoon tea."

"Tell Granny I said hello."

"I will. Love you, Bastian."

"Love you too, Mum."

Melancholy threatened to cloud my thoughts as I continued toward the coffee shop. I wanted to fix things between my parents, but they stubbornly refused to discuss what had happened to create this split.

It was maddening and depressing.

However, the sight of Lily standing outside the coffee shop made all those dark feelings crumble away. Warmth radiated through me at the sight of her texting someone, her head bowed over her phone. She'd tied up her hair in a messy knot that was falling over to one side, a loose strand caressing her cheek. She wore a T-shirt knotted at the waist and skinny jeans that accentuated her narrow waist and lush hips.

Two blokes passed her, one of them eyeing her up, even

turning back to look at her as he passed. Lily didn't even notice. Totally oblivious.

"Are you texting with a secret admirer?" I teased upon approach.

Lily startled, her head jerking up from her phone. Her large hazel eyes were round with surprise. Then she let out a huff of laughter. "You scared me."

"You were rather engrossed."

"Oh." She waved her phone before tucking it into the back pocket of her jeans. "Sierra has been on at me to start dating again for the podcast, so I swiped right on this guy last night and he messaged to ask me out."

A prick of some unfamiliar feeling niggled me. It wasn't a pleasant sensation. "Oh. You said yes?" I pushed open the coffee shop door, holding it for her.

Lily nodded as she passed, and I inhaled the delicious floral scent of whatever shampoo she used. "I did."

"You're interested, then?"

"Not really." She shrugged. "I've got a lot on my plate this year and could do with a break from dating. But if it'll shut Sierra up for another month, I'll do it."

My smile felt a little forced. "Right. Well, you know you shouldn't do something you don't want to do."

"It's fine. What are you drinking?"

"I'm buying. What do you want?"

"You don't have—"

"Nonsense. I invited you."

Lily sighed but capitulated. "Hazelnut latte. Thank you."

"You go grab a table. I'll be right over."

A minute or so later, I settled across the small table from her, my legs bumping into hers beneath it. "Sorry." I chuckled. "These are rather cozy, aren't they."

"You have very long legs." She pointed out the obvious. "And mine aren't exactly short."

I smiled, watching her add sugar to the latte, making a mental note about how she took her coffee. "What music do you like?" I blurted out.

Lily smiled at the question, those adorable, dimpled cheeks somehow sexy at the same time. "Random, but okay. I have eclectic taste. You'll find me listening to rock, dance, pop, country. Pretty much everything but heavy metal and jazz."

"Note to self, hates heavy metal and jazz."

"What about you?"

"Indie rock mostly."

"Is music important to you?"

"I play a little piano. But it's not something I ever wanted to make my life in. Yet, it is important. I listen to music almost every day, and I like going to gigs."

"Me too."

"There's this really good cover band playing Whistlebinkies next Friday. Would you want to go?" Whistlebinkies was a live music bar on South Bridge. "A few of us are going," I hurried to say at her hesitation.

"Oh. I would like to ... but that's when this dating app guy wants to meet."

"Bring him," I insisted. "It'll make it safer."

Lily raised an eyebrow. "Safer?"

"Yes, safer." I'd never really thought of it before, but it didn't sit well with me Lily meeting some stranger off a dating app. I'd never used the apps myself, but it suddenly occurred to me how much less safe it was for women than men. I wondered if Juno used dating apps and what precautions she took when meeting strangers. I'd ask her later.

"Okay." She shrugged. "I'll think about it."

"Good."

"So ..." Lily took a sip of her latte while searching my face. She wiped a smear of coffee off her lips, almost distracting me from her next question. "You mentioned you have a sister. What's she like?"

"Juno is two years older than me, but you'd think she was ten years older. We grew up close, she grew up protective." I chuckled. "She's one of my closest friends, really. Not sure that's very cool to admit, but it's true."

"I don't care about cool. I love that you're so close to her."

"She's mad as a hatter. Ballsy, take no prisoners. Says the most preposterous things and mocks me relentlessly. But I love her."

Lily's expression softened. "She sounds wonderful. She sounds like she'd get on really well with January."

"Your little sister?"

Lily nodded. "She's a fresher this year. And my complete opposite."

"Plain, stupid, and unkind?" I teased.

She grimaced. "No, I meant she's loud and überconfident, assertive, blunt. She's also hilarious. But from the outside in, I think people find her intimidating. I'm as intimidating as the saber-toothed tiger in *The Croods*."

Chuckling, I pulled out my phone to google the movie. "I've never seen it." An adorable animation of a saber-toothed tiger appeared on my screen, and I burst out laughing. "Yes, you are definitely as intimidating as that."

"He's so cute, isn't he?" Lily peered over the table at my phone, her dimples melting me.

"Not as adorable as you."

She wrinkled her nose. "That's me. Adorable."

"It's not a bad thing, you know."

"Hmm, if you say so."

"I do say so. Have you seen *Rise of the Guardians*?"

"Uh, aye. Queen of animations over here."

Grinning, I nodded. "It's one of my favorite movies, but that's just between you and me. If anyone else asks, my favorite movie is *The Godfather*."

"Have you even seen *The Godfather*?"

"Of course. Once."

Lily burst out laughing and I found myself grinning like the Cheshire fucking Cat. And that's how our morning went. Easy, natural conversation over three coffees. She told me more about her love for romance novels and I insisted on a list of recommendations. She sent me a few links, looking very much like she thought I never intended to click on them. She was wrong.

I could've sat there for hours talking nonsense with Lily.

When she announced she had to leave to get ready for an afternoon class, I wanted to plead with her to stay a little longer. Instead, I walked her out of the coffee shop and down the street to her flat.

"So, this is where you live?" I stared up at the building as noisy traffic passed behind us.

"This is it." She glanced over her shoulder at me, her key dangling in the main entrance door. "So ... I'll see you."

"I'll text you," I promised her firmly. "If you've got time, I'd love to see you before Friday."

"I might come on Friday. Might."

I sighed. "Please. It'll make me feel better to check out this bloke and to know you're surrounded by friends. Safe."

"Thorne, you do realize I've been on many dates?"

I smirked at her use of my surname. "Yes, Sawyer, I do. But that was before you knew me and I'm overprotective of my friends."

Lily rolled her eyes. "I'll talk to you soon. Thanks for coffee." And then she was inside, the heavy entrance door shutting behind her.

A pang of something weird spread across my chest.

I didn't like the feeling.

Pulling my phone from my pocket, I quickly sent Lily a text.

> Lunch. Teviot. Thursday. You free?

I turned and started walking back toward home.

A minute later, my phone beeped.

> I can do 1 p.m.

A massive grin split my face as I quickly texted back.

> See you then.

CHAPTER ELEVEN

LILY

For some reason, I woke up feeling a wee bit overwhelmed about trying to juggle my coursework with the podcast. However, I had a meeting with my advisor, Anna, a research grad student and tutor who was my advisor in third year too. On top of my dissertation, I had a general paper to write, a tutorial course, and then I had to select three classes over the course of the two semesters. I decided to take two classes this semester, leaving me extra time in the second semester for my dissertation. My plan was also to do most of my interviews for the dissertation this semester as well. Anna thought in general it was a good plan but told me to consider spreading out some of the interviews so my first semester wasn't so top heavy.

I came out of the meeting feeling better but also worse because I had a nagging feeling I needed to chat with the girls about giving more airtime to January and Aiysha this year than we'd originally planned. The idea of trying to date on top of all this work made my head spin.

After my meeting, I had a seminar—Emotions: Social and Neuroscience Perspectives.

Since the course was smaller than previous years, the lecture was held in a classroom instead of a hall. I spotted an acquaintance from a class last year and she waved me over. Her name was Esme and she was French. I was always so impressed by students who chose to study in a foreign country. We shared some pleasantries and then the professor and his TA walked into the room, hushing the small group of students. It felt more like a tutorial than a seminar.

"Good morning. We have two new students this week who are a little late to the game, so a quick reintroduction. I'm Professor Andrews. My TA, Penny." He gestured to the young woman who waved and took a seat at the front of the class. Professor Andrews had taught my Psychology 2B class in second year, so I'd been happy to see his name on the course since I was already familiar with his teaching style. "Welcome to Emotions: Social and Neuroscience Perspectives. A few admin pieces first. There is a tutorial for this course and you all should have your tutorial groups and times. Find them on the school hub. There is a midterm paper and a final paper. Above and beyond that, I love a quiz, so expect one at the end of every seminar. Moreover, I expect everyone to get involved in discussions during our seminars and tutorials. Consider it part of your grade. No hiding behind iPads."

He eyed each and every one of us like he'd done last week when he said this, and I did my best not to look away when his gaze caught mine. "Now. Let's get to it. Over the next few weeks, this course should hopefully provide you with an understanding of the social functions of emotions." He turned to write the latter on the whiteboard in front of him. "The influence of culture on emotion ..."

I opened my iPad as I listened and watched him draw

out the list of topics we'd cover. When he asked questions, I raised my hand to answer along with most people in the seminar. Professor Andrews looked pleased and when he called on me and approved of my response, I got a buzz from it. What could I say? I was a bit of swot, really.

As we packed up at the end of the seminar, Esme turned to me. "Do you have a class next?" she asked in her musical accent.

"No, I have work." The podcast counted as work to me since it took up so much headspace and I made wage from the ad money. "You?"

"Library. I'll see you next week."

I was heading out of the building toward my bike when I heard, "Lily, right?"

Turning around, I searched the main reception and locked eyes with a guy who was staring right at me. Familiarity hit and I racked my brain for his name. "Zac?"

He grinned as he approached. "Yes, Zac. How are you?"

I remembered Zac from the night Sebastian approached me at the bar. After I'd told him to fuck off, Zac apologized to Sierra and then me before leaving. Sierra had told me Zac was Harry and Sebastian's roommate. He wasn't involved in the podcast drama, but he knew Sierra via Harry via Olly.

"I'm good. How are you?" I asked politely.

"Grand, grand, yeah." He had as posh an accent as Sebastian, but it didn't do *things* to me like Sebastian's did. "Are you a psychology student, then? I'm sure I recognize you from Psychology 1B in first year."

"Oh." I was surprised and a bit embarrassed because I hadn't noticed him. I'd switched to psychology my second semester of first year. "Are you a psychology student?"

"Cognitive science. Leaning heavily on the AI side."

That was surprising. For some reason, I'd assumed he was an engineering student like Sebastian. "Very cool."

"Yeah, I think so. You know I've seen you around."

I felt even worse that we'd spent the last three years in the same school building on campus and I'd never been aware of him.

"You're Sebastian's friend."

Zac gave me a wide, toothy grin. "That's me. Room-mates, actually. I live in a flat with him and Harry on the Royal Mile."

My eyebrows rose. "Fancy."

He laughed, seeming a little embarrassed. "Well, it's Harry's place, really. So where are you heading off to?"

"Podcast duties."

"Ah, of course. I've been a longtime listener. You're very good."

I wondered if Sebastian had put Zac up to this to make me even more amenable to a friendship with him. Like a *"Look how nice my friends are! Let's be friends too"* kind of thing. "Thank you. I appreciate it. I really better go. It was nice seeing you again."

"You too. Hopefully I'll be seeing more of you."

"Sure. Bye."

As I got on my bike, I chuckled to myself. Sebastian had texted me every day since our coffee "date." I'd never met anyone so determined to be my friend. And weirdly, despite my attraction to him, talking with him was so easy. I didn't overthink every word I spoke or typed. But perhaps that was because he'd friend-zoned me, taking all the romantic pressure out of the situation.

I'd decided to follow my mum and Aunt Jo's advice and just go with it. Which was why I had decided to not only meet him today at Teviot but also to bring my date to Whistlebinkies tomorrow night.

Sierra was waiting with Jan at the recording studio when I hurried inside. Kenny gave me a wave as I darted into the recording booth.

"Where's Aiysha?" I practically fell into the seat.

"Class." Jan narrowed her eyes. "You're late."

"I had a seminar way across campus. Your face is late."

"What does that even mean?"

I shrugged, smiling at my immaturity.

"You're in a good mood. Is this about the date?"

"No, shut up." Sierra waved a hand at us. "Wait for us to start recording."

A few hours later, the podcast session was done, and I'd told Sierra we all needed to meet to figure out a fixed schedule that would allow the three of us more time for our dissertations and coursework. Thankfully, my friend agreed that the podcast was going to have to take a back seat, as much as it pained us. It meant a lot to me, and I didn't make the decision lightly.

Jan, however, seemed all too happy at the prospect of taking it over early. Her episodes so far had been a revelation. She was crazy and hilarious, but she'd surprised me by being sensitive when she needed to. I guess it was just me she didn't feel the need to be sensitive with.

I strode toward Teviot feeling a lot less stressed than I had this morning. I'd spent an hour in the library scheduling my first interview for my dissertation. I'd reached out to a few social media influencers of different genders, some I knew who'd already spoken out about their trials on social media, some who hadn't but who had varying degrees of followers. Yes, I wanted to interview people who had a ton of followers, but I was just as interested in chatting with people with smaller followings who seemed to dedicate a lot of time to their platforms.

So far only two people hadn't gotten back to me, but the interviews were scheduled, and I'd gotten a positive response from a university who had conducted a huge research project for the UK government on the correlation between the mental health crisis in the country and social media. I was feeling a lot more organized and on top of things.

I spotted Sebastian as soon as I walked into the Library Bar. He was sitting at a table by himself, but a girl stood by his chair, her hand on the back of it. Everything about her body language screamed *flirt*. Sebastian grinned up at her and whatever he said made her laugh, her body bowing closer to his.

Ignoring the spike of white-hot jealousy, I reminded myself he and I were just friends. And that he was the world's biggest flirt. I had to get used to seeing him with other women.

Feeling awkward about approaching, I hovered for a minute, wondering what to do.

Then I heard Jan's voice in my head telling me that Sebastian asked me to lunch, and I should pull up my big-girl knickers and walk over there!

Adjusting my backpack, I tried to infuse casual into my stride. I wasn't sure I was successful, but I was pleased my smile felt natural as I stopped at the table.

Sebastian looked at me before I could even say hi. He grinned broadly. "You came."

My attention flicked to the girl who stared at me with undisguised distaste. I gave her a small smile because I was incapable of being rude unless absolutely provoked. Then I turned to Sebastian. "You thought I wouldn't?"

"I don't know. You're still an enigma." He motioned to the pretty blond. "This is ..."

She frowned. "Hermione."

"Parents big Harry Potter fans?" I asked.

Hermione curled her lip. "What do you think?"

Sebastian's brows pinched together. "Well, Hermione, my friend is here, so ..."

"Are you two ..." She gestured between us.

I opened my mouth to say no, but Sebastian cut me off. "About to have lunch? Just the two of us? Yes. Thanks so much. Nice to meet you, though."

She grimaced and strode off without saying goodbye.

"Sorry."

"Lily, please sit. And no need to apologize." Sebastian shook his head. "Why are some women like that? She was nice until you appeared."

Chuckling, I sat down at the table, dumping my backpack at my feet. "I'd like to think most of our generation has evolved past catty competitiveness, but it still exists." I snorted. "How the heck do you forget the name *Hermione*?"

Sebastian laughed, abashed. "She came up to me and introduced herself so quickly. Said she followed me on socials and always wanted to meet me. Didn't know I was so famous," he muttered.

"My sister googled you." I winced in apology. "She told me you have quite a few followers."

"Not of my doing. Now and then some tabloid or magazine will do an article on the royal family or something repulsive like a list of the best- and worst-looking members of the royal family. It's pretty bloody awful when someone you care about is on the worst. Anyway, I get a flood of new followers from those things."

I'd never really paid attention to tabloids or lists like

those, but I couldn't imagine someone listing me as the worst-looking member of my family on a public forum. "That's atrocious."

"I know. Thankfully it doesn't happen all that often. My family aren't exactly black sheep, but we stay away from a lot of public events and only attend the musts. Weddings, funerals. Ascot. That sort of thing." His expression hardened as he looked away. "But that might change."

I was about to ask why when he tapped the menu in front of me. "Choose something."

Going with the change of subject, I picked a sandwich and salad.

"Is that what you really want or what you think you should eat in front of me?" he asked bluntly.

Taken aback by the question, I replied quietly, "It's what I really want. Why would you ask that?"

Sebastian pressed his lips together, then sighed before explaining, "I notice you seem a little self-conscious about your body and I know you talk about it on your podcast."

My cheeks burned. "*Okay?*"

"I ... first, you should know you're absolutely gorgeous just as you are, and you have no bloody reason to be self-conscious."

My cheeks burned even hotter.

"And second, I want you to be comfortable around me."

Irritated and *uncomfortable*, I decided to be honest about it. "I am the opposite of that right now." I glowered at him. "I don't have a problem with food. I order what I want to eat and don't really think about people thinking about me eating. Pointing out my self-consciousness only makes me embarrassed and self-conscious and now all I'm going to be thinking about when I'm eating is the fact that you are, in fact, thinking about what I'm eating."

He gaped at me. Then blanched. "Bugger, that's a clusterfuck, isn't it."

Before I could respond, he got up, and for a second, I thought he was about to leave. Instead, he rounded the table and slid onto my bench. He rested his arm along the back of it so we were cocooned on this side.

"What are you doing?" I looked him up and down, my skin buzzing with awareness at his sudden proximity. I made a mental note to ask him when it was less weird what cologne he wore.

"I felt very far away from you during an important discussion."

My lips twitched. "You're kind of an odd duck, do you know that?"

Sebastian's eyes twinkled and I noted his shoulders drop a little, as if he was visibly relaxing. "I'm sorry for making you uncomfortable. Believe it or not, it was the exact opposite of my intentions."

His eyes roamed my face as if marking every detail in his mind for later. It was confusing. The way he looked at me was confusing, considering he only wanted to be my friend.

"What were your intentions?"

"We're friends now," he said, as if he'd read my mind and was making things absolutely clear. "And I care about my friends. I want you to see yourself the way you really are and the way you really are ... You are gorgeous, Lily Sawyer. Inside and out. Nothing to be self-conscious about. Ever."

Then why don't you want me?

I shoved out the melancholy thought and smiled. "I appreciate that. And I'll take it on board. I promise. But just so you know when I was sixteen...someone made me feel self-conscious about my weight. From then, I was always on some fad diet because I thought I was fat. I've finally gotten to a place where I just want to be healthy, and I stopped the fad dieting and just try to eat well. But people being weird about food reminds of that time so—"

"Lily, I'm so sorry." Sebastian leaned in close. Close enough to kiss. His expression was anguished. "I won't ever bring it up again. I'm an arsehole."

"You're not an arsehole." *You are very close and way too good-looking, though.* His eyes were a mossy green around the iris, but the green melted into a Mediterranean Sea blue. Beautiful eyes.

"Good. So, we're still friends?"

"We're still friends."

"I'll go order the food."

"Let me pay—"

"Nope." He slid off the bench.

"Thorne, if we're to be friends, we need to share the cost of stuff."

"Not today." He was gone before I could argue further.

While Sebastian waited at the bar to place our order, the girl from earlier, Hermione, approached me with a girl at her side. They had their bags, so it seemed as if they were leaving.

"Hi again," she said, a little friendlier this time.

"Hi."

"Sorry about earlier. I didn't know he was taken."

Knowing it would be dishonest to pretend he was, I shook my head. "We're just friends."

Her pretty eyes lit up. "Really?" She stuffed her hand into her bag and pulled out a pen and paper. Tearing a corner of a sheet of A4, she leaned on the table and scribbled on the piece. "Will you give him this? I tried reaching out on socials, but he apparently doesn't answer his messages."

I looked down to see her name and number on the paper. Feeling like I'd swallowed a brick, I nodded and took it. "Of course."

"Thanks. You're a sweetheart." She grinned at me and sauntered off with her companion.

Less than a minute later, Sebastian returned. "What did Hogwarts want?"

Laughing, I held out the paper to him. "She gave me her number to give to you."

He frowned and took it. Then he crumpled it up.

At my shocked look, he huffed. "I do have some standards. She was ugly to you."

"She was nicer when she found out we're not dating."

"Oh, well then, that makes all the difference," he replied dryly.

Warmth filled my chest.

Sebastian did that intense staring thing again.

"What?"

He shrugged. "I like looking at you."

Confusion replaced the warmth until I reminded myself that Sebastian was a self-confessed flirt. He flirted with everyone. Wanting to find some even footing again, I asked tentatively, "What did you mean earlier?"

"Earlier when?"

"You were talking about your family not being involved in the institution." I referred to the royal family. "You said 'But that might change.' What did you mean?"

Sebastian ran a hand through his hair, disheveling it and making me think naughty thoughts I immediately threw out of my head when he leaned across the table and confessed, "My parents separated over the summer."

The crushed look on his face made my chest ache. "I'm so sorry."

"They haven't gone public with it. And I ... I haven't told anyone. Not even Harry. Juno and I talk about it, but ... anyway, it was a big shock."

"You can talk to me about it."

Frustration hardened his features. "It came out of nowhere, Lily. I mean, my parents used to joke that Juno and I had to be adopted because neither of us are interested in monogamy while our parents were attached at the hip. Our childhood was idyllic. We had parents who adored each other. Yes, I went to boarding school, and it wasn't always fun, but going home was magical. I had two parents who loved us and loved each other. There were no clues, no disagreements or strangeness between them. There was no buildup to this separation. Of course, Juno and I are out of the house now, so if there was anything going on, it happened quickly. Sometime between last Christmas and this summer. It shocked the hell out of us."

"Did they give you a reason?"

"They won't talk about it."

Sympathy had me reaching over to squeeze his hand. "I'm sorry."

He patted the top of my hand with his other. "Thanks. It's ... I'm a grown man and it shouldn't bother me this much, but it is messing with my head a little."

"Of course it is. If I was forty years old and my parents turned around and told me they were divorcing, it would mess with my head. Never mind not explaining why."

It was an interesting case. There had to be a reason, of course, and one Sebastian and his sister had to let their parents work through before they were ready to explain. It was also interesting that Sebastian was a commitment-phobe considering his description of his parents as such a loving couple. Usually, people were less likely to want serious connections with people if there was some kind of trauma, either parental divorce or familial loss.

At Sebastian's grim expression, I switched off my analytical wannabe-therapist thoughts and pulled back my hand. "Why does that mean things will change with the royal family?"

Before he could respond, our food arrived.

He'd ordered a cheeseburger and fries, and honestly, I did have food regrets as soon as I saw it.

Sebastian seemed to read me. "You are very welcome to my fries."

Grinning, I reached over and took one. "Don't mind if I do."

After a bite, he swallowed and answered my last question. "My mum made herself a little bit of a black sheep by marrying my father, a commoner. We weren't ousted or anything, but my parents didn't partake in a lot of the royal events because of it. We saw our family at private affairs all the time, though. However, Mum decided she wants back *in*. Apparently, that means trying to set Juno and me up with 'suitable' partners."

"What does *suitable* entail?"

"So far, the last remnants of the aristocracy. She tried to set me up with Lady Amelia Shrewsbury who is only eighteen years old and in her first year here."

I tried not to laugh at his expression, like he'd just tasted sand in his burger. "You can tell her to stop, you know."

"Oh, I have. But I don't recognize her right now. She's not the mum I grew up with."

At the sad bitterness in his tone, I reassured him, "It'll

pass. This separation and whatever has caused it must be devastating for your parents, no matter if they say it's not. And I imagine they'll act in all kinds of uncharacteristic ways until they themselves make peace with the change. You need to be patient. As difficult as it might prove. And know I'm here on the days it is more difficult to deal with. You can always talk to me."

Sebastian tilted his head, studying me.

"What?"

"Nothing. I'm just so glad you decided to be my friend."

CHAPTER TWELVE
SEBASTIAN

> This guy is an arsehole.

I frowned down at the text Lily had sent. I was surprised it got through, considering I had one bar of signal on my phone. Courtesy of being deep in the Vaults. The Vaults were hidden beneath Edinburgh's Old Town and were once slums and criminal dens. Some of them had been turned into nightclubs and bars. Whistlebinkies was loud and crowded as people drank and waited for the band to come on. Harry and Zac were talking to a couple of girls at the end of the long bar near where the band would play, while my gut knotted at the possibilities of why Lily's date was an arsehole.

When she'd reminded me yesterday she was bringing her date tonight, I'd ignored my irritation. But I was irritated again. And concerned.

Another text came in before I could reply.

> Just preparing you so you know he's a dick.

Will be there in 2 mins.

Fan-fucking-tastic.

My focus remained on the stairwell entrance.

"Bas. Bastian!" Harry nudged me.

I turned to find him gesturing to one of the three girls. "Alana is asking if you've seen Vistas live?"

"Yes." I nodded absentmindedly. We'd caught a gig or two of the local rock band in first year. My attention returned to the stairs.

Harry nudged me again.

"What?"

He widened his eyes as if to say *"What the hell?"*

"I'm waiting for Lily."

Zac pushed off the bar. "Lily's coming?"

I nodded and glanced back as a pair of shapely legs came into view on the stairs. I was about to turn away when I recognized the long, thick dark hair spilling down the woman's shoulders. It was Lily. Alone. I pushed away from the bar and held up an arm so she could see me as she turned. I saw her expression melt with recognition before she walked around well-guarded tables and the cluster of people at the bar.

Heat licked down my spine at the sight of her. She wore a tartan pleated miniskirt with an oversized long-sleeved band T-shirt. The sexy casual look shocked the hell out of me because I'd never seen her bare legs before. Now I couldn't understand why. My God. She wore Nike trainers because the woman didn't need heels to accentuate anything. I tried not to ogle the sight of her long, olive-toned legs but then got stuck ogling her face instead. At uni, Lily didn't wear a ton of makeup, but tonight her eyes were all done up and she looked incredible.

She also looked flustered and annoyed. As she reached me, she tucked a strand of hair behind her ear and huffed loudly, "He's outside on a call."

Settling a hand on her lower back, I drew her into my personal space.

So I could hear her better.

"What happened?"

"Och, what didn't?" Lily rolled her eyes. "His name is Kyle. He works in finance. He was twenty minutes late and didn't apologize. He didn't ask me one question the entire drink at the bar or the walk here. I don't think he knows my name. But he managed to make a bunch of passive-aggressive comments about me being a student, and he is now talking to his friend on the phone."

"What a prick." I pressed a sympathetic kiss to her temple. She smelled amazing. A different perfume tonight. Something headier. "Let me get you a drink."

Harry and Zac said hello and introduced Lily to the girls they'd met while we waited for the bartender. I caught the older guy next to us staring down at Lily's legs and glared at him in warning. He blanched and turned away.

"There you are!"

The booming male voice had us all turning around.

Something sharp and ugly swept through me at the sight of the finance guy named Kyle.

He was very good-looking, and I was very glad Lily thought he was a prick.

Well-mannered, however, Lily introduced us all and asked him what he was drinking.

Once we all had a glass in hand and were huddled in a group, I casually rested my free arm around Lily's shoulders as we chatted.

Kyle the prick didn't say much, but I could feel his eyes on me.

Finally, he blurted, "I'm sorry, but I thought you and I were on a date."

Lily gaped at him. "That *was* the intention."

I smirked at her smart response.

"But you're with this guy?" He pointed to me.

"We're just friends." I took a casual sip of my pint, but I couldn't resist the challenge in my expression. And I didn't remove my arm.

Kyle the prick shook his head in aggravation. "I knew I shouldn't have swiped right on a student. Sorry, you're gorgeous, but this is not my scene, and I can't deal with the drama." He slammed his half-drunk pint on the bar and abruptly pushed through the crowds to leave.

"Good riddance." I raised my glass to his departure.

"Drama?" Lily gestured after him. "*He* turned up late. *He* barely talked to me. What an absolute turd!"

"Aw, sorry about the bad date, Lil." Zac gave her a sympathetic nudge. "Let us buy you another drink to cheer you up."

"Are you two not dating, then?" the girl Harry had spoken of before—Elaine or Illan or something—asked. Her eyes were fixed on my arm around Lily's shoulders.

"Sawyer and I are just good friends." I pulled her closer so her warm, curvy body pressed to mine. "Aren't we, darling?"

She clinked her pint against mine. "That we are."

We chatted among ourselves, about classes, music, plans for the future. We laughed and joked and took the piss and Lily seemed to fall in with my friends as easily as she had with me. I could tell Harry and Zac really liked her, which pleased me.

Then the band started to warm up, so we edged closer to the stage.

"Who are these guys again?" Lily asked.

"Local band. I think you'll like them. Here." I pushed closer to the stage so we had a good view and positioned Lily in front of me. "Lean on me. Get comfy," I urged, sliding my arms around her waist to draw her back against my chest.

After a second or two, she relaxed. I gave her a squeeze and leaned down to murmur in her ear, "You're not upset about that prick earlier?"

She shook her head slightly and I thought I heard her breath hitch.

Awareness flooded through me.

Just friends, I reminded myself.

Just bloody good friends.

I liked this woman too damn much to mess it up with sex.

"He wasn't my type," she replied so quietly I almost didn't hear her.

"Hi, folks." The lead singer's voice crackled into the mic, halting my follow-up questions. "Thanks for coming out tonight. We're the Steel Pennies." They launched immediately into their first track, a fast rock song that had everyone around us bopping their heads and shifting their feet. The rhythm caught Lily, her body moving to the beat without thought. Her curvy arse moved against me, and I sucked in a breath, taking a step back with what I hoped was casualness. I rested my hands loosely on her warm hips instead so I could feel the movements without her undulating against me in a way that made me hard.

Feeling like someone was watching me, I glanced left and found Zac. His frown turned to a knowing smirk.

I ignored him and focused on the band because if I focused on the woman in front of me, I'd be unable to hide the physical representation of my appreciation for her.

———

"They were fantastic!" Lily cried happily as we all tumbled out of Whistlebinkies and into the much cooler night air. For the bar being deep in the Vaults with its stone walls and floors, it got bloody hot.

I smiled, happy she'd enjoyed herself, and watched as she pulled out her phone. "I'm going to follow them on socials."

I peered down at her phone as our group walked toward the Royal Mile. Lily quickly tapped on the app, searched the band, and followed them. "Are you following me?"

She looked up at me in surprise. "No. Do you want me to?"

"Of course." I pulled my mobile out of my pocket. "I'll follow you. Follow me back."

"I'm warning you now, my feed isn't exactly exciting." She proceeded to give me her handle.

Finding her, I clicked follow and then scrolled through her photos. I paused on one of her with a good-looking blond bloke with whom she appeared very cozy.

"Who's this?" I asked, as the notification popped up on my screen to tell me she'd followed me back.

"Who?" Lily leaned in to see what I was looking at.

Her face glistened with sweat and her cheeks were flushed from the heat of the bar. I looked away quickly before I let very dirty thoughts take over my mind.

"Oh, that's my cousin Luke. Well, he's not technically blood related. But I think of him as my cousin."

"But you're not related? You look close."

Lily laughed. "As close as cousins. Even if we didn't think of each other like family, Luke would never be attracted to me."

I scowled at that. "Anyone would be attracted to you."

She shot me a look of confusion. But it melted away as she grinned cheekily, those adorable dimples tempting me to madness. "Luke prefers men."

"Ah." I laughed huskily at my strange possessiveness. I really needed to get over myself if Lily and I were to make a go at this friendship thing.

Lily suddenly frowned as we turned on the Royal Mile heading toward my flat. "Where are we going?"

"Our place."

"Oh, I should head home."

"Come back for a bit. Then I'll walk you home."

"I can grab a taxi."

"No, I'll see you home." I threw a look at the girls following Harry and Zac back to our place. "If you leave, then I'm left with Illiana."

"Alana." Lily's lips twitched. "She's very pretty."

"I'm not interested and not in the mood to reject someone tonight. And I did rescue you from Kyle the prick, so you owe me," I teased.

"How did you rescue me?" She shoved me playfully. "I think it was pretty clear the evening would end that way from the moment he showed up with his phone glued to his bloody ear."

"Moron," I muttered under my breath.

"What?"

"Nothing. Will you come?"

She turned around suddenly, walking backward so she could face me. The short hem of her little pleated skirt bounced around her thighs, and it took everything within me to keep my eyes on her face. "Fine. But only because I'm nosy about this flat on the Royal Mile." She gestured around her. "Very fancy."

I narrowed my eyes. "You're not going to think too badly of me when you see it, are you?"

"Why? Do you have a butler called Wakefield who waits on you hand and foot?"

Laughing, I shook my head. "Not quite."

"Then I'll only gently mock your fanciness, I promise."

Lily didn't mock me at all, but I found myself watching her every reaction as the lads and I led her and their companions into the penthouse. Lily took everything in with a guarded expression and then strode across the living space to the three tall windows overlooking the Royal Mile.

I sidled up beside her. "What are you thinking?"

"It's so modern. You wouldn't think it was from the outside." Lily smiled at me. "It's fantastic. What a view." She pressed a hand to the glass, her pretty, polished nails making a tapping sound on it. A sudden flash image of those nails raking down my back had me squeezing my eyes closed. "I've lived here my whole life, and I never tire of the history."

I opened my eyes as I watched her lean to look farther up the thoroughfare that led to the castle.

"Do you know the last time the castle was inhabited was 1633?" She looked up at me. "Can you imagine what life was like then?"

"Smelly," I joked. "I imagine it was very smelly."

Lily laughed, those dimples deeply indenting her cheeks, and I decided my new mission in life was to make her laugh every time we met. Which would hopefully be often.

"Harry's asking if you guys want a drink?"

We turned to the voice to find the girl from the bar staring at me. "I'm fine. Lily?"

"I'm good."

"We're good, Illiana, thank you."

The girl's face fell. "It's Alana." She grimaced and strode off toward the kitchen where the others were.

"You do that deliberately, don't you?"

At Lily's odd tone, I replied, "Do what?"

"Get their names wrong. When you're not interested in a woman, you deliberately get her name wrong."

Christ, she was way too perceptive for my own good. I shrugged guiltily. "It seems like the least shitty way to make it obvious."

"It's not." She gave me a disappointed look.

The thought of Lily finding anything about me disappointing stung. "Then I won't do it again," I promised.

She squeezed my arm to let me know she wasn't mad at me. Then she sighed. "I really should get going."

"Bloody hell, where have you all been?" a familiar and unexpected voice asked. "I've been waiting here for ages."

CHAPTER THIRTEEN
LILY

A pixie of a woman stood in the entrance of the open-plan living area of Sebastian's impressive flat. She was petite but stunning with her short blond hair and doll-like features.

"Juno!" Harry crossed the room to pull the woman into his arms.

She laughed and hugged him back. "Well, that's a nice greeting."

"My sister," Sebastian told me with a pleased grin before he strode toward her.

Nervousness fluttered in my belly as I followed him.

Juno released Harry as Sebastian reached her and he bent down to lift her off her feet in a bear hug.

"Put me down, you big softie!" Juno cried happily.

Sebastian set her down but cuddled her into his side, pressing a kiss to her temple as he proudly introduced, "This is my sister, Juno. Juno, you know Harry and Zac. These are their recently made friends Alana, Katie, and Shan." His gaze moved to me, and he beamed. "And this is my new best friend, Lily. Lily, meet Juno."

He was so disarmingly boyish sometimes it made my chest ache.

"Hi." I waved shyly.

Juno grinned, shrugging off Sebastian's arm to pull me into a hug. "I've heard so much about you."

"You have?"

"Mmm-hmm." She released me but only to study me like a prospective mother-in-law might. She stared and then announced, "You're frightfully attractive, aren't you?"

I bit my lip against teasing her for using the word *frightfully*. "You are too."

"Oh, I know." She tilted her head cockily. "Did I hear you were leaving? You can't leave yet. Stay for a bit, please. I'm only in the city for one night."

"What *are* you doing here?" Sebastian asked.

"I have a meeting with an art gallery who might be interested in showcasing and selling my latest pottery collection."

"You're a potter?" I asked, genuinely curious.

"You didn't tell her about me?" Juno smacked her brother's arm. "What's wrong with you?"

He snorted. "I did tell her about you. I somehow forgot the potter part."

"I feel so loved."

Sebastian hooked an arm around her again, crushing her into his side as he guided her toward the kitchen for drinks.

For the next hour, we lounged and chatted in the living room on the giant sectional. Juno seemed only to be interested in me, so I felt a little under the microscope. At first, I was worried she thought I wasn't somehow good enough for Sebastian. In friendship or otherwise. Seeing his penthouse flat here on the Royal Mile reminded me of something I often forgot when we were together, unless we were directly talking about it: Sebastian was from money. A lot of it. And not just money. He was the son of Lady Clarissa Hanover, the daughter of a princess.

To my relief, however, Juno, despite her posh accent and manner, wasn't a snob. She was hilarious and kind. I'd just finished telling her about my bad date that evening.

"Dating is the worst." She leaned against Sebastian on the couch. "I once had to climb out of a ladies' restroom window to escape a bad date."

I chuckled at the imagery. "It must have been pretty terrible if you had to do that."

"Oh, awful. It started off as little 'icks.' If you know what I mean. Talking with his mouth full, ogling my breasts."

"Yes, that's enough, thank you." Sebastian wrinkled his nose.

"It got much worse. He suddenly started talking about what he wanted to do to my breasts—"

"I think I might be sick." Sebastian did look a little green, and I struggled not to laugh.

"Anyway, when he asked me what my safe word was, I got out of there." Her eyes twinkled with devilishness. "It was far too soon to share a safe word. And who wants a man who talks while he eats to tie them to a bed? Will he keep talking while he eats, I ask? It's rather a distracting and ineffective use of his tongue."

Sebastian squeezed his eyes closed. "I beg of you, stop talking."

I, on the other hand, cackled so hard, I had to wipe tears from the corners of my eyes.

Juno grinned unapologetically.

"You and my sister January would get on so well," I told her as my laughter melted.

"What are you lot giggling about?" Zac asked from the other side of the sectional.

It seemed Harry and one of the girls had disappeared.

"Juno is torturing me. I don't know what I did to deserve it." Sebastian mock glowered at her.

"I'm not torturing you. I'm bonding with Lily. I thought that would please you."

In answer, he pressed an affectionate kiss to her temple.

And that's finally when the confusion I'd felt for weeks dissipated. In its place I felt deflated, and I had to keep smiling to cover it up. I hadn't understood Sebastian's affection toward me. His physical affection. Putting his arm around me tonight. Holding me while we watched the band. Kisses to my temple and cuddling me close.

However, watching him with Juno I realized it was just who he was. He was a physically affectionate person. And I should count myself lucky that he liked me so much, he treated me as he treated his sister.

Unfortunately, at that moment, I realized I had been holding on to a wee bit of hope that his behavior toward me meant he was actually attracted to me. That maybe our friendship would develop into something more.

But Sebastian hadn't lied to me. Or to himself.

He needed a friend and he'd chosen me.

I'd take that for the compliment it was and get over myself.

"I really do need to get going." I stood slowly. "I'll call a cab."

"I'll walk you," Sebastian spoke up.

"I can do it," Zac offered. "Your sister is here."

"No, no, don't mind me." Juno waved Zac off. "Bastian, see her safely home. Crash on the couch when you get back because I'm stealing your bed."

"Of course you are."

CHAPTER FOURTEEN

LILY

Sebastian insisted I borrow a hoodie, and I was glad because the early-morning air held a chill that announced the start of the autumn. At this time of the morning, there were a few stragglers hanging around. At three, when the nightclubs closed, there would be a spill of noisy, drunk people. Considering there were a few nightclubs on our path home, I wanted to get by them before they shut. Sebastian with his long strides easily kept up with my quick ones.

"I like her a lot," I confessed as we cut through Upper Bow onto Victoria Street. "Juno."

"Yes, she's wonderful when she isn't talking about her sex life in front of me."

Chuckling, I nodded. "She really is like Jan. We need to introduce them."

"I'm afraid of the chaos that would occur if we did."

At the sight of two drunk lads wobbling their way uphill toward us, Sebastian protectively put his arm around me to draw me into his side. The hard heat of his body stole my breath again. Just like it had at the bar.

I really needed to get over this unrequited crush. Pronto.

After we passed the drunks, he released me and I tried not to let out a whoosh of breath. Distraction would help. I hesitated a second before daring to broach the subject. "How ... How is Juno coping with your parents' separation?"

He stuck his hands in his jeans pockets, unconsciously hunching his shoulders inward as he replied quietly, "She likes to come off tough and irritated to cover the fact that she's sad and angry. And confused. We're both just really confused."

"I'm sorry." I squeezed his arm in comfort, then quickly moved on because I didn't want to make him melancholy. "I'd love to see Juno's pottery."

"Oh. Here." Sebastian pulled out his phone, tapped the screen a couple of times, and handed it to me. "Her socials."

I scrolled through her feed only to discover she not only made beautiful vases and dinnerware, but she also sculpted art pieces. At the top of her profile, it said she had over sixteen thousand followers.

"She's incredibly talented." I handed his phone back to him as we strode down the cobbled road of the Grassmarket. A girl in a tiny minidress stood screaming in another girl's face while a guy sat on his haunches nearby with his head in his hands.

Sebastian and I shared a wince at the drama before he continued about Juno's art. "Yeah. She started doing those time-lapse videos on her pottery last week and her followers shot up. That's probably why the gallery has reached out with interest. Power of social media."

"You sound like my cousin Beth."

"The one who runs the social media management company?"

"Aye. She's actually helped me make some contacts with a few influencers I want to interview for my dissertation."

"What's your dissertation subject?"

"The impact of social media on self-esteem across genders."

Sebastian's eyebrows rose. "Heavy stuff."

"My choice of career is heavy stuff."

He seemed to ponder that. "How will you cope? How will you compartmentalize all the awful stories you're going to hear day in and day out?"

"I hope I cope well, but I won't know until I do the job." I was pragmatic about the reality of being a psychotherapist. "I know that I want to do something meaningful with my life. And while social media is something you and I were raised with, our parents' generation wasn't, and I've read all these articles on how far-reaching its impact is. Mental health issues are on the rise. I want to know what part social media is playing in that. Not merely online bullying but what else is it about social media that triggers negative feelings. Is it the platforms themselves deliberately fudging the algorithm to show their users content they know will trigger a negative response because we tend to engage more when we're angry or upset about something? Is it the universal fantasy content? And since it's well documented that men find it harder to talk about their mental health, is the impact on self-esteem different across genders?"

Sebastian was silent at my side, and my cheeks heated.

"Sorry. I can get a bit carried away by the subject."

"No, no. I'm just thinking, I'm a little in awe of you, to be honest. I've never really considered any of that stuff. I just post ... now and then ..." He drifted off.

"What is it? Aren't you content with your degree? What made you decide to be a civil engineer?"

He shrugged. "I've always been good at maths and physics. And I like building things. Working out how to engineer a structure. My dad and I built a few of the structures on our estate back in Norfolk. A couple of sheds, chicken coops." He grinned. "And even a summer house."

"Well, I'm in awe of you," I told him honestly. "My brain does not work like that. I was useless at physics."

"I have a secret," Sebastian suddenly blurted out as we crossed the main street and took a shortcut through the cobbled lane I wouldn't have dreamed of taking alone at night.

I raised an eyebrow at his boyish outburst. "What kind of secret?"

He rubbed his nape, huffing in bemusement. "I don't know what it is about you ..."

"Okay ...?"

"Only Juno knows. I lie quite easily to everyone else about this." He stopped in the middle of the lane. "But I trust you, and I don't quite understand it."

"It's because I'm trustworthy." I pointed to my dimples as I grinned. "These are the dimples of a truly trustworthy person."

Sebastian chuckled, his eyes twinkling warmly. Whatever this lie was, I didn't believe for a second it was harmful.

Because ... despite our inauspicious start ... I trusted him too.

He started walking again but tapped on his phone screen. "It's easier to show you."

I took the phone, brimming over with curiosity. When I

tripped on a cobble, Sebastian took my arm, guiding me so I could keep looking at the screen.

Once more, it was a social media account. I scrolled through the feed of beautiful time-lapse videos. I stood there for what could have been minutes watching a man whose face never turned to the camera, create impressionist paintings using a mix of techniques from splattering the paint on canvas and then finessing the details with palette knives and brushes. What started out as an abstract mess turned into extraordinary works of art by the end. There were lots of scenes from Edinburgh's cityscape but also places I didn't recognize. A quick scroll to the top of the account showed it had fifty-seven thousand followers. There was a link in the bio to a website. A quick click on it showed me it sold originals and prints.

I recognized the back of the man doing all the painting.

Understanding, I gaped at Sebastian, suddenly seeing him in a new light. "You're an artist too."

His lips curved upward. "Yes. A secret one."

"And a phenomenal one." I glanced back down at the phone, clicking on a painting of a lamppost in St. Mary's Close in the snow. The way the light caught the snowflakes was eerie and beautiful. "Thorne, these are stunning."

"Thank you." His voice sounded extra gruff. "I'm glad you think so."

"But how do you pull this off without anyone knowing?"

"I rent a tiny studio not far from your place. It's actually a one-bedroom flat with a massive bay window in the living room that lets in a ton of light. I use an online printer for the prints, but I pack all those up myself and post them out. It can be time-consuming if one of my images or Reels takes off, since I then get a surge of purchases. The originals have been selling well too. I have a company do the professional packing and shipping for those. The prints are the most time-consuming part. Last night I got fifty orders. I need to go to the flat tomorrow morning and start packaging them up."

"I'll help," I offered without thinking, more than curious to see this studio of his.

"Lily, you have your own stuff to do. I can manage."

"Let me help."

Sebastian began walking again. "You really want to?"

"I really want to. Did you know my dad is a professional photographer?"

His eyebrows rose. "Yeah?"

"He does private events mostly, but he's started something similar to what you're doing on socials. I've helped him curate wedding albums."

"Wow. I'd love to see his work."

"I'll show you sometime. So? Can I help tomorrow?"

"Of course you can help."

I asked him what his plans were for his art in the future, and Sebastian shrugged as we approached my flat. "No plans, really. It's a passion project. I'll forge ahead with my degree."

His words rang false to me. Almost like he was lying to himself. "Juno is making money from her pottery. Why shouldn't you continue to make money from your art? You should do it if it would make you happy."

"Being a painter is not the practical choice. Juno loves the struggling artist shtick because we have a trust fund, so it's not exactly struggling. But I want the trust fund to be a backup. I don't want to be living off it." He grimaced. "Tell me if I sound like a privileged arsehole."

I let us into the building, lowering my voice to a

whisper so as not to wake my neighbors. "You are privileged, but you don't sound like a privileged arsehole. A privileged arsehole wouldn't ask if he sounded like a privileged arsehole. You have to do what feels right to you. But if you're in the position to do what makes you happy, I would. If you ever want to talk to my dad about turning it into a business, I'm happy to arrange that."

"I won't," he said, uncharacteristically abrupt. Then he softened. "Thanks, though."

So busy mulling over his weird attitude about his art, it wasn't until we'd reached my flat that I realized we hadn't said goodbye.

As if he'd read my mind, Sebastian smirked. "Let me see your flat. You saw mine."

"Okay. But you'll need to be quiet because Maddie will be asleep."

He pressed a finger to his lips in promise and I let us in. I kicked off my trainers, leaving them by the door, and locked the door behind us. Sebastian removed his shoes and wandered off. I shook my head, smiling at his nosiness as he poked his head into the kitchen and bathroom and then the airy living room. The bedrooms were off the spacious hall, mine abutting the living room.

"Can I see?" Sebastian whispered, gesturing to my bedroom, having guessed it was mine because the door was open, and Maddie's door was closed.

I nodded, hoping like hell I hadn't left underwear lying around.

The room wasn't huge. While it had high ceilings, the double bed was tucked up against the window so you could only get in on one side. That left room for a wardrobe and a desk and a little floor space to maneuver around. Because of that, I kept the room organized and tidy. Except for my books. I had piles of them under my bed, neatly stacked. My e-reader sat on the desk by my lamp, my TBR pile of paperbacks lying next to it.

Sebastian's gaze danced across the walls where I'd tacked up posters of the city and of my favorite bands. Interspersed between them were photographs of my friends and family. Photos that spanned years.

I sidled up to him as he bent to peer at a photograph of me in high school. It was my fifth-year prom, and I'd worn a red dress that was way more daring than anything I'd worn since. Jan had talked me into it. My dad had a fit when he saw me in it, and Mum had reluctantly allowed me to leave the house. My boyfriend at the time was older and he'd picked me up after the prom and ... well ... let's just say he hadn't been very nice to me about the dress.

But the photograph of me and my high school buddies was one I tried to look on fondly. I was proud of the girl who had dared to wear that dress. Mum said I looked like a dark-haired Jessica Rabbit in it. I didn't know who that was, so I'd googled her and had been weirdly flattered by the comparison to a cartoon.

"My fifth-year high school prom," I told Sebastian.

Sebastian raised an eyebrow and grinned cheekily. "I imagine you made the male teachers in attendance very uncomfortable."

"Don't say that," I whisper-shouted, smacking his arm.

He laughed unrepentantly. "You're the stuff of fantasies in that dress. Did you have a date?"

Just like that, my mood dimmed. "Nope." I shrugged. "Well, this is it. Do you want to call an Uber?"

His brows drew together but after a few seconds, he went with the subject change. "Actually, since I need to be at my studio around the corner tomorrow first thing, would you mind if I stayed here? Juno is in my bed."

My heart jolted. "Stayed here, here?" I gestured to my bed.

Sebastian lifted his palms. "I promise I'm not making a pass. I'm just shattered. I meant I'll sleep on the couch."

Our couch was a tiny two-seater that had seen better days. Plus, the extra blankets and pillows were in the cupboard in Maddie's room. I said as much.

"It'll have to be my bed." I bit my lip.

"No funny business, I promise." Then he grimaced. "Bugger, I'm sorry. I don't mean to make you uncomfortable. I'll go."

"No." I reached out to grab his arm. "It's fine. But you're taking the window side."

"So you have easy access to get out to pee, right?"

I narrowed my eyes. "Well ... actually ... shut up."

His laughter followed me out of the room as I left to go pee.

Once I'd brushed my teeth and washed my face, I gave Sebastian one of the spare new toothbrushes Maddie kept in the bathroom. He raised an eyebrow, and I explained, "They're for family guests, not one-night stands."

"The guests you have nowhere to put? Yes, I don't believe you," he teased. "I've listened to your podcast, remember."

Rolling my eyes, I shut the bathroom door in his face and on his laughter.

Quickly, before he returned, I changed into pajamas. I didn't let myself overthink what I chose.

I waited awkwardly on the edge of the bed for him to return so he could take the window side. Butterflies fluttered crazily in my belly, and I shook my head at myself.

What was I nervous about? It wasn't like we were about to have sex.

Sebastian treated me like a sister.

When he returned, he flashed me a weary smile before closing the bedroom door. "God, the tiredness just hit me."

Did it?

Because I *was* tired until this scenario.

I gestured to the bed and Sebastian got in. Not over-thinking it, I slipped in beside him, keeping my distance as I pulled the duvet over us. Then I switched off the bedside lamp. Moonlight shafted through the too-thin curtains over the window.

Sebastian lightly plumped the pillow behind his head, and he closed his eyes with a smile. "This is cozy, Sawyer."

He was completely unbothered by the fact that he was in bed with me.

I stared at the ceiling, trying to stave off the ache in my chest. Maybe Mum and Aunt Jo were wrong. Maybe I shouldn't have pursued this friendship when my feelings were too friendly.

"Lily?"

"Oh, good night, Thorne. Sleep well." I turned on my side, giving him my back.

"Night, Sawyer. Thanks for sharing your bed."

His rumbly voice wrapped around those particular words caused a tingling between my legs. I shifted rest-lessly for a moment and then started counting to a hundred in my head.

By the time I was done, Sebastian's breathing had evened out into sleep.

Turning around to face him, I rested my cheek on my hands. Because of the light spilling in from outside, I could make out his features clearly in the dark of the room. He looked younger in sleep. And so bloody handsome, I could cry at the absurdity of my current situation.

I'd met my unicorn.

The guy who made me feel so comfortable I could talk to him about anything.

And yet whom I was so attracted to, I felt like every fiber of my being came alive in a way it never had until him.

A bloody unicorn.

Yet he didn't feel the same way.

Of course not.

I should have known when I finally found him, he'd only want to be friends.

CHAPTER FIFTEEN
SEBASTIAN

At first, when I awoke staring at curtains I didn't recognize, my immediate panicked thought was: *Bugger. Who did I sleep with last night?*

It was as I gingerly turned around in the unfamiliar bed and saw the posters and photographs on the wall that last night came back to me on a wave of relief.

I was with Lily.

Curiosity had my head whipping right.

There she was.

Long hair sprawled across her pillow, and mine, in fact. I rested my head near it and inhaled the scent of that delicious shampoo she used. My gaze trailed across her face. Her dark lashes were incredibly thick. And she had a freckle on her right cheekbone I'd never noticed before, which seemed impossible since I was pretty sure I'd studied her face until it was imprinted on my brain. Perfect little button nose. And her mouth ... my attention snagged on her lips, lips meant for kissing. They were parted in sleep, her light breathing filling the bedroom. The urge to press my mouth to hers forced me to drag my eyes off her.

Unfortunately, my attention was ensnared by the rise of her right breast. Her loose pajama top had slipped during the night. It dipped low over one side and pulled taut on the other. Lily was generously endowed. Her large chest was what made her narrow waist look even tinier. I drew in a shuddering breath as need tightened in my gut. She was all smooth olive skin, elegant limbs, and then lush curves.

I squeezed my eyes closed.

I would pick the most stunning woman to be my best friend.

It was true, then. I was a masochist.

My eyes flew open at the sound of her mumbling in her sleep and shifting.

This is Lily, I reminded myself sharply. Lovely, kind, smart, funny Lily who was the only person I felt truly myself around.

Something as animal and basic as physical attraction was not going to drive a wedge between us.

I needed her too damn much.

No, I still didn't understand why I'd attached myself to her like a fucking barnacle, but it was what it was, and I wouldn't ruin our friendship.

Even if the urge to nuzzle my face in her neck and cuddle her was almost as strong as the urge to bury my body inside hers. God, I hoped this want for her dimmed over time. It would get damned exhausting denying it.

Not wanting Lily to wake only to find me with the hard-on I was currently sporting, I drew off the duvet on my side and then tried to ninja my way over her. My breath caught as I hovered over her for a second. Cursing inwardly, I practically jumped off the bed and hurried from the room.

As soon as I was behind the bathroom door, I sighed in relief.

Then looked down at my cock straining against my jeans.

Bloody Nora.

———

Thankfully, a few minutes of thinking about the Queen of England (who was literally my great-aunt) solved my situation. Lily was oblivious about my reaction to waking up next to her. She had a quick shower without washing her hair and while I waited, I started reading one of the romantasy novels on her shelves. The fae romance sucked me right in. When she came out, I asked if I could borrow it, and she smiled in delight and said yes. Then I washed up as best as I could. I had extra clothes at my studio, so I'd change there. We grabbed a quick bowl of cereal and left before Maddie woke.

I think Lily just didn't want to answer any leading questions about my presence.

Before heading to my studio, I bought us a coffee from the shop across the street from Lily's flat, discussing the book I'd already read the first few chapters of. Lily grew more animated as she declared the next three books were even better than the first.

We made our way around the corner onto Glengyle Terrace across from the Meadows.

"It's strange to think I've been coming to this studio for two years and never bumped into you. I'm a little annoyed about it, to be honest." I grinned before sipping my coffee.

Lily chuckled, rubbing sleepily at her makeup-free eyes. "Fate wanted our meeting to be a wee bit more dramatic, it seems."

I eyed her. "You're sure you want to come help? You could go back to bed. You've had hardly any sleep."

"I want to," she insisted. "I'm curious."

Nodding, I led her halfway down the terrace before stopping at one of the townhouses.

"This is it?" Lily asked incredulously.

I led her up the steps. "This is it." I opened the main door and led her upward to the top floor of the building.

"The truth is an art studio is considered commercial, so it's more expensive to rent. I found a light-filled one bedroom flat for cheaper instead." Turning the key in the lock, I strode into the kitchen slash living space. The bedroom and bathroom were off the kitchen.

Lily stepped inside, eyes wide as she sipped her coffee.

The large living area had a ton of natural light not only from the large bay window but from the large window by the kitchen too. The only piece of furniture was a leather sofa, worn but comfortable, easels of varying sizes, and my ladder for the larger pieces. Pots of paint and my painting tools laid scattered by the work I was in the middle of.

Lily stepped toward the painting. It was in the early stages so you could only just start to see the image of the bridges at South Queensferry appearing through the paint. "I can't wait to see it finished," she said, admiring it quietly.

Her genuine appreciation for my work made me feel better than the one hundred positive comments I'd gotten on last week's Reel.

"The packing room is this way."

Lily followed me into the bedroom that didn't have a bed but was filled with boxes of prints and packing material.

Pulling out my phone, I ran through the orders with her, picking out the prints we needed to pack. I had an address label maker set up in the corner that I could use through my phone. We got into a rhythm of packing, while my ego grew to unimaginable sizes at Lily's oohing and aahing over different paintings I'd created.

"Oh." She breathed as I handed her a print of my painting, *The Vennel*. It was an iconic spot in Edinburgh. Many a photograph had been taken of the castle from the top of the Vennel Steps because of the way the castle towered over the old buildings, the Victorian lamppost situated in just the right place.

Last winter, there was frost in the air and on the ground. You could see it sparkling on the lamppost glass. As the sun was setting, I'd started taking photographs at different angles. A couple, oblivious to me, passed. She had stopped at the top of the steps to take a photograph while he ventured down the first flight. He turned back to her and held out his hand to help her down the icy staircase. I'd taken the photograph of them and captured the adoration on his face when he looked at her.

Afterward, I'd returned to the studio and began work on a painting that attempted to catch the romance in one of Edinburgh's most romantic spots. It was one of my bestsellers.

"How much?" Lily looked up at me.

"Twenty-five pounds."

"Done."

Realizing she wanted to buy it, I smiled so big, I probably looked insane. "You're not buying a thing." I pulled another copy from the stack and handed it to her. "It's yours."

"I have to pay for it."

"Consider it a wage for helping me this morning."

"Really?" Her hazel eyes were bright with joy.

Well, that could get addictive quickly, I thought with slight alarm. Because in that moment, making Lily happy felt like a bit of a kink.

Bloody hell.

I looked away. "Of course."

"Thank you." She wrapped an arm around me, giving me a squeeze.

Incapable of ignoring said gesture, I pulled her more tightly into my side and kissed the side of her head. "You're welcome."

A few seconds later, after she'd set aside the print like it was made of bone china, Lily opined, "I think you should seriously consider this as a career, Sebastian. I don't know if you realize how talented you are. How you look at a canvas and imagine what you then bring to life by flicking and scraping paint around on it ... it's kind of genius."

Uncomfortable with the subject, I replied quietly, "I appreciate that. I do. But I'm going to be a civil engineer."

"Sebastian—"

"Lily." I cut her off and then bit back my impatience because she didn't deserve it. My expression softened. "I don't want to talk about this."

"Why?" she pushed.

"Isn't it enough that I don't want to talk about it?"

My friend considered this, then ominously replied, "For now."

CHAPTER SIXTEEN
LILY

For how strangely attached to him and vulnerable I felt, I might as well have slept with Sebastian last night. Perhaps it was the act of sharing a bed with him, or the fact that he'd let me into this private world no one knew about. Whatever the reason, once we'd finished packaging up the prints and dropped them off at the post office, I didn't want to part from him yet.

"What are you up to for the rest of the day, Thorne?" I asked as we ambled in the direction of my flat.

His long strides were edging mine out and I smiled at the side of the romantasy paperback tucked into his back pocket.

"Other than going home for a quick shower and change, I don't really have plans. I suppose I should do my coursework for my Research Methods class."

I nodded, not wanting to distract him from schoolwork. In fact, I should probably work on my Science of Close Relationships essay. However, I knew by how restless I felt that I wouldn't be able to concentrate.

"What are your plans?" Sebastian asked.

"I'm going for a bike ride," I decided. "I need the fresh air."

It was a dry, mild day and soon we wouldn't have many of those.

"Do you fancy some company?"

Yes, yes, I do!

I hid my excitement. "Sounds good. Do you have a bike?"

"I'll hire one."

"Are you sure?"

"Absolutely." He grinned, seeming enervated by the idea. "I've never ridden around Edinburgh. I bet you know places I don't."

"I do know the city like the back of my hand."

He considered this and then nodded. "Okay, Sawyer. Show me your world."

———

Two hours later, after Sebastian had showered and changed and we'd located the nearest e-bike hire, we found ourselves in Dean Village. To my surprise, Sebastian had never ventured to Dean Village.

"I've seen lots of photographs, but I've never wandered that way," he explained.

First, I led him down the cobbled lane of Damside and to the bridge over the Water of Leith to Hawthornbank Lane so he could take some quintessential Dean Village photographs as inspiration for any future artwork.

There were a few tourists already there, taking photographs.

"It feels like we're suddenly in a Harry Potter version of Amsterdam." Sebastian marveled as we got off the bikes.

I chuckled. "That is the perfect description."

It was fascinating to watch Sebastian snap into artist mode. He suddenly got very intense and serious as he moved up and down the lane, taking shots from different angles with his camera phone. As he wandered upward, I leaned over the wooden fence to watch the water calmly flow by. I wish someone could explain why the sound of water was so lulling and peaceful. Maybe it was something I could research for general psychology class. Or maybe my professor would think it was too new age science-y. *Maybe she'll think science-y isn't a word.* I snorted to myself as I scanned our surroundings. On the bridge was an old man who had stopped to watch the water flow beneath him.

He had to be in his late seventies, immaculately dressed in a three-piece brown suit. On his head was a brown tweed flat cap. I wondered where he was off to in his suit. Or if he was the kind of man who'd worn a suit every day of his life and couldn't break the habit. My curiosity was even more piqued when he plucked the flower pinned to his breast pocket and dropped it into the water. He pressed a kiss to his fingertips and smoothed those fingers over the top of the bridge railing. With a tip of his cap to the water, he strode back the way he'd come and disappeared up Damside.

It was clearly a tradition. Or a goodbye maybe. Or a remembrance.

"Where did you go?" Sebastian's voice rumbled in my ear.

I startled, whipping my head around to find him leaning against the railing at my side.

He grinned. "You were off in a dream somewhere."

"I people-watch to the point of forgetting where I am."

"I'll need to keep that in mind." He lifted his phone, pointed the camera side at my face.

"Don't." I groaned, turning away.

"Okay, I won't."

I turned back and heard the fake camera shutter noise of a photo being taken. "You lied!"

Sebastian chuckled as he lowered it. "It was worth it."

Shaking my head at his nonsense, I gestured to the bikes. "Shall we move on?"

"Where to next, Mistress of Auld Reekie?"

I wrinkled my nose. "Let's not call me that."

"I rather like it."

"You do know Auld Reekie means Old Smokey?"

"I do." His smile was unrepentant as he took another quick photograph of me.

"Stop doing that." I shoved him and he nearly dropped his phone as he righted himself. My lips pursed to stop my laugh at his indignant expression.

"If I'd dropped my phone, you'd pay for it and not monetarily," he warned, lips twitching with amusement.

"Since you're so precious about it, I'll try to be more careful in the future."

"Precious?" He guffawed.

Giggling, I got on my bike and watched him slip his precious phone into his shirt pocket before getting on his hired bicycle.

He shot me a mock beleaguered look.

"I know from your social media feed that you've been to Arthur's Seat."

"I have," he drawled as he pulled up beside me. "Hasn't everyone who lives here?"

"Depends." I tilted my head. "But have you been to Dr. Neil's Garden?"

"Why does that sound like somewhere sinister? Like he lured children there with lollipops."

I sniggered. "You have such a crooked mind. The garden was created by two doctors and it's beautiful. Do you want to go there or not?"

"So, there are no lollipops on offer?"

"Are you five?"

"I like to keep my tongue agile." Sebastian leaned in, the devil twinkling in his eyes. "I'm a very good licker, don't you know?"

My cheeks heated at the images his words inspired. At once turned on, irritated, and reluctantly amused, I pushed off on my bike. "Keep up, lollipop!" I called over my shoulder.

Thankfully, the rest of the day, Sebastian kept his overt flirting to a minimum. We rode around Arthur's Seat and ventured into the garden that sat on the banks of Duddingston Loch. While Sebastian strolled off to take photos, I sat down on a bench that faced the water.

When I was here, it felt like I wasn't even in the city anymore.

I had a million things to do when I got back to the flat, but for now I was enjoying slowing down for a few minutes. And showing Sebastian new places in a city that was abundantly inspirational.

Taking my phone out to snap a few shots of my own, I realized I must have accidentally switched it to silent because I had a missed call from January and a couple texts from her and a few friends. There was also a bunch of notifications from social media and my group chat for my general psychology class.

Sighing, I opened January's text first.

> Maddie said you brought a guy home last
> night and then you disappeared before she
> could say hi this morning.

At my lack of response, she'd sent another.

> At least tell me you're alive.

And another.

> You better be having the best sex of your
> life. No other excuse for this silence will do.

And ...

> LILY SAWYER TEXT ME BACK!!

Snorting, I quickly texted her.

> Sorry, you overprotective nutter. My phone
> was on silent. Out with a friend. Talk later.

There was a text from Maddie asking much more calmly and less dramatically if I was all right. I assured her I was and got a notification that January had replied.

> A friend with a dick?

I sent her the middle finger emoji in response.

The rest of my notifications could wait. Sighing, I took a photo of the loch and slipped my phone back in my pocket. I didn't know how to explain Sebastian to my friends and January. Jan would say I needed to cut him loose if I was still attracted to him, and Maddie and Sierra would probably agree.

But ... no one of any gender had ever pursued a friendship like this with me. Sebastian apparently enjoyed being around me. Maybe even needed me a little. And I couldn't say I didn't like the feeling. I could get over this crush and be his friend.

I could.

I was determined to.

"There you are." Sebastian appeared between the trees, that sexy curl of his lips awakening the butterflies in my belly.

Okay. So, I would *eventually* get over it.

He sat down beside me on the bench, his arm pressed against mine. Together we stared out at the water for a bit.

"Thank you for bringing me here." Sebastian broke the silence. "I didn't even know this little gem existed."

"You're welcome." Feeling a hunger pang, I stood up slowly. "I think I need to grab some lunch."

"Why don't we go to the Sheep Heid Inn? I've always wanted to."

I stared out at the water, smiling a bit at the sound of Sebastian's posh accent on the very Scottish word *heid*. And maybe at the fact that he wanted to keep spending time with me. "Sounds good."

I turned to look at him as he stood. He took another photo of me before I could even react.

"Will you stop doing that?"

"I can't." He shrugged. "You are incredibly photogenic, and I click where I must."

It was much, much later, after we'd eaten at the pub and then ridden off our lunch by cycling back into Old Town, after Sebastian returned his hired bike and invited me to his flat for drinks with Juno before she returned to London. It was after Sebastian insisted on walking me home again but departed to work in his studio around the corner. After discovering Maddie and Sierra had gone out dancing without me but left me a bunch of voicemails demanding to know where I'd been.

I'd changed into my PJs and snuggled up in bed to do some coursework and dissertation research. As was my process so I didn't get too overwhelmed, I switched from uni work to the romantic suspense novel I was reading that was like the *Bourne Identity* with more romance. An hour later, eyes heavy with exhaustion, I'd finished my book and had a quick look on socials before bed. Curiosity compelled me to search Sebastian's pseudonym artist account.

To my utter shock, there was a new post.

It was a photograph of me by Duddingston Loch. It was a closer shot than I'd realized. A headshot. The breeze had blown a strand of hair across my face and my eyes were lit up at just the right angle by the sun, making the green in the hazel more prominent.

The caption read:

After three and a half years here, I finally found this city's real beauty.

My heart lurched in my throat at his meaning. It was quite possibly the most spectacular compliment anyone had ever given me. It was unbelievably ... *romantic*.

Confusion rioted through me once more.

Sebastian had to know I'd see the photograph and the caption.

Switching out of the app, I settled my phone by my bed and turned off the light. Staring up at the ceiling, I let my turmoil of emotions sort themselves out. Finally, I decided it was my own crush on Sebastian that was making me read into things. Sebastian was affectionate and complimentary as a person. He didn't mean to be romantic. Just ... sweet.

It didn't mean anything beyond what he'd said.

Perhaps he really did find me beautiful.

That didn't mean he was interested in anything but friendship.

After all, I found Sierra and Maddie beautiful. That didn't mean I wanted to sleep with them.

Melancholy washed over me, and I sighed into my pillow. This whole friendship thing must be considered. I'd give it a few more weeks and if I still felt this aching longing, I'd reevaluate the situation.

CHAPTER SEVENTEEN
SEBASTIAN

The cab couldn't get me to Lily's parents' house in Kirkliston fast enough. I was glad the airport wasn't far from the village.

Even though it had been a mere four days, it felt like I'd been gone for longer. Maybe it was because I'd seen so much of Lily over the last few weeks. Or maybe it was because being home to see my parents' latest craziness in action was so bloody exhausting and upsetting.

I felt like I no longer knew the people who'd raised me.

My insides churned and I tried to throw the thoughts away.

The truth was I shouldn't have gone home for a long weekend, but my parents had insisted. Lily knew I wasn't particularly looking forward to it and wanted to check in on me, so she'd invited me to Sunday dinner at her parents' house upon my return. I could have said no. Probably should have, given my foul mood.

Yet, I couldn't help my curiosity. I wanted to see where Lily grew up. I'd met her mother briefly and saw her now and then at the library, but I was interested to know more about how Lily became *Lily*.

The street the cab driver pulled onto was like many streets in the country. Rows of closely packed detached villas most likely timber-framed and clad with light-colored bricks. They were perhaps fifteen to twenty years old, going by the style. I knew which one was Lily's parents' house by the blue bicycle chained up outside. The sight of it lightened my grim mood.

After paying the driver, I grabbed my backpack and strolled up the Sawyers' driveway. I looked around the neighborhood, imagining Lily as a little girl riding her bike up and down the street. It was a good thought. From everything she'd told me (and she'd seemed reluctant to at first because of the state of my parents' relationship), her folks were still very much in love. She remembered a bad patch when she was little, when they seemed to fight quite a bit. But they'd gone off on holiday to the US and returned closer than ever. There had been disagreements here and there over the years, like with any couple, but none that made Lily feel like her parents would ever split. I hoped for her sake that was true because it turned out, it was shit watching your parents go through that at any age.

I rang the doorbell and perhaps only five seconds later, it flew open.

A girl not much younger than Lily stood in the doorway, one eyebrow raised comically as she looked me over. She was dressed in a sequined rainbow-colored minidress with big puffy sleeves, like something out of a Disney movie. Black tights and black Doc Marten boots were a dichotomous choice to pair with the sugary-sweet confection of a dress. She looked like a lollipop on top of two sticks of black licorice.

Her outfit was so startling it took me a minute to realize she was as beautiful as Lily. Same olive skin, same dark hair. Her eyes, however, were dark brown, not light hazel.

"You must be January. I'm Sebastian, Lily's friend."

"I know who you are." Her eyes dropped down my body and back up again. "I haven't decided yet."

Confused, I asked, "Decided what?"

"Whether you're worthy to be in my sister's life."

My lips twitched. Lily had warned me her younger sister was overprotective. "Ah."

"Ah." She mocked me, eyes narrowing hilariously. "You do know my sister is the greatest person who ever lived and that I'm like a sneaky elven watchdog who can curse your dick to fall off if you hurt her?"

Trying desperately not to laugh, I nodded. "I do now."

"Good. You may enter." She stepped to the side to allow me into the house.

"You'd get along well with my sister Juno," I told her. "And nice dress."

Before she could reply, Lily appeared at the end of the hallway that branched off into several doors. The sight of her made me realize I'd been carrying this huge weight on my shoulders all weekend, because it suddenly felt as if she'd taken it from me.

I smiled affectionately. "Hey, Sawyer."

"Thorne." She strolled down the hallway. "I hope my sister wasn't interrogating you at the door."

"Not at all." I dropped my backpack so I could pull her into a hug. Her hair was down, and I buried my face in it as we embraced. Lily gave me a squeeze and I ignored other *feelings* at the press of her body to mine and took comfort in her affection.

"All okay?" she whispered before I forced myself to release her.

I gave her a tight smile, not wanting to talk about it in front of her sister.

She seemed to understand and smoothed a hand down my arm. "Come meet my mum and dad."

Lily led me into what appeared to be a new addition on the house. It was a large open-plan family kitchen/dining/living area with bifold doors onto a larger garden than I would have expected. The kitchen was fairly new, very modern, and a bit of a showpiece, really. Gleaming white quartz countertops, dark green cupboards with brass fixings, and an expensive white and brass range oven.

Beyond noticing that, my attention was taken up by the couple in the kitchen.

I knew Lily looked like her mother but now I realized she was a perfect combination of her parents. Her father was grinning at Lily's mum, and he had dimples.

His grin, however, disappeared when he turned to find me standing next to his daughter.

He eyed me behind a pair of smart spectacles with the same suspicion January had.

Didn't her family realize we were just friends?

"It's okay, Dad," January announced as she strolled in behind us. "I warned him. He's duly terrified."

Their father nodded. "I trust you did."

"Sebastian, it's so nice to see you again." Lily's mum put down the knife she was using to cut vegetables and rounded the island to greet me. She pulled me into a hug, and I relaxed a bit when she said, "It's always nice to meet one of Lily's friends."

"It's nice to see you again, Mrs. Sawyer."

"Oh, call me Liv, please. I'm not even Mrs. Sawyer at the library." She gestured to her husband. "Nate."

Lily's dad wiped his hands on his apron and strolled over. He was shorter than me, perhaps only five ten or eleven, but for an older guy he was all lean, wiry muscle. I remembered then Lily told me her dad was a martial artist.

"Sebastian, is it?"

"Yes, sir. Nice to meet you."

Her dad nodded. "I hope you like veggie burgers."

"Sounds great."

"Lil tells us you're a member of the royal family."

"Dad!" Lily looked as if she wanted the earth to swallow her whole as Liv groaned at her husband.

"What?" He shrugged. "It's the only thing I know about him so far and it's interesting."

Chuckling, I smoothed a reassuring hand down Lily's back. "It's fine."

Nate Sawyer zeroed in on my hand on his daughter's body so fast and sharply, I dropped my arm back to my side.

"Yes." I shrugged, sticking my hands in my pockets. "My mother is the daughter of Princess Mary."

"The Queen of England is your great-aunt?" Nate was visibly surprised as he rounded the island again. "When Lily said you were a distant member of the royal family, I thought she meant distant, distant."

"Well, I am distant. I'm thirtieth in line to the throne."

"That's not that distant." Nate chuckled.

"So, you've, like, talked to the Queen of England?" Jan asked, hopping onto a stool at the island.

"Stop it." Lily turned to me, true concern in her eyes. "I didn't tell them in a gossipy way. I'm so sorry. I shouldn't have told them at all."

"Forgive my family for being rude." Liv shot her youngest daughter a scolding look. "Subject change."

"It's fine. Really. I understand why people are curious about it. And yes." I looked at January. "I have spent lots of time with Queen Anne. We get on well."

"Surreal. That's very surreal," she said. I supposed to her it was.

"Subject change," Lily repeated her mother's words.

"I know a way to get to know your young man." Nate pointed a knife at me, and I almost took a step back.

"He's not my young man." Lily gritted her teeth. "Sebastian is my *friend*."

"Sorry. You've never brought a male *friend* home before. I'm struggling to readjust my perspective." Nate lowered the knife but smirked, even though the amusement didn't reach his eyes. "Usually, I hate the blokes my daughters bring home. Dad prerogative."

"Absolutely." I felt agreeing was the best thing to do since he was holding a weapon.

"Dad—"

"Sebastian gets it."

I gave Lily another reassuring look.

"Anyway, as I was saying ... let's play Would You Rather."

"Oh yes. Genius idea, Dad." January held a fist out to her father, and he reached over to bump it with his own.

"Um, no." Lily shook her head.

"Oh, come on, it'll be fun," Liv agreed.

Bemused, I queried, "What's Would You Rather?"

"A game Nate and I started playing when we first dated and then it became a family game. Here, we'll start." She nudged her husband. "Would you rather read *The Iliad* for the rest of your life or not read at all?"

"*The Iliad.*"

"Really?" Jan asked. "*The Iliad*? It's like five million pages long and barely understandable."

"It's better than not having anything to read. And if you concentrate, there are some interesting stories in that poem."

"What poem?"

"*The Iliad.*"

"That's a poem?"

Liv pointed a spatula at her youngest. "I'm going to pretend you didn't say that."

"What? What did I say? I'm not a history student. I'm a fashion student." She gestured to her rainbow confection.

Until Lily told me her sister was doing a BA in fashion, I didn't even know that was a course Edinburgh offered.

"Did you make that?" I asked.

"I make most of my clothes."

"That's really clever."

She considered me, her chin lifted haughtily as she looked down her nose. Then, "Okay, a point in your favor. Well done."

I tried not to laugh, but it was a struggle. Lily's little sister was funny without even trying.

Soon we were gathered around the dining table and hopefully, I'd won some points helping Lily take the food, drinks, and cutlery over to it.

"You understand the premise of the game?" Liv asked.

"Sure."

"Okay, this is for everyone," January said as she held her burger to her mouth. "Would you rather eat nothing but kale for the rest of your life or eat what you want but have chronic diarrhea forever?"

"Really?" Liv glowered at her. "We're eating and you start with that?"

"It was the food that inspired the question."

Smothering my grin, I looked at Lily across the table and saw she was struggling not to laugh around her bite of burger.

"Chronic diarrhea," Nate answered seriously.

"Agreed." I nodded.

"Me too." Jan took an aggressive bite of her burger.

Lily and her mother exchanged a look and then nodded in unison. "Me too."

"Would you rather live in *Stranger Things* or *The Last of Us*?" Nate asked.

I frowned because I hadn't seen *The Last of Us*.

"*Stranger Things*. Eleven and I would be BFFs," January said with authority and seriousness.

"*The Last of Us*," Liv said.

Her husband glanced at her. "Pedro Pascal?"

"Maybe."

"Then I better choose *The Last of Us*, so you don't run off with the bastard."

"He's probably going to die in season two," January opined. "If that helps."

"Lily-Billy?" Nate asked.

I almost choked on my burger. "Lily-Billy?"

Her eyes narrowed dangerously. "Don't even think about calling me that."

"But it's so very tempting."

"I will end you. I will drag you into *The Last of Us* with me and end you."

Shoulders shaking with laughter, I replied, "I've never seen it."

Nate gestured at us. "Lil, you need to fix that. Watch it with him. It's a great show."

I nodded because I'd use any excuse to spend time with my friend. "We should definitely do that."

Lily smiled. "We'll pencil that in to our already bursting schedule. Anyhoo, would you rather spend one month out of your entire life living your version of a perfect, blissful existence, knowing the rest of your life would be mediocre? Or live a mediocre life never knowing bliss?"

"Trust the psychotherapist to go deep." Jan groaned in exaggeration.

"Well?"

"You know I'm picking a month of bliss."

"Me too," Liv decided.

Nate considered it. "Aye, a month of bliss is better than nothing."

"Agreed." Lily leaned into her dad with a smile and then they stared expectantly at me.

I shrugged. "I'd rather not know. Mediocre life never knowing." I sensed Lily's attention turn scrutinizing, so I changed the subject. "Would you rather spend eternity at a philosophy lecture or at a concert where they play the same song over and over again?"

———

"They like you," Lily announced as we walked to the bus stop hours later. "My family likes you."

Mid-October meant it was dark at this time and getting chillier by the day. January had left not long after dinner to record a podcast episode. She'd needled Lily for being more absent on the podcast than she'd expected her to be. "But then you'd have to date to have anything interesting to say, wouldn't you?" she'd said pointedly to her big sister.

Lily glowered at her.

Now I let her words about her family penetrate. They felt good. After dinner and the fun Would You Rather game, Nate had shown me his photography studio at Lily's urging. His passion projects were my favorite. He played around with filters and digital art to make his photographs almost painting-like. We had fun and I was relieved Nate seemed to like me. I told Lily as much. "I'm glad. I like them too."

We stopped at the empty bus station and Lily shivered against the cold. I reached out and buttoned up the last button on her coat.

She smirked. "Thanks, Mum."

"You looked cold. So ... the podcast. You haven't spoken much about it these last few weeks."

Lily sighed. "I feel terrible because you know how much it means to me, but I haven't had time."

"To do the episodes or to date?" My heart hammered in my chest, and I didn't want to think about why.

"Both. This year ... the coursework is more than I even expected."

"Yet you still find time for your friends?" For me.

"Of course. Dating is different, though."

"In what way?"

"The mental energy it takes, for a start."

I frowned, genuinely confused.

Lily laughed, but it was humorless. "You wouldn't understand, Sebastian. You only have to look at a girl and speak to her in that posh voice and she's telling everyone it was the best date of her life."

Feeling rather smug she thought so, I couldn't help my answering grin.

She smacked my arm. "Ego!"

I snickered. "You were the one who said it, not me."

"My point is, when I go on a date, I overthink what I should wear. I overthink what I'm going to say. I then beat myself up mentally when I say something that was stupid or banal. By the time I'm done with a date, I'm exhausted. Drained. And then I spend the rest of the next few days worrying about what he thought of me. How I could have been a better date. Why didn't he like me? Why I told him I liked peanut butter and pickle sandwiches when I was thirteen. It's horrible."

"I agree, peanut butter and pickle sandwiches sounds disgusting," I teased.

Lily playfully shoved me, her lips curling ever so slightly. Yet there was sadness in her eyes.

My gut clenched at the idea of Lily putting herself through such mental gymnastics for something as simple as a date. "You didn't seem all that bothered with that finance guy that night at Whistlebinkies."

"No, because I didn't like him from the moment he showed up. But if I think someone has potential, I'm a nervous wreck on the first few dates. It takes me ages to relax."

"It didn't take you ages to relax with me."

"Because there's no romantic intention here." She shrugged as if that were obvious.

I mean, she was right. There was no romantic *intention*. Didn't mean we both weren't fighting an attraction to keep our friendship afloat.

Then I remembered something. "You were pretty nervous when we first met."

Lily groaned, covering her face with her hand. "Don't remind me."

I tugged gently on her wrist, uncovering her gorgeous features. "Look, we're friends, so I feel like I can tell you this and it might help."

"Okay ..."

"I found your nervousness adorable. Truly. You should stop worrying so much what blokes are thinking and just be you."

"Oh, if only I'd thought of that."

Her sarcastic response made me grin. "I'm serious."

"I wish it were that easy." She sighed again and contemplated me. "How was home?"

"You don't want to know."

"I do actually." She squeezed my arm. "I saw the look on your face when you first got here. It was bad, wasn't it?"

Letting out a slow exhale, I leaned back against the bus stop shelter. "Lil ... I ... I feel like these people I thought I knew better than anyone have turned into complete strangers. It's fucking with my head."

"Of course it is." She settled beside me, her side pressed to mine. "What happened?"

"Dad has moved into one of the cottages in their village. I was to spend Thursday night and Saturday with him and then Friday and Sunday with Mum at the house. Juno came up on Friday too. Dad was very, very drunk for the most part. He rarely ever drank before. A whisky at special occasions. Maybe share a pint with the locals during the village on Field Day. It's like a day of celebration. There are activities and a parade and all that stuff. Anyway, suffice it to say Dad is not dealing with the separation at all well and has turned into a very angry drunk who said nasty things about Mum and said something so cutting about Juno, I almost punched him."

He'd called Juno a flaky waste of space just like Mum. I

knew he was drunk, and I hoped when he was sober, he'd feel awful about it. I was glad Juno wasn't there to hear him speak of her like that.

"Sebastian." Lily tangled her fingers in mine, squeezing them. I laced my fingers through hers, seeking her warmth, her comfort.

"Mum, on the other hand, veered between talking shit about Dad and discussing her busy social calendar. Oh, and there were the boxes of my father's stuff she was throwing out without telling him, so I had to rescue those. To top it all off, Juno discovered Mum's on a dating app. When that became a discussion, I heard more about my mother's sexual needs than any son ever, ever bloody well needs to hear.

"The pièce de résistance was Saturday evening. We heard loud rock music blaring from out on the estate and discovered my father there. He was rip-roaring drunk again, he had one of those old boom boxes I didn't even know still existed, blaring Led Zeppelin, and he was digging up all the beetroot. Beetroot he insisted he was the one who wanted to plant so it was his to take. Juno and I stood there while they got into a physical tug of war over fucking beetroot. The shrieking and yelling ... I'm surprised they didn't hear them all the way to the village. Christ, it's like they're caricatures of a separated couple. And anytime Juno and I try to press for a real answer as to why they separated, my dad just shouts and stomps around and Mum zips up tight like a fucking airlock bag." I looked down at Lily. "You don't understand ... these are two people who were so mild-mannered ... and, like, unusually content with life. It would be like your parents suddenly turning around and telling you they were getting a divorce."

Her fingers tightened around mine. "I am so sorry. I

think parents have this bad habit of assuming because their kids are grown up that their actions and words don't affect us the same way. But it's a bond unlike any, and you can't change that drastically on someone you love without it hurting them. What you need to keep in mind is that they were and still are, deep down, the parents you love and remember, and so for them to change like this ... they must be in so much pain.

"Whatever happened between them ... well, things always have a way of pushing their way to the surface. Like a splinter beneath the skin. And it'll hurt like hell while it's in there, but when it comes out, when the truth comes out, there might be some pain, but there will also be relief. The truth will come out, Sebastian. It just takes time."

A swell of emotion tightened around my chest, crushing almost in its intensity. My voice was gruff when I eventually replied, "I was in a shit mood before I got here. But you and your family ... you made it better. Thanks for inviting me."

"You're welcome anytime, Thorne."

We sat in silence for a while, and it wasn't until the bus arrived that I finally let go of her hand.

CHAPTER EIGHTEEN

LILY

I'd known the final year of my MA would be brutal, especially considering I needed to maintain my grades to keep my spot on my postgraduate, but I hadn't realized how time-consuming it would be. The girls and I found ourselves relying heavily on January and Aiysha to keep the podcast going. Thankfully, audiences were loving my sister's nutty dating antics and Sierra was still dating enough to share some of her own funny stories.

Maddie had started seeing someone six weeks ago and it had developed into a serious relationship. His name was Shaun. He was a six-foot-two, rugby-playing Scot who seemed so reserved, I'd been shocked at the pairing. However, the more I got to know him, the more his sly sense of humor came out. Maddie always did love someone who could make her laugh. I'd marvel at how she was managing to juggle it all, but then I was somehow still managing to see Sebastian every other day and text and talk with him daily.

By the time November rolled around, Sebastian had become the closest person in my life, and I think the feeling was mutual. Had my crush dissipated? Not even a wee bit. However, I think I'd finally made peace with the fact that ours would only ever be a great friendship and nothing more.

As busy as I was with work, friends, and avoiding my true feelings, when Beth told me she was bringing her new boyfriend to a big family Sunday dinner at her parents', I knew I needed to be there to support her. Beth's boyfriend wasn't just any bloke. He was Callan Keen. If I was more into football, I'd have known who he was before I googled him. Callan Keen, as it turned out, was only Scotland's most famous football player and captain of Edinburgh team Caledonia United. The relationship had started unconventionally (as in they were fake dating for *reasons*) but had turned into something real. Beth introducing him to her parents was a big deal.

I don't think she was expecting every member of our extended family to be there. Or for the dads (mine, Uncle Braden, Uncle Cam, Uncle Marco, Uncle Adam, Uncle Cole, and Uncle Logan) to surround Callan like a pack of wild dogs.

To be fair to Callan, he handled it with such cool affability, I think he impressed our overprotective fathers and uncles.

I hadn't expected Beth and Callan to bring Caley United goalie Baird McMillan along with them. If I hadn't been so consumed with Sebastian and school, I might have developed a whopping crush on the goalie. He was well over six foot, broad of shoulder, powerfully muscled, and we shared a similar dark coloring. Baird's longish dark hair was piled on top of his head in a messy man bun, and he had a neatly trimmed beard.

I had no time for crushing on the gregarious Scot who

insinuated himself into the family like he'd known us for years. I left that to my wee sister. January eyed the goalie like she'd love a chance to fondle his foot*balls.*

"I'm so glad you're here," Beth said as she sat next to me at the dining table. "Callan, this is Lily, one of the few sane members of my family. Lily, Callan."

I laughed and reached out to shake the very attractive football player's hand. Callan had the most beautiful green eyes I'd ever seen. "Thanks, and nice to meet you."

He flashed me a handsome grin and shook my hand. "You too. I've heard your podcast. You're funny."

My cheeks heated. "I appreciate that, thanks."

We chatted among ourselves, but Callan soon got pulled into conversation with Beth's brother Luke. Baird seemed to have recognized my sister's interest and for whatever reason decided to avoid her. Instead, he pissed off all the men flirting with our mothers and then flirted outrageously with Beth's brother Luke, which did not go down well with Luke's boyfriend Afonso.

"Is he bi?" I'd asked Beth quietly.

She laughed, shaking her head. "No. He's just a big flirt."

"Afonso is going to kill him."

"He should kill Luke." Beth frowned at her brother. "He's the one flirting back."

"To be fair, Luke is a Caley United fan and Baird McMillan is flirting with him."

My cousin chuckled, shaking her head as she turned from the drama unfolding at the end of the table. "What's going on with you? How's uni? My last year was such a bitch."

"It is a lot of work," I agreed, tired merely thinking about it. "I feel guilty. I'm getting my cut from the ad sponsorship for the podcast, but I'm not on it nearly as much as everyone else." I needed the money, however. It covered my rent and bills. Sierra, Maddie, and I took turns editing each episode, so I was still pulling my weight in that respect ... but the guilt remained.

Beth frowned in thought. "Lily, you helped build it into what it is. It was a fun dating advice show when I started it. You've turned it into a real place of commiseration and consolation. You make people feel seen and not alone. That's incredibly important. You might have taken a step back, but that doesn't erase what you've achieved."

I loved my cousin. There was no bigger cheerleader on the planet than Beth Carmichael. "Thank you for saying that."

"So ... any other news? That guy on your Instagram is awfully familiar," she teased.

I assumed she referred to the photo of Sebastian I'd posted. He wasn't alone in it. The photo was of me, him, Harry, and Juno. Juno came up again last weekend and we got a bit tipsy at Sebastian's flat and played board games like eight-year-olds. Zac had snapped the shot of the three of us trying to tear cards out of Sebastian's hand as he laughed uproariously. It was a wonderful photo, and I'd asked Zac for it.

Funny how Beth zoomed in on Sebastian and not Harry.

"Which one?" I played coy.

She wrinkled her nose at me. "The tall blond who I met before the summer."

With a huff, I replied, "We're just friends. He's commit-ment phobic and I'm not looking for anything casual."

"Shame. He's delicious."

Don't remind me.

Beth was soon pulled into conversation with Baird, and

I was left to my own thoughts. I glanced around the table at my large family, at our parents who all were tight knit, close, still obnoxiously in love. Maybe it was growing up surrounded by the kind of love you only read about that made me believe I'd eventually find it too. Maybe it was reading all those romance novels. Maybe it had given me a false sense of hope and optimism.

It suddenly occurred to me that I could end up being the person in our family whose love was unrequited.

Love.

Pfft.

I waved off the thought.

I was not in love.

I'd find my person. I would! It just wasn't going to be Sebastian Thorne.

My attention shifted to Callan and my curiosity sparked. He'd been staring at Beth earlier with longing and affection. Now his expression was completely blank. He didn't look at anyone, instead stared into his glass. He was giving off very weird vibes. It was like he'd disappeared inside himself. I looked over at Beth to see if she'd noticed there was something wrong with her boyfriend, but Baird was monopolizing her attention.

I glanced around and noted my aunt Joss's focus on Callan. She watched him with taut features as if she knew something I didn't. Had something happened while I wasn't looking? I hoped not. Beth seemed so happy. The happiest I'd ever seen her.

When Callan excused himself before dessert, I watched curiously as Aunt Joss followed him out of the room. They were both gone for a wee while and Beth left the kitchen to check on them.

"You're Lily, right?" Baird asked once Beth had disappeared between us.

My cheeks heated. I might not be interested in the goalie, but my goodness, he was attractive. He flashed me a white-toothed, cocky smile. "I am."

"Baird." He gestured to himself.

"I know."

"So, is your family part of some weird experiment?"

I frowned. "What do you mean?"

"You're all gorgeous. If I wasn't so good-looking myself, I might feel like a melted welly in comparison."

Chuckling at his charming nonsense and that he'd basically called me gorgeous, I blushed inwardly. "Something in the water, I guess."

"You're the podcaster?"

"I am."

"You know if you're looking for fresh material, I am ready and willing." He spread his arms as if to say, *"Here I am, come get me."*

I almost choked on a swallow of water.

"No," a gruff voice said from behind me.

Baird peered past me as I turned to find Uncle Cole glowering at Baird. Uncle Cole was Aunt Jo's younger brother. He was also over six feet, covered in tattoos, and a judo champion.

Oh, and extremely overprotective.

"No?" Baird quirked an eyebrow.

"No, as in look at Lily again and I'll end you, mate."

"Fair enough. I respect that." Baird was completely unfazed by the threat in Uncle Cole's voice. In fact, he leaned past me, eyes on the sleeve of artwork on Uncle Cole's left arm. "Like the ink. I thought mine was good, but the art ... man. Where did you get it done?"

"I'm part owner of INKarnate. The tattoo studio in Leith. I'm one of the artists."

What he didn't say was that he'd won a ton of awards over the years for his tattoo artwork.

"No way!" Baird was so loud, I eased right back so he could talk to Cole. "I pass that place all the time. Fuck. I should have gone to you last time."

Just like that Uncle Cole relaxed, and they started chatting over me. Men were weird.

"Why haven't you two gone Instagram official?" The loud question came from January. It did the job of quieting Baird and Cole. Baird relaxed in his seat, giving me my personal space back.

I groaned softly when I realized January had asked this question of Beth and Callan, who had returned to the kitchen with Joss.

"Jan," Beth huffed. "You don't just ask people that."

"Why not?" My sister crossed her arms over her chest. "You've been in the tabloids. Callan has two hundred thousand followers, and a lot of the comments are people drooling over your man, Beth. You should claim him."

Saying preposterous things like that made Jan very popular on *Seek and You Shall Find*. Saying it in real life ... I groaned loudly. "You read too many MC romance books."

Beth laughed as Jan shot me a dirty look. Then my cousin turned to her partner, who seemed much more relaxed than he had before he'd left the kitchen. "Why aren't we Instagram official?"

"I'm letting you lead the way. We can post our relationship on socials if you want. I'm quite happy to let the world know you're mine."

An ache spread across my chest at the romantic words.

Everything drowned out around me as I stared at Beth and Callan.

I'm quite happy to let the world know you're mine.

It was the reminder I needed, even if it was slightly painful. Perhaps there was a tiny part of me holding out hope for Sebastian to become more. But it had been almost two months of close friendship. If something was going to happen, it would have already. And I shouldn't hang around for someone who didn't want to shout from the rooftops that I was his and he was mine.

CHAPTER NINETEEN

LILY

Guilt got to me about the ad sponsorship money and not pulling my weight. Even though Beth's words had helped, when January gently needled me again as we were leaving the Carmichaels' that Sunday, I agreed to go with her to record the next episode.

It was late, I was tired, and I didn't want to, but I took a cab to the university with Jan.

Sierra and Aiysha were there and were surprised to see me, which made me feel worse.

Aiysha stood to hug me, her soft, dark tight curls tickling my nose. As always, January's best friend and fellow fashion student looked like she was ready for the runway. Her bright yellow cropped sweater was amazing against her umber skin. "I'm so glad you're here. We have a couple of call-ins tonight that I think you're better suited to deal with."

"Than whom?" Jan teased as she took her seat at the recording table.

"I love you, babe, but you have all the subtlety of a cartoon anvil," Aiysha replied drolly.

Chuckling, because, wow, it was true, I took my seat next to Sierra. "How goes it?"

"Busy as hell." Sierra ran a hand through her hair. "I want this year to be over, but I don't, you know."

I did know. I reached to squeeze her arm because I was going to miss her so much when she left after our final semester.

"Nope. No sad crap before we even get started," Jan admonished with a wag of her finger. "I just spent the day in a kitchen with two smoking-hot famous footballers and got nowhere. So, I need a pick-me-up, not a bring-me-down."

"Explain yourself," a wide-eyed Aiysha demanded.

I wrinkled my nose. "Callan is Beth's boyfriend. Where did you think you'd get with him?"

"Oh, pfft. You know I meant Baird. I noticed he drooled on you. I guess younger women aren't his thing." She pouted and shrugged nonchalantly. "Och, I can wait."

"What is she talking about?" Sierra leaned into me.

"Something that's never going to happen," I murmured back.

"I heard that!"

I turned to my sister. "Baird is a player, Jan. You're not going there."

"Who is Baird?"

"Ladies, we're ready and I have places to be," Kenny, our producer, huffed into our headphones.

With that, we started the episode. A few call-ins got the ball rolling and discussion flew between us.

"So, we're talking Sierra's ... what... tenth date since the start of the semester?" Aiysha said into her microphone. "Lily, she's making you look like an old spinster. No offense."

"I think it's more than ten, actually." Sierra grinned at me. "Come on, Lil. Tell us all why you're going through such a long dry spell. Does it have a name?"

At the wicked glint in her eye, I stared back stonily. I did not want to talk about Sebastian on our podcast. "I'm just busy."

"I think it has a name," Jan agreed.

This time, my quelling look made the smile drop from my sister's face.

"Okay, well, it can't only be that you're busy," she recovered.

Deciding now was a good time to bring up the discussion of peer pressure, I asked, "Why is it young women are under pressure from society to actively pursue romance? If we're not actively trying to date, it's worse than if we are and are failing." I looked at my cohosts. "Can't I just take a break from the exhausting process of dating? I have a lot going on with school and I'm tired. Sorry, that's not a funny or charming answer ... but I'm tired, guys. I'm tired of looking for Mr. Right and I need a break. I'm not giving up. I just need a break. And I think we should normalize women making the decision to focus on themselves instead of pursuing a romantic connection."

My cohosts were silent for a few seconds.

Then January slow clapped. "Well fucking said, big sister. I bow to your feminist wisdom."

My lips curled at the corner. "For those of you who don't know my wee sister well, that is not her sarcastic tone, though you might think differently."

"No, I'm sincere. I can accept being put in my place when it's done as well as that. We should all shut the hell up and let you be you. Note that, listeners. If the people in your life are pressuring you into anything, they should all shut the hell up and let you be you."

––––––

A few days later, after the episode aired, I was gratified by all the comments on our socials from listeners telling me I'd made them feel seen. That they often needed to take breaks between long periods of serial dating, and family and friends made remarks and comments that were unhelpful. Like how "They weren't getting any younger" and "You won't find anyone if you don't look." There was even a comment from a person who identified as asexual and how she was constantly pressured to date by family who didn't understand. She'd turned my quote, "I think we should normalize women making the decision to focus on themselves instead of pursuing a romantic connection" into a reel that got so many thousands of likes, I was blown away.

It reminded me that I didn't need to be dating to be useful on the podcast. That I had things to say and shockingly, people wanted to listen. That night, I sat down and rearranged some of my schedule to fit in more episodes. Just as I was finishing up, I got a few texts from Sebastian.

Listened to your episode. You're amazing.

But I miss you.

It's been four days without Lily.

Come over to the flat tomorrow.

I'll order takeaway.

And because I was apparently a masochist, I replied.

Make it Thai and I'll be there.

Two seconds later, my phone beeped again.

You got it. Can't wait to see you.

CHAPTER TWENTY

SEBASTIAN

During a slow moment in the football match the lads and I were watching on TV, I glanced at my phone again to see if Lily had texted to say she was on her way. It felt like forever since I'd seen her.

Harry nudged me. "What's going on?"

I frowned at him. He was lounged next to me on our large sectional, a can of cold beer in hand. Zac was sprawled at the other end of the sofa, sipping on his beer, eyes on the Caley United game.

"Nothing's going on."

"You keep looking at your phone."

"Lily's coming over. I was checking if she'd texted."

"You didn't say Lily was coming." Harry scowled. "Thought this was a lads' evening in."

Considering we lived together and saw each other every day, I wouldn't be guilted about inviting Lily. "No one said that. I haven't seen Lily in ages."

"Since you became friends with that girl, you have become the shittiest wingman ever," Zac opined, eyes still on the screen. "And I have a suspicion you haven't gotten laid since."

Harry grimaced. "I don't get it. Why are you spending time with this girl if you're not getting anything from her? She's a little fuller"—he gestured with his hands—"than my usual taste, but those curves are nicely compacted. Any bloke with a working dick would hit that."

Zac groaned under his breath.

Probably because he could tell I was seconds from punching my best mate in the face. "You talk about Lily like that again, and you and I will have problems, Harry. Real fucking problems."

Harry blanched. "We talk about girls like that all the time."

"No, *you* talk about girls like that all the time. I just haven't called you on your bullshit until now. Lily is my friend. You don't disrespect my friends. You hear me?" I seethed.

Raising his palms defensively, Harry nodded. "You're right, you're right. I'm sorry. I like Lily. You know I do. I just … I don't get it. Why aren't you dating her? You're not sleeping with other girls, so you might as well be in a committed relationship."

"We're just friends." I scrubbed a hand over my face as I looked back at the game. "I think my mum pushing all these girls on me has messed with my head. I'm afraid if I even try to go home with someone, it'll turn out she was sent by my mother."

"That's disturbing," Zac offered.

"I know."

Harry clamped a hand on my shoulder and squeezed. "I get it. Why don't I do some reconnaissance on some luscious ladies so you can get laid?"

I shot him a look. "Harry, mate, I love you like a brother. But you are not setting me up with a woman like a pimp."

Zac snorted on a swallow of beer and started coughing.

Harry grinned. "Shit. Sorry. Didn't mean for it to come off weird. I was thinking—"

"Keen's got the ball!" Zac rasped out, throwing an arm toward the TV.

With that we were dragged back into a game that suddenly got exciting.

Before moving to Edinburgh, none of us had been into Scottish teams because we supported English teams. I'd been a Merseyside FC supporter my whole life. I'd indoctrinated Harry and Zac into my love of the club. However, when we'd moved to Edinburgh, we started following the Scottish Professional League and had become firm fans of Caledonia United. They were the underdogs, always third behind the two largest Glasgow teams, but with Callan Keen, the country's top midfielder, in their ranks, Caley had become a force to be reckoned with.

So engrossed in the game, I didn't hear the knock at the door or the door opening.

"I just had dinner with him," a familiar female voice announced behind Zac.

We turned to find Lily standing between the couch and the kitchen, gesturing to the TV. She gave me a smile. At the sight of her, of those dimples, I ignored the flutter in my chest.

"You had dinner with who?" Zac asked, grinning up at her.

"Callan. He's dating my cousin Beth."

Harry and Zac erupted into a million questions. Lily laughed, surprised by their excitement. I literally cut through them by getting up to cross the room to her.

Reaching for her, I took her by the upper arms, bending my head so our faces were inches apart.

"My darling Lily, are you telling me you know Callan 'the Flash' Keen?"

Her full lips trembled with laughter at my intensity. "I do."

"You had dinner with the man?"

"Him and Baird McMillan. They came to Beth's parents' Sunday dinner."

Harry and Zac exploded into renewed excitement behind me and Lily shook with laughter.

"What will it take to be invited to one of these Sunday dinners in which people you know entertain Caley United heroes?"

Her grin got wider. "You're fangirling!"

"Uh, yes." I gave her a gentle shake. "He's Callan Keen."

"Oh. My. Goodness."

"My darling Lily." I pulled her into my arms, squeezing her tight and comically stroking the top of her hair. "I'll do anything. Do you need a kidney? I have two."

I could feel her laughter thrumming through my chest.

"A foot rub for life? Because I could get over my aversion to feet for you."

"I have nice feet," she mumbled against my chest, still laughing.

"Back massage? Every day for six months."

"I think that's more of a treat for you, Bas," Zac cracked.

Lily snorted and shoved me away. "In all this time I haven't seen you watch a game or even talk about football."

Harry huffed. "How is that possible? Bastian was on course to be a professional football player."

My gut tightened and I cut Harry a dirty look.

"No way." Lily gaped at me as if she'd never seen me before.

"Yes, bloody way. Sebastian played forward on a team at our boarding school and while he was on the team, they slaughtered all the others. He was scouted at sixteen but ..." Harry suddenly stopped talking, his expression tightening as he realized the subject he'd almost stumbled onto.

"But?" Lily queried, eyes wide at this new information.

"But nothing." I shrugged nonchalantly. "I didn't want to play professionally. Now, let's order some food. I'm starving."

Everyone, thankfully, let it go, and we watched the rest of the game while we waited for our food to arrive. Zac and Harry pestered Lily with more questions about Callan and Baird, and Harry googled Beth and Callan.

"Jesus. Fuck me. Keen is a lucky bastard." Harry gaped at his phone. "Lily, your cousin is a prime piece. I'd give my left nut to hit that."

He was rewarded with a smack across the head from Lily.

"Ow." Harry rubbed at the spot. "I'm only saying she's a gorgeous girl, for fuck's sake."

"Women aren't pieces, Harry." Lily glared at him over the top of a forkful of red Thai chicken. "We're not walking holes for your cocks to 'hit' like they're targets."

I almost choked on a bite of food.

Harry wrinkled his nose. "Well, when you say it like that, it sounds disgusting."

"See, to my ears what you said sounds equally disgusting."

My friend's brow furrowed as he sincerely seemed to contemplate that. He stared at Lily like he'd never seen her before. "I'm going to take this on board," he assured her.

Lily visibly fought a smile. "I'm glad."

"Hey, so, Lil." Zac nudged her. He was sitting on her other side. "I downloaded that album you recommended. That band. White Lies."

"Oh aye, did you like them?"

I frowned, because since when did Lily and Zac share music recommendations?

"Really good. Any more recs?"

"We Are Scientists. Album: *With Love and Squalor.*"

"Noted. Thanks."

I nudged her now. "Would I like them?"

She turned to me, considering. "Actually, yeah. We Are Scientists more so than White Lies."

"I'll check them out too."

The four of us ate and chatted and I was grateful that the lads were welcoming to Lily and didn't bring up what they'd brought up earlier. About our friendship. About my monk-like existence since Lily and I had become close.

Afterward, needing her to myself for a bit, I asked if she wanted to go for a walk. It was a dry but chilly November evening. We couldn't see much of the stars in the middle of the city, but the moon was shining bright, illuminating our way as we walked down South Bridge together. Buses and cabs passed us, as did pub goers and diners, while we strolled quietly. Sometimes that's what I loved most about Lily. She never felt like she had to fill the silence. At least not with me. She'd told me she was different on dates. That silence made her panic. That she worried her date would find her boring. I told her if he did, then he was a clueless arsehole and not worth her time.

The thought of her on a date, as always, twisted me up inside.

"So ... you were very weird when Harry brought up your school football career."

Now my gut clenched. "Lil—"

"And Harry looked panicked before he abruptly stopped talking about it. Did something happen at school with your football team?"

She was too bloody perceptive for her own good.

Lawrence's face flashed before my mind and that awful ache he inspired scored across my chest like the blade of a knife.

I never talked about him.

Harry knew because he'd been there. Zac knew nothing. Everyone we'd gone to school with remembered. My parents knew. Lawrence's parents knew and loathed me. Loathed me and all the lads on the team.

"Sebastian." Lily's hand curled around mine. "You can talk to me."

"I know." The words were hoarse. "It's not something I particularly enjoy dredging up."

"You don't have to," she assured me.

I looked down at her beautiful, upturned face. Those eyes so full of compassion and care. Perhaps the masochist in me wanted to push, to prod, to see if Lily Sawyer really was the most nonjudgmental person I knew.

Maybe it was self-sabotage that prompted me to tell her.

"I killed a boy at school."

Instead of dropping my hand, Lily's hold on me grew bruising. "Excuse me?" she breathed, the color leaching from her cheeks.

I gently removed my hand from hers and stuffed it into the pocket of my jacket. Hunching into the chilly breeze blowing down South Bridge, I continued to walk and talk.

"There are multiple teams at our boarding school. Sport is a big part of the culture at the school. We play each other and we play internationally."

"That's how you got scouted?"

I nodded. "I was in the middle of discussions with Merseyside Under 18s."

"Oh my God, that's huge."

"It was. I was ecstatic."

"I don't understand. You've never talked about football. I've never seen you watch a game until today."

I shrugged. "I watch with the lads. I follow my teams. But it's not a part of my life in the way it was before."

"Because ... you killed someone?" Her tone was filled with disbelief.

I nodded, nauseated, the Thai food suddenly roiling inside me. "Lawrence was new to our team. Our captain, James, was a year older. He was a prick. It was tradition that you pranked new team members and James pushed it further than most would."

"Like pledging?"

"Kind of. We were all aware that going into the team, you'd get pranked. You didn't know when it was coming or what it would be. Every time we did it, James seemed to up the prank. He liked me because I did well for the team and was on the path to playing professional football. But he could be a swine to others. I didn't speak up when I should have because I didn't want to mess up my own chances. If James didn't want you to play, you didn't play. He was the master of manipulation and had the coaches wrapped around his finger. So, I didn't stop him."

Lily curled her hand around my forearm. "What happened?"

I swallowed hard, seeing Lawrence ... "James found out

from Lawrence's roommate that he was terrified of spiders."

I felt Lily tense at my side.

"James thought it would be funny to watch Lawrence piss himself in fear." Self-loathing filled every word. "I went along with it. There was a cubicle for changing in one of the locker rooms that was floor to ceiling, no getting out except by unlocking the door. We stuck him in there with a bunch of spiders the lads had collected and locked the door." Nausea started to rise as I remembered his shouts of terror. Tears burned my eyes, and I blinked rapidly trying to fight them back. "I felt so sick, and I knew I should stop them, but I didn't move quickly enough. The others were so busy laughing and joking, we didn't hear that Lawrence was struggling to breathe. By the time I decided to do some-thing, it was too late. James wouldn't let me open the door. I eventually punched him and got the door open. But like I said, it was too late. He'd been in there for about five or six minutes."

I stopped in the middle of the pavement, a tear escaping before I could stop it as I looked down at Lily. Part of me wanted her to hate me. To judge me. The other part was terrified of it. "Lawrence was asthmatic. He'd hid it from us. All of us. We would eventually have found out on the field. His panic caused him to hyperventilate. And he didn't have his inhaler with him. He died while we barricaded him in a cubicle with his worst fear, struggling to breathe as we laughed and joked outside."

"Sebastian." Lily's eyes misted over as she reached for me. "You didn't laugh and joke. You tried to help him."

I pulled away, storming up the street.

"Sebastian!"

"Don't look at me with compassion. I don't deserve it," I

spat out. "I should be in prison, but our school didn't want an international scandal. It all got swept under the rug as a boyish prank that went wrong."

"It *was* a prank that went wrong." Lily tugged me to a stop. "And I fully understand your guilt. But, Sebastian, you did not intend to kill someone. You didn't come up with the prank. It was someone else's ugliness that led to a terrible tragedy."

"You know, that's what Lawrence's father said to me. That it was a terrible tragedy. I was crying uncontrollably as I confronted his parents, and his father smacked me hard. 'Man up, boy. My son's weakness was not your fault.'"

"Bloody hell," Lily muttered, appalled.

"Lawrence's dad was alumni. Hard, cold man. I often wondered if Lawrence hid his asthma because of him."

"I think that's a fair bet." Lily soothed a hand over my back.

"But his mother ..." I stared at Lily in anguish, remembering the look on Lawrence's mum's face. "She looked at me and James like she wanted to wipe us from the earth. And I didn't blame her. That poor woman."

"Weren't the police involved?"

"Yes. I told them the truth, even though the school told me not to. And nothing happened. A slap on the wrist. That's what money and privilege buys you," I sneered in self-directed disgust.

"What happened with James?"

"He was furious. Turned the boys on me. Said I was a snitch, a traitor. I didn't care. I quit the team, and I didn't pursue the Under 18s, even though it would have gotten me out of there."

"Why quit football if you loved it?"

"Because I didn't deserve it. Lawrence would never play again. So why should I get to?"

Lily brushed a tear away and I reached for her hand, squeezing it.

"Don't cry for me, Lily."

"I hate that you're holding on to this. You would never intentionally hurt anyone."

Relief warmed me as I tucked her arm through mine and held her close as we walked. "You always see the good in me."

"Because you are good."

I grunted. I'd never be sure of that again.

"What happened with James?"

"We spent the rest of our time at school in a cold war with one another. I wasn't afraid of him anymore and because of Harry, I had all the lads on the rugby team at my back. He tried at first to get to me. Then I saw him and some lads trying to tape another lad to a tree. Lesson not learned. Something came over me and I beat the utter shit out of him."

"Good." Her features were hard and angry. "He deserved it."

"He did," I agreed. "It was my second strike, though. Third and they'd expel me. But after that, James stayed out of my way. He graduated that year and my last year at the school was better. It was better for everyone without him there."

"But you never returned to football?"

"Haven't played a game since."

At Lily's silence, I glanced down at her. "What?"

"You're punishing yourself."

"Maybe I am." I shrugged. "Maybe I deserve to."

"Sebastian—"

"I don't really want to talk about it anymore," I cut her off, my tone soft, placating. "Please."

Frustration lit her eyes, but she nodded. "Okay." Then she did something that made my chest ache unbearably. She rested her head against the top of my arm, cuddling in close as we walked.

Accepting me.

Accepting my past and my truth.

And still caring about me even so.

Grateful, I pressed a kiss to the top of her head and fell into peaceful silence with her as we ambled aimlessly through Old Town.

CHAPTER TWENTY-ONE
LILY

A Few Weeks Later

"Okay, if Thanksgiving is this bloody delicious, why aren't *we* doing it every year?" Harry asked as we all pulled on our coats.

"Actually, we used to, and I believe it was the English that introduced it in North America," I told him as I fumbled over a coat button.

"How so?"

"Thanksgiving was important during the English Reformation."

At his blank look, I continued, "During the reign of Henry VIII."

"Is he an ancestor of yours, then?" Maddie asked Sebastian.

He shot her a droll look.

Harry crossed the room to me. "You're telling me we

started Thanksgiving but stopped while the North Americans continued the tradition?"

"It evolved in North America from what it was, but aye."

"How do you know this?"

I turned to Sebastian to find him smiling fondly at me as he tied a scarf around his neck.

"Lily is a sponge," Sierra offered. "Anything she reads, she soaks right up."

"Well, I vote we petition the government to bring it back." Harry patted his stomach. "That was delicious, Sierra, thank you."

"I had help from my girlies. And Sebastian."

Sebastian bowed his head comically.

Because Sierra could only afford to return to the US at Christmas every year, it meant she missed out on Thanksgiving with her family. Maddie and I had surprised her in our first year with a Thanksgiving dinner. The following years, Sierra organized it. Sometimes we invited fellow Americans to join us. This year, we'd invited Sebastian, Harry, Zac, and Shaun.

I'd also invited Jan, but she was hard at work on a project for one of her fashion courses.

The dinner came at a good time because we were all gearing up for exams. Needing a wee break, we'd organized the dinner and everyone bought tickets to The Stand, a legendary comedy club. They were doing a Thanksgiving special with four US standup comedians.

We all piled out of our flat, bellies too full from our feast. Even though it was a thirty-minute walk from Leven Street to York Place, we all decided we needed to walk off the turkey and plethora of sides we'd inhaled at dinner.

Sebastian fell into step beside me, and we chatted about

our current workload for a bit. Then I asked, "How's Juno?" I hadn't seen her in weeks.

"The gallery in Edinburgh changed their minds about her pottery collection."

Disappointed for her, I said so.

"The truth is she's doing wonderfully well selling them herself. And she doesn't have to pay fifty percent commission to a gallery to do it. I think it's the prestige thing, though. I think she feels people might take her seriously if she's in galleries."

"That doesn't sound like Juno."

"My sister is very good at putting on a front, making people think nothing bothers her. But she has her own insecurities."

I thought about that. "Jan's the same. When we were kids, she was more open about her vulnerabilities, but as we got older, she started to hide them more. I often wondered if it was because I was so sensitive and she felt she needed to be strong for me." And I'd always felt guilty at the thought. I was her big sister. Not the other way around.

"I don't think you're overly sensitive at all. I think you're very pragmatic."

"Maybe now." Experience had thickened my skin. "But when we were kids, I was always getting my feelings hurt. But ... Jan's like Juno. The insecurities are there. I once caught her crying reading the book *A Thousand Boy Kisses*."

Sebastian grinned. "A tearjerker?"

"The biggest. I'm going to make you read it."

"Add it to my now never-ending TBR," he replied drolly. It was true. I'd successfully converted Sebastian into a romance fan.

I glanced up to make sure our friends were far enough ahead. "How are things with your mum and dad?"

We'd been so busy with school lately that our interactions were usually quick lunches at Teviot or dinner with our friends. We hadn't had the time or privacy for me to ask.

Sebastian scowled at the pavement as we walked. "No different, I'm afraid. Did I tell you a girl my mum contacted ambushed me coming out of my steel structures lecture?"

Horrified on multiple levels, I shook my head. "You never said."

"Poppy Danvers. Daughter of a viscount. Prelaw. Very pretty. According to my mother, perfect for me."

My heart plummeted. "Oh?"

He grimaced. "I have no idea what my mother said to that poor girl, but she seemed convinced we were a sure thing. She also was not amused when I made it clear we were not."

Relief shook me. "Oh dear." I sounded a little too breathless. Clearing my throat, I said, "I hope she wasn't too put out."

"Oh, I think I'm definitely on her shitlist. Fourth year is hard enough ... my mother is being so selfish doing stuff like this. I'm honestly considering not going home for Christmas."

"Really?"

He sighed heavily. "I say it, but I don't mean it. I can't leave Juno to them."

"Well, you and Juno are welcome at my house over Christmas if you find you need to escape."

Sebastian cut me a tender smile. "Thanks, Sawyer." He nudged me with his elbow. "How's your family doing? How's Beth and Mr. Keen?"

I laughed. Unfortunately, there hadn't been a chance to introduce Sebastian to his football hero yet. "I think they're doing well. She seems really happy. The rest of my family are the same. Busy. I haven't seen them in a while because of school. At least I get to catch moments with Mum at the library."

We chatted more about our family and then suddenly we were on York Place, entering the club. Sebastian insisted on buying my drink and Zac did a valiant job of securing a table for all of us. It was at the back, but I was thankful because the very thought of being picked on by a comedian made my insides shrivel up. Coats and scarves off, we settled around the table. I was at the edge with Sebastian on my other side.

I scanned the crowded club, people-watching as I often did. That's how I found him.

Standing at the bar, sipping on a pint. There was a petite brunette with him.

"Lily? You all right?" Sebastian asked in my ear.

But I was frozen.

My gut twisted and my chest tightened as the good-looking, dark-haired bloke I couldn't take my eyes off suddenly caught me staring.

Recognition lit his face. Then the psychopath raised his pint to me with a hard smirk curling the corners of his mouth.

I looked away from him, staring stonily ahead, suddenly lost in memories I'd rather cast out into Dumbledore's pensieve than have festering inside me.

"Lily." Sebastian curled his hand around my wrist, and I reluctantly looked at him.

He sucked in a breath at whatever he saw on my face. He peered past me to the bar. "Who is that bloke?"

I shook my head, tone brittle. "No one."

His eyes flared but thankfully, the house lights went down as the comedians took the stage.

I couldn't concentrate on their sketch. I was wholly aware of the man at the bar, and I didn't want to look at him, but I needed to be alert in case he approached me. Needed my armor up.

Staring in stony silence, I heard my friends laugh all around me.

Except Sebastian.

I sensed his tension at my side.

However, I could do nothing to snap myself out of my panicked stupor.

I wanted to leave.

Yet I knew that would give the bastard satisfaction of knowing how much he still affected me.

Instead, I stayed put out of stubbornness, but I was so bloody thankful when the house lights went back up again.

———

"Let's go grab another drink somewhere else." Harry bumped Sierra playfully as we stood outside the comedy club.

She nodded. "Sure, I'm up for it."

"We're going to head back," Maddie said, leaning into Shaun.

"Yeah, I'm actually done in." Zac scrubbed a hand over his face. "Think I ate too much."

We laughed at that because we all had.

"Lily? Bas?" Sierra asked.

"Lily and I are going for a walk," Sebastian said before I could respond.

"Okay. Just us, then." Sierra threaded her arm through Harry's and they waved goodbye as they headed down York Place toward Queen Street. There were a bunch of bars in New Town where they could grab a drink.

"Who wants to place a bet that they'll sleep together tonight?" Zac snorted.

"I'll take that bet. Twenty that they do." Maddie grinned slyly.

Shaun chuckled. "You know something, don't you?"

She shrugged. "Sierra might fancy Harry. She might have suggested to me that she'd like to get him out of her system."

Zac whistled. "Lucky Harry. Well, it's not a fair bet, then, if we know it's a sure thing."

Maddie zeroed in on me suddenly. "Are you all right, Lily?"

"I'm fine." My tone was flat even to my ears.

My friend narrowed her eyes. "Are you sure?" She scrutinized Sebastian with a frown. "You can walk back with Shaun and me."

Not wanting her to think my problem was with Sebastian, I waved her off. "I'm good." Even though I knew I was about to be interrogated by my best friend.

A few minutes later we were all going our separate ways.

"Where are we walking?" I queried as I fell into step beside Sebastian.

"We're just walking. And talking. Who the hell was that, Lily? The bloke at the bar. Did he do something to you?"

The fierceness of his expression bordered on murderous.

"His name is Christian. Chris." Just saying his name made me shudder. I wrapped my arms around my waist.

Sebastian waited quietly if not impatiently for me to continue.

"I haven't told anyone about him. Only Jan knows, but after the fact. And my cousin Luke."

"What happened?"

"I didn't always used to be this self-conscious, you know." Bitterness filled my tone, and I hated it. I hated that Chris had that power over me. "I grew up with a family that told me I was beautiful all the time. I didn't have much of an ego about it, but I was also pretty laid-back about my appearance. Like it wasn't something I had to be overly concerned about."

"You don't," he assured me.

I huffed inwardly.

"I met Christian when I was sixteen. At the library of all places. He was four years older. A college student."

"What was a twenty-year-old doing with a sixteen-year-old?" Sebastian sneered. "The thought turns my stomach. Four years isn't a lot. But at that age it is."

"I didn't think anything of it then. I was young and naive and excited that this older guy liked me. That's why I didn't tell my parents or Jan. Or anyone. My dad would have killed him."

"Jan would have killed him."

I laughed humorlessly. "You're right."

"Anyway, it didn't take long for me to realize he had a lot of problems. Trauma. His father abandoned him and his mum, and one of his mum's many boyfriends ... he abused Chris. Sexually."

"Wow."

I nodded, still feeling deeply sad about it even after everything Chris had done to me.

"That's a lot to put on a sixteen-year-old."

"I tried to help him. To be there for him. But he pulled me down with him into his black hole. He would love-bomb me. Intensely. Gifts, texts, he even wrote me a couple of long letters. When he felt me pulling away, he wrote me letters telling me he'd kill himself if I ever left him."

"What a manipulative prick."

That was the understatement of the year.

"Before we got to there, he started belittling me, making me feel less than. Sometimes it was about my intelligence, my personality ... other times ..." I exhaled heavily, my cheeks heating. "When we were in bed, he'd tell me that I was lucky he wanted me because most guys would want me to lose a bit of weight before they'd sleep with me."

Sebastian halted abruptly.

I turned, almost afraid to look at him.

Sure enough, his features were taut with anger.

I shrugged helplessly, tears in my eyes. "That's not the worst of it."

"Tell me," he bit out.

I gestured for him to walk with me again because it was easier to tell him without looking him in the eye. "He'd say stuff about my weight a lot in bed. I won't go into it, but I will say I refuse to be on top now." If I was a blusher, my cheeks would be beetroot.

Sebastian's next words were said in a low growl. "I'm going to rip this bastard apart if I ever see him again."

"I hope we never see him again." A chill shivered through me at the thought. "He's the reason I got weird about food and needed to talk to someone about it. But he didn't just poke at me about my appearance. It was everything. He wanted me to believe that he was the only one who could put up with me. Knowing what I know now, I realize his self-esteem was nonexistent, so he was trying to obliterate *my* self-esteem so I wouldn't leave him. Then I found out he was cheating. I tried to break up with him, but he told me he was scared of his feelings for me. That he'd never do it again. And he wrote those letters threatening to kill himself if I did leave. So, I took him back."

I hated remembering how scared I was then. Even as I returned to him. He changed me into an anxious ball of insecurity. My parents knew something was wrong, but they thought I was suffering an eating disorder. Plus, I kept telling them I was stressed with school. "It all started up again. The ups and downs were too much. I couldn't take it anymore. I couldn't take the Jekyll & Hyde act or how miserable and anxious I was all the time. The final straw was him accusing me of cheating on *him* after my prom. We couldn't go together obviously, but I'd worn that red dress … do you remember from the photo?"

"I do. You were beautiful."

"Well, he thought I'd dressed up for someone else. I spent ages curled up on his sofa while he screamed himself hoarse, calling me a whore, a slut. I was terrified to move in case he suddenly got physical." My voice shook with the memories, and I heard Sebastian inhale sharply. "His neighbor, this big bloke, came banging on the door. I told him I wanted to leave, and he warned Chris he'd call the police if he didn't let me. His neighbor put me in a cab. I thought that was it. But … he started to harass me. Stalk me. I was afraid to tell my parents. Afraid of what my dad might do—"

"Kill the motherfucker, that's what."

"Aye, well, I didn't want to be the cause of my dad

getting in trouble. I didn't want my parents to know how stupid I'd been dating Chris in the first place. I went to my cousin Luke instead. Luke and I are the same age, and when we were younger, we were closer. Even at seventeen, he was a big guy, on the rugby and football teams. He rounded up a few of his teammates and they confronted Chris. I don't know exactly what happened, but Chris backed off. I never heard from him again. I think he realized I had too many people around me who would hurt him if he didn't leave me alone. Maybe he concluded I was the wrong target."

"Target ..." Sebastian bit out a curse. "He's the reason you don't realize how beautiful you are." My friend tugged me to a stop. "He got in your head and you can't get him out."

"It's not just him. Every guy I've ever dated has cheated on me. You start to think maybe you're not enough. Not pretty enough. Smart enough ..."

"Lily—"

I waved him off, feeling unbearably vulnerable. Trying to lighten the tone, I told him, "I know rationally that's not true. Anyway, the last bloke who cheated on me got a nice surprise. January planted a dead fish in the back of his closet."

"Remind me never to get on your sister's bad side." Sebastian suddenly pulled me into his embrace. He kissed the top of my head and gritted out, "I want to go back to that club and kill him and every arsehole who's ever hurt you."

I held on tight to this man who made me hurt with each passing day. It wasn't his fault, though. It was mine. I'd let our friendship continue when I knew I wanted more. More than he could give me.

"Lily Sawyer, listen to me and listen good." Sebastian

gently eased me back so he could look deep in my eyes. "You are hilarious, thoughtful, so bloody smart, and absolutely knee-tremblingly gorgeous."

My lips twitched. "Knee-tremblingly? Try saying that five times fast."

He grinned but shook me a little. "I'm serious. That arsehole took something from you and it's your job to take it back. Okay?"

That ugly thing in my gut, that thing that tightened my chest, unfurled, and the constriction eased. And I knew ... Sebastian's friendship and the good it did me was worth the ache of an unrequited crush.

"Okay. I'll try to take it back," I vowed.

"Good." He drew me against him and kept his arm around my shoulders as we strolled toward Princes Street. "No one messes with my best friend, Sawyer. Not even my best friend."

I smiled, leaning into him, enjoying the feel of his hard, comforting body pressed to my side in the only way I'd ever have him.

CHAPTER TWENTY-TWO
SEBASTIAN

Several Weeks Later

When I handed over my paper and stood, I felt calm, relaxed. I usually did well with exams, and I felt in my gut I'd passed this one. Classes finished up at the end of November and for the first week in December, I'd been studying nonstop with Lily, either at one of our places or at the library. Lily was a big advocate for flash cards and how they helped her memorize, so she'd put together a bunch with me, even though she was busy herself, and I found them incredibly helpful.

Now, with my first exam over, I was eager to see her. She was upset for Beth. Unfortunately, the Caledonia United goalie, Baird McMillan, had suffered a terrible head injury during their game yesterday. It made national news. He'd been carted off unconscious and Beth had witnessed it. Baird wasn't just Beth's friend, he was Callan Keen's best friend. As a Caley United fan, I was gutted for

Baird. As Lily's friend, I was concerned for her and the people she loved. Baird was recovering, but it was an awful accident. Lily was still shaken for Beth. I'd decided to take her mind off it and treat her to lunch after my exam.

As I was leaving the exam hall, a girl, not looking where she was going as she stuffed her phone and pen into her backpack, ran into me. Her phone clattered to the ground.

"I'm so sorry," she huffed in what I assumed was self-directed annoyance.

We both lowered to our haunches to pick up the phone. I got it first.

"It's fine."

The girl looked up as she took the phone. Her blond hair was piled in a messy, sexy knot and her large black framed glasses sat at an angle, like they'd been knocked slightly too. Her wide gray eyes were gorgeous.

"Thanks." She took the phone and we stood, getting out of people's way. "Am a flustered mess after that exam. No' sure I did aw that well." The girl had a Scottish accent. It was thicker than Lily's.

"Are you studying civil engineering?"

She nodded. "That I am. But this Finite Element Methods course has kicked ma arse aw semester."

There was a lot of calculus in this course, which is why I took it. I was good at it. If you weren't, I imagined it would be torture. "Sorry to hear that."

The girl grimaced. "*You* sailed through it, didn't ye?"

I chuckled. "I'm afraid to admit it."

She sighed heavily. "Ah wish ah hud a math brain." Suddenly she held out her hand. "Am Julianne. Ah've seen ye in ma classes over the years."

I suddenly felt bad for not noticing her because she had

a fresh prettiness that usually caught my eye. "Sebastian," I offered, shaking her hand.

A little tinge of red brightened her cheeks. "Ah ken who ye are." Julianne shrugged her backpack higher on her shoulder. "Ah dinnae suppose ye'd fancy grabbin' a coffee sometime? Maybe ye could help meh understand that crap." She gestured toward the exam hall.

Smiling, I was contemplating how to turn her down when Zac and Harry's recent needling infiltrated my mind. They'd grown insistently annoying about my lack of a sex life. Truthfully, they were right. I was going through a long dry spell. The reason for that dry spell was masochistic. Extremely.

Maybe it was time to get back to normal in that respect. "Sure, I'd like that."

She grinned and it was very pretty, though I missed the lack of dimples. Pulling a pen out of her pocket, she then tugged my wrist and did something old school and charming. She wrote her number on the back of my hand. "Call meh."

I laughed. "I will."

Julianne gave me a little wave and then strolled off with a definite swing in her hips.

Smiling to myself, I turned toward the exit and halted abruptly.

Lily stood before me. It was clear by her strained expression she'd seen and heard everything.

Guilt tightened in an ugly knot in my gut.

I felt like I'd been planning to cheat on her.

What the hell?

Lily gave me a small smile. "Hey. I thought I'd come meet you. See how the exam went."

I swallowed around the sudden thickness in my throat

and forced a smile. "It went great. Your flash cards worked a treat."

"I'm glad."

I started walking and she fell into step beside me.

An awkward silence settled between us as we strolled out of the building. I sought to fill it. "I thought we'd do lunch at Bubba Qs. You like their burgers, right?"

"I do."

Glancing down at her, I found her nibbling her bottom lip in thought.

My gut clenched.

Suddenly, Lily looked up, her hazel eyes searching my face. Whatever she found there made her smile soften into something more genuine. She bumped me with her shoulder. "You know we talk about everything except your dating life." Her tone sounded breezy, natural.

Maybe she wasn't bothered by my interaction with Julianne. Maybe she was merely surprised by it.

I didn't know how I felt about that.

"There hasn't been one in a while." I shrugged. "I haven't even been to my studio in weeks. I'm regurgitating the same videos on social media."

Lily nodded. "Aye, it's been crazy busy lately."

More awkward silence I did not like in the least. Lily and I never had awkward silence between us.

"So, the girl?" she asked.

"Julianne." Did my voice sound strained? "She was nice. She gave me her number." I flashed my hand at her.

"Old school. Nice." Her gaze darted away from my hand as if she didn't want to look at it for too long.

"It doesn't mean anything," I found myself assuring her. "If I met up with her, it would be casual."

"Why doesn't it ever mean anything?" There was something brittle about Lily's tone. "It seems strange to me that you grow up in a house with two loving parents—at least during your formative years—but you end up being commitment phobic?"

"It's just the way I am."

"Sebastian."

I exhaled heavily. "Lil, I don't know why I am the way I am. I know I don't want that kind of responsibility. And seeing what my parents are going through has only reinforced my belief that relying on one person to make you happy is asking to be destroyed."

Lily stopped in the middle of the street to gape at me. "You can't believe that. Being in a relationship doesn't mean relying on that person to make you happy. That *is* asking for disappointment. You have to make yourself happy. Aye, you can find a portion of that happiness in the person you love, but being in a relationship is having someone at your side to support you while *you* find the things that will make you happy on this strange, bloody planet—"

"Lily!" I cut her off, raising my voice. Because what she was saying ... it made me want to yank her into my arms and kiss her until neither one of us knew where the other ended.

And I couldn't.

Not with her.

If it was anyone, it would be her.

But it could never be anyone.

Her lips clamped shut, her eyes wide with hurt.

I reached for her. "I didn't mean to shout." When she retreated, it felt like someone punched me in the gut. "Lily, I'm sorry. I'm just tired. Can we ... can we drop it and have a nice lunch together?"

She considered me and then nodded tentatively. Yet she kept a physical distance between us as we walked in silence through Old Town toward the Royal Mile. And I hated every millimeter of that distance.

Worse, I loathed the tangled mess inside me that I feared might ruin everything between us one day.

CHAPTER TWENTY-THREE
LILY

As I walked out of my last exam yesterday, I'd felt lighter than I'd felt in a long time. It was only temporary, of course, but it was the start of winter vacation for me. Three whole weeks off and I planned to spend it at my parents' house. Sierra had already left for the US because her last exam had been three days before mine. Maddie was leaving for Newcastle tomorrow. I would depart tomorrow too, along with the rest of our new group of friends.

I had a pep in my step as we filed into the posh bar on George Street. Maddie and I couldn't really afford to buy drinks in New Town, but Shaun, Harry, Zac, and Sebastian were adamant the drinks were on them. We argued because we liked to pay our own way, but they insisted it was a Christmas present. Which was kind of sweet.

Things had been a wee bit off between Sebastian and me for the last few weeks, so I allowed it this once. Ever since I stumbled upon him flirting with that blond, it had hit home for me how much I was currently endangering my heart. Like, *really* hit home. I was in a foul, depressed mood for days after it, driving myself crazy with wondering if he'd taken her up on her invitation. It was then I knew I had to do something about this situation. Slowly, but surely, I needed to create a bit of distance between us.

Unfortunately, Sebastian didn't make it easy. He was used to us texting constantly and seeing each other every other day. I made the excuse that exams were keeping me busy and I knew it confused him because up until that point, we'd studied together. I told him I needed some solo studying because I felt like my first exam hadn't gone well. It was a lie, but a necessary one. He accepted it, but that didn't stop him from checking in all the time, and it would be rude and hurtful to ignore him.

I missed him.

Which proved how necessary some distance was.

Harry grabbed us a large high-backed velvet booth we could all fit in. We shrugged out of our coats and scarves.

Zac suddenly whistled.

I looked up as I laid my coat over the back of the booth and to my shock found him gazing at me open-mouthed. My cheeks heated. Zac grinned goofily. "Sorry, Lil, but ... you look hot."

Sebastian scowled and smacked him lightly across the back of the head. "Watch it."

"It's fine." Honestly, the compliment was bolstering. "Thanks, Zac."

This time I felt Sebastian's frown turn my way, but I ignored him and made sure I was sitting between Zac and Maddie in the booth. Sebastian was stuck on a chair opposite and I could feel him watching me.

Maddie and I always dressed up for our last night of term. My friend was in a tight-fitting, red-sequined, long-sleeve dress and platform Mary Janes. I'd taken a break from studying last weekend to go shopping with January and she'd convinced me to buy the velvet green minidress I currently wore.

"Your legs are amazing from biking it everywhere. You should show them off more often," Jan had insisted.

The dress came to mid-thigh and the velvet was shot through with subtle glitter, so it sparkled under the lights. It wasn't just my legs it flashed, though. It had a flattering sleeveless square neckline and spaghetti straps. Earlier, Maddie had taken one look at me and pretended to fan herself as she declared, "Your tits look phenomenal."

I'd left my hair down and styled it into soft waves and paired the dress with green velvet low-heeled boots January had spotted in the same store. The dress made me feel good, and I think I needed to feel good about myself in a "single woman" kind of way.

Harry insisted on buying the first round, and Sebastian got up to help him order.

"Sorry if I was rude." Zac leaned into me. "I should have said you look beautiful."

I smiled at his sheepishness. "It's fine. Thank you."

"Are you glad exams are over?"

"Unbelievably glad. Are you heading home tomorrow?"

"I'm heading to LA. My mother is in the middle of shooting a movie at one of the studios." He curled his lip in an uncharacteristic sneer. "I'm unlikely to see much of her at all, so I told her I could go home with Harry for Christmas, but she said it would look bad to the public."

Oof. That's horrible. I rested a hand on his forearm. "I'm sorry."

He gave me a warm smile. "Don't be. I have some friends out there. I'll just party with them."

Despite his words, I could see the melancholy he tried

to mask. I wondered if Zac longed for a normal family Christmas Day.

"And I'll be back in Edinburgh for New Year. You're coming to our party, right?"

I frowned. "What party?"

"Bas didn't ask you?" Zac scowled. "We always come back to the city for Hogmanay and host a party. The Royal Mile is usually heaving with the Hogmanay street party and we can watch it from the rooftop garden."

A strange ache scored across my chest. Why hadn't Sebastian invited me? I usually spent New Year with my family and extended family, but ... it was nice to be invited.

"I'm inviting you." Zac must have seen something on my face. "I want you there."

A pity invite. Wonderful. "Thanks."

"Lily, what's the name of that Christmas movie with Kurt Russell?" Maddie asked from my other side. "I'm trying to convince Shaun to watch Christmas movies with me via video call once we're apart for the holidays. He'll like that one, right?"

Trying not to laugh at Shaun's less than convinced expression, I replied, "*The Christmas Chronicles.*"

"Oh, aye, that sounds right up my street," Shaun deadpanned.

I laughed as Maddie shoved him playfully.

Harry and Sebastian returned with the drinks. Sebastian placed a glass in front of me. "Mojito for the lady," he drawled, as he searched my face.

I muttered my thanks.

"Why didn't you invite Lily to our Hogmanay party?" Zac asked accusingly.

Sebastian shot him an annoyed look as he settled into his seat but then his expression softened on me. "I was planning to," he assured me. "I just haven't seen you in person in ages."

"It's okay." I trusted he was telling the truth.

"Will you come?"

"I'll need to see. I usually spend Hogmanay with my family."

"I'd really love for you to be there."

I smiled and promised, "Then I'll really think about it."

The next hour passed a bit less awkwardly, though I was glad for the physical distance from Sebastian because it meant we were engaged in discussion as a group rather than one on one. Maddie and I wanted to buy a round, so I sneakily pretended to go to the restroom and stopped at the bar on my way back. The good-looking bartender finished up with a customer and ignored those who'd been waiting so he could serve me. Despite the dirty looks and muttered complaints from the other customers, it made me feel good and I couldn't help my grin as I ordered our drinks.

The bartender smiled at me as he mixed the mojitos. "Those dimples are lethal."

Oh, be still my heart, he had an Irish accent.

Buzzed from two mojitos, I flirted back. "Lethal how?"

The bartender chuckled, his eyes twinkling with interest. "My heart skipped a beat at the sight of them. They provoked a literal heart palpitation."

I part groaned, part laughed. "What a line!"

He laughed, setting another drink on the counter. He'd opened his mouth to say something when he glimpsed over my shoulder and his grin fell.

I'd know why when a warm, familiar hand settled on my lower back and Sebastian leaned in, pressed to my side. He shot the bartender a tight-lipped smile and then looked down at me, his hand smoothing up my back. "Need help with the drinks?"

"Sure." I forced myself not to tense against his touch. He smelled so bloody good, I could bury my nose in his throat and live there. Or just stare at his stupidly too handsome face. It was like staring into the sun. It burned to be this near him.

The bartender finished up the drinks without flirting. Sebastian handed over his card to pay before I could.

"Hey, the whole point was Maddie and I wanted to pay for one round."

Sebastian shrugged. "Sorry. You can pay for the next round."

I grumbled under my breath, and he snickered. "You're so fucking cute."

"Don't be patronizing."

"I'm not trying to be. Unfortunately for you, you are adorable when you're annoyed."

I stuck my middle finger up at him.

"See? Adorable."

The bartender returned with the card so I couldn't respond. However, he said to Sebastian as his eyes darted between me and my companion, "You're a very lucky man. Enjoy your night."

I opened my mouth to deny what was insinuated: that I was here with Sebastian as his date, but my friend replied, "Thank you. I know." Then he gestured for me to walk ahead of him.

Irritated, I stopped in the middle of the crowded bar. "Why did you make it seem like you were my date? And don't call me adorable when I'm annoyed. It fucks me off."

His eyes flared because I rarely cursed. "I'm sorry. I

really didn't mean anything by it. The adorable comment. I just find everything about you adorable."

Aye, unfortunately. Not sexy or charismatic or alluring.

Adorable.

Like a kid sister.

Or a bunny rabbit.

"Well, the bartender found me hot, and he was hot, and you made it seem like you and I are together."

Sebastian's expression blanked and his tone flattened. "I can go back and let him know we're not."

"No. Never mind. Just ... never mind." I didn't want to argue with him or even think about our relationship right now. I just wanted a nice night with my friends.

Returning to the table, I stupidly downed my drink, and it went straight to my head. The next couple of hours were a blur. As soon as I realized I was hitting the "very drunk" stage, I switched to water. After a few glasses, I sobered up a bit. I noted Sebastian switched to soda, even though I was trying not to pay too much attention to him.

When the evening ended, coats on, we huddled outside on George Street. Trees and buildings were lit up with Christmas lights and it was a frosty winter night. I sucked in a breath of crisp air, listening to the hoots and laughter of drunk partygoers wandering up and down the wide street. The nippy fresh air helped me sober up even more.

Maddie and Shaun were hailing a cab that I planned to share with them, and Zac was hailing one for him, Harry, and Sebastian.

Sebastian took my arm and pulled me aside, concern etched into his taut features. "I don't want to say goodbye like this. Will you come back to my place for a bit?"

"I should really go home."

"Please, Sawyer." He dipped his head toward mine. "Things feel weird between us, and I really don't like it."

"Sebastian—"

"You're one of the most important people in my life. You know that, right?"

Guilt knotted inside me.

Part of me knew I wasn't being fair to him and our friendship. "Okay. I'll come back for a bit."

He seemed to slump with relief. "Good." He pulled me into his side, wrapping his arm around my shoulders to huddle me close. His lips brushed familiarly against my temple.

As the first cab pulled up, Maddie turned to me. "You coming, Lil?"

"I'm going to go to Sebastian's. I'll see you in the morning."

She frowned. Maddie and Sierra didn't know I was half in love with my best friend, but I think they suspected, and I suspected they were worried. "Okay. If you're sure? My train leaves at ten, so please return in time to swap Christmas presents."

"I'll be there. Love you."

"Love you, babe. Bye, guys!" She waved at the lads. "Merry Christmas!"

"Merry Christmas!" the three of them boomed enthusiastically.

Sebastian squeezed me closer. "Fancy a hot chocolate when we get back?"

There were those butterflies again, raging wildly to life. "Sounds nice."

CHAPTER TWENTY-FOUR
LILY

In my attempt to avoid Sebastian over the last two weeks, I hadn't been to the lads' flat in a while. In that time, they'd decorated for Christmas. It was like a tinsel shop had thrown up in it. It was everywhere. The tree in the corner of the living room was practically suffocating in it.

Sebastian saw my amusement and chuckled. "Hey, at least we made an effort."

"That you did."

"You guys hanging out in here?" Zac asked, sounding almost hopeful.

I nodded, but Sebastian cut me off. "We're going to hang out in my room. I'm making hot chocolate. You want some?"

Harry had already disappeared into his room and passed out drunk.

Zac swayed on his feet. "Nah, I'll grab some water and head to bed, then."

Five minutes later, I found myself curled up next to Sebastian on his king-size bed with a mug of hot chocolate between my palms. Alone with him, I was much more aware of how short my party dress was. I sat sideways so the skirt covered my thighs, but there was nothing I could do about my cleavage.

Sebastian glanced down at my breasts a few times before he quickly glanced away.

I didn't think it meant anything.

Weren't straight men genetically programmed to look at tits no matter who they were attached to?

He stared at the wall opposite the bed after taking a sip of his hot cocoa. "Are we all right?"

Ignoring a niggle of guilt, I replied, "Of course."

Sebastian searched my eyes. "It doesn't feel like we are. I feel like you've been avoiding me."

"I'm not," I lied. *I am the shittiest friend ever.* "I swear I've been stressed out about exams. I freaked out at that first one and I needed to go solo. Sometimes I do that. I didn't mean to make you feel like I was avoiding you."

"No, no. I'm sorry if I'm coming across like a first-class cling-on." He rubbed the nape of his neck self-consciously. "Our friendship is really important to me, and I ... I don't want to lose you, so if I ever do something that upsets you, I want to know."

Apparently, it was possible to feel more remorseful than I did already. "We're good. I promise."

Once Sebastian seemed convinced that all was right in Thorne and Sawyer land, we fell into easier conversation, catching each other up on the last few weeks. It turned out his mum and dad were fighting so much over who was hosting him and Juno for Christmas dinner that Sebastian and his sister had decided to do Christmas brunch with their dad and Christmas dinner with their mum. Their parents still weren't entirely happy about it but had accepted the compromise.

"You finished?" Sebastian asked, gesturing to my mug.

I nodded and he took it, disappearing out of the room to put them in the kitchen. I'd been in his room many times and always marveled at how cozy it was. My exes' rooms were usually practical and cold with little in the way of soft furnishings. The room was not only big enough for a king bed but a two-seater sofa at the end of it, facing the TV on the wall. There were cushions and throws, a rug, and even bed cushions. There was framed artwork, a vase Juno made, and illustrated scenes from Steven Spielberg movies on the wall. I knew from our many conversations Sebastian was a fan of the director. "I know it's not particularly cool to be a fan of a legendary successful artist," he'd told me at the time. "It's cooler to admire the more obscure, lesser known. But I love his movies."

"My dad would say it's cooler to love what you love no matter what anyone else thinks," I'd replied.

I remembered the conversation because Sebastian had looked at me in that way I found so confusing. That tender, awed way. Like I really was special to him.

It turned out Juno had added the 'lived-in' feel to the flat. He'd returned one day to discover she'd decorated the living spaces and his bedroom with all the soft furnishings and artwork. He said he didn't mind. That she made it feel more homely. Harry had blustered a bit but was the first one to hog all the cushions on the couch.

When Sebastian returned from the kitchen, he had a small, wrapped package in his hand. He gestured with it as he approached the bed. "I got you something for Christmas."

Warm delight filled me. "Oh, I've left your present at my flat."

He shrugged. "You can get it to me anytime." He settled down beside me and held out the package. He seemed weirdly nervous. "Merry Christmas, Lily."

Biting my lip against a pleased smile, I took the present. "Thank you."

"I hope you like it."

Excited to discover what he'd thought to buy me, I carefully tore open the wrapping ... and then gaped at the jewelry box. The name of the jeweler was stamped on it, and it was a very old, prestigious jeweler in Edinburgh. Like ... everything in that store was bloody expensive.

"Open it," Sebastian demanded gruffly.

I did, my fingers trembling.

Tears of surprise, dismay, joy, and confusion blurred my vision. I blinked rapidly to clear them and held the jewelry box up for a better look. On a delicate white gold chain was a small white gold lily encrusted with diamonds. It sparkled beautifully in the light.

"Well ... do you like it?"

My lips opened and shut like a gulping fish.

"Sawyer?"

I looked up at him, eyes wide. "This is too much."

His eyebrows furrowed. "No, it's not. I saw it and I knew it had to belong to you. If ... if you don't like it, I can return it."

"I love it." I clutched it protectively to my chest. "It's so beautiful and thoughtful. Thank you."

Sebastian's expression melted into a sexy, relieved smile. "Good. I'm glad. May I help you put it on?"

Slightly discombobulated by the extravagant gift, I

nodded and handed the box to him. He carefully removed it, and I shifted onto my other hip.

His fingers tickled against my upper back as he gently swept my hair aside. I shivered as his fingertips caressed the nape of my neck and hoped he didn't notice. My friend took his sweet time making sure my hair was out of the way.

Then his arms were around me, the necklace dangling from his fingers as he settled it against my chest and then clasped it at my nape.

I glanced down at the glittering lily, a wee bit in awe. It took me a second to realize Sebastian's palm clasped the back of my neck. Then he squeezed it affectionately and a shudder of arousal moved through me.

Oh hell. I really hoped he didn't notice *that*.

"You like it?" he asked gruffly.

Desperately trying to ignore the tightening in my breasts, I nodded and cleared my throat. "It's stunning. Thank you."

He released his hold on my neck, and I settled back against his headboard, slightly shaken by how quickly one little touch from him had turned me on.

Sebastian stared at the lily nestled against my cleavage, and he swallowed hard. "Looks good." His voice was hoarse.

"It's still too much."

"Hmm?" He reluctantly drew his eyes up from my chest to my face. "What?"

"The necklace is too much."

"Nothing's too much for you. You deserve beauty in your life, Lily."

"Thank you," I whispered, overcome.

"Stay. I'm exhausted and I know you must be. I'll set my alarm so you get back to Maddie in time."

I shouldn't.

I really, really shouldn't.

The diamond lily felt warm beneath my fingertips as I touched it. "All right."

————

It was not atypical of me to wake up during the night after an evening of alcohol consumption. It nearly always disrupted my usual good sleeping habits.

When my eyes fluttered open, it wasn't only the lingering alcohol in my system that woke me, I knew. I was too hot. There was a giant hot water bottle surrounding me.

It took me a second to get my bearings.

To realize I was in Sebastian's bedroom.

And that the giant hot water bottle wrapped around me was in fact Sebastian Thorne.

His arm rested over my waist, his palm curled into my stomach, his face nuzzled in the crook of my neck, his breathing light and steady, warm and damp against my skin. His chest was pressed tight to my back and—

"*Oh* ..." The sound wheezed out of me before I could stop it.

There was something hard prodding my arse.

Sebastian's dick.

My cheeks flushed as my inner muscles rippled with excitement. An answering tingle flared to life between my thighs. Breasts suddenly tight with awareness, my breathing increased beyond my control.

Calm down, calm down.

It's just an erection.

An erection that was turning me the heck on!

I shifted against his hold and Sebastian's arm tightened. He drew me closer. This caused his hard-on to push between my ass cheeks and I couldn't help the gasp that escaped me.

Sebastian suddenly groaned in my ear and flexed his hips against me.

Rhythmically.

Heat scored through me. My lower belly clenched, and I felt the rush of dampness wet my underwear. "Sebastian." His name escaped my lips in a tone I didn't even recognize. Needy. Wanting.

Totally turned on.

Sebastian abruptly froze.

"Lily?" His voice was hoarse with sleep.

Call it mindless desire, but all rational thinking fled my mind.

I shifted my lower body, pushing my arse into his dick.

His fingers flexed on my belly and he groaned, his head burying deeper into my neck.

It wasn't enough. I needed more.

I flipped over in the dark, barely making out his features in the sliver of light escaping the crack in his curtains. More boldly than I'd known I could be, I clenched the front of his shirt into fists and pulled him toward me as I hooked my left leg over his hip. He'd changed into sweatpants to sleep in, and his dick strained against the material as it met the heat of my underwear.

"Oh God, Lily," Sebastian gritted out. He gripped my hip, drawing me against him.

The pressure wasn't enough. I needed more stimulation. I rocked my hips against him. "Sebastian ..." I sounded breathy and pleading.

His fingers bit into my hip for a second and then I was suddenly pushed onto my back and Sebastian's mouth found mine.

Yes, yes, yes, yes. I groaned with relief into his kiss as he undulated against my spread legs. For so long, I'd needed this. The hot, desperate taste of him on my tongue. I was lost. He kissed me with a hunger that matched the thrust of his hips against mine. Searching, ravaging. No one had ever kissed me like that before. We were completely lost in each other with passion I thought only existed in books and movies. Jerking my head back to catch my breath, I huffed out on a plea, "Touch me."

"Lily …" Sebastian panted heavily against my lips. "Lily … Oh … fuck!"

A cool breeze whooshed over me as Sebastian scrambled off me and the bed.

Confused by the abrupt distance, I lay panting against the pillows. It was only when he reached over and pulled my dress down from where it had risen to my waist that cold, hard reality returned. A light flared from his bedside table.

Sebastian stood over the bed, scrubbing a hand down his face. Despite the erection still straining his sweatpants, dark tension radiated from him.

When his hand dropped back to his side, he wore the countenance of a destroyed man.

Just like that my arousal was extinguished.

I was suddenly nauseated.

He regretted touching me. More than that, he was appalled that he'd touched me.

Desperately needing to be anywhere but there, I fumbled across the mattress to get out on the opposite side.

"Lily." Sebastian rounded the bed as I searched frantically for my shoes and coat. He took me by the shoulders. "Lily, please don't rush out. We should ... we should talk about this."

"Apparently, what just happened was repulsive to you, so I'd really rather not." I couldn't even look at him.

He gave me a shake. "Lily, stop."

I did, trying not to cry.

Sebastian's hold on my upper arms tightened as he bent his head to mine. "Sawyer, it was anything but repulsive. But you're my best friend, and I don't want to ruin that because of some fumbling in the dark."

Fumbling in the dark?

I yanked out of his hold.

As if he realized what he'd said, his face paled. "I didn't mean it like that. You know I think you're gorgeous. Clearly," he bit out dryly. "But is an attraction worth ruining our friendship? No, absolutely not."

Considering it was already awkward as hell, I asked the question that had been burning in my mind for months. "Why are you so adamant that friendship is all you and I can have?"

His expression hardened. "Because with friendship, I'm less likely to lose you."

"Are you?"

That's when I saw it. Panic. Real panic. "Lily, don't even joke about it."

His words suggested I was important to him and he was attracted to me ... so ... "I don't understand," I murmured sadly. I didn't get it at all. As I reached for my boots, Sebastian attempted to steady me. I pushed him away. Instead, I leaned a palm against the wall and pulled on my footwear myself.

When I picked up my coat, he tugged on my hand. "Lil,

please. I can't lose you. If ... just know if it could be anyone, it would be you."

Fury shot through me as I whirled on him, wrenching free of his hold to yank on my coat. "You think that makes me feel better?"

Anger tautened his features. "I'm trying to be honest with you."

"Honest with me? You told me that if it wasn't for your messed-up commitment issues, you would be with me."

"It's the truth."

Abruptly something terrible and heartbreaking dawned on me.

Sebastian Thorne was set on punishing himself for life. "This is about Lawrence."

His head snapped back like I'd hit him. "What?"

I ignored the warning edge in the question. "You love football, but you gave it up because Lawrence can't play. Lawrence lost his future. You love art, so you allow just enough of it to torture yourself with but are intent on a career that won't make you happy. And me? Do I fall into the same category? Are you giving yourself just enough of me ... but refusing to give yourself all of me ... as some kind of punishment for what happened to Lawrence?"

Sebastian turned chalk white and stumbled away from me. "Don't. Don't fucking psychoanalyze me, Lily. That's not fair."

It was true, then.

"Wow," I whispered tearfully. Because in punishing himself, he was punishing me.

The debt he'd conjured in his mind toward Lawrence was more important than his feelings for me.

That's when what wee bit of hope I'd tethered myself to over the past few months died.

"I need to get back to the flat."

"Lily."

I moved toward his bedroom door, feeling numb. "Happy Christmas, Sebastian."

"No." He yanked me back around, his strong hands gripping my arms as he pressed his forehead to mine. "I can't lose you, Lily. That's not a lie."

The thing was, he was right. He hadn't lied about our friendship. He'd made it clear from the start that it was all he'd give me. I just hadn't understood why until now.

Could I forgive him for it? Could I forgive him for not being able to forgive himself?

My heart ached for him as much as I raged at him.

I didn't know.

But even as heartbroken as I was, I didn't want to hurt him like he'd hurt me. I didn't want to leave him thinking it was hopeless.

Maybe I could find a way to recalibrate my feelings for him. If it meant some distance, that's what it would have to mean. Sebastian would have to compromise.

I leaned up to press a sad kiss to his cheek. "We'll talk soon. Happy Christmas," I repeated as I drew back.

Reluctantly, Sebastian let go. His words were strained with anxiety as he replied, "Happy Christmas, Sawyer."

CHAPTER TWENTY-FIVE

LILY

It was probably a good thing we had plans to spend Christmas Eve at the Carmichaels'. My family was picking up on my vibes and pestering me with questions about why I'd come home so "glum." I deflected. I lied. Stress, I said. My exams. It was taking me a while to decompress, that's all.

They didn't believe me, and Jan, in particular, looked as if she was gearing up to tie me to a chair and interrogate me.

I didn't want to ruin anyone's Christmas. The black cloud over my head wasn't going anywhere, but I didn't need to infect anyone else with its inky dreariness. Christmas Eve, I pasted a bright smile on my face and filed into the car with my family. Jan decided she wanted to be cutesy this year and had insisted she and I wear the same dress in different colors. She'd made them herself—long-sleeve, velvet skater girl dresses with oversized white collars. Mine was Christmas red and Jan's was Christmas green. The thing that pushed our outfits over the edge into ridiculous was that she'd talked me into wearing green tights while she wore red. We looked like frickin' elves. But I was trying to keep the peace between us, so I wore the outfit and endured the good-natured teasing from our parents and extended family.

"This is adorable," Beth greeted me as we entered her parents' busy kitchen. My cousin's lips strained against laughter.

"Don't." I rolled my eyes before leaning in to kiss her cheek. "I'm doing a sisterly favor is all. Jan is on some weird cutesy kick this Christmas."

"Uh, weird cutesy kick?" Jan appeared at our side. "We look fucking delightful."

"Language!" Mum yelled across the room.

Jan's eyes widened. "Her hearing is supernatural."

"You do look adorable." Beth leaned into Callan, who wrapped an arm around her waist. "But you also look like Christmas elves."

Jan looked us up and down in consideration. "Crazy-hot Christmas elves," she decided.

Callan and Beth grinned while I sighed in my best beleaguered big sister way.

"Anyway, I didn't do it for me. I did it to inject some humor into Lily." Jan patted my shoulder sympathetically. "Something happened to Lily that she won't talk to us about. Maybe you'll have a better chance getting it out of her so the rest of us can enjoy our Christmas." On that, she flounced off to engage Belle in a tight hug.

I hadn't seen Belle in ages and was glad to see Jo and Cam's daughter was here without the boyfriend everyone hated.

"She dumped him," Beth informed me.

"Huh?"

"Belle. She dumped the arsehole after she found out he was cheating on her."

"I'm glad she got rid of him," I murmured.

"Now, what's this Jan is talking about?"

Callan cleared his throat and released Beth. "I think I'll go grab another drink."

She smiled gratefully at him, then turned to me as her boyfriend departed.

"Beth—"

My cousin took my arm before I could stop her and shuffled me out of the kitchen.

The Carmichaels' townhouse was mammoth. The ground floor had a grand vestibule that led into a hallway with a wide, opulent curving stairwell. Three doors split off to the huge kitchen my aunt and uncle had renovated a few years ago, a TV room, a guest bedroom, a bathroom, and Uncle Braden's office. On the next floor was the primary suite, a huge second living room, and Aunt Joss's office. The top floor had been my cousins' floor growing up. They each had a bedroom and shared a bathroom. When I was a wee kid, I thought my cousins lived in a palace.

Beth led me into the TV room and shut the door. They'd color drenched the room with a moody blue. The sofa was a sumptuous corner unit that could seat about ten people and was in a mustard-gold velvet that worked beautifully against the blue. Scatter cushions in blues and yellows and coppers made you want to dive on it so you could enjoy the enormous flat-screen TV on the opposite wall.

Beth sat down and I reluctantly followed suit.

"What's going on?"

I shrugged unhappily. "I'm fine."

"That was the least-sounding *fine* I've ever heard in my

life. Why aren't you telling Jan and/or your parents what's up?"

"It's Christmas and I don't want to bring anyone down, okay."

Beth raised an eyebrow. "Clearly, that plan is working great."

"If they knew what was wrong, they'd watch me like a bird with a broken wing for the rest of Christmas break and I can't stand the thought of that."

"Then tell *me*. Maybe it'll help. Has it got something to do with Sebastian?"

Groaning, I rested my face in my hands for a few seconds and then dropped them to meet Beth's sympathetic stare. Maybe telling Beth would help me figure out my next move.

I told her about the last few months of very confusing signals from Sebastian. The Christmas gift he'd given me that was currently hidden in a drawer in the bedroom back at my flat. And without going into too much detail, the kisses we'd shared and the resultant aftermath.

While I hadn't told Beth the details of Sebastian's trauma, I did tell her there was something in his past that he blamed himself for. That it was big, and he was punishing himself over it.

"Oh wow." Beth considered this. "You really think he won't pursue a relationship with you because he's punishing himself for some past transgression?"

"All evidence points to it. I don't even think he realized that's what he's doing until I said it out loud." My gut twisted. "When I said it, he looked like he was going to be sick."

"Oof."

"Oof indeed." The ache in my chest intensified. "I don't

know what to do. I mean enough to him that he wants my friendship. But I don't mean enough to him to work through his issues to be with me romantically."

Beth took my hand. "Lily, forget about Sebastian's feelings for a second. I'm interested in yours and what's best for you. If you think you can continue being his friend, then do it, but I suggest putting boundaries in place. If you think you can't, then you should sever all ties."

"It would hurt him."

"If remaining his friend hurts you, I'm sorry, I don't care if ending the friendship hurts him. Sometimes we have to be selfish to protect our own mental health."

Neither option made me feel any better. In fact, the thought of not seeing Sebastian anymore was like a crushing weight on my chest. "I ... I think I want to keep him in my life. But ... with boundaries. Not like before. We were in each other's pockets before."

"He was acting like a boyfriend without the benefits," Beth opined dryly. "That boy is in serious denial. You know Callan was in denial for a while."

"You said." I smiled unhappily. When Callan and Beth started dating, it was casual. With an end date and everything. Callan didn't want the casual dating to stop but Beth was falling for him, so she broke it off. It didn't take Callan long to realize he was in love with her and to come groveling back.

Remembering the haunted look on Sebastian's face, I shook my head. "I don't think Sebastian's ready to let go of the past. I'm not sure he ever will be."

Beth patted my hand. "Then you start living life for you. I know you're busy, but maybe dating would be a good way to move on from this nonrelationship with Sebastian.

Hogmanay is the perfect night to start. No-strings fun can be found anywhere on Hogmanay."

There was a desperate part of me that wanted to do just that. To find some quick fix to get over Sebastian Thorne. "I did get invited to a Hogmanay party."

"Then you should go. You're twenty-two, Lily, and you look like you're carrying the weight of the world on your shoulders. You should start enjoying yourself and stop putting life off because you have exams and papers and a dissertation. Trust this former workaholic who had no life. Find the balance now so you don't wake up at forty wondering why all you have to show for your time on this planet is work. I mean, that's great if that's all you want, but I know that's not all you want."

Her advice settled on me with gravity.

She was right.

Even if Sebastian hadn't come into my life, I knew I'd still have buried my head in school. Maybe it was burnout from dating. Or maybe it was easier to stop looking for love than to endure the heartache of continuing to look for it.

I didn't want to live my life like that.

I wanted to keep searching, even when it hurt. Because I had something some people didn't. I had living proof from my parents, from my aunts and uncles, and from Beth ... true love existed. And it was worth the growing pains and the inconvenience and all the disruption it brought.

It was worth searching for.

CHAPTER TWENTY-SIX

SEBASTIAN

I couldn't remember a worse Christmas.

The incident with Lily had already cast a pall over the holidays and I had this niggling sense of dread that wouldn't abate. It was like waiting for medical test results. When I returned to Edinburgh, would I still have Lily, or would she choose to walk away? What would I do if she did? Because at this point, it would be like losing a limb.

Then there were my bloody parents.

Mum was surprisingly taciturn. Not in an unpleasant way but in a distracted, preoccupied way. She didn't complain about Dad once. The royal estate wasn't far from ours, so Mum left for church on Christmas morning to spend it with my grandmother, my great-aunt, and the entourage of princes and princesses who were my cousins. I'd spoken to my grandmother that morning on the phone and she'd asked me to come to church and Christmas lunch with the family at the Hillingham House, the royal estate. I'd told her I'd promised to spend Christmas morning with my father.

"A bad business that." Granny had sighed heavily in

response. "I do wish your parents would stop being so moronic."

I'd snorted unhappily. "Me too, Granny. Me too."

It was a relief to leave the house without Mum watching us go. To know that she was preoccupied with the family while we visited with Dad. Juno and I didn't have to deal with watery eyes or pinched lips that made us feel guilty for loving our own father as we stepped out.

"I met someone," Juno announced abruptly as we got into Mum's SUV.

I raised an eyebrow. "Met someone, met someone? You?"

My sister's eyes were comically wide with dazed panic. "I'm as surprised as you are. I think I'm still surprised."

Confused, I asked, "When? When did you meet this person?"

"Two months ago. At a friend's dinner party. I thought it was only friendship, but it's turned into more."

Hitting uncomfortably close to home with her words, I shifted in the driver's seat. "I don't understand. You were set on a life of singledom. Of freedom. Especially after witnessing this rubbish." I gestured toward the house.

"I ... I was." There was a hesitant silence from my sister before she blurted, "Until I met Leona. That's a woman's name, by the way, because she's a woman."

I almost hit the brakes. "You're gay? Since when?"

"I won't insult you by suggesting that tone is judgmental."

"It's not!" I hurried to assure her. "I'm just taken aback. I mean, Juno, you're not exactly a person who would be concerned with hiding your sexuality. I know more about your sex life than any brother should ever have to."

Juno gave a bark of laughter. "True. To be honest ... I've

never fancied a girl before Leona. I fell in love with *her*. She just happens to be a woman."

My pulse raced a bit. "You're in love?"

"Weird, isn't it? But yeah. I was trying to deny it, but I'm totally in love with her and kind of scared shitless but also, like, possibly the happiest I've ever been in my life."

Pulling up outside Dad's cottage, I turned to my sister. She was uncharacteristically threading her fingers nervously together in her lap. "Why do you look so worried about it, then?"

She shrugged. "I'm kind of half expecting you to naysay the whole thing, and the truth is, little brother, your opinion matters to me whether I want it to or not."

Affection cut through my surprise. I reached over to pull my sister into a tight embrace. "I'm happy for you, Junebug. I will always be happy when you're happy."

"Yeah?" Her question was muffled against my chest.

"Always." I kissed the top of her head and released her. "I don't ever want you to be afraid to tell me anything."

She nodded, giving me a small smile. "Thanks. You're kind of an all-right brother, you know that?"

I chuckled, pleased. "So ... when do I get to meet Leona?"

"I really wanted to bring her home for Christmas, but with our parents acting like imbeciles, that was impossible. And she gets it. So ... I was thinking I could bring her to your Hogmanay party?"

"Of course. I can't wait to meet her." I meant it.

However, I felt a little unsteady as I got out of the SUV. Like something set in stone had freed itself and left the ground beneath me unsettled.

"Don't tell Mum and Dad yet. I don't want their bullshit to ruin anything."

"You know they won't care you're dating a woman."

"Mum might. She has her heart set on you marrying Lady Whatshername and me Lord Whathisfuckingface so she can return to Aunty Anne's inner fold. Still strange that Aunty Anne's queen." Juno wrinkled her nose. "Our relatives are really weird."

I wrapped my arm around her as we walked to Dad's door. "Yes, they are. But Mum will get over her ambitions when she sees how happy you are. She told me if I was gay, she'd support me."

"Did she? When did she? Why did she? Never mind. It's different with her and me. Do you remember that speech she gave two years ago about how I needed to give her grandchildren someday because sons notoriously allowed their wives to push the son's parents out of the grandparental bubble?"

"Being gay doesn't mean you're suddenly unable to provide grandchildren."

"Yes, but Leona doesn't want children."

"What age is Leona?"

"Twenty-eight."

"Maybe she'll change her mind."

"This is a stupidly big conversation to be having. Let's reconcile ourselves with the idea that your commitment-phobic sister is in love. Yes?"

Nodding on a still slightly stunned smile, I agreed.

Dad opened the door, ending the conversation. "Come in, come in." He gestured us inside, already walking away. "Happy Christmas and all that blasted nonsense."

Juno and I exchanged a grim look.

Happy Christmas, indeed.

———

"He's drinking too much," Juno observed as I drove us back to the house.

"I know," I replied darkly.

It wasn't yet one in the afternoon and Dad was drunk.

And bitter.

And sarcastic.

And generally unpleasant to be around.

Juno and I made our excuses to leave after brunch, which consisted of burnt toast and fried eggs.

"We need to do something."

"I know that too." The reality of my father's drinking, however, was so big, so heavy, I didn't even know where to start.

Mum returned home about an hour after we did, and I saw her note the grim atmosphere between us. But unlike the mother I'd grown up with who wouldn't settle until she'd fixed every single one of our problems, I saw her silently question what had happened … then bury her head in the sand about it.

Instead, she enlisted us in making dinner and chatted away to us about Penelope Chiltworth, a nineteen-year-old home from St. Andrews University for Christmas.

"That's not far from Edinburgh. And she was very pretty. Her mother is Lady Pillbroke. Daughter of the Earl of Kennilston."

"I don't care, Mother," I'd muttered under my breath.

She either didn't hear me or ignored me.

"And, Juno, Lord Thirsk was at the church service this morning. Did you know his eldest son is getting divorced? Very handsome man. And no children."

"Isn't he forty?"

"A very fit and handsome forty."

I caught Juno's eye. *Tell her*, my expression said. My

sister shook her head frantically, nonverbally threatening me to keep my mouth shut.

Per her wishes, I let my mother torture us both with long-winded speeches about the wonderful attributes of aristocratic strangers she felt compelled to foist upon us.

It might have been a nice reprieve to have Dad show up out of the blue. If it wasn't so bloody horrible. We were halfway through the turkey dinner when Dad burst into the house. Still drunk. And apparently ready to fight.

He strode into the dining room, angrily observing the beautifully laid table.

Mum shot out of her chair. "What are you doing here?"

Dad yanked off his coat and scarf. "Having Christmas bloody dinner in my house," he announced belligerently as he swayed on his feet.

"Paul, are you drunk?" Mum glowered at him. "Again?"

"I've had a tipple. What are we eating?" He pulled out a chair and sat down.

"Get out!"

"Mumsy." Juno threw her a pleading look. "Please let him stay."

"No, I will not. Get out of this house, Paul."

"This house is mine!" he yelled back, his face suddenly mottled with rage. "Just because you've allowed that bitch to twist your mind with her lies doesn't mean I get to lose everything!"

I tensed at this sudden window into what was between them. "What's he talking about?" I asked Mum.

Her face bleached of color. "Nothing." She primly sat back down. "You can stay if you'll shut up."

"Shut up?" Dad laughed bitterly. "Why? Hmm?" He turned to us now. "Do you want to know why your mother upended all of our lives?"

"Paul—"

"Because Gemma—"

"Paul, don't—"

"An old flame of mine, bumped into your mother last winter and said, I quote, 'It's awfully good of you to forgive Paul for our little affair when we were younger.'"

Betrayal and anger rushed through me. "You didn't?"

Dad slapped a hand on the table, so hard cutlery bounced. "I didn't! I dated that witch before I met your mother! Nothing happened after!"

"What about the letter? That letter you always told me meant nothing!" Mum cried.

"Because it did!" Dad pushed back from the table, veins popping in his head, spittle flying from his mouth as he roared, "I wrote that letter before I even met you! When I thought Gemma was a good person!"

"Dad, stop yelling," I demanded quietly.

"Stop yelling?" he huffed. "Your mother chose to believe that woman's lies over your father. She threw me out of my own life without a discussion. But yes, let's mind ourselves not to yell about it." He pushed his chair hard against the table, making Juno and my mother flinch. Then he glared at Mum. "I'm taking my house back. If you want to leave, you know where the door is." With that, he stomped upstairs.

Stunned, I turned to Mum. Tears rolled down her cheeks. I pushed my chair back and rounded the table to pull my mother into my arms. "It's okay," I soothed as she clung to me.

"It's not okay." Juno's chair scraped with a squeal against the floor as she stood.

She glowered at Mum.

"Juno—"

My sister ignored my warning tone as Mum pulled from my arms to look at her.

"Please do not tell me that you left Dad based on the word of a woman who clearly has ulterior motives?"

Mum tensed in my arms. "Don't use that tone, Juno Thorne. You have no idea what you're talking about. This goes way back."

"Then explain it to me or I will never talk to you again."

"Juno," I growled her name in outrage.

"No. I'm done, Sebastian. If I don't get answers right now, I'm walking out of here and never coming back."

Mum straightened, pulling out of my embrace. "Very well." Her tone was brittle. "Before your father and I married, we split up for a time. I found letters between him and Gemma, his ex-girlfriend."

"Are we talking about Gemma Hartwright?" Juno gaped.

Mum nodded.

My sister and I exchanged a look. Suddenly, everything was a bit clearer. Gemma Hartwright was married to a wealthy London financier. She ran in our parents' circle, but Mum had been very vocal about how much she didn't like her. Dad always seemed weirdly unfriendly around her too. I remember being at a party when I was fifteen and Mrs. Hartwright telling me I was handsome and Mum pulling me away like the woman had tried to solicit me for sex.

"The letters between your father and Gemma were love letters. Then I caught him in a lie. He'd told me he couldn't see me one evening because he was working. So, I went out in the city with friends, and he was there with Gemma. We split up. But then he told me that Gemma had manipulated him. That she'd informed him her mother died and she needed someone to talk to. It turned out to be a lie, a manipulation to try to get him to talk to her so she could win him back. I was young and in love, so I believed him.

"Then last spring, I was in London and bumped into Gemma. She let it slip that they did have an affair. That your father was confused about whether he was ready to move on from her. He chose me, she said."

Juno's cheeks tinged with red, and her eyes blazed with anger. "And you believed that lying, pretentious hag? Everything about that woman is fake, Mother!"

"You don't understand." Mum sobbed. I reached for her again and she clung to me as she explained through her tears. "You don't understand what it's like to have these doubts living in the back of your mind for years. To love someone as much as I love your father and wonder if the person you trust most is capable of deceiving you so badly. And why would she lie after all these years? No one would do that!"

"Yes, they would. And you're a faithless idiot for believing her!" Juno yelled, almost a shriek, that shuddered through us both. Then she stormed out, her footsteps stomping through the house until the front door slammed hard behind her.

Mum collapsed against me, her hiccupping cries like a vise around my chest.

CHAPTER TWENTY-SEVEN
SEBASTIAN

I t seemed utterly selfish to call Lily on Christmas evening, especially after how we left things between us.

Yet, as I walked through the fields on our estate that evening, the moon the only thing lighting my path, I kept reaching for the phone in my pocket.

Thirty years ago. That's how long ago the incident my mother spoke of happened.

It boggled my mind to think that something that happened so long ago, something seemingly long buried, could unearth itself abruptly and cause so much damage.

Juno had returned only to lock herself in her bedroom.

Dad was locked in the primary suite.

And Mum was staring at the flickering TV, not processing anything but the emotional muddle in her head.

I'd taken myself for a walk.

Happy fucking Christmas.

The only person I wanted to see right now was Lily. She made all this shittiness disappear.

Bugger it.

I'd never pretended not to be a selfish arsehole. Swiping the lock screen off my phone, I found Lily's name right at the top of my video call list. An ache scored through me as I hesitated.

What if she didn't pick up?

I tapped her name.

I shivered against the freezing cold air as a particularly bitter breeze nipped at my cheeks. The app rang out and I was just about to end the attempted call when the screen changed.

There was Lily's beautiful face.

"One second," she told me breathlessly, and I watched as she shrugged into her coat, moving the phone from one hand to the other, and stepped out of the back patio door of her parents' house. I could just make out her family gathered around the living area in the kitchen before she ventured farther into the garden. "Happy Christmas," she said, giving me a small, strained smile.

Things were definitely still weird between us.

But maybe my family problems might help ease the awkwardness. "Oh, if only, Sawyer. If only."

Her expression tightened. "What's happened?"

My breath puffed visibly in the cold air as I let out a long exhalation before I proceeded to recount my day to my friend.

"Sebastian." Her tone was quiet with sympathy afterward. "I'm so sorry."

"I just ... I don't know what to do. Not about my dad's drinking. Not about this woman and this bomb she dropped on my mother."

Lily cocked her head to the side, her dark hair tumbling over her shoulder with the movement. "Do you know who this woman is?"

"I do. She runs in my parents' circle. We've always avoided her. Now I know why."

"You and Juno should find her. Make her tell your mother the truth."

I raised an eyebrow. "You think my dad is telling the truth? That this woman is lying?"

"Don't you?"

"I do." Tears of frustration, sadness on behalf of my father and my mother, burned in my eyes, and I looked away for a second so I could get myself together.

"It's going to be okay," Lily promised quietly.

"I don't think so. Even if we got to the truth, I don't think my father will forgive my mother for not believing him."

"I don't know ... I think a man so heartbroken he's driven to drink might forgive quite easily if it means getting the love of his life back."

Hope flickered at Lily's words. "How would we get this woman to tell the truth? I mean, she tried to manipulate my father with a terrible lie when they were younger. I'm pretty sure she's a narcissist."

"Well—and this is something I will never advise my patients when I become a licensed psychotherapist—" She wagged her finger comically at the camera. "You could dig up some dirt on her."

A surprised smile curled my lips. "Lily Sawyer, are you suggesting I blackmail this woman?"

She grinned sheepishly, holding up her forefinger and thumb. "Maybe a wee bit."

My laughter rang out across the field.

Lily always made me feel better.

Then as a cold fleck hit my cheek, Lily let out a little

gasp. "Oh, Sebastian, it's snowing here!" Her beautiful smile filled my screen. "It's snowing on Christmas."

I looked up from my phone to find snowflakes falling around me. "It's snowing down here too."

We shared a long look, my chest aching with gratitude and maybe something else.

"Happy Christmas, Sebastian," Lily murmured.

"Happy Christmas, Lily."

CHAPTER TWENTY-EIGHT
SEBASTIAN

Lily's idea sparked another. If there was one person who knew everything about everybody in my family and our social circle, it was my grandmother. Princess Mary might have once been a bit of a party girl "black sheep," but she was a working member of the royal family. She had power. And I believed she'd be equally motivated to help us.

"I cannot believe you're enlisting Granny to help us blackmail someone. It's a bonkers idea." Juno sighed as the guards let us onto the grounds of Hillingham House. "I'm so annoyed I didn't come up with it."

We parked the SUV outside the porticoed entrance of the Jacobean-style mansion that was bought by a Victorian ancestor. Truthfully, Juno and I had spent more time at Hillingham than any other royal residence because it was closer to home. Moreover, it was a favorite among the family. They alternated Christmases between here and the estate in the Scottish Highlands, so we were lucky that this year they'd stayed in England.

Staff appeared to take the car keys and usher us into the house.

While we waited in the wood-paneled drawing room with its arched pillared gallery walkway above it, Juno tapped her foot nervously.

"It's unlike you to be anxious."

"I've never asked my grandmother—a royal princess—to help us blackmail someone before."

"Well, that sounds very mysterious and interesting."

We both jumped to our feet at our grandmother's voice. She was tall and walked with the straight-backed stride of a much younger woman. Her light brown hair had been dyed her once-natural color to hide the gray and styled in flattering waves around her still pretty, wrinkled face.

She strode across the drawing room in a Christmas green sweater and skirt.

"Granny." Juno curtsied and then bridged the distance between them for a far more informal hug.

I bowed as Granny embraced my sister.

Then she reached for me, cupping my face affectionately between her palms. "You get more handsome every day, Sebastian."

"Thank you, Granny."

"Now." She looked between me and my sister. "It sounds like we're in luck that the queen and the rest of the family are out on the estate riding ... if there's blackmail afoot?"

I cleared my throat. "Let me explain ..."

———

Ten minutes later, I'd finished explaining what had happened between our parents when Granny pressed a button under the side table next to her armchair.

"I'll deal with it."

Relief churned with my guilt. "I know my mother will be angry with me for sharing these details—"

Granny cut me off with a wave of her hand. "Your mother is my daughter. I have a right to know when she's ruining her life over the word of a vicious social-climbing leech. Gemma Hartwright has enough ghouls in her closet to frighten a decent person into removing herself to some far-off place where no one knows her. She's miserable because her husband is divorcing her for someone who won't drain his coffers dry, and she decided to make your mother miserable because your mother made herself an easy target."

I scowled. "Granny, I don't think that's fair. I think this is a doubt that has sat between my parents for a long time."

"Only because your mother doubts herself and cannot see how wonderful she is. She always thought she was lucky to marry Paul, not the other way around."

Well, that was rather nice. "Have you ever said that to her face?"

My grandmother narrowed her eyes. "Of course I have." Her expression softened ever so slightly. "Do you know your mother was bullied at school? I didn't find out for two years. She was bullied for being the daughter of a princess and the school kept it from me. My darling Clarissa kept it from me because she was afraid of disappointing me. I found out from another parent whose daughter had grown quite concerned for your mother's well-being. I pulled Clarissa from that school so fast ... along with my money. It doesn't exist anymore. The school. Unfortunately, the damage those girls wrought on your mother's self-esteem does."

"I didn't know that," Juno murmured, something like guilt crossing her face.

"No, that doesn't surprise me. You know we didn't use to talk about things like that and how they affect you. We were told to toughen up and get on with it. I'm glad your generation talks about these things. Though I do think you all could do with a little more resilience. There's got to be a balance, you know. There aren't trigger warnings in real life."

My lips twitched with amusement that my grandmother even knew what a trigger warning was.

Suddenly, the drawing room door opened and the butler, Mr. English (really, that was his actual name), strode into the room.

"Your Royal Highness?" Mr. English gave a bow of his head.

"English, I'd like you to contact Ms. Gemma Hartwright on my behalf and ask her to attend afternoon tea here at Hillingham House tomorrow at two o'clock. Make sure she understands the importance of her accepting my invitation."

"Very good, Your Highness."

"My grandchildren will be leaving in ten minutes. Have Anderson bring their vehicle back around."

English bowed his head and departed the room.

Juno leaned forward in her seat. "What are you going to do, Granny?"

Our grandmother wore a wicked little smirk. "Let's just say, I know something that will nullify her prenuptial agreement. We wouldn't want that happening mid-divorce battle, would we?"

I let out a bark of laughter. "You are my hero."

She nodded, accepting the compliment as if it was her due. "We'll have your parents back together in no time." She stood, signaling the end of our discussion. "Oh, and, Sebastian, Candice Winchester is moving to Edinburgh for some job in finance. She's your age and very attractive. I told her mother I would give her your phone number so you can show her around the windy city. The girl shouldn't be alone on New Year. You must invite her to that Hogmanay party you host every year."

It didn't even surprise me that my grandmother knew about my annual party. "I'm not interested in a serious relationship."

"Oh, neither is she. She's very busy. Very driven. I quite admire that. Her mother does worry about her being alone so far from home, though. Especially on New Year."

Juno nudged me. "Give her his number, Granny. It's the least he can do after what you're doing for us."

Sighing inwardly, I nodded. "Of course. Happy to invite her to the party so she can meet some people."

"Wonderful. Now, let's get you home to Clarissa. She'll need you both right now." She turned to Juno. "Daughters are always hardest on their mothers. Try to be forgiving, dear Juno. We mothers are only human too."

I slid an arm around my sister at the slightly stricken look on her face, and she leaned into me as she promised, "I will."

CHAPTER TWENTY-NINE

LILY

Sebastian: Sawyer, you'll never guess what.

Lily: I'm useless at guessing games so you're right, I never will.

😆 I won't lay the suspense on thick then.

Mum and Dad are talking.

I think Granny pulled it off.

You mean … she got that woman to admit to lying?

Sounds like it. Mum got a phone call last night.

She was weird about it.

Then an hour ago, my parents locked themselves in the bedroom.

There was some yelling. But they've calmed down.

That's a great sign!

Yeah. And it was all your genius idea.

Princess Mary was the one who executed it.

You can just call her my grandmother, you know.

Can I? Really? Isn't that illegal?

Anyway, Juno and I are going into London to leave them to it.

I'm meeting Juno's new girlfriend. Leona. Whom she's in love with.

You can't just drop two info bombs like that! What??

I'll tell you all about it when I see you.

Okay. Well, tell Juno I'm happy for her. Have fun.

Thanks, Sawyer. Miss you.

CHAPTER THIRTY
LILY

Having lived in Edinburgh my whole life, I had, along with my family, participated in the four-day Hogmanay festival multiple times. However, the last few years, we'd avoided the city on Hogmanay if we could because it was packed with people from all over the world. In particular, we avoided the Royal Mile because everyone congregated there for the street party.

It took Jan and me ages to even reach the high street and then we had to "politely" shove our way through the crowds to get to the main entrance of Sebastian's building.

Two massive doormen blocked our way. I'd never seen them before, and they both had a rough, intimidating demeanor. One held a tablet computer and barked, "Name?"

"Oh, uh, Lily and January Sawyer."

He scrolled through the screen and nodded, stepping aside. "Go on up."

"There's a list?" January hissed as we hurried into the

building. "Bloody hell, you didn't tell me this was a VIP party."

"I think it's to stop randoms from coming inside." I shrugged. "There's never been a list before." Not that I'd been to any of Sebastian's parties. I was thankful I'd asked Sebastian if January could tag along and not just shown up with my sister.

January had agreed to attend the Hogmanay party with me as support but also because she was nosy and wanted to see Sebastian's Royal Mile penthouse.

While my friend and I had exchanged multiple texts over the holidays, we hadn't talked again since Christmas Day. Instead of moping over how much I missed him and worried about him and his situation with his parents, I attempted to look at the time apart as a good thing. It helped me gather my emotions and put the boundaries in place I needed to continue a friendship with him.

The door to the flat was wide open, probably because of the doormen downstairs halting any "undesirables" from walking in. Music pumped loudly from inside. Surprisingly, it was Dua Lipa, not the boys' usual indie rock. Catering to the masses, I assumed. I enjoyed a bit of Dua Lipa; the catchy beat of the song put a much-needed swing in my step.

We strolled up the wide hallway. People I didn't recognize lingered near the entrance to the open-plan living space. As soon as we reached the strangers, I sucked in a breath. There were so many people crowded into the apartment. Way more than I'd anticipated.

"Holy shit." January gaped around at the teeming kitchen and living room. "This place is huge." Quickly, she unbuttoned her coat. "I'm getting a drink. Want one?"

I nodded, still a bit dazed as I scanned the room in search of my friend.

Zac suddenly appeared in front of me. Sebastian's roommate grinned as he pulled me into a tight hug. "Lil, you made it."

"I did." I returned his embrace before pulling loose, too hot in my coat.

"Let me get that for you." Zac gestured as I hurriedly unbuttoned it. "Did you come alone?"

"No, I came with Jan. She's …" I glanced over my shoulder into the kitchen where my sister was already laughing and chatting away with some cute guy. That was fast! "Getting us a drink. Or supposed to be."

I shrugged out of my coat and Zac reached for it. My cheeks heated at the hungry expression on his face as his eyes swept down my body.

"You look gorgeous." He gave me another quick grin before he strode off with my coat. I watched him throw it into his bedroom and tried not to overanalyze the overt appreciation he'd shown me.

Smoothing my hands down my dress, I searched the main room again. Where the hell was Sebastian?

My outfit was armor. After the sting of his rejection, I needed to feel good about myself. Sexy. In control. Nobody's reject.

However, my plan failed. As I took in the female guests dressed in similarly sexy party attire to my own, I felt stupidly self-conscious. There were so many überslender beauties in the room. I'd never have gently sloping hips and elegant curves. The dress I wore was body-forming, accentuating my exaggerated curves. I had boobs, an arse you could sit a coffee cup on, and hips in abundance. Jan called my figure an "hourglass." She reminded me famous people paid surgeons to make their body look like mine. I held on to that thought as I took in the stunners who made up half the guest list.

Zac's compliment did give me a boost, but I couldn't help but wish I'd worn some jeans and a cute top.

"Here." Zac appeared with a bottle of chilled beer. "Your sister is preoccupied."

"Thanks." I looked back into the kitchen to find Jan shoving her male companion playfully as they flirted. "Less than a minute."

"What?" Zac leaned in, his brow wrinkled with confusion.

"My sister. It took her less than a minute to find a bloke to snog at midnight."

He snickered. "That's like Harry. The guy is charmed."

I snorted because I didn't know how. Harry had all the subtlety of a battering ram, but I guessed some girls liked that sort of thing. "Where's Sebastian?"

Zac wouldn't meet my eyes as he took a swig of beer.

My gut knotted. "Well?"

He glanced at me before searching the room. "He was introducing some girl around."

The beer I'd sipped sat unpleasantly in my belly. Before I could find an airy response to the implication in this information, Sebastian's bedroom door opened, and he stepped out.

He was accompanied by a tall, beautiful strawberry blond. She was dazzling. As tall as Sebastian in her glittering heeled sandals. Her dress was sophisticated and sexy at the same time. Modest neckline with bell sleeves, but a mini-miniskirt and cutouts at the waist so everyone could see her torso and waistline were as toned as her long, long legs.

Thankfully, neither of them appeared disheveled and her lipstick was still firmly in place.

That didn't alleviate the crushing sensation pressing on my chest.

I wanted to burst into loud, messy tears.

I wanted to leave. Immediately.

"Lily!" Sebastian's voice boomed over the music seconds before he crossed the crowded room. His arms came around me as he embraced me tightly, lifting me off my feet a little. "Christ, I missed you." His words were growly and full of sincerity.

His welcome made me want to cry even more.

Instead, I pulled out of his embrace and explained hurriedly, "Don't want to spill my beer all over you."

Sebastian's hand lingered on my waist, so I stepped back, bumping into Zac who stayed put, like a supportive wall.

Sebastian's eyes narrowed ever so slightly. Then he grabbed my free hand, apparently forgetting about the strawberry blond at his side. "Come with me."

Discombobulated, I let him tug me toward the exit. I caught January's eye as I passed the kitchen, but she merely grinned evilly at my silent plea for help. Sebastian's hand was strong and warm in mine, his fingers flexing in tight wee squeezes as he guided me out of the apartment and into the quiet hallway.

I took a fortifying swig of beer as he turned to face me, dropping my free hand. His gaze swept down my body and back up again. The little flush high on his cheeks wasn't my imagination, nor was the way his eyes lingered on my breasts before he swallowed hard and looked back into the flat.

"What's up?"

Sebastian turned to me, those startling eyes roaming my face. "I haven't seen you in a while. I missed you."

"Aye, it's ... been a while," I repeated stupidly, my smile tight as I refused to say I missed him back.

I needed my boundaries, after all.

Especially if he was going to be coming out of his bedroom with gorgeous blonds. Or redheads. Or whatever strawberry blond was categorized as. It didn't matter. All females in Sebastian's bedroom made me want to pour my beer over the top of his perfectly formed head.

Sebastian frowned, searching my face. Then he stared fixedly at my cleavage again. I scowled until I realized he wasn't ogling me.

He was looking for something.

The necklace.

I stiffened.

He was looking for the lily necklace he gave me.

It was tucked away in the back of a drawer. I'd worn the locket January got me for Christmas instead. It was gold and shaped like a book. It opened to reveal an engraved quote from one of my favorite childhood novels. "'Why, sir. I think—I don't know—but I think I could be brave enough.'" It was from *The Lion, the Witch, and the Wardrobe*. And it made me cry because January always had a way of telling a person something meaningful without actually saying it out loud.

I didn't know if she was right.

My fingertips grazed the locket. "It was a gift from Jan."

Sebastian gave me a strained smile. "It's nice."

I shifted awkwardly. "How are your parents?"

"Talking. So at least that's something."

"Good."

"Thanks for that, by the way."

"I didn't do anything."

"It was your idea to force Gemma to tell the truth."

"I'm glad it worked. How's Juno?"

Sebastian shrugged, his mouth tilting upward in one corner. "In love with Leona. So strange. The love part, not the Leona part. She's cool. I get the attraction. They were supposed to be here tonight, but Leona surprised Juno with tickets to New York. Can't really compete with New Year in Times Square."

"I dunno. I'm a wee bit biased, but a Scottish Hogmanay is a special thing."

"Is that because it lasts longer?" he teased.

"We Scots do like to draw things out, don't we?"

"Sebastian!"

We turned to find the strawberry blond leaning casually against the entrance of the flat. Her eyes flickered over me, dismissing me, before warming on Sebastian. "Do you know what you did with that prosecco I brought?" Her accent was as crisp and classy as Sebastian's.

"Uh, sure. Candice, this is my friend Lily. Lily, this is Candice. She moved to Edinburgh for a job and is a friend of my grandmother."

A friend of Princess Mary?

Wow.

Okay, then. So she was gorgeous and ran in the same circles as Sebastian.

"Nice to meet you," I said politely.

She gave me a small smile. "You too. Love your dress."

"You too."

"Prosecco, Bas?"

Bas?

She was calling him Bas like she was one of his close buddies?

"Sure." He gestured for me to go inside first, and Candice stepped aside to let me pass. When I glanced over my shoulder, the newcomer slid her arm around Sebastian's waist. I quickly turned away.

I wanted to go home.

I wouldn't give him the satisfaction of seeing how much it hurt.

However, I'd leave before midnight.

I doubt he'd even notice.

———

Candice and Sebastian ended up on the other side of the flat talking with a bunch of people. It was a blessing because she was fawning all over him, touching him, and he was allowing it to happen. His behavior was uncharacteristically cruel considering what happened between us before Christmas.

I saw Harry at one point before he joined Sebastian's wee group.

Zac and Jan seemed to take it upon themselves to recover my night and apparently that meant getting me drunk.

I downed a pint of water in between each beer they set in front of me and I ate the party food. It was catered and delicious and I needed it to soak up the alcohol. Between the crowded room, the drink, and my indignant fury, I grew uncomfortably hot.

"Are you okay?" Zac asked suddenly, his brow furrowed.

I probably looked like a bronzed tomato. "I need some air."

"Oh, come this way." He took my hand before I could agree, and I found myself being led into his bedroom. Zac closed the door, dropped my hand, and crossed the room to open the large window near his bed. His room was slightly smaller than Sebastian's and way less cozy. There was hardly anything in it and his furniture choices were on the severe sterile side of modern. The only item that looked somewhat comfortable was his bed.

As if he read my mind, he smirked. "I grew up with a mother who hates clutter and loves clean lines. Her tastes rubbed off on me."

Nodding, I moved to the window and sighed in relief as the wintry air seeping in through it fluttered over my skin in a cooling caress. "Thanks for this."

"No problem." He leaned against the wall.

Feeling his penetrating stare, I turned from the window. "What?"

"I can snog you at midnight," Zac offered matter-of-factly.

I snorted. "I don't need a pity snog, but thanks."

"Lil, you've seen you, right?" Zac gave me a very serious look, despite the drunken glaze in his eyes. "You're gorgeous. It wouldn't exactly be a chore to kiss you at midnight."

"You're sweet." I reached out to squeeze his arm. "But I'm good. I promise." It was an absolute lie.

"Right." His tone suggested he knew it was a lie too.

Wanting desperately to change the subject, I asked, "How was LA?"

Zac's entire demeanor changed. His features hardened

and he pushed away from the wall. "Exactly as I imagined it would be."

Sympathy filled me at his dull tone. "Do you want to talk about it?"

His eyes and mouth softened. "There's not much to say, Lil. I realized a few years ago that my mother is a narcissist who loves herself more than she'll ever love anyone else, including her son. One day my heart will catch up with my brain and it'll stop hurting."

I didn't say I was sorry. I had a feeling that would piss him off. But I was sorry. It baffled me that some people had children and then forgot to love them. "You'll do better with your own children."

"I hope so. Harry and I say that all the time."

Surprised, I asked, "Harry wants children?"

Zac chuckled. "Unbelievably, yes. At some point. Later. Much, much later in life. But he gets it, you know. His mum is all right. But his dad is an utter prick. It's harder for Bas to get it. He's had this amazing childhood with wonderful, loving parents. Like something out of a children's book."

I frowned because I heard a hint of bitterness in his tone. "He's not had it easy with his parents this year."

"Oh, I know." Zac nodded. "I feel bad for the guy. But at the same time, his parents were good when he needed them to be. Not much to complain about there. Bastian's kind of ... things come easy to him. I love the bloke, so I'm glad for him, but I think he takes things for granted."

I wasn't sure I agreed at all. The one thing I'd admired about Sebastian was that he recognized his privilege and had a great perspective.

"I'm feeling better," I replied quietly. "I'm going to find January."

"Sure," Zac agreed easily and strode across the room to

let me out. As we did, he said in my ear, "Lil, you deserve better than Sebastian."

My heart flipped over in my chest. "Zac——"

"She's the type of girl he'll end up with." Zac gestured across the room to Sebastian and Candice who stood near one of the large floor-to-ceiling windows in the main room. "I don't say this to be a shit but to help. She's from old money. Aristocratic. Known and liked by the royal family. That's the kind of woman he'll choose to be with. Someone who gets it. Not someone like you or me who exist on the fringes of that world. I mean, my mum might be Hollywood royalty, but it's a totally different thing to be an aristocrat. They tend to stick to their own because bad things happen when they don't. Like you said, Bastian's parents are falling apart now. You don't think it's partly to do with the fact his mum married outside of the nobility? Why else would she be constantly pushing noble women at her son?"

His words hurt so bad, I had to bite my lip to stop my tipsy tears from trembling it. "We're not that," I wheezed out.

"No? Because he's certainly been all over you for months. Look, he's my friend, but what he's doing to you is screwed up. He's strung you along when he has no intention of ever being with you."

Those tears sprung to my eyes before I could stop them. It was humiliating to realize everyone was aware of my unrequited feelings for Sebastian.

"Shit, Lil, I'm sorry."

"No." I blinked away tears, looking down. "You're not wrong."

"I could have been more sensitive about it, though. It just ... it pisses me off because you're so great and you deserve better."

"Thanks," I muttered.

Zac sighed heavily. "I'll be back in a sec. Need the loo."

I nodded, but I wouldn't be there when he returned. I was going home. This was too embarrassing and if I stayed, I might get drunker and start shouting at Sebastian for being such a dick.

Just then, however, Harry suggested we go up to the roof garden to see the street party and wait for the fireworks to go off at the castle.

"Come on, you!" Jan grabbed my hand, tugging me along with the crowd of moving partygoers. I slipped free of her on the stairwell, but with everyone heading upward, I had no choice but to follow or be crushed. When we reached the rooftop, it was bloody freezing. Once everyone had filed onto the roof, I reopened the exit to the stairwell to make my escape. I turned to find Jan to tell her I was leaving, but she was nowhere in sight.

"Cold?"

I whirled around to find a familiar-looking man grinning down at me.

He held out his jacket. "Here, put this on."

Like magic, his Irish accent flicked the recognition switch. "You. You were my bartender a few weeks ago."

"I was. I recognize you too. Hard to forget you in that green velvet dress. It's imprinted on my brain." His eyes dragged down my body, lingering on my legs. "This one is good too." He grinned unrepentantly at my raised eyebrow. "But then you'd make a bin bag look amazing. Where's your boyfriend tonight?"

There was that aching sharpness in my chest again. With a will of their own, my eyes found Sebastian at the edge of the rooftop. He was laughing with Candice as she rested a hand on his chest, smiling up at him with "screw me" eyes.

I felt sick. And enraged.

"He's not my boyfriend."

Following my gaze, Bartender huffed. "He moves fast, huh?"

Ignoring that, I asked a little snippily, "What are you doing here?"

"I work with Chaz, who apparently knows one of the lads who lives here." The Irishman smirked. "How the other half live. I'm Lorcan. You are?"

"Lily."

His lovely eyes twinkled with overt interest. It soothed my ravaged self-esteem. Lorcan was incredibly good-looking and there were many attractive women at this party. Yet, he'd zeroed in on me.

Ugh, I replayed that thought in my head.

January was right.

I really needed to work on my self-esteem.

January would see things the opposite way around. Like, Lorcan was the lucky one for getting to breathe anywhere near her. I thought about the quote she'd inscribed in my locket. Maybe bravery meant walking away from something you wanted but knew was bad for you.

A kernel of doubt had me looking over at Sebastian again.

My heart plummeted at the sight of his lips pressed to Candice's. Her arms were looped around his neck, her body crushed to his, and they were kissing like no one else was there.

Tears burned in my throat. I felt gutted. Like I was watching my boyfriend cheat on me.

Another one.

Even though I knew that wasn't rational, it's how I felt.

And once again I wondered what was so wrong with me that the guys I liked always ended up hurting me.

"Lily?"

I wrenched my eyes from the awful sight of Sebastian snogging another woman to the Irishman.

Lorcan was a sexy distraction.

And I needed to be brave enough to walk away from the thing that was bad for me for a sexy distraction that wouldn't leave me feeling like shit in the morning. Forcing the pain from my tone and my expression, I gestured toward the street with a tip of my head. "I know it's kind of crazy out there, but would you fancy getting out of here?"

His eyes lit up and I felt a flutter of butterflies in my belly.

That was encouraging.

It was a much better feeling than the crushing ache of seeing Sebastian all over Candice.

"You don't want to wait for the bells up here? Watch the fireworks. Kiss at midnight."

I chuckled at his cockiness. "How about we kiss at midnight ... just not here?" Then recklessly I threw out, "My flat is empty. We could go back to my place."

"Hell yes." Lorcan held out his arm in a gentlemanly fashion, incongruous to his enthusiastic response and the unspoken plans between us.

I was about to embark on a one-night stand.

My first ever one-night stand.

Jittery nerves almost stopped me.

Go for it, big sis! I heard my sister's voice in my head.

I took Lorcan's arm and headed toward the rooftop door. Zac stood near it chatting up a pretty brunette. "Hey, Zac, can I grab my coat from your room?"

His eyes flickered over me and Lorcan and narrowed ever so slightly. But he flashed me a grin, like whatever that thought was he'd wiped it clean. "Sure. I left it unlocked before we came up. Go in and grab it. You're leaving, then?"

I nodded. "Aye. I don't feel like staying."

Zac peered across the rooftop. "Good for you, Lil. Happy New Year when it comes."

"You too."

CHAPTER THIRTY-ONE
SEBASTIAN

I broke the kiss with Candice.

She stared up at me, eyes smoky, turned on. Ready for more.

I'd wanted to feel something kissing her.

Instead, I'd felt nothing.

Unlike when I woke up in bed with Lily in my arms and my whole body felt like it was on fucking fire.

I released my grip on Candice.

The woman was stunning. Yet looking at her elicited hardly any feeling. Like I was looking at a beautiful sculpture and could recognize its beauty but felt nothing about it otherwise. However, she'd made it clear upon her arrival that she was only looking for fun. That she'd broken up with her fiancé and needed a rebound. Despite the weirdness with Lily, or maybe because of it, I'd thought *Why not?*

It would make a statement about what was or was not between me and Lily.

She'd get it.

We'd get over it.

And we'd go back to the way things were before I'd messed up and dry-humped her in my bed.

The urge to search the crowded rooftop for my friend was too insistent to resist. A prickle of an ugly feeling hung over me as I glanced around.

It wasn't guilt. Why should I feel guilty?

I was single.

My stomach knotted, however, the longer I looked and couldn't find Lily.

"What is it? Who are you looking for?" Candice asked, sounding slightly irritated.

"Uh, one sec, yeah." I gave her a tight-lipped smile. "I'll be back in a second."

As I pushed through the crowd, I spotted January snogging Geoff, who I'd befriended on my civil engineering course in second year. Not wanting to interrupt them, I headed over to where Zac chatted with a couple of girls. I'd noted he'd been hanging out with Lily all night. I'd kept my distance because I was still getting weird vibes and didn't want to push myself on her.

"Hey, where's Sawyer?" I interrupted my friend's conversation.

Zac glanced up at me, a smirk curling his mouth. "She took off with some guy."

He might as well have shoved me toward the edge of the rooftop for how unbalanced I felt at this information. Some bloke? Lily? No way. "What do you mean?"

Zac shrugged, frowning. "What do you think I mean? She hooked up with some guy. I don't know who he is, but they were all over each other."

Lily? My Lily? Who had never had a one-night stand in her life? "Are you kidding?"

"No."

I moved on instinct toward the door.

A strong hand gripped the back of my shirt, jerking me to a halt. I glanced over my shoulder to find Zac glaring at me. "What are you doing?" he bit out.

I shrugged him off. "What are *you* doing?"

"Stopping you from being an utter arse to Lil. She saw you snogging Candice."

I swallowed hard. "So?"

Zac's disgust was obvious, and I felt about two feet tall. "You know, I've never thought you would deliberately hurt someone, but the way you've strung that girl along is shitty. Let her be. Let her hook up with someone else and get over you. Because we all know Lily Sawyer deserves better than you."

Stunned, I couldn't speak as Zac turned his back and started chatting away to his companions like he hadn't torn strips off me.

He was right.

Lily deserved so much better.

I should walk back across the roof and kiss Candice at midnight.

My hands fisted at my sides as an image of Lily in bed with some faceless bloke filled my mind. It made me sick. It made my blood boil and my skin flush hot.

It made my feet walk through the door and down the stairwell before I could think better of it.

———

LILY

Guilt swamped me as I let myself into my flat.

Alone.

Lorcan and I had made it halfway to Leven Street before my bravery fled and I started to feel nauseated by the thought of some strange bloke taking off my clothes. I'd stopped in the middle of the street, blurted out what was happening with Sebastian, and how I was so sorry, but I was upset and I couldn't sleep with him.

Thankfully, the Irishman was a decent guy. He told me he understood. Then he'd given me his phone number and told me to call him if I ever changed my mind.

A gentleman might have walked me the rest of the way home at eleven forty-five in the evening in the middle of a city, but whatever. At least he didn't have a shit fit at being led on. Och, he'd probably return to the party and find someone else to sleep with.

Which was exactly why I couldn't do it.

For some stupid reason, I needed to believe the guy sleeping with me wanted to sleep with *me,* not just that he needed to stick his cock in the nearest available vagina.

Tears spilled down my cheeks as I slammed my flat door shut behind me. I kept seeing Sebastian kissing Candice. Was that what I was, then, that night in his bed? Was he merely turned on because I was female? Could I have been any girl in his bed, and he would have kissed me?

And why did I care?

I hated him right now!

Maybe all it was between us was physical attraction and I was the one mistaking it for something else.

I swiped at my tears and kicked off my heels. Flattening my aching soles into the cold floorboards, I braced against the wall and tried to get a hold of myself. I was not going into the new year feeling like shit over a guy.

No way!

BANG, BANG, BANG! "Lily! Are you in there?!"

Startled, I squeaked at the sound of Sebastian battering his fist against my front door. What the hell? I crossed the room and unlocked it, throwing it open.

He stood with hands braced on either side of the doorway, white knuckling the woodwork. His expression was taut with some intense emotion as he inspected me and then peered over my shoulder as if searching for something.

"What the hell are you doing here?"

Sebastian glowered at me, practically growling as he grunted and pushed past.

"Aye, sure, come in, Thorne." I crossed my arms over my chest. "That was sarcasm, by the way." Blood rushed in my ears, my skin turning hot as I watched Sebastian march around my flat, checking in doorways. "Looking for something?"

He whirled on me, nostrils flaring. "Zac said you left with some guy."

What. The. Heck?

This was not happening.

Blazing indignation crawled up my legs, rapidly igniting my entire body. "I did," I bit out between clenched teeth.

"Where is he?"

"Probably back at the party. What are you doing here? I thought you'd have Candice under you by now."

"Did you fuck him?"

"I think you should leave before I kill you."

Sebastian's chest heaved as if he'd run a marathon. On closer inspection, I noted his skin was a little dewy, his cheeks flushed, like he'd run all the way here. Relief blazed in his eyes. "You didn't fuck him. So you're alone?"

"I was until my insane ex-friend just showed up." I whirled around and grabbed the edge of the door. "You should go. You're about to miss sticking your tongue down Candice's throat *again* for the bells."

His eyes narrowed. "That bothered you, huh?"

He did not.

"Sebastian, again, I'll repeat: Get out before I'm arrested for murdering you."

"No."

I gaped at him. "No? When a woman asks you to leave her apartment, the answer is not no. Get out!"

Features etched with anger, he bridged the distance between us, and I backed up to let him exit. Instead, he grabbed the door out of my hold and slammed it shut, locking us inside together.

"W-what are you doing?" I spluttered.

"I don't know what I'm doing," he breathed out raggedly. "I just ... I heard you left with some guy and ... and ..."

My heart raced so hard, I was sure he could hear it. "And what?"

Pain crossed his expression. "I don't know. I ... I hated the idea. Like, fully wanted to punch my fist through a wall hated it."

"But you were okay about eating Candice's face in front of me." I shoved past him. "What is this, Thorne? You don't want me but no one else can have me? You need therapy!"

He wrapped a hand around my biceps, pulling me back. His face bent to mine. "I didn't feel anything for Candice. For fuck's sake, I abandoned her on a rooftop to come to you. What does that tell you?"

"It tells me this is fucked up!" I yanked my arm from his hold, and he flinched at my uncharacteristic cursing.

"I know." Sebastian scrubbed a hand over his face. "Don't you think I know that? Don't you think I want what's best for you and know it's not me? Don't you think I know I'm a selfish bastard when it comes to you?"

"Then stop being selfish."

"Then stop making me want you so much."

I huffed, my cheeks turning hotter. "You did not just say that. You don't blame a woman for your attraction."

"I don't blame you. But don't you wish you weren't attracted to me?"

"Aye!" I yelled. "I have never wanted something more!"

We stared at each other in sullen resentment, even as the air between us crackled with the most intense sexual tension I'd ever experienced.

My earlier thought returned.

What if it was only sexual attraction?

What if ... what if we scratched the itch and discovered it was enough to put our feelings to bed?

"Fine," I whispered, my knees shaking even as I kept my tone cool and confident. "Let's just do it."

His lips parted as he inhaled sharply. "Are you ... what?"

"Let's sleep together." I shrugged with more casualness than I felt. "Let's scratch the bloody itch and be done with it."

Sebastian swallowed hard as his gaze dragged down my body slowly as if he was memorizing every inch of me. "You mean ... I mean ... you mean ..."

"A one-night stand. No strings attached."

He straightened, his eyes flaring hotly. "And you'd still be my friend afterward? It wouldn't ... wouldn't it get weird?"

"No." I shrugged. "It's messing things up. So, let's do it and be done with it."

He stared at me so long, I thought he would deny it.

Instead, it was like some string holding him back snapped and suddenly I was in his arms.

Sebastian Thorne kissed me with a passion that rocked me back on my heels.

CHAPTER THIRTY-TWO
LILY

He kissed me like it was the last time we'd ever see each other—a sensual place caught between wild longing and desperate hunger.

It was lips, tongue, *need*.

Sebastian held my head to his, his fingers threaded through my hair. I could do nothing but hold on to his arms as his kiss ignited my body in a way I didn't know existed outside of my romance novels.

His kiss tasted of yearning and frustration. I moaned as his other hand gripped my arse, hauling me against him. His erection dug into me, making me moan even louder.

Sebastian grunted, slipping his hand from my hair to join the other one on my butt. He squeezed it and we stumbled back against the wall. It broke the kiss and Sebastian stared down at my mouth, his eyes hooded. His voice was thick as he confessed, "I've fantasized about doing many a filthy thing to your gorgeous arse."

My belly clenched, low and deep. "Like what?"

"I'd prefer to show you. But first ..." His mouth crushed over mine again. He tasted of champagne and something all him. I'd never been much a fan of kissing. It wasn't that I disliked it, but it wasn't my favorite part of foreplay. Yet with Sebastian, it was different. His tongue caressing mine was turning me on in a way a kiss never had.

I needed him inside me.

Before I changed my mind.

Sebastian's mouth left mine as I fumbled for the zip on his jeans. His breath puffed against my forehead as he looked down between us. Sliding his hand under my dress, his thumb pressed the fabric against my clit. I shivered, arousal squeezing my inner muscles. "Let me take care of you first."

I shook my head. "I ... after. I just want ..."

"What do you want?" He ducked his head to press a kiss to my throat. "Lily, what do you want?"

"You inside me."

"Sweet holy hell." His mouth was on mine again as we stumbled across the hall toward my bedroom. Then we were on the bed, hands pawing and ripping while lips and tongues ravaged each other's mouths. He pushed the hem of my dress up and gripped my knickers, hurriedly drawing them down my thighs. My usual self-consciousness seemed to have taken a vacation, overwhelmed instead by heady lust.

Sebastian moved to draw my dress over my head, but I slid my hand inside his jeans instead. "Just get inside me."

"Fuuuuccck." He growled seconds before he kissed me, impossibly hungrier than ever as I fumbled to pull the zipper down on his jeans.

I arched into him as he slipped his hands between my legs, sliding his fingers into me. The wet he found there made him groan against my mouth. "Lily, God, Lily." He drew away to watch my expression as he pumped in and out of me. The look on his face ... He watched me as if I was the sexiest, most exciting woman he'd ever seen in his life.

"Sebastian!"

His features hardened, tautening with need, and he sat up straddling me, the movement forcing my hands to fall to my sides. I couldn't take my eyes off him or the way his hands shook. All composure gone, he tugged out his wallet from his back pocket, flipped it open impatiently, and removed a foil package.

A small voice prodded the back of my mind, screaming at me this was a terrible idea and I'd regret it. We'd both been drinking. We both knew our reasoning for doing this was beyond flawed.

Yet I was too far gone. I'd never experienced sexual desire like this, and I might never again. For once I wanted to be brave and soak up life. No matter what.

I panted beneath Sebastian as he threw away the wallet and tugged the zipper on his jeans down the rest of the way. His eyes locked with mine as he shoved down his jeans and boxers just far enough to release his thick, swollen erection. He was ... there was ... girth *and* length.

Wow.

No wonder he was so confident walking around with that thing in his trousers.

My fingers clawed the duvet beneath me as he rolled on the condom. I let my legs fall open, inviting him to settle between them. He did, bracing his elbows on either side of my head as we kissed.

I moaned into his mouth at the feel of the hard heat nudging into me.

Sebastian tore his mouth from mine again, his features etched with something akin to pain. "Lily ..." He clasped my thigh, spreading me wider. "My Lily."

My heart throbbed at the possessive words and raced as Sebastian pushed into me.

That overwhelming fullness I'd been desperate for shot electric sparks of pleasure down my spine. It ached but in a really delicious way.

"Sebastian," I breathed out his name, sliding my hands down his arse, pushing his jeans further out of the way so I could curl my fingers into his muscular cheeks.

He grunted, his head bowing into my neck as he pushed up onto his hands and moved his hips.

If everything was out of control before, it turned utterly wild. Forgotten was our friendship, our doubts, the complication of attraction. Everything distilled down to abject need, centered around the hot, fast, hard drive of him inside me. My hips rose in shallow thrusts to meet his, my cries filling his ears as his groans filled mine.

I loved the taut look on his face, the heat burning in his blue-green gaze. The tension inside me tightened, tightened, tightened every time he dragged his cock out and thrust back in. So full. It was everything. It was heaven. Perfect. Coiling bloody ecstasy.

I'd never come with only sex before. Usually, I needed some action on my clit to come.

This was ... this was unbelievable.

"I'm close," I gasped, shocked.

Sebastian pulled my thigh up against his hip, changing the angle of his thrust. "Lily, Lily," he gasped my name over and over, pleasure suffusing his expression.

The tension inside shattered, lights exploding behind my eyes as I cried out. My orgasm rolled through me, my inner muscles rippling and squeezing around Sebastian. His hips pounded faster against me, falling out of rhythm, and then momentarily stilled before he let out a guttural cry, his grip on my thigh bruising as his hips jerked with the swell and throb of his release.

"Lily!" His eyes rolled as his climax shuddered through him with surprising and impressive lengthiness.

Finally, he let go of my thigh and slumped over me. His weight was heavy but warm, and I closed my eyes.

Holy heck.

Our labored breathing filled my bedroom.

My heart pounded against my chest.

Finally, the blood rushing in my ears calmed and I became fully cognizant of our situation.

I was sprawled on my bed with Sebastian between my legs, still inside me. My dress was pushed up around my waist and he was still fully dressed with his jeans halfway down his legs.

It had been frantic.

Unromantic, frantic, needy, animal sex.

And it was the best sex I'd ever had.

CHAPTER THIRTY-THREE
SEBASTIAN

As I took off the condom and threw it into Lily's bedroom wastebasket, she wouldn't look at me and started pulling her duvet up to cover herself. "We're doing that again," I told her, "so I wouldn't bother covering yourself."

She bit her lip, glancing nervously at me.

That made my chest twinge with some unknown emotion. But I knew I didn't like it. I didn't want her nervous with me. I wanted her flushed with need like before, crying out my name and coming around my cock with such exquisite tightness, I thought I'd never stop climaxing.

Seriously, it was the best orgasm of my life, and I felt more than a little unbalanced by it.

Lily bit her lower lip and then released it to whisper, "Maybe we shouldn't."

Irritated that she didn't want to do it again when all I could think about was getting her naked, I huffed. "You said scratch the itch. The itch has not been scratched. Not for me, at least. Are you saying you've had enough?" *Please, God, let her say no.*

Her breathing picked up, making her breasts tremble against the strained fabric of her dress. They'd quivered with my thrusts earlier and if I hadn't been so desperate to come inside her, I'd have taken time to rip that bloody dress right off.

This time I would. I wanted her naked so I could kiss and lick and suck every inch of her.

My brain grew fuzzy with desire.

"Sebastian—"

"One night." I tried to keep my tone casual and not desperate or pleading. "One night, Sawyer."

She considered me and then sat up, letting the duvet fall away. The sexy dress might have covered her torso but not the rest of her and heat flooded my cock.

Lily licked her swollen lips. "All right. One night. Only one night."

In answer, I pulled my sweater over my head and threw it behind me. Lily's eyes devoured me as I kicked off my jeans and boxers.

"Up," I commanded gruffly.

Lily stood slowly, eating up every inch of me with her stare, even as her fingers trembled as they tugged at her dress.

Impatient to see her naked after having fantasized about her for months, I took over, fisting the material and yanking it up and over her head. The black bra she wore was gone with a flick of my fingers and every inch of me heated with need.

Lily Sawyer was the most erotic thing I'd ever seen.

All curves and dips and softness. Her dark pink nipples

tightened in the cool air, and I reached out to cup her large breasts in my hands.

"Oh." She arched into me, her head falling back, causing her hair to tumble down it.

"My God, do you even know how sexy you are." My thumbs rolled over her nipples, as I watched the pleasure suffuse her beautiful face.

"Sebastian ..."

I loved hearing my name on her lips in that breathy, needy tone.

I edged her back to the bed. "Lie down, my love, and spread your legs. I've been dreaming of burying my face in your pussy for months."

Her eyes flew open, her lips parting in surprise. "Sebastian ..."

Some girls loved dirty talk while others did not. I wanted Lily to love it. I wanted to make her wet merely by whispering filthy sweet nothings in her ear. But I'd stop if she didn't like it. There was nothing in the world I wouldn't do for Lily Sawyer.

"Really?" she asked in a hushed voice, eyes wide.

I slid a hand down her silky soft belly and down between her legs. She wasn't completely bare, my hands skimming over her neatly trimmed hair to find her wet. So wet, I squeezed my eyes closed to curb the sudden urge to shove inside her again. "Lily, you feel amazing. Tell me when it feels amazing for you." I moved my thumb over her, searching for that bundle of nerves.

She jolted when I found her clit, reaching out to hold on to me. "Yes," she said hoarsely.

I circled my thumb over her clit, watching her face as her arousal grew. Her fingernails bit into my waist. I wanted them scoring down my back as I fucked her, but it would have to wait because I wanted her a million ways before the night was through.

"Ah ..." Her moans started to grow in decibels. "Ah, ah ... aah!"

I'd never known such pleasure in giving it to a woman. I loved foreplay but not with this savage satisfaction. I wanted to give Lily orgasms for Lily's sake. Not for my ego or because I got off on it. Okay, I definitely got off on it. But I ... in this small way I didn't want to be selfish with her.

"That's right, my love." I gently pushed two fingers inside her as I continued to circle her with my thumb. It was an awkward position for me because I was so tall, but I didn't care. I'd keep at it until Lily shattered around me.

"Sebastian!"

"Yes, *Sebastian*," I whispered against her mouth. "Scream it, Sawyer."

"Sebastian ... Sebastian!" Her eyes squeezed closed as she cried out again, shuddering against me as her climax took her.

Lily swayed on her feet, and I eased her down on the bed, pushing her thighs apart as she continued to shiver through her orgasm.

Before she'd even finished, my head was between her thighs and my mouth was on her pussy. Her female taste coated my tongue as I pushed inside her wet heat.

"Oh!" she cried out, her hands pawing at my head as she drew her knees up in surprise.

I didn't lift my head.

Instead, I devoured.

I licked and played with her until she was squirming and panting with need. Sucking at her clit, I drew it between my teeth, making her hips jerk harshly. Holding her down, I kept at her, looking up to find her moaning desperately, her breasts trembling, nipples peaked.

Lily Sawyer really was the sexiest woman I'd ever seen in my life.

I needed to come.

Preferably inside her pussy or her mouth.

But I wanted to send her to the goddamn stars first. If I only got one night with her, I'd make it the best night of her life. She'd never be able to forget me then.

Lily screamed in release as I suckled at her clit. Wet flooded her and I lapped it up. Her clit was swollen and overly sensitive and I kept at it even as she begged and pleaded in senseless murmurings. When she came again, tears on her cheeks, I sat up and watched the climax roll through her.

"Lily," I breathed her name, in awe of her.

I wondered if any man had ever brought her to tears of pleasure before.

Possessiveness roared through me at the thought, and I stood abruptly, my cock straining with painful need.

Lily stared up at me beneath lowered wet eyelashes, her chest still heaving, her belly quivering.

I wanted to be inside her, but I wanted to see every inch of her.

Getting onto the bed, I pulled her up and she gave me the sexiest blissed-out smile, her dimples appearing. "God, Lily," I murmured, guiding her so she straddled me. My hands coasted up her back, as her breasts bobbed in my face. She was so luscious it was hard to believe she was real.

I saw the moment reality of our position cut through her bliss.

Her hands tensed on my shoulders, and she shoved at me. "Not like this."

For a moment, I thought she meant to end the situation entirely.

But then she said, "I'll get on my back."

My hands fell to her hips to stall her as I tried to work out what the problem was.

"Sebastian, not like this." She tried to move again, but I wouldn't let her. Then her arms dropped to wrap around her waist, covering herself, and that thing prodding the back of my mind became clear.

Her ex.

Telling her she was fat when she was on top of him.

That son of a bitch.

I swear if he were in front of me, I'd rip off his fucking balls.

Reaching for her, my grip on her chin was just hard enough to force her to look at me. It took me a second to cover my anger at her ex-arsehole of a boyfriend. "I'm not him," I bit out and then softened my gruff tone when she tried to pull away. "Lily, I'm not him. I think you are the sexiest woman alive and the thought of you riding me makes me want to come all over you right now like a callow youth."

Her beautiful eyes widened. "You don't have to—"

"Lily, can you not feel how hard I am right now?"

Her lips twitched. "Yes."

I rolled my hips beneath her, and she gasped, need tightening her features. "I love your body. I love it so much I want to see every inch of you as you fuck me."

Lily jerked her chin from my hold but only to brush her lips over mine. "You have a very dirty mouth, Sebastian Thorne."

I smoothed a hand down her back and over her perfect, round arse. I gave it a little slap and she squeaked, eyes dilating. "You love it," I growled against her lips before I took her in a hungry, desperate kiss.

Soon we were fumbling for my bloody wallet. I was so desperate to have her I almost dropped the condom.

"Let me." Lily took it from me, her eyes locked onto my cock and the precum dripping from the tip. She seemed delighted by the sight and squirmed a little as she rolled the condom over me. She gave me a hard, confident tug that made me grunt and then swat her arse again.

"Oh," Lily huffed as she raised her hips over me. "I think …"

"You think?"

She bit her lip in hesitation.

"You can tell me anything."

"I think … I might like that."

God, she was adorable. "You mean this?" A smile tugged at my lips a second before I cracked my hand over her arse again.

"Oh!" Her hands fell on my shoulders as surprised pleasure flooded her expression.

My God, why did she have to be so bloody perfect? "Lily, get on my cock before I lose my mind." I smacked her arse again for good measure.

"I really do like that," she murmured as she reached to guide me between her thighs.

Then her wet heat pushed down on me, and I muttered a million filthy curse words as lust tightened my balls. She felt amazing. Snug and wet and hot. I bowed my head, reaching for her nipple to suck into my mouth. I played with her, my head moving between her breasts until both her nipples were swollen and she'd adjusted around my cock nicely.

I laid slowly back on the bed and Lily gasped at the

change of angle. Her hands fluttered nervously over her body.

"I want to see you." My grip on her hips tightened. "Ride me, angel."

She studied me, as if searching for some truth. Determination suddenly glittered in her warm hazel eyes and her hands dropped to my belly. Her fingertips followed the grooves of my six-pack and her inner muscles fluttered around my cock.

"Sawyer, please move," I huffed out, thrusting up into her.

"Ah!" Lily cried out, her fingernails scraping across my abs. Something flashed in her eyes, and she started to raise her hips up and then down.

"Oh fuck!" I panted as sensation tugged at my groin. "Arch your back. I want to see you."

My lovely Lily took direction well, arching her back as she began to ride me. Her breasts bounced with her as she moved over my cock, and I swear to God I could have died with happiness, my heart raced so fast at the perfect sight of her.

"That's right, ride me, angel. Touch yourself if you need to."

Her hand slid between her legs, fondling her clit.

Bloody hell fucking heaven fuck fuck!

"I'm going to come," I growled out in sudden panic. "You have to come first."

As if taunting me, she fondled her breast with her free hand. Any hint of the self-conscious woman from seconds ago was gone. Her cheeks were flushed with pleasure, her eyes glazed with need and ... power.

With me, she believed she was sexy.

And she was ruining me with it.

I would have applauded her if I wasn't so near to climaxing.

Sitting up, I smacked her arse. Hard.

Lily let out a startled groan, her lips parting on the long sound of pleasure as she climaxed around me.

I was a goner.

My orgasm ripped through me, and I couldn't hold back my hoarse cry of relief. I throbbed inside her as she tightened around me. It was sensational.

The ecstasy of coming shuddered through us as Lily leaned her forehead against my shoulder, while my hands roamed over her with a mind of their own. When the pleasure eased, I realized I was squeezing her breast in my hand. I gave it another gentle squeeze before I released it and pressed a kiss to her damp cheek.

I groaned, flopping back on the bed, pulling her with me. She eased off my cock and I couldn't help the little grunt I released at the feel of losing her heat. Lily moved as if to roll away, but I wrapped my arm around her, cuddling her close.

"Sebastian?"

I stared down at her as she looked up at me, uncertainty now having overtaken her earlier lust.

I cared about this woman. It wasn't just sex, even if it was. "You're my friend. I don't want to get up and leave like you mean nothing to me, even if this is only a onetime thing."

Lily dropped her gaze. I could see her swallow hard either against words or emotion. Or both.

"Sawyer?"

She nodded and relaxed against me, pressing her cheek to my chest.

I sighed with relief, caressing my hand over the magical exaggerated slope of her waist.

We lay in silence for a while and I desperately fought the indignation and rage churning in my gut as each second passed, taking me slowly away from her.

"Happy New Year, Sebastian."

I squeezed my eyes closed, the ache in my chest intensifying. "Happy New Year, Lily."

CHAPTER THIRTY-FOUR
LILY

I t might have been ten or twenty minutes that passed as we lay in my bed. I wasn't quite sure. I just knew that I dreaded each minute that moved us further into the new year.

Finally, Sebastian let out a ragged breath, pressed a kiss to my forehead, and gently moved out of my arms. "Stay in bed," he told me quietly.

Reaching for the duvet, I pulled it over my naked body as Sebastian got up to deal with the condom. He grabbed the wastepaper basket and disappeared out of the room, presumably to dispose of them properly. When he returned, he put his clothes back on. We watched each other as he dressed until he sat on the end of the bed to tie his shoes. I waited as he finished and stared at my open bedroom door out into the hall.

"We're still friends, aren't we?" he asked dully.

Part of me still wanted to rage at him. To ask how he could not want to explore what was between us after that. Then again, he'd had more sex than me and maybe it was normal for sex to be this good for him. He *was* a very generous lover.

The thought of his head buried between some other woman's thighs nauseated me.

My promise to remain his friend nauseated me.

I'd let blinding passion guide me tonight. It had overtaken my rationale and allowed me to talk myself into something I knew I'd regret.

I wanted to hate Sebastian for not being willing to give me more.

But he'd been honest about what this would be for him.

Scratching an itch.

His itch had clearly been scratched.

Mine had turned into an open, bleeding wound.

"Aye," I muttered. "Friends."

Sebastian turned his head to look down at me. A sad smile curved his mouth upward. "I suppose kissing you goodbye wouldn't be very friend-like?"

Maybe his itch wasn't scratched.

Maybe I was right all along.

He wouldn't explore what was between us out of penance.

Shoving down my growing anger, I shook my head. "Better not. Goodbye, Sebastian."

His nostrils flared as he stood. "Good *night*, Sawyer."

———

When my flat door snicked shut with the automatic lock behind him a few seconds later, I let the tears burning my nose free. I cried silently for a while until realization hit.

I shouldn't have agreed to stay friends.

This was going to be agonizing.

A sob burst out of me like an animal's wail, and I cried until my nose was stuffed up and my head throbbed.

Eventually, I eased out of bed to shower. To scrub the smell of Sebastian Thorne off every inch of me.

CHAPTER THIRTY-FIVE
SEBASTIAN

One Month Later

S tepping down from the ladder and away from the painting, I cracked my neck.

It was my largest piece yet.

Edinburgh skyline in the rain. With the impression of a gorgeous brunette's head and upper body peeking through the image.

She'd jumped from my mind onto the canvas without true intention or thought.

All instinct.

The brunette was Lily. If you knew her well enough, you'd recognize the curve of her profile.

I scrubbed a paint-splattered hand over my face, feeling the scruff of a short beard scratch my palm.

Every inch of me ached and it wasn't because I'd holed myself up in my studio for weeks. I'd barely been back to my flat since returning in the early hours of New Year's Day to find Candice leaving Zac's bedroom.

"I had sex with your friend," she'd told me with a sneer.

Too devastated about Lily to care, I gestured lazily at the door for Candice to leave. She'd given me the middle finger and stormed out.

Truthfully, I had treated her rather poorly. Leading her on and abandoning her to go sleep with another woman.

Not just any woman, though.

I rubbed my chest where it ached unbearably at the thought of Lily.

A look at my phone told me it was February 2.

It had been a month.

A month without Lily had left me grief-stricken. I'd missed classes and was barely keeping up with my coursework and dissertation. My advisor called me into give me a "tough love" speech yesterday. The lads were irritated with me, calling me a mopey bastard, and the only place that offered escape was my studio. My art.

I could fall into a piece for days—doing videos for social media—and only think of her now and then. At least that's what I consciously believed.

Apparently not, I realized as I stared at the painting of her.

We'd texted after our night together. Or I'd texted Lily. She replied a day later with a polite response but no encouragement for further conversation. So I'd texted again. She replied two days later and again, there were no inquiries after my well-being or questions to lead to further discussion.

Like a pathetic arsehole, I attempted it one more time, but she didn't text back for days and when she did, her response was courteous but distant.

Before, I would have called her out for it. Demanded she get over herself. Push my friendship on her like a codependent arsehole.

But this time, I couldn't.

I had to stop being selfish with her.

Lily deserved that from me.

A month, though ...

It might as well have been a year.

And I couldn't seem to bring myself to care about anything.

Reaching for my phone to switch off the recording I'd use for my socials, I closed it out and saved it. To record, I switched off all other notifications, including phone calls, so it didn't interrupt the video. Now I could see I had ten missed calls from Juno and several texts.

Guilt swamped me as I called her back.

"Dear bloody buggering hell!" Juno snapped in my ear. "Mumsy and Pa called me to say they haven't heard from you in days, so I thought I'd try. I was this close to telling them to call the police. Where the hell have you been? Harry said you haven't been back to the flat in days and that you weren't picking up your phone."

"I'm in my studio."

"You can't do that, Bastian! There are people who care about you. You can't disappear on us!"

Juno rarely showed serious concern, so I knew I'd screwed up. "Junebug, I'm sorry," I muttered wearily. "I'm really sorry."

Her answering sigh was heavy with questions. "It's not like you. You've been weird for weeks. What's going on?"

I looked at the painting. The brunette was like an ephemeral moment of beauty the city couldn't hold on to. Like Lily for me.

I missed her so much I was changed from it. I didn't even recognize myself anymore. Was this life from now on? A black hole of depression and misery?

"Bastian?"

"I slept with Lily on New Year's Eve," I blurted out, my voice ragged around the words. "And I think we've come to a nonmutual decision on her side to no longer be a part of each other's lives."

My sister was silent for what felt like an age.

And then she huffed out, "I love you, but you're an absolute moron sometimes."

"I do adore our talks."

She ignored my sarcasm. "I want to reach down the phone and shake some sense into you."

"I—"

"No. It's time for some truths. You have never been this way about a woman. Ever. I knew from the moment you signed up to a psych experiment to win back her friendship that she was different and then when I saw you together, do you know what I thought?" She didn't give me time to reply. "I thought, oh my God, he's in love with this girl and doesn't even realize it."

That ache in my chest intensified.

"And before you argue, can I ask if you've showered, eaten, or slept in the last month?"

"I—"

"It's called heartbreak. Depression brought on by heartbreak. Because you love her and you're too stubborn to get over it and be with her!"

I glared sullenly at my painting.

"Sebastian?"

"Oh, am I allowed to talk?"

"Sorry. You just exasperate me sometimes."

My mind threw back to the night Lily had spent in my bed. When she'd accused me of punishing myself over Lawrence. I didn't know if she was right.

But I did know I didn't deserve Lily.

"How's Leona?" I changed the subject.

"Happy now that Mumsy and Pa know about her."

Shit, I was a terrible brother. "Yeah, how have they been about that?"

"Thank you for asking," she replied dryly. "They're fine. Too caught up in their own drama to be overly in my face about it. A bit like you. You know Pa moved back in, yes?"

My pulse leapt. "What? No. When?"

"While you were stewing in your pit of denial, our parents called me two nights ago to let me know Pa moved back in and they're seeing a couple's therapist."

"Shit." I pulled my phone from my ear to check my call list. Sure enough, there were two missed video calls from my parents a few days ago. "I'll call them back. That's great news."

"Yes, and when you're not nursing a broken heart, brother, you'll actually mean that."

"I mean it now."

"You don't mean anything now."

"Juno—"

"Go home, shower, eat something, and let your friends know you're alive. Blokes are stupid about this stuff, but beneath Harry's devil-may-care attitude, I can tell he's worried about you. Go fix that. He can be a wanker sometimes, but I'll forgive it because he treats you like a brother."

LILY

"Our next caller is Fran. Hi, Fran, how can we help?" January asked into the mic.

A girl's voice filled our headphones, her accent much like Maddie's. "Hi, ladies, thanks for having me on. Big fan. Never miss an episode. Jan, I love you. You're hilarious, babe."

"Thanks!" Jan beamed smugly. "Much appreciated."

"Fran and Jan." Maddie snorted.

Impatience rode me. "What's the problem, Fran?" I insisted.

"Oh. Well. See, I like this guy, but he's in my friend group. He likes me back but doesn't want to jeopardize our friendship. But I don't think I can just be friends with him anymore. What should I do?"

Was this a setup? I glowered at Jan and Maddie. They both knew what happened with Sebastian. With raised eyebrows of surprise, they shook their heads, nonverbally telling me this was a coincidence.

"You should cut him out of your life, Fran," I advised.

"Just snip, snip, snip, right out. Trust me. It'll save you a lot of heartache."

Maddie gaped at me.

"Isn't that a bit brutal, sis?" Jan asked, eyes wide as if to say *What the hell?*

"Nope," I replied dully. "If he doesn't want to risk your friendship, he doesn't feel the way you feel about him and you're only going to end up getting hurt. If you stay in the friendship, you're going to pine for more, lose out on opportunities with other guys, and get hurt watching him move on easily with other girls. Get out now while you can."

Maddie glared at me. "That advice tasted strangely bitter."

"Or wise," I argued.

"Both. It was both." Jan cut off our disagreement. "Fran, maybe you should talk to him again. Make sure he realizes how much you like him."

"Don't do that, Fran," I sneered. "He'll break your goddamn heart."

"Lily Sawyer, everyone!" Maddie clapped sarcastically near her mic. "She came back from winter break as the Ice Queen."

Guilt-riddled, but too stubborn to apologize, I pinched my lips together.

"Fran, are you there?"

"Uh, she hung up, ladies," Kenny informed us from the editing booth.

"Well done," Maddie huffed. "What the hell kind of advice was that, Lily?"

"Good advice."

"I think it was more the delivery than the advice." Jan cocked her head in thought. "Maybe it would be good for you if you talked about what's going on. Give our listeners some insight into this strangely dislikable version of you and unburden yourself at the same time."

Hurt drenched me at my sister's words. She'd always been overprotective of me, but now that I was *actually* heartbroken, Jan treated me with impatient callousness. I wasn't the even-tempered Lily she was used to. I was depressed, pissed off, and despairing that the ache in my chest over Sebastian would never go away.

There were moments I remembered our night together and wanted the floor to swallow me whole. The spanking. Riding him. This completely uninhibited self I'd tapped into with him. There was a man walking around in my city who had seen me at my most vulnerable and he was someone I'd never be with romantically. He didn't ... I didn't want him to have that part of me. I felt ... indignant and, aye, bitter, that it was him who'd experienced that side of me.

Mostly, though, I missed him.

Sebastian had clearly decided it was best we no longer be friends too.

He didn't push his friendship on me when I created distance between us.

Our last text string was two weeks ago.

It was over.

And I had never been more miserable in my life. Mum had taken one look at me in the library and known. Now I'd been fielding constant texts and calls from her and Dad checking in, worried about me. I wouldn't tell them what was wrong, which only worried them more.

Jan knew, though.

I'd told her.

And a little patience from a sister I'd been nothing but patient with my whole life would have been nice. "Okay. I'll unburden myself. I've stood by your side through every drama you've either incited or participated in with patience and love. I'm sorry that for the first time in my life, I'm putting myself before you and what you need from me, but you can go screw yourself, my dearest wee sister." I yanked off my headphones and threw them at the table as January gaped up at me in pale-faced shock.

"Lily!" Maddie called for me, but I ignored her too, slamming out of the recording room and marching past a wide-eyed Kenny.

For at least five minutes, I felt liberated by my outburst.

Then the guilt hit.

Because I knew I was pushing everyone away, cocooning myself in my fortress of solitude.

However, I couldn't seem to stop.

CHAPTER THIRTY-SEVEN

SEBASTIAN

When I came out of my shower, I found Harry lounging on my bed reading one of the books Lily had lent me.

"Mate, do you know this is filthy?" Harry muttered as he turned the page, seemingly engrossed.

"It's a romance book." I scrubbed the towel through my hair as I crossed the room to slump in my armchair.

"One of Lil's?" he asked tentatively, still not looking up from the page.

"Yeah."

"It's pretty funny. Can I borrow it?"

I smirked sadly, thinking Lily would get a kick out of turning our flat of blokes into a romance book club. "Knock yourself out."

Satisfied, Harry closed the book. "Glad you're back."

"Thanks. Sorry if I ... I didn't mean to make anyone worry."

He nodded, studying me. "You've lost a bit of weight."

I sighed. "Haven't been eating much. Or going to the

gym." Thinking about it, I missed the exercise. "I think I'll go tomorrow."

"I'll come with."

"Sounds good."

"We're going out tonight." Harry swung his legs off the bed. "You're coming with us."

The thought exhausted me. "I'm not in the mood."

"I invited Maddie, Sierra, and Lily. They said they'll be there."

My heart turned in my chest. "Lily will be there?"

Harry nodded grimly. "Yeah, she'll be there. Maybe ... maybe you can talk to her. Sort out this shit between you."

"You're sure she knows I'll be there?" At his silence, I groaned. "Harry, I can't ambush her. Sorry, I'm not going."

"Okay, I didn't want to have to do this, but I overheard Zac listening to Lily's podcast and I think you need to hear this morning's episode."

"Harry—"

He cut me off, producing his phone with a flourish. Seconds later, Lily's voice filled my bedroom, and I squeezed my eyes closed.

I missed her so much.

"If he doesn't want to risk your friendship, he doesn't feel the way you feel about him and you're only going to end up getting hurt," Lily was saying. My eyes flew open as the words hit very, very close to home. "If you stay in the friendship, you're going to pine for more, lose out on opportunities with other guys, and get hurt watching him move on easily with other girls. Get out now while you can."

"That advice tasted strangely bitter." That was from Maddie.

I frowned. "What are they talking about?"

"Some bird called in asking for advice about liking a guy in her friend group."

Scowling, I listened to a Lily who sounded bitter and angry and not at all like herself. When she told Jan to go screw herself and a few long seconds later Maddie explained Lily had walked out, I stared stonily at the carpet.

Jan's voice filled my room, explaining to their audience they'd decided not to edit the moment out of their episode because it was real. Then she said, "And to the person who screwed with my sister's head, I'll make sure Karma gets you, arsehole."

"That would be you," Harry needlessly pointed out as he switched off the episode.

"I gathered that, thanks." I scrubbed a hand over my face, feeling that terrible pit in my gut swell into something unbearable.

"Look, she's in just as bad a shape as you. I don't know what you're thinking or what the details are ... but you've got to fix this. For both your sakes."

"I wouldn't even know what to say."

"Just show up and let nature take its course." Harry stood and gave me a pitying look. "Bloody hell, Bas. If this is love, I hope it never happens to me." He clapped a hand on my shoulder, giving me a comforting pat before he strode from the room. "Be ready to go in two hours!"

————

LILY

Jan stood in our living room, arms crossed over her chest as I stared up at her from the couch. Maddie had let her in. She and Sierra shared the armchair, watching me and my sister like we were a tennis match.

The truth is I wanted to apologize to Jan, but I also didn't think I was entirely wrong earlier.

"We didn't edit the episode," Jan announced. "We aired it with you telling me to go screw myself and storming out."

We rarely edited the real stuff, so I shouldn't have been surprised. Still, it wouldn't take our audience much to deduce I was heartbroken. For some reason, this time having my private life in the public arena made me feel naked and vulnerable, and I resented all of them for not editing the episode.

"Are you going to speak at some point?" my sister prodded with a huff of annoyance.

I shrugged. "I shouldn't have told you to go screw yourself, but you're treating me like I'm being a drama queen who needs to get over this. Proof, January Sawyer, that you've never felt about someone the way I, unfortunately, feel about Sebastian."

"Bastian is a bastard."

"I'm sure he's never heard that before," I mumbled.

"Oh, I'm sorry, are my insults not witty enough for you?"

I narrowed my eyes. "I have never felt our three-year age gap more than I do right now."

Jan's expression veered between indignant and considering. Finally, her shoulders slumped. "Fine. I'm being immature. I ... I'm not used to seeing you like this. Anytime a guy hurt you in the past you bounced back with this inspiring determination to move on. You're acting ... lovesick. And it's not very inspiring. It's pathetic."

Hurt, I sneered. "Pathetic? Do you even hear yourself sometimes? I'm not allowed to be infallible? To be human? I have to be the poster child of feminism even while I feel like I've lost a limb? Inspiring in my heartbreak to make me worthy of your affection and respect?"

My wee sister's expression tightened. "I didn't … I didn't mean it like that."

"Didn't you?"

Uncharacteristic tears brightened Jan's eyes. "I'm sorry. You're right. And I'm sorry. I … maybe there's a part of me that resents Sebastian."

"For hurting me?"

"That. But … for taking you away." Her gaze cast downward, and she looked so young and lost.

I sat forward on the couch. "Taking me away?"

"From me." Jan shrugged. "It started happening when you began uni without me. New friends, new life. Finding the guy who's *the* guy is the beginning of everything really changing. I'll never be your priority again. I know how selfish I am making this about me, believe me. But I hate it, and I hate that he changed you."

Pushing up off the sofa, I crossed the room to pull my sister into my arms. She embraced me so tightly, it was almost painful. Jan rarely made herself vulnerable. When she did, I wanted to roll her in bubble wrap to protect her from the world. Or at the very least, make her feel safe in sharing her vulnerabilities. "You will always be my priority," I whispered. "Sisters forever. No one can ever come between that. You could be thousands of miles away on some adventure and we'd still never be apart."

Jan sniffled as she nodded. Then she gave me one last painful squeeze and released me. She wiped at her nose, her cheeky grin appearing along with her dimples. "Okay, enough cheesiness."

Sierra and Maddie chuckled, reminding me they were in the room.

"We're good?" I asked them all.

"We're good. I'm sorry," Jan said sincerely.

"I'm sorry too. I know I haven't been myself lately."

"And we're all going to be more patient about that." Sierra gave Maddie and Jan a stern look before turning to me. Her expression softened, but there was still a hard glint of determination in her eyes. "And we will be patient. But you also have to try to return to the land of the living. No more burying yourself in schoolwork and your dissertation. These are our last few months together," she reminded me.

Remorseful, I winced. How I felt about the situation with Sebastian had made me forget that we were all going our separate ways after this semester. Four years we'd spent as close as sisters. Even if I had to force myself, I needed to be more present and enjoy what time we had left. "You're right. I'm sorry."

Sierra gave me a relieved nod. "We're going dancing tonight and you, my gorgeous friend, are coming with us."

I glanced between them all. While I was tired and dreaded the idea of being in a busy club ... I also wanted to get out from under this black cloud. The thought of feeling this depressed for months to come made me want to rock in a dark corner. I had to try to break out of it. It wouldn't miraculously happen overnight, but baby steps toward it might help.

"Okay. We're going dancing."

CHAPTER THIRTY-EIGHT
SEBASTIAN

The lads led me into Cabaret Voltaire on Blair Street, only a two-minute walk from our flat. Upstairs was the café with live music and down in the Vaults was the club. I felt like I'd been in some weird sluggish daze for the past month. While I'd attended a few classes, being around this many people after isolating myself was a bit disconcerting. Between my nerves at seeing Lily again and this, I was nauseated. I didn't feel like myself at all.

"It's a drinks' deal night!" Zac shouted over his shoulder. "That's why it's packed!"

Down in the Vaults, I swept the subterranean club as light strobes glanced from dancer to dancer. The techno music was already giving me a headache.

"By the bar!" Harry tapped my shoulder and pointed.

My eyes landed on the crowd around the bar and zeroed in on Lily. Sierra had her head bent toward Lily's ear and whatever she said made her laugh. A viselike sensation around my chest made it difficult to breathe.

She didn't look very miserable without me.

What if she wasn't?

What if she had realized she really was better off without me in her life?

Harry patted me a little hard on the back and urged me through the crowds toward Lily. I couldn't drag my eyes off her and as I neared, even in the frantic lighting of the club, I could see her earlier amusement was replaced by a dull weariness. It was the same dull weariness I'd heard in her voice on the podcast episode.

Harry pulled Sierra into a hug while Zac nodded hello to Jan and Maddie.

Lily's eyes locked with mine, her nostrils flaring with surprise.

It took everything in me not to haul her into my arms.

"Hullo, Sawyer," I greeted loudly enough to be heard.

———

LILY

Several realizations hit me at once.

One, either my friends didn't know Sebastian was going to be here and they'd been lied to, or they did know, and I'd been lied to.

Two, Sebastian did not look like himself. He had a short scruffy beard, and his clothes hung a wee bit loose on him, like he'd lost weight. There were dark circles under his eyes, and he appeared exhausted.

Three, his appearance suggested distress.

Four, his distress might be related to me.

I didn't know what to do with any of that. The part of me that loved him wanted to fix everything for him. However, he didn't want to be fixed. He wanted to wallow in his masochistic need to punish himself in penance for something he wasn't to blame for in the first place.

My knees trembled as I shifted on my feet and I found I couldn't quite speak. So, I settled on a nod of hello before turning to accept Harry's and Zac's affectionate hugs. Thankfully, the bartender finally got around to serving our drinks. I could feel Sebastian's attention as I threw mine back.

"You two are talking again, then?" Harry asked loudly, gesturing between me and Jan. At my frown, he grinned cheekily. "Oh, we all heard the episode today."

Even Sebastian?

Damn it.

Hyperaware of him towering by my side, I desperately tried to ignore the flood of images from our night together suddenly filling my head. I grabbed my sister's wrist, in need of an escape. "I want to dance!"

Jan nodded enthusiastically and together we pushed through the throng to find ourselves in the middle of the dance floor.

I didn't really want to dance, but I let the techno music that usually made my head thump take hold of my body and I started bouncing around like everyone else, attempting not to spill my drink. Finally, I settled on throwing the alcohol down my throat in one big gulp.

January cheered, did the same, then took my plastic cup from me to throw it in the air with hers. People around us yelled, their arms reaching above their heads. Suddenly, the music changed from techno to a Calvin Harris tune I liked. I grinned at my sister as the crowd whooped at the song change. The beat thrummed through us all in time as we jumped up and down in rhythm with one another.

The weight that had been crushing down on my shoulders lifted for those few minutes and I found myself laughing in relief. Suddenly, Maddie and Sierra were with us. Sierra took my hand, finding her way into the rhythm easily. My friends danced and sang along, Maddie shouting the lyrics, "I feel so close to you!" in my face, wearing a cheesy grin, and I took a mental snapshot, storing the memory away. A beautiful reminder that I didn't need a bloke to make me feel loved or connected to people.

It was a perfect moment.

Until it wasn't.

He appeared out of nowhere.

The sight of his familiar face inspired a jolt of dread.

Chris. My ex.

Years I hadn't seen the arsehole and now twice in as many weeks. Edinburgh was a small city, and it had never felt more so than now. He bounced right up to us, pushing between me and Sierra so she had no choice but to let go of my hand. Chris's head bowed to mine, and I jerked back as he yelled, "We keep bumpin' into each other! Must be fate!"

I sneered in disgust, bolstered by the fact that he couldn't hurt me anymore and I had my friends and sister with me. "Or not! Piss off, Chris!"

He grinned lazily and I realized by the glaze in his eyes, he was drunk. "Not very friendly!"

"Chris, you're drunk! Go sober up somewhere else!"

"I forgot how gorgeous you are, Lily Pad!"

Nausea rolled through me at his ridiculous pet name.

When I was seventeen, I'd thought it was cute. Now it sickened me. Everything about him sickened me.

"Piss. Off." I pushed him away.

He bounced back and snaked his arm around my waist, yanking me against him. I struggled, but he was too strong. A flashback hit. A memory of him holding me hostage in his flat, his grip on my wrists bruising as he threatened to kill himself if I left him.

All the old feelings of terror and entrapment flooded me. Panicked, I struggled like a wild thing.

"Calm the fuck doon!" he yelled in my ear. "I just wanna dance!"

"Get off my sister!" I heard January.

And then I was free, stumbling back into a hard body. Gentle hands gripped me, and I looked up, dazed, to find Zac. "You okay, Lil?"

I nodded, confused, then glanced back at my ex.

My breath whooshed right out of my body.

The crowd of dancers had all stumbled away from the skirmish that had broken out between Sebastian and Chris. Considering my ex was drunk and Bastian wasn't, it wasn't a fight as much as it was an annihilation.

Sebastian was pummeling Chris, his expression tight and wild all at the same time.

"Stop him!" I lunged toward the fighting men, but Zac held me back.

"No, you'll get hurt."

However, Harry seemed to sense what I could.

Sebastian wasn't going to stop.

He braved the fighting men and grabbed Sebastian under his arms, gripping him by the chest for leverage. Sebastian tried to resist, but Harry was as determined to get him away as Sebastian was to stay and kill my ex. Finally,

Harry yelled something that made Sebastian give in a little. He hauled him off and shoved Sebastian through the crowd toward the exit.

Chris lay groaning in the middle of the dance floor, blood spilling from his nose, one eye already swelling shut.

"We need to get out of here now!" Zac started guiding me after Harry and Sebastian, the girls hurrying along with us. I barely remembered getting out of the club I was in such a shaken daze. My stomach roiled as we hurried up through the building and out onto Blair Street.

"Keep moving." Zac's grip was hard around my biceps. "We need to get away from here."

Harry and Sebastian stormed ahead, eating up the ground with their long legs.

"What just happened?" Jan was at my side as Sierra and Maddie huddled along with us.

"That was Chris." My voice shook. "My ex."

Jan halted. "The son of a bitch who stalked you?"

"What?" Zac snapped, horrified. "And keep moving."

Jan started running after us. "Well?"

"Aye, the same," I bit out. It wasn't exactly something I wanted to be public knowledge.

"Does Bastian know who Chris is?" my sister asked.

My heart turned over in my chest as indignation began to douse my shock. "Aye."

Harry and Sebastian finally stopped outside their apartment building, and I yanked my arm free of Zac's grip. Marching toward Sebastian, I took in his defiant, hard expression and felt an uncharacteristic wildness rise. I wanted to tear at something. Shake him! Scratch and claw at him.

I didn't.

But the words seethed from me as I hissed, "What the hell was that?"

He glowered right back. "I recognized him. I know who he is."

"And you thought pummeling him to death in a club was an appropriate response?"

Sebastian took a step toward me, baring his teeth like an animal. I sensed that same wildness in him, but I wasn't afraid. I was too enraged and disappointed and mad at the world—specifically at Sebastian—to fear anything right now.

"He grabbed you! The arsehole who messed with your fucking head was touching you against your will, and I lost my mind for a second. I'm only human!"

I shook my head, letting my disappointment drip from my words. "You're not angry at him. You're angry at yourself. Because you know that you're messing with my head too, just in a different way than he did." A crushing finality settled over me and I felt it in the slump of my shoulders. "The thing is, Sebastian, you can only have your head messed with for so long before you realize that you're *allowing* your head to be messed with. And I'm done. I'm done with you. I need you to stay out of my life, and I need everyone here to respect the fact that I don't want to see you anymore."

I turned on my heels, wrapping my arms tightly around my waist as I strode away from him.

The crushing expression on his face tugged at me.

However, for once, I didn't want to put someone else's feelings before mine.

I kept walking and heard my sister's and friends' footsteps follow.

As much as it hurt, I recognized in the long run I'd done

the right thing. It wasn't up to me to protect Sebastian from himself. If he loved me like I loved him, I'd be more important than some subconscious vow of penance he'd made when he was sixteen years old.

But I wasn't.

I had to let him go.

CHAPTER THIRTY-NINE
LILY

Butterflies raged in my belly as I approached Sebastian's flat, but I needed a clean break.

The doorman recognized me and stepped aside to let me up. I shook my head instead and held out an envelope to him. "Can you make sure this gets to Sebastian Thorne in the penthouse flat?"

"Uh ..." The doorman frowned but tentatively took the envelope. "Of course. Shall I tell him who it's from?"

"He'll know." Tears thickened my throat and my voice cracked as I thanked him before turning back around. The tears finally fell as I rode off on my bike. Wasn't I supposed to feel lighter? Like I'd just freed myself from something?

I didn't feel lighter.

If anything, I felt as if the weight of the entire world was riding alongside me.

CHAPTER FORTY
SEBASTIAN

Royal Mile was bleak beneath the darkened sky, the cobbled road slickened and shiny under the street-lamps that were inspired to blaze to life earlier than usual.

I sat on the window seat in the living area, staring down at the familiar view. February weather in Scotland was dreary as hell. To match my mood. People hurried by with umbrellas or wearing oversized hoods, and I wondered where they were going.

It was better than wondering about Lily.

Or focusing on the necklace wrapped around my fingers.

She'd returned my Christmas gift.

As if what she said last night wasn't enough. She wanted to make it very clear we were never to see each other again.

My attention wandered back to the necklace. It shone against my olive skin and the dark bruises of my knuckles. I'd iced them last night, so they weren't as swollen.

"Bugger." I squeezed my eyes closed.

I didn't recognize the person I'd turned into in the club.

One minute I'd been watching Lily have fun with her friends, happy to see her happy, and then the next I saw some bloke approach her. A light strobe flashed over his face, and I recognized him as her ex from that night in the bar. When he grabbed her ... seeing her struggle in his arms, knowing the damage he'd already caused her, I lost my mind.

Yet ... I think Lily was right.

I think I lost it so badly because this anger at myself had been building for weeks.

I'd wanted to take it out on someone, and Chris had been the perfect target. I could punish him for what he'd done to Lily. For what *I'd* done to Lily.

The front door opened and slammed shut, footsteps approaching.

"Good news." Harry strode into the living room. "I did a little investigating, and the police weren't called. Chris and his mates left the club without reporting it. The club didn't want any bad press, so they didn't report it either."

"That's good," I replied flatly. Though truthfully, it was good news. I might not be an oft-talked-about member of the royal family, but the tabloids would definitely print a story about Princess Mary's grandson almost beating a man to death in a Scottish nightclub.

"Did ... did he really stalk Lily? That's what Zac said Jan said." Harry sat down on the sofa, his expression uncharacteristically concerned.

I nodded. "He was her ex. He treated her ... badly."

Anger flashed in Harry's eyes. "Glad you beat the shit out of him, then."

I huffed bitterly, raising my hand with the necklace. "I lost her for good because of it."

"What's that?"

"The necklace I gave her for Christmas. She dropped it off with the doorman."

Harry winced. "Sorry, man ... So, does that mean you guys really were a thing?"

A thing? We were so much more than a bloody thing.

My mobile rang, saving me from having to answer. I reached for it. "It's Juno."

My friend nodded and stood. "I'll give you some privacy."

"Thanks, Harry."

"For what?"

"For always having my back."

He smirked. "Remember that after you answer your phone."

I frowned, watching him disappear into his bedroom as I picked up. "Junebug."

"Harry said you beat up some bloke that used to stalk Lily. What the hell?"

Bloody Harry. I sighed. Heavily. And rested my head against the wall, closing my eyes.

"Sebastian?"

With a grumble of weary impatience, I launched into the story without giving away too many details about Lily's ex. That was hers to tell, not mine.

Juno's tone was careful. "And she ended your friendship?"

A sharp, agonizing ache flared in my chest. "Yes."

"I feel like I'm missing something."

Bugger it. There was no point hiding anything now that everything was a giant mess. "Lily thinks I'm punishing myself for what happened to Lawrence." Juno was one of the few people who knew about the incident.

"I don't understand."

"She thinks I gave up pursuing a football career and a career as an artist because I'm punishing myself for what happened to Lawrence. She thinks I think I don't deserve real happiness and that's why I refuse to choose the things that will make me happy, including ... well, her."

Juno was silent so long I asked, "Are you still there?"

"Yes. I'm ... wow. Bloody hell, that woman is smart. She'll make a brilliant therapist. I didn't even put two and two together, but it does make sense. Any big choices you have to make, life-changing decisions, you never choose the path that will make you truly happy. When you gave up football after Lawrence died, you wanted to study in the US. You had grand plans to study art at Yale. But when the acceptance letter came in, you chose Edinburgh instead. And instead of pursuing art, you chose a civil engineering degree just because you're good at physics and maths. I never pushed you about it because I thought maybe you really had changed your mind."

"But if I hadn't gone to Edinburgh, I wouldn't have met Lily."

"And it all comes back to her. So why aren't you with her? Is she right, Bastian? Do you still blame yourself for Lawrence, and because you don't think you deserve her, deserve happiness, you're pushing her away?"

"Maybe."

"Maybe or yes?"

That old self-directed rage flared as I snapped, "Yes. All right. I don't deserve her."

"What is this nonsense about deserving someone? Lily doesn't care if you deserve her or not. She's chosen *you*. Out of every bloke in the world, she's chosen you, Sebastian. You don't get to say she doesn't deserve you. It's condescending. It's saying that you know better than one of the most emotionally intelligent women you've ever met."

My body jerked like I'd been shot by her words.

"And do you realize what you're losing now by being so bloody stubborn? This isn't giving up football or Yale or art. You're giving up a person who makes you happier than I've ever seen you. Can you live with that? Can you live without Lily?"

Emotion thickened my throat as my fist clenched around her necklace. "I feel like she's died. Every inch of me hurts and I'm angry. I'm so angry at myself. I haven't ..." I huffed, embarrassed by the coming confession. "I haven't even looked at another woman since I met her. Not in any real way. The thought of being with someone else after being with her makes me physically sick, and the thought of her with someone else makes me want to eviscerate whoever he is with my bare hands."

"Then you have to get over this."

"How? I wasn't even cognizant of doing it until Lily pointed it out."

"Maybe it's as simple as realizing that you've found something you want enough to stop punishing yourself." Juno suddenly snort-laughed. "When this family falls, we fall hard. It's a little unnerving."

"It's atrocious. I hate every second of it."

"Oh, it's much lovelier once you're actually in a relationship with the person you love. So, time to get over yourself, little brother. You're going to pull up your big-boy knickers and tell her everything you just told me."

My pulse leapt at the thought. "What if she doesn't want me now?"

"Oh, please. Lily Sawyer is mad about you. She's also the sweetest human I've ever met and considering she's the one who perceptively worked out your issues, I think she'll forgive you for them." At my hesitation, she bit out impatiently, "Go tell her or I will get on a plane to Edinburgh and come sort this mess out myself."

"I hurt her. Badly. She might not want to talk to me. Last time I hurt her, I had to sign up to do a psych experiment just to get close enough to get her to listen."

"Well, make sure she can't walk away from you. Better yet, do something big and grand like the ending of some cringeworthy romantic film. She'll listen then. She'll have to. And bonus—I'll get to dine out on the story for years. Mock you on your wedding day, when your children are old enough to hear it, your grandchildren ..."

Heart racing as I stood, I felt the hopeless dreariness begin to fall away from me as a plan formed in my mind. "I know you're trying to freak me out, but it isn't working."

"She really has broken you like a filly, hasn't she?"

"Before you mock me any further, maybe I should talk to Leona. I have a feeling she has you wrapped around her little finger."

"Ugh." Juno groaned. "How did this happen to us? We were both perfectly normal a few months ago."

"Normal, but a little lost, maybe," I muttered truthfully.

"No, normal and in our right minds. Love makes you crazy, brother."

"I thought you said it was lovely."

"Oh, it is. But it also makes you crazy."

"I already know that." I lifted Lily's necklace, examining it in the light. "But I'd rather be crazy than live one more day without Lily Sawyer."

"Awww ... This is me notifying you that I'm adding that line to the list of things I'm going to mock you about for the rest of your life."

CHAPTER FORTY-ONE
LILY

Ironically, Professor McAvoy's lecture today wasn't penetrating. Ten minutes in, I switched the recording on my phone, hoping it would pick up the seminar. Because my brain certainly wasn't. And it was ironic because she'd handed our Gender and Psychology papers back to us as we came into the lecture hall, and she'd stopped me when she handed over mine. Professor McAvoy had taught a few of my courses over the years and we'd met to discuss my future career. Moreover, she was my dissertation advisor since she specialized in gender and psychology.

She'd pulled me aside as I approached her desk for my essay and told me in concern, "This isn't your best work, Lily. Now is not the time to drop the ball. It's not awful by any means, so there's no need to panic, but I want you to know I noticed a shift. Let's get things back to where they should be for you. Do better with your research proposal."

I was an A student.

The essay was a B.

I really needed to pull myself together. My career would be there long after some guy who ...

Throwing Sebastian from my mind, I tried to focus on Professor McAvoy. But my mind kept going back over the events of the last few days, including getting a B on an essay.

I'd been staring dazedly at my tablet, so it took me a second to realize someone had interrupted our class.

My classmates' murmuring brought my attention to the front of the class and my heart faltered in my chest.

The sight of Sebastian standing next to Professor McAvoy caused a flush of heat through my body so strong, my palms started sweating.

What the ...

"I'm in the middle of a class," Professor McAvoy stated impatiently, as if it was not the first time she'd said it to him.

"I understand." Sebastian's voice carried upward through the smaller lecture hall. "And I respect your time, but this is incredibly important. And possibly educational for any would-be therapists in the room." There was a teasing note in his words.

Professor McAvoy, it seemed, was not immune to Sebastian Thorne's charms. "Fine. Enlighten us, Mr. ...?"

"Thorne. Sebastian."

"The floor is yours, Mr. Thorne. I'm eager to hear what is so important that it warrants interrupting my fourth-year class."

I sat upright, as if my body was preparing to flee before my mind even considered it.

However, Sebastian nodded and turned forward, his eyes finding mine immediately, like he'd known where I was from the moment he stepped into the room.

My breath caught.

He'd shaved his beard since I'd seen him a few nights ago and I could see now in the sharp angles of his handsome face that he *had* lost weight.

What the hell was he doing? My eyes widened with the nonverbal question.

His lip curled up in one corner, but there was a panicked edge of sadness in his expression that made my chest throb. "Hullo, Sawyer."

The physical evidence of the impact our estrangement had on him, along with the gently affectionate words, made me want to burst into tears.

I couldn't speak around the thickening in my throat.

"I'm sorry for interrupting your class, but I didn't think I could get you to listen any other way. I thought about calling into the podcast, but you could easily walk out or hang up ... and really, I need to say this face-to-face. Also, apologies to your classmates." He gestured to them. "But hopefully, no matter which way this goes, they're thoroughly entertained. I'm about to get metaphorically naked in front of them, after all."

"*Literally* would be better!" a girl shouted from the back, and everyone tittered but me.

I was too much in shock.

Sebastian grinned. "Sorry, but I only have plans to get naked for one woman for the rest of my life ... if she'll have me." His gaze returned to mine and softened with such tenderness, I swear I heard the girl two seats down from me sigh cartoonishly.

What ... what ... I think my brain exploded.

Why wasn't Professor McAvoy putting a stop to this?

Instead, my lecturer sat on her desk, smiling like she found my ex-best friend incredibly amusing.

Sebastian moved slowly toward the stairs. Toward me. "Lily Sawyer, I have been a thickheaded, stubborn, unforgiveable moron. You know this. I know this. Our friends know this." He waved to the room as he climbed the auditorium stairs. "And now this room of complete strangers knows this."

More tittering.

Again, not from me.

I glared at him, my cheeks flushed hot. I was stuck between being infuriated with him for making me the center of attention and furious with him for making me feel hope.

"You were right. I thought I didn't deserve you." The teasing note left his tone. "I thought I didn't deserve anything that made me truly happy." Sebastian stopped a few steps down from my row so we were on eye level. His were pleading. "Lily, I ... I didn't think I'd ever meet anyone like you, so I wasn't prepared for you or what you make me feel."

"Dude, what the fuck?" a guy behind me sniggered.

"Shut up!" someone hissed.

Sebastian ignored them. "I thought I could have just enough of you for it to be okay." His expression was meaningful, and I understood even though everyone else around didn't. "It wasn't fair to you, and I ended up hurting the one person I *never* want to hurt."

"Sebastian..."

He took the rest of the steps up to me but lowered onto his knee at my side. "I'm done being a masochistic arsehole. You are so much more important than some stupid vow I didn't even know I made to myself. If you ... if *you* think I'm worthy of you, then who the hell am I to disagree?"

Oh my goodness. Oh my ... I was having difficulty breathing.

"Forgive me, my love. Forgive me and let me love you. Because I do. Lily, I am ..." His voice grew low and gruff as his eyes shone with emotion. "I'm so in love with you, I cannot imagine my life without you. I don't want to. It's an awful place. It's bland and boring and I'm very monk-like there."

My lips twitched even as my hope turned to utter euphoria. "You mean it? Really, truly mean it? You're not planning to self-flagellate again tomorrow once reality hits?"

"No, no plans for that." He moved closer so our faces were mere inches apart. He searched mine. "Be my girl-friend, Lily, and I promise I'll make it my mission to make you happy. I'll even allow you to make me a research subject in your dissertation."

I laughed, but it was cut off by Sebastian's hungry kiss. His hands clasped my face as he kissed me breathless. For a moment, I was swept up in it and the resultant whistles and whoops of my classmates.

But then I reluctantly pulled away. "I didn't say yes."

His fingers caressed my cheeks. "You should."

"After this mortifying display?"

"It was more mortifying for me."

"You're not in the least bit embarrassed by this."

"No, I'm not. I don't care who knows I love you. Apparently, everyone already did."

"I didn't."

"Well, that's because you're blind to the fact that you are the most lovable ..." He brushed his lips over mine. "Sexiest ..." Another caress of his mouth. "Smartest, kindest, funniest woman in the world. How could I not love you?"

"If she doesn't want you, I'll have you!" some girl shouted from behind us.

I scowled.

Sebastian chuckled and then leaned his forehead against mine. "I only see you, Lily Sawyer. Say yes. Before your professor has me forcibly removed."

A glance toward Professor McAvoy revealed her amused smile was starting to strain. I looked back into Sebastian's eyes. I ... I found I couldn't quite tell him I loved him back. Even after his grand confession. Not because I didn't ... but because my heart was still badly bruised.

"If you ask me out on a date," I said, "I'll probably say yes."

He pressed another kiss to my mouth. "I'll wait for you after class and take you to lunch."

"That wasn't asking," I complained as he stood up to leave.

"You said you'd say yes, but I'm not taking the chance you'll say no." He winked and hurried down the auditorium steps.

"Sebastian!" I hissed.

"I love you, Lily Sawyer!"

Oh my goodness. I laughed, my cheeks hot as I buried my face in my hands.

"Thank you, Professor, for giving me the space to declare myself in this humiliating and cringeworthy fashion that will make my grandmother rethink leaving me an inheritance. Much appreciated."

Everyone laughed.

I peeked between my fingers to see my professor thankfully give him an amiable nod. "You're welcome. And you're right. I think I can turn this into a teachable moment."

"Always happy to be of help." He glanced back up

toward me, flashing that sexy smile. Except this time, I recognized what I'd been too insecure to realize before. His smile was not a new smile. It was the smile he'd given me for months.

It was a smile filled with love.

I bit my lip against my own and Sebastian reluctantly left the hall.

I could feel everyone's eyes on me.

"Well, that was an entertaining respite, but let's get back to it. Or should we expect more suitors interrupting to declare their love for you, Ms. Sawyer?"

One day, I'd get revenge on Sebastian for this. I groaned and slid down in my seat, shaking my head with a mortified no.

As my professor launched back into her lesson, I couldn't say I was listening. I was too busy trying to keep the stupid grin off my face and the butterflies in my belly from lifting me right out of my seat with the frantic flapping of their wings.

Then, as the lecture ended and I packed up, taking my classmates good-natured ribbing on the chin, I realized my phone had recorded the entire incident.

I laughed to myself as I saved it with glee.

"You're so lucky." A girl whom I'd shared classes with for the last four years but who had never spoken to me before approached as I strode toward the exit. "He's so gorgeous. And that accent. And what he did and said ... it was like a movie."

"Aye, it was like a really embarrassing, corny movie," I agreed.

Her face fell. "It's just a pity we were all too engrossed in the moment to film it so you could see it from our perspective. It was really brave of him. I hope you appreciate that."

It was brave, but Sebastian wasn't easily embarrassed. He was too confident to care what strangers thought of him. What he'd done was more smart than brave, really. Because Sebastian did know me. Once I made up my mind about something, I could be a stubborn arse. He knew he'd have to do something like this to get me to stick around long enough to listen. "Who says I didn't appreciate it?" I shrugged and pushed out of the auditorium doors to find Sebastian leaning against the opposite wall, waiting for me as promised.

The sight of him filled my chest with possessiveness.

And to prove I appreciated him, I strode across the hall, aware of the eyes on us and not caring in the least for once.

He pushed off the wall to greet me, but I got there first, dropping my bookbag at our feet so I could hop into his arms. It was a move I'd have been too self-conscious to make with any other boyfriend, but Sebastian caught me with ease, eyes lit with happy surprise as he cupped my arse in his hands. I tightened my legs around his middle, my fingers moving through his hair, as I crushed my mouth over his. While giving my classmates a second show, I kissed Sebastian Thorne with all the love I wasn't quite ready to confess out loud.

CHAPTER FORTY-TWO
SEBASTIAN

Our laptops and books littered my bed as we ate Chinese takeaway straight from the cartons.

Since Lily had agreed to date me, my appetite had returned. For the last two days, I'd eaten everything in sight and then burned it all off at the gym.

What I hadn't done was burn it off in bed with my girlfriend.

Girlfriend.

Last year, the thought of calling any woman that would have sent me running for the hills. Now, with Lily, the word filled me with an overwhelming affectionate possessiveness.

However, I was trying not to push her too fast, too soon. This wasn't about the instant gratification of the best sex ever. It was about reassuring Lily that I wanted her in a very permanent way.

Since we were both extremely busy with the last semester of school, we'd decided we'd study and work on our dissertations together. That way, we could easily spend our breaks with each other.

Lily dug into her kung pao chicken, her long silky hair tied up into a messy knot. She was making "yummy" noises that were driving me crazy. I couldn't stop staring at her, marveling at the fact that she was here with me. That I'd somehow, incredibly, managed to talk this amazing woman into giving me a second chance.

She looked up from beneath her lashes and swallowed a bite of food. "You're staring again."

"You're stare-worthy." I shrugged, taking another bite. I observed the necklaces nestled between her breasts. Next to the book pendant January gave her was my diamond lily. I gave it back to her yesterday and she put it on right away. Lily then gave me my belated Christmas present—a vintage Stephen Spielberg *Empire of the Sun* film poster. It was framed and everything. I knew how expensive those things could get, so I was very moved that Lily had spent her hard-earned cash on something so thoughtful for me.

We spent the entire day after my public declaration of love catching up with each other and what we'd been up to for the past month. There was more apologizing, some kissing and petting, but nothing more, even though I was desperate for her.

Suddenly, Lily reached out with her free hand to stroke my cheek. "You shaved."

"Had a bit of a grizzly bear thing happening."

"I quite liked it."

"Really?"

She grinned, her dimples appearing. "I did. I also like you with a bit of scruff. You look all rugged and sexy unshaven."

Pleasure filled me. "Oh really?"

"Hmm."

"I'll keep that in mind."

"You do that." Lily cocked her head in thought, the hair on top of her head bobbing adorably. "Would you rather spend every minute of every day shaving or never be able to shave again?"

Being invited back into Lily's Would You Rather discussions felt symbolic, so I took the question seriously. "Never shave again."

"Wouldn't you constantly trip on your beard?"

"Well, if I choose to spend every minute of every day shaving, then that means I never, ever get to make love to you again ... so I'd rather never shave and you could braid my beard into weird and wonderful creations."

Her eyes glittered flirtatiously. "Who's to say I'd be attracted to a man with a very long beard?"

"Are you saying your attraction to me is entirely dependent on my appearance?" I teased.

She laughed and shook her head. "You know it's not. I'll braid your beard, Gandalf."

I gave her a nod of imperious thanks. Then asked, "Would you rather write a dissertation for the rest of your life or listen to 'I Saw Mommy Kissing Santa Claus' every day for eternity?" I'd learned over the holiday season that Lily couldn't stand the Jackson Five Christmas track.

"That's just cruel." She let out a heavy sigh. "Dissertation."

"Really? You hate it that much?"

"Aye, I hate it that much."

Chuckling, I took another bite and murmured around the mouthful, "Good to know."

"Would you rather eat vomit for the rest of your life or embarrass yourself and your girlfriend with romantic declarations in a public place?" Lily asked with a straight face. Then she snickered like a five-year-old. "Oh, I'm sorry, you already did the latter."

"I am never going to live that down, am I? And thank you for mentioning vomit while we're eating kung pao chicken."

"You're welcome. And never. Ever. Ever."

"I wasn't embarrassed in the least. And you shouldn't be at all embarrassed by my public declaration of love." I watched her carefully as she smiled but dropped her eyes.

It was, of course, not lost on me that Lily had not returned my avowal of love. Not because she didn't love me. I knew that. She was ... afraid to say it out loud. In case I hurt her again.

I hated that.

More than anything else in the world, I wanted her to tell me she loved me.

Yet I understood.

It didn't mean I wasn't determined to get her to confess it sooner rather than later.

Lily leaned away, putting her carton on the bedside table. The action caused her cropped sweater to rise, revealing an expanse of creamy olive skin I wanted to press a million kisses to. When she sat back, I knew she'd caught me ogling by the curve of her smile.

I shrugged unrepentantly and she let out a little laugh before settling back against my pillows.

"Would you rather spend the rest of your life as a civil engineer or in an art studio creating the most beautiful art I've ever seen?"

I tensed at her pointed question. Our eyes held and locked, hers serious and searching.

Her expression softened. "I know this week has been a big week for you emotionally and I don't want to push, so tell me to back off if you need to. But ... if you can pursue me, then maybe it means you're ready to pursue other things you want."

"I don't know," I answered honestly. "I've been working toward my civil engineering degree for four years."

"And yet you haven't pursued a part-time job in the industry. Not even an internship or work experience."

No, I hadn't, and many of my classmates had.

"You'll finish your degree, and you'll always have it. But is it what you want, Sebastian?"

"You know it isn't." The idea of giving my art my full-time attention excited me as much as it terrified me. "It's not a stable career, Lily. And I have you to think about now."

Her lips parted in shock. "What do you mean?"

"This isn't a passing fancy. I didn't put myself through the emotional wringer for someone I see as temporary." I gestured impatiently between us. "This is it for me, and I want to be able to take care of you."

Lily's brow wrinkled and she appeared to be suppressing a smile as she shimmied over to me. She smoothed a hand up my thigh, momentarily distracting me from the serious subject matter. "You will take care of me by supporting me through *my* career choices and being my shoulder to cry on and ... helping me decompress with many, many orgasms."

Heat flooded my groin. "Is that right?"

She chuckled. "I thought that part would get your attention. But my point is ... I don't need you to support me financially. In fact, considering who your family is, I'd really prefer not to be thought of as a person who needs your financial support."

I scowled. "But—"

Lily pressed a finger over my lips, shushing me. "I've worked extremely hard for four years and will spend another four years working even harder to get my doctorate in psychotherapy. I know everyone thinks I'm Mother Teresa, but I'm not actually quite as self-sacrificing as that. I'm ambitious. Eventually, I want to work for myself and have my own practice. If I pull it off, I won't need anyone's financial support."

"I know." I did know that. Lily had told me all this before.

"That means you won't need to support me in that way. Don't make this decision based on that. If your art doesn't pay enough to support you—"

"Us," I insisted.

Lily's eyes lit with affection. "Us. Then you can go back to school or find an engineering job."

My chest was suddenly tight with *feelings*. Overwhelming feelings I wasn't quite sure I'd ever get used to. I placed my carton of takeaway on the bedside table near me and turned back to her, brushing my thumb over her full lips. "What did I do to deserve you, Sawyer?"

Her breath hitched at the gruffness in my voice. "We deserve each other."

Need fogged my mind, and I knew if I kissed her now, I'd want to take it further. After all, I'd quite like to brand myself on this woman's soul like she'd branded herself on mine.

"You ..." She licked her lips, catching my thumb, and causing a jolt of lust to harden my cock. "You don't need to be careful with me. If you're holding back ... don't."

That was all the invitation I needed.

Our lips were millimeters from touching when my bedroom door crashed open. Lily and I jerked away from each other in surprise.

There was my sister in the doorway, Leona at her back. Juno grinned deviously. "I hope I wasn't interrupting anything."

"Don't take this the wrong way, Junebug, but I currently hate you."

My sister cackled with sadistic delight.

Lily shoved me playfully. "Be nice!" She hopped off the bed while I covered my current situation with a pillow. "Juno!"

My sister and girlfriend enfolded each other in a thrilled hug. On any normal occasion, I'd be delighted they liked each other so much.

"Lily, this is my girlfriend, Leona." Juno introduced the tall, brown-skinned beauty who had stolen my sister's heart.

"It's so lovely to meet you."

"You too." Leona pulled her into a hug. "I've heard so much about you." She beamed over Lily's shoulder and waved. "Hi, Bastian."

"Good to see you." I nodded gruffly. "Now all of you, except Lily, get out."

Lily whirled on me. "Sebastian, manners." Then she slid her arm around Juno's shoulders and guided them out of the room. "Tea? Wine? How long are you here for?"

I groaned, closing my eyes in despair as their voices drifted away. "I love my sister," I reminded myself between gritted teeth. "One cannot kill one's sister."

"Hey, Bas."

My eyes flew open to find Zac leaning against my door frame. "Do you know your sister is here?"

"Painfully, painfully aware of the fact."

CHAPTER FORTY-THREE
LILY

One of my favorite perks of having a mum who's the university's head librarian was getting my hands on the much sought-after study room. It was almost impossible to book one, but Mum tried to allocate me one whenever I needed it. My dissertation was almost finished. Most of the interview requests I'd made at the beginning of the year had come through, and yesterday I'd completed my last interview with the author of a bestselling book about the impact of social media on our mental health. I was proud of myself for being so ahead of the curve because I knew from talking to my peers that some of them were way behind on their dissertation.

Being this close to finishing meant I could send it to Professor McAvoy in plenty of time to get feedback.

My conclusions were interesting and worrying. While there *were* differences between genders with regard to the impact of social media and that was my primary focus, there was one unifying conclusion to my research. Governments needed to step in and regulate social media apps more effectively. The platform themselves, and not merely individual users, needed to be held legally accountable not only for the harassment, bullying, and grooming that were allowed to run rampant, but also for the intentional negative targeting of their algorithm. I'd interviewed several experts who all confirmed the platforms, having deduced people engaged more with negative content, were deliberately amplifying negative content on everyone's algorithms to encourage engagement, regardless of the adverse effects on our mental health.

It was complicated and, honestly, a political and social quagmire. If I thought about it too much, it depressed the heck out of me. Instead, I chose to focus on helping where I could. Getting my degree and graduating onto my postgrad was the next step toward helping people with their mental health.

First, though, I had to finish my dissertation, and Mum had promised me a study room at the library when I called to beg for one. Maddie and Shaun had been fighting a lot recently. Maddie was convinced something had happened between him and some rugby fan when he was in Europe two weeks ago, and Shaun was convinced she was causing fictional conflict to cover the fact that she didn't want to leave him behind when she moved back to Newcastle for the job waiting for her in her dad's architect firm.

Their arguing was loud and interspersed with even louder sex, and I couldn't take it anymore. I would have hauled my arse over to Sebastian's, but yesterday his sister's arrival interrupted impending sexy times. If I went anywhere near him, no work would get done, other than the work of stripping him naked and having my way with him.

I groaned under my breath as I approached Mum's office. The truth was I desperately wanted to have sex with him. Sebastian reluctantly parted ways with me last night because of his sister's impromptu visit, so I'd spent the night alone and had a very, very vivid dream about him.

As giddy and excited as I was to be embarking on a real relationship with Sebastian when I'd long given up hope we'd ever have that, I had a dissertation to finish. I couldn't let myself be distracted by my extremely primal need to repeat the best sex I'd ever had.

Not wanting carnal thoughts showing on my face in front of my mother, I tried to shove said thoughts about my boyfriend (boyfriend!) out of my head. I knocked and entered at her *Come in*. Usually, Mum was out on the library floor somewhere, but today she was hunched over her computer, rubbing a frown from between her eyes.

"Hey."

She looked up, her expression clearing into a welcoming smile. "Hi, sweetheart. Keys? Right." Mum pushed back from the desk, opened a locked cabinet, and pulled out a set of keys. When she handed them over, she said, "Room five."

Ooh, the best study room. "Thanks. Are you okay?"

She tucked her thick, dark hair behind her ear. "Budget stuff. Total headache. I guess I'm supposed to pull what we need out of my ass."

I winced. "Sorry."

Mum reached out to stroke my cheek. "Thanks, sweetie. You look ... you look great." A smile twitched her lips. "It wouldn't have anything to do with a certain guy declaring himself in front of an entire lecture hall, would it?"

My lips parted in surprise. "How did you know?"

"Faculty gossip."

Guilt flashed through me. "Mum, I was going to tell you. It's been a crazy week."

"I know. So ... you happy?"

Biting my lip against the cheeky grin that wanted to overtake my whole face, I nodded.

"Look at you." Her eyes misted over. "My baby all grown up and falling in love."

"Mum—"

"I know, I know. Don't get sappy." She hauled me into a hug, and I embraced her tightly, breathing in her familiar perfume. I felt safe in her arms. Always had. And I knew how lucky I was to have that.

"I was going to tell you today," I promised. "I wanted to tell you face-to-face."

"I believe you." She kissed my temple and released me. Laughter lit her eyes. "Your dad knows."

I grimaced. "And?"

"He had his suspicions when you brought Sebastian over to the house. But suspecting and knowing are two different things, so he would like to re-meet your young man and instill in him the utter terror of knowing the consequences that awaits him if he hurts you."

I rolled my eyes, remembering the way Dad and my uncles acted around Beth's boyfriend Callan. "That's ridiculous."

"No, it's not." Mum shook her head. "Your dad loves you more than he ever thought he could love anything, including me, which is saying a lot."

"Mum—"

"That's the way it should be. The love you have for your children is like the universe. Constantly expanding and overwhelming and mysterious and terrifyingly beautiful."

Tears brightened my eyes.

"One day, you'll get that. And one day you'll understand why your dad needs to threaten your boyfriend with bodily harm if he hurts you."

Laughing, I nodded. "Okay. I love you."

"I love you too. Bring your young man over to meet us soon, okay."

"I will." I kissed her cheek and pulled her office door open. "Don't work too hard."

"You too, sweetheart."

———

Study room five was in the back corner, far from the others. It was a sanctuary for those of us trying to finish dissertations. The first thing I did was switch my phone to silent before I plugged in my laptop.

I'd perhaps been in the room for twenty minutes of my allotted ninety minutes when someone tried to enter, rattling the locked door handle. It was followed by a knock.

"Occupied!" I yelled out in impatient annoyance. There was a freaking sign on the door that said as much.

"Lily, it's me."

My pulse leapt at the familiar, deep voice and its posh accent. I quickly saved my document and got up from the table to unlock the door. Sebastian pushed his way in as soon as I did and then slammed the door shut behind him, locking it.

"What are you doing?" I gaped up at him.

"I texted you."

"My phone is on silent. Did my mother tell you I was in here?"

"No, you told me this morning you'd booked a study room. I knocked on every single one until I found you."

If he'd made this effort to hunt me down, something must be wrong. My mind jumped to the worst conclusions. "Did something happen?"

"Well, I have a problem," he said with grave seriousness.

"What's wrong?"

Sebastian gently took hold of my hips and started backing me toward the table as he spoke. "A few days ago I reunited with the love of my life and on the day she told me she'd welcome my amorous attentions, my sister showed up and cock-blocked me."

I burst into laughter even as heat licked through my lower belly. "Is that right?"

"Yes. And now I can't stop thinking about your eyes or your laugh or your smile or the way you moan when I'm inside you." His voice thickened. "So, when you reported you would be locked in a room with no windows at the library, I must confess I didn't imagine you in it studying."

My knees trembled as Sebastian maneuvered me onto the table. My lower belly clenched with need. "Oh?"

"No. And while a better man might wait to get you in his bed where he can gently make love to you ... I need you, Lily." He leaned his forehead against mine. "I need you so much it's all I can think about."

Honestly, when my mum had told me stories of booting horny couples out of study rooms or quiet corners of the library, I'd wrinkled my nose in disgust. Who would have sex in a library? A library was to be respected and the people who were there using it to further their education were to be respected.

Yet I did not think any of those things as I opened my thighs, welcoming Sebastian between them. Truthfully, I couldn't think beyond how much I wanted him. He seemed to release some kind of magical pheromone that made me instantly needy.

He gripped my hips, pulling me against him so I could

feel how much he wanted me too. "Lily, Lily ..." His voice was hoarse around my name. Then his lips brushed my throat, and my head fell back on a gasp. Who would have thought the mere feathery caress of his mouth would elicit such a deliciously shivery reaction?

"You smell incredible," he murmured as he kissed beneath my chin. "You *are* incredible. You're all I can think about."

"Sebastian," I moaned, my fingers digging into his back, pulling him closer.

"I love the way you say my name. I want to hear you say it as you come." Hot determination glinted in his beautiful blue-green eyes and his hand slipped between my thighs. At the tug of the zipper on my jeans, tingles exploded to life right where I hoped he was aiming to explore.

A loud knocking lingered on the periphery of my awareness, but Sebastian's fingers were dipping beneath my underwear so—

"Lily Sawyer, this is your mother!"

Her voice was an icy shower of reality blasting over us both. We froze, eyes wide, and the heat of foggy lust dissipated.

Oh my goodness, was I actually about to have sex in the library?

"Lily!"

"Coming!"

Sebastian's lips trembled with disgruntled laughter. "Well, you were about to."

"Get off me," I hissed, swatting his hand out of my jeans.

His broad shoulders shook with amusement as he moved away while I zipped up my jeans. Sebastian murmured, "Granny naked. Granny naked in a shower with

English. Granny naked in a shower with English." He shuddered in revulsion. "That'll do it."

At my mum's insistent knocking, I threw my boyfriend a harried look before unlocking the study room.

Mum had her arms crossed over her chest as she glanced from me to Sebastian who stood behind me. Her expression was one I knew well from my childhood— unamused and trying not to lose her shit.

"Hi, Mum," I squeaked out. "What's up?"

She pressed her lips together and Sebastian took that opportunity to place his hands on my shoulders in support. "Nice to see you again, Mrs. Sawyer."

She didn't tell him to call her Liv this time. Instead, she glowered at his hands.

"Stop touching me." I shook him off.

I heard him try to cover a snort of laughter.

Mum grimaced. "Isn't this the highlight of my career? Who would have thought the first time I kicked a pair of horny students out of a study room that one day one of them would be my own kid?"

"Mum, we were—"

"I don't want to know."

Stupidly, I asked, "How did you know Sebastian was here?"

"I was coming to bring you a coffee." She raised her hand, and I noted the coffee cup in it and felt even more guilty. "And I saw your boyfriend scurry in here with ill intent."

"My intentions toward your daughter are in fact honor—"

"Sex with someone's daughter will always be considered as ill-intended by said parent. Do you understand?" Mum glared at him. "Even more so in my library. Now, usually I have a pretty good sense of humor about these things, but Lily is my baby girl, and I'd quite like to maim you with a letter opener."

Oh boy.

"I can assure you, I wasn't here to—"

"Don't lie to me. Please. It'll only make it worse. Just leave."

My belly swooped at the unpleasant altercation. Sure, I half expected this was how it would be with Dad, but Mum was always so laid back with my boyfriends.

Then again, I'd never tried to have sex with one of them at her place of work.

I grimaced, my cheeks burning hot.

Sebastian sighed at my back and then stepped around me. He had the gall to cup my face tenderly in front of Mum. His expression told me not to worry. Then he brushed his mouth over mine in a gentle promise before releasing me to leave.

However, he halted at Mum's side before departing. "I love Lily, Mrs. Sawyer. My intentions really are honorable."

Mum softened infinitesimally and she let out a long sigh. "I know. I can see that. I think I saw that before you saw it. And we'll be fine. Just don't do *this* again." She gestured in a vague way to our surroundings.

"Of course." Sebastian threw me another reassuring smirk and then walked away. He was almost around the corner when he glanced back. Even from a distance I could read the hot promise in his expression.

Once he disappeared, I reluctantly turned to Mum. "I really am sorry."

"I know. You're a good girl. Which means you really must be in love to lose all sense of common decency."

My cheeks were on fire with embarrassment, and even if I wasn't a blusher, I knew my mum could sense it.

She chuckled, softening even more. "Don't let it happen again."

"I won't. I promise."

"Bring him over to the house soon. He sounds very serious about you, so I want to get to know him better."

"Okay."

"Fine. Here's your coffee."

"Thanks, Mum."

"Do some work." She waved a hand toward the room.

"I am sorry."

"I know, kid. Forget about it. Anyway, it's kind of hypocritical of me considering what your father and I got up to in there."

Horror most definitely saturated my features and Mum covered her mouth to stifle a bark of laughter as she strode away.

"In here *here*?" I hissed after her.

Her shoulders shook harder.

"Mum!" I whisper-shouted.

But she was already walking around the corner.

I turned back and stared at the table where I'd almost had sex with Sebastian and the thought that my parents might have had sex on the same table had me quickly packing up my things.

I'd just have to work on my dissertation at home.

"Ugh." I shuddered as I locked the room behind me.

CHAPTER FORTY-FOUR

LILY

The awareness of a warm, heavy weight filtered into my consciousness and my eyes flew open in a sudden panic.

My muscles locked for a moment as I stared up at my bedroom ceiling and then lowered my gaze. It took me a second to process what I was seeing but once the sleepy fog lifted, I relaxed into the mattress and pillow beneath me.

Sebastian.

I remembered stirring awake in the middle of the night to find him spooning me. He'd murmured at me to go back to sleep.

Now Sebastian sprawled over me, pinning me to the bed. His face nuzzled against my breasts, one of his legs tangled between mine, and while one arm rested near my face, the other was tucked around my waist as if he was holding me close even in sleep.

As adorable as waking to find my boyfriend with his face buried in my boobs was, he was kind of heavy.

I stroked my fingers through his thick, blond hair, possessive tenderness my overarching emotion.

Yesterday, I'd ended up writing in a study cubicle after returning the study room key to a gloating, smug mother who was delighted her revenge had worked so well. Sebastian had texted that he had a meeting with his advisor, but he'd try to come over to mine afterward. I had to put him off because I'd promised the girls I'd do a podcast episode. People wanted to know what had happened to make me storm out. Now rumors were flying about Sebastian and his declaration of love in my psych lecture, and the girls wanted me to address them. Sebastian hadn't told his parents or his family about us yet, and since his family wasn't a "normal" family, I didn't want to go public about our relationship.

Instead, I agreed to do the episode but only to assure our audience I was fine, Jan and I were good, and that some personal stress had gotten to me. The girls weren't entirely happy with that (surprise, surprise, neither was our audience), but I wasn't ready to share more details.

Sebastian and I needed time to acclimate to our relationship without inviting the whole world into it. I mean, I knew he kind of had by making it so public, but I assumed he hadn't thought about the ramifications of that beyond trying to get me to listen to him and making a grand gesture to win back my affection.

I needed to discuss it with him first.

End of story.

By the time I'd gotten home, I had a voice note from Sebastian to say Juno and Leona had a massive fight and he was hanging out with Juno for a bit until Leona returned to the flat. I'd gotten on with a little more work until my eyelids started to drift closed.

Maddie must have let Sebastian into the flat after I'd gone to bed.

I stroked his hair, trying to decide whether his heaviness was worth the loveliness of having him sleeping on me.

The decision was taken from me when his lashes fluttered. He dopily blinked a few times and his cheek pushed deeper against one of my boobs. I'd gone to bed in a cropped T-shirt that fully covered my breasts, but I was also braless underneath it. I made a wee noise of amusement as his eyebrow rose in question. We locked eyes and his expression relaxed into such awe and tenderness, my amusement was taken over by affection.

He lifted his head, studying my face before ogling my chest. "Well, this is a very nice way to wake up."

"Aye, apparently you zero in on my boobs even when you're unconscious."

Sebastian's laugh was low and husky with sleep as he slid his hand up my waist to cup my breast. "Who can blame me? They are spectacular. And very comfy." His brow drew together. "I can't remember the last time I had such a good sleep."

"Me too." My fingers drifted from his hair down his cheek.

That's when I felt the subtle change in his body. A tension. I studied him carefully as his gaze lowered and glazed over slightly. He looked abruptly ... lost.

Maybe even a wee bit afraid.

Venturing a guess as to why, I wanted to do nothing but reassure him. I caressed him, bringing my other arm up to smooth over his shoulder. "You know, all those old feelings don't just disappear overnight."

Sebastian's eyes flew to mine, surprised. "How did you know what I was thinking?"

Glad my insight had been on point, I brought my knee

up so I could tighten my thigh around him, attempting to cocoon him in every way I could. "I feel like I know you better than I know myself. Feelings as big as you had about Lawrence, about yourself, they don't just disappear because you've decided to work through them. It's a process. But I'm here, Sebastian. Anytime you start to feel the pull of those dark thoughts ... tell me. And I'll remind you why you deserve all the happiness in the world."

Sebastian suddenly moved, bracing himself over me and in doing so nudging his hardening cock between my legs. His voice was thick with emotion and need. "Do you know how much I love you, Lily Sawyer?"

My hands fell to his waist as I bent my other leg, shifting my hips, urging him closer as heady desire warmed through me. "I have an inkling."

He kissed me, uncaring we'd just awoken from sleep. Too needy to care.

All my usual overthinking flew out the window when it was just me and Sebastian.

By the time he broke the kiss, I gasped for air, my lips tingling. I barely had a chance to catch my breath when Sebastian undressed me, hauling my tee off, urging my pajama shorts and underwear down my legs. Then he was shoving out of his boxers and T-shirt, throwing them on the floor beside the jeans, boots, and sweater he'd discarded last night.

"I'm on the pill," I informed him on a rushed whisper as I shivered and trembled with want.

Sebastian was in the middle of pulling a condom out of his jeans pocket. He glanced back at me, his features taut with lust. He let out a harsh pant. "Fuck, you don't even know how much I want to take you bare ... but ..." He winced. "I should get a health check first. I haven't ... I haven't been with anyone since last summer, but I also haven't been checked since last winter."

Damn.

What was I thinking?

I should have been the one to bring that up before ever suggesting we not use a condom. It was true, then. Falling in love had officially made me stupid.

I gave him a sheepish smile, grateful to him for having my best interests in mind. "Then after we both get checked."

"For damn sure," he agreed, dropping the condom on the pillow beside me.

"What are—"

"Let me take care of you first."

I curled my fingers in his hair, kissing him back like I needed his kiss to breathe. A hand slipped between my legs. His thumb circled my clit, and I whimpered into his mouth. Sebastian took over the kiss while I sighed and panted and murmured his name, my hips pushing into his touch.

My thighs trembled.

My abdomen tightened.

Sebastian's thumb slicked over me and I was close. So close. "Lily, my love," he murmured against my lips, "do you know how good you feel? How tight? How hot?" He groaned and rested his forehead against my chest. "So wet. So ready."

I didn't want to bloat his ego by telling him it usually took a lot more work than this to get me to this point. Magical pheromones, indeed. Or I loved him in a way I'd never loved a man, and it made all the difference. Probably both.

Easing his fingers from me, Sebastian moved down my body. "Spread," he demanded in that posh accent. The incongruity of an accent that embodied British politeness with his crude command made my belly clench.

Sebastian made a guttural noise of desire seconds before his tongue touched my clit.

Need slammed through me, and I undulated against his mouth. His fingers dug into my thigh, and his groan vibrated through me.

He suckled my clit, and I panted as beautiful tension built deep inside me. His tongue circled and then slid down in a dirty voracious lick before pushing inside me.

I cried out, as I climbed higher and higher toward climax.

Feeling my desperation, Sebastian returned to my clit and gently pushed two fingers inside me.

It was like an explosion, the sensational release sliding through me as I shuddered against Sebastian's mouth.

Sebastian wiped his lips against my thigh and the slight roughness of his unshaven cheeks rasped deliciously against my skin. I trembled in the aftermath of climax, holding his smoldering gaze.

"Tell me you love me," he demanded.

Surprise shot through me. "Sebastian ..."

He waited.

The words stuck in my throat.

His jaw set with a ferocious hunger. "By the time I'm done with you, Sawyer, you're going to *scream* those three little words for me."

My pulse leapt at the vow.

He moved upward over me. "I can't believe I spent God knows how long with my face buried between these gorgeous tits, completely unaware."

I chuckled throatily, arching my back in instinct. My nipples peaked and my breasts were swollen with want of attention. But his touch wasn't greedy. It was loving as Sebastian trailed his fingertips with excruciating slowness across my collarbone and down toward the rise of my breasts. His cock was hard and hot against my leg, the tip wet with precum.

"Sebastian."

Gently, he cupped my face in his hands and kissed me so deeply, I could taste myself. This time his kiss was slower and filled with so much love, it brought tears to my eyes. My hands curled around his biceps, feeling his strength, his adoration, and those three important words pushed their way up from inside the depths of my soul.

With light strokes, Sebastian relearned every inch of me —my ribs, my waist, my stomach. Almost in habit, I tried to pull his hands away from my soft belly, but he shot me a chiding look. "You're beautiful. Every inch of you," he reminded me. Then his hands glided around to my arse, and his kiss deepened again as he drew me against his arousal. The hunger returned tenfold, his tongue caressing mine in deep, wet strokes. It was like he was determined to make love to me, but another part of him wanted to fuck me until I couldn't breathe.

I was happy with either, truthfully.

As I stroked my hands down his arms, the touch seemed to calm him, and his kiss grew gentler. Sebastian eventually eased away, and my lips stung in the air, swollen from all the attention. His own mouth appeared bee stung. The earlier possessiveness I'd felt roared through me as I stared hotly at his lips. Then he was kissing me again, but this time wet, hungry kisses down my throat and chest.

Desire rippled low in my belly as he played with my breasts, sculpting and kneading them, stroking and pinching my nipples. All the time his eyes vacillated between my face and my breasts. I thrust into his touch, muttering my need for him.

"Tell me you love me," he demanded again.

"Sebastian ..."

"Tell me." His mouth closed around my nipple and he sucked on it. My thighs clamped around his hips as my lower body arched into the sensation scoring through me.

"Sebastian!"

Suddenly, whatever war he'd been fighting to go slow was lost. He reached for the condom and ripped it out of the wrapper. He sat up, expression taut with fierceness.

I devoured the sight of his strong body above me. His tight abs and broad shoulders. The impressive cock he rolled the condom onto.

Sebastian Thorne was beautiful.

And he was mine.

His eyes flashed with something. Something I didn't quite understand. Whatever it was it had him pulling me gently up to straddle him. Then he guided me over him, his arousal hot beneath me.

Sebastian touched my chin, bringing my head up. My fingers curled into the back of his shoulders as I took in his expression. "I love you. I know you're afraid to say it back. But I need you to know I ... I wasn't lying when I said you're everything to me, Lily. *Everything*. I didn't ... I didn't know it was possible to love anyone this much."

Tears filled my eyes. I had to let go of that final barrier between us or this was never going to work.

"I love you too, Sebastian. I'm so in love with you." My confession ended on a gasp as Sebastian slid his hand along the back of my neck, tangling in my hair to grab a handful. His kiss was bruising, desperate.

He broke it only to murmur against my lips, "Thank

fuckity fuck." He seemed to shudder in relief. Then he gently tugged my head back, arched my chest, and covered my right nipple with his mouth.

I gasped as sensation slammed through me, my hips rocking as he sucked, laved, and nipped at me. Tension coiled between my legs, tightening and tightening as he moved between my breasts, his hot mouth, his tongue—

"Sebastian ..." I was going to come again with only this.

He stopped, and I lifted my head to beg, to plead for him to keep touching me, but halted when he gripped my hips. Guiding me, he lifted me up, and I stared down at him, waiting as he took his cock in hand and put it between my legs.

Taking his cue, I lowered myself onto him, feeling the hot tip of him against my slick opening. Electric tingles cascaded down my spine and around my belly, deep between my legs.

Sebastian took hold of my hip with one hand and cupped my right breast with the other, and I gasped at the overwhelming thick sensation of him as I lowered.

"I love you," he said gruffly as he thrust upward.

The words apparently were so powerful, I suddenly came.

I cried out and clung to his shoulders as my climax tore through me, my inner muscles rippling and tugging and drawing Sebastian in deeper.

"Oh God. God! Lily!" Sebastian abruptly pushed me onto my back and started driving into me through my orgasm.

He moved inside me with powerful thrusts of his hips, wearing a dazed, consumed look as he held my eyes. Sebastian gritted his teeth as he moved inside me. "You're going to come again."

"You come," I panted. "It's okay."

That seemed to be the wrong answer because I quickly found myself on my hands and knees facing the headboard. "You'll come again," he commanded harshly before his hand cracked against my arse, seconds before he gripped me by the nape and thrust back into me.

"Oh my ..." I shivered with arousal as he took me hard and rough. My arms trembled with the power of his drives, and I could feel the quickening of my inner muscles. "Sebastian!"

"God, I love you." There was something enticing about the dichotomy of his loving words and the way he powered into me.

And I loved it.

I loved him. "I love you!" I gasped out, pushing back into his thrusts.

The tension built in me again with every thick drag of him in and out.

"Come around me, Sawyer," he demanded, his hand sliding between my thighs to find my clit. His finger pushed down on the bundle of nerves as he continued to thrust. "I want to feel it. Nothing feels better than your precious pussy coming around my cock."

Just like that I shattered. Lights exploded behind my eyes as I yelled out his name and fell onto my elbows. I could feel how hard I rippled around him. The sensation was overwhelming and apparently for him too.

"Lily ... Lily ... my God!" Sebastian swelled to impossible thickness. His fingers bit into my hips as he tensed and then I felt him throb exquisitely inside of me. "Lily!" He jerked and shuddered, his climax juddering through him.

I slumped against the pillows, trying to catch my breath. Sebastian came down over me, his chest to my back, his cock still inside. His lips lazily caressed my shoulder as he thrust his hips shallowly against me.

Finally sated, we settled on our sides, spooning.

I had the vague thought that I hoped Maddie wasn't home and had heard our energetic and very loud sex.

Then I decided I couldn't care less and smiled to myself.

"Say it again," Sebastian whispered in my ear, his embrace tightening.

Knowing exactly what he wanted, I turned to meet his tender look. "I love you, Sebastian Thorne."

He squeezed his eyes closed, almost as if in pain. Then he let out a sigh of deep relief. "I love you too, Lily Sawyer."

CHAPTER FORTY-FIVE
LILY

"Are you sure you're ready for this?" I squeezed Sebastian's hand.

As per usual, my boyfriend appeared way calmer than I was. He grinned. "Are you embarrassed by me, Sawyer?"

I glowered at him. "You know I'm not. But this"—I gestured to the beautiful townhouse on Dublin Street—"is bigger than meeting the parents."

After the incident in the library, it seemed Mum wanted everyone to inspect Sebastian. Instead of having him over to our house, Mum had insisted I invite Sebastian to Uncle Braden and Aunt Joss's anniversary party. Aunt Ellie, Uncle Braden's half sister, was the mastermind behind the event. She was hosting at the Carmichaels' townhouse and she'd invited all of their closest friends and family. All my aunts and uncles and cousins. Even Sara, who was back at Aberdeen Uni for the semester. She'd gotten a train to Longniddry last night to spend the weekend with her grandparents so she could attend the party.

While I was looking forward to seeing her after such a

long time, I was extremely nervous about introducing Sebastian to everyone. For his sake.

We'd been dating for two weeks.

In those two weeks, he'd told his parents about our relationship. They were eager to meet me, even though I could read between the lines from Sebastian's tenseness that his mum might not be all that happy about it. Juno and Leona were over their fight (Sebastian still had no idea what the root cause of it was) and had returned to London. Juno had promised to come home whenever Sebastian decided to take me there to meet his parents.

Our workload didn't disappear overnight, so we were both extremely busy. However, we studied together whenever we could, slept together most nights, and we'd socialized with our friend group who were enjoying mocking us for our movie-worthy romantic saga over the last few months.

Everything was great between us. Sebastian was talking about pursuing his art for real after graduation. He'd even shared his secret social media profile with Harry, who told him in his very Harry-like way that Sebastian was a moron if he didn't commit to his art. Whatever my boyfriend planned to do, he was staying in Edinburgh. Not only for me, he promised, but because he loved the city and it's where he wanted to live.

Thankful that I didn't have to worry about our impending separation (I was already dreading saying goodbye to Sierra and Maddie), I was enjoying the heady, passionate beginning of our new relationship. I'd had more sex in the last two weeks than I had my entire life. Fantastic sex. Mind-blowing, utterly addictive, phenomenal sex.

I wasn't ready for our bubble to burst under the

weighty reality of overprotective parents and aunts and uncles.

Sebastian squeezed my hand again. "Are we going in or are we just admiring the architecture?"

My smile trembled, but I nodded. "We're going in."

————

Mum, to my everlasting gratitude, was as lovely as ever to Sebastian, the incident in the study room completely forgotten. I was pretty certain she hadn't told Dad about it. Nevertheless, he and my uncles surrounded Sebastian like a pack of velociraptors.

When Uncle Adam demanded to know when Sebastian's last sexual health check was and Dad's face turned purple at the implications, I intervened.

"Okay, we're done here." I glowered at each of my uncles and pinned my dad with a pleading look before I yanked Sebastian free from the circling predators.

Sebastian appeared a wee bit dazed as I guided him across the kitchen to my mum, sister, and female relatives. "I don't understand." My boyfriend shook his head. "Your father liked me before."

My sister snorted and offered way too loudly, "Well, that was before he knew you were boffing his daughter."

"Jan!" I protested.

She cocked her head in mock innocence. "No? Boinking? Banging?"

"Stop!"

"Plowing? Violat—" Mum clamped a hand over her youngest daughter's mouth.

"Thank you." Sebastian nodded gratefully at Mum. "A gentleman never *plows*."

Aunt Joss and Beth burst into laughter while Mum grimaced.

My sister freed herself from Mum's hand and gave Sebastian a nod. "You're going to survive here. I can tell."

Groaning because I was stuck somewhere between mortification and laughter, I buried my face in Sebastian's shoulder. He cuddled me close, his body shaking slightly with his own amusement. The chuckle vibrated through his chest. I enjoyed the feel and sound of it. Much to my relief, he'd put back on the weight and muscle he'd lost during our estrangement.

"Let's stop torturing Lily and her mother with sex talk." Beth turned to Sebastian. "My cousin tells me you're a Caledonia United fan."

"I am." He nodded to the ring that glittered on her finger. Beth and Callan had gotten engaged a few weeks ago. "Congrats on the engagement to Scotland's finest midfielder."

"Well, I love him in spite of that," she joked. "Anyway, anytime you want to attend a game, let me know. I can always get tickets."

"Thanks. I appreciate it."

"You don't strike me as a fangirling type, but I'm forewarning you that Callan and Baird will be here in about five minutes."

I felt Sebastian tense and bit my lip against a snort as his voice strained a bit. "Here? In five minutes?"

Beth raised an eyebrow. "Was I wrong about the fangirling?"

Remembering the day he almost tackled me when he found out I knew Callan, I gave a bark of laughter. "Very wrong."

"Hey, I do not fangirl. I'm ... appreciating how jealous

Harry and Zac are going to be when I tell them I met Keen and McMillan."

Unsurprisingly, Sebastian was unflappably cool with *Keen* and *McMillan* when they arrived at the party fifteen minutes later. He greeted them with his usual laid-back affability and told them, as if it was no big deal, that he was a Caley United fan. The footballers took it in stride. When I first met Baird McMillan, he'd been loud and gregarious, and I had the impression he would flirt with a wooden pole if it was the only object in the room. However, this was my first time seeing him since his traumatic head injury. While he was still somewhat flirtatious, he was quieter. More introspective. There was a shift in his eyes. A somber, sober quality in him that hadn't been there before. Perhaps the accident had changed him. It hadn't been that long since the incident, so it was possible he was suffering psychological side effects. A near-death accident will do that to a person. Only time would tell if the change was permanent.

Sebastian was chatting easily with the footballers and my cousin Luke and his boyfriend. Uncle Cole and Uncle Cam had broken away from the other older men to discuss football with them.

"How is Baird?" I asked Beth. "He seems a bit different."

My cousin's expression tightened with concern. "He is different. For the first few weeks after his injury, he was like a totally different person, snarling at everyone, wanting to be alone. You know how social he is, so it was worrying. But the last few weeks, he seems to be getting back to himself. He returns to the game in a month. They think it'll be okay by then."

"You're still worried about him."

"I am. So's Callan. Baird is socializing, but he's ... changed."

"He needs time. And if time doesn't work, then maybe group therapy with some people who have been through something similar," I offered.

"So, you don't think the injury did something to his personality?"

"I'm not a medical professional, so I don't know. If the doctor said there wasn't any brain damage, then it's doubtful. Psychological impact is not out of the question, though. It would be unusual if it hadn't affected his mental well-being. Don't you think?"

"You're the psychotherapist."

"Not yet, I'm not. Four more years to go."

Beth winced. "Doesn't that fill you with horror? I was desperate to finish uni and get out into the world to make my mark."

I chuckled. "Another four years does sound exhausting. But it's what I need to do to get to where I want."

"I'm in awe of you."

Pleased, my cheeks heated. "That means a lot coming from you."

Beth nudged my shoulder with hers. "You seem happy. Is he treating you well?"

I looked over at Sebastian who grinned at something Baird said. "He makes me so blissfully happy, it's terrifying."

"Oh, aye." Beth slid her arm around me, giving me an affectionate squeeze. "You're definitely in love."

I nodded, not denying it.

"It's true he's a member of the royal family?"

"Aye, but I don't want anyone mentioning it. He doesn't like to make a big deal of it. He's not a working member of the family, you know. Only thirtieth in line to the throne."

"Oh, only thirtieth in line to one of the oldest monarchies in the world. Aye, that's not a big deal at all."

"Japan's monarchy is way older," a new voice interjected.

We turned to find Maia, my uncle Logan's daughter, smiling at us in greeting. The three of us embraced, talking over one another as we did so.

Uncle Logan was Aunt Shannon's brother. When Aunt Shannon hooked up with Uncle Cole, Logan became a part of our family. He hadn't known he had a daughter until Maia showed up on his doorstep when she was fifteen years old. Maia kind of brought Logan and his wife Grace together. Grace had been his neighbor and she stepped in to help him through the process of sudden parenthood. Maia hadn't had the best start in life, but she claimed Uncle Logan and Aunt Grace had changed her life for the better. She'd attended university in London and then returned to Edinburgh upon graduation.

Now Maia, at only twenty-nine years old, was a senior fashion buyer for one of Edinburgh's most exclusive department stores, Pennington's. She was also engaged to some financial bigwig I'd yet to meet. I don't think anyone but Maia's parents and her brother Lachlan had met the bloke.

Maia had grown into a striking beauty. She'd inherited her dad and aunt's unusual violet eyes and in adulthood she'd tamed her thick dark hair so it was enviously sleek and shiny, lying so perfectly down her back I had to think there was some magic involved.

Because of her job, Maia always looked amazing. Her style was professional with a sexy, feminine twist. Today she wore wide leg pants, high heels, and a cropped oversized cashmere sweater.

"You didn't bring the fiancé?" Beth asked, staring past

Maia as if looking for him. "When are we going to meet him?"

Maia's expression turned irritated. "Will was supposed to be here, but a work thing popped up at the last minute. At this rate, you all will meet him at the wedding."

"I thought I heard your voice."

I glanced up to see Baird had crossed the room and was smiling flirtatiously down at Maia.

To my surprise, she beamed back at him and gave him a familiar hug. The goalie embraced her and held on a wee bit too long to be merely friendly.

Beth shook her head, smirking, as I shot her a questioning look. I recognized her silent "I'll tell you later" face.

"You look great. How are you?" Maia asked as she pulled away.

Baird remained in her personal space as he stared at her in a very nonplatonic fashion. "Much better. Especially now you're here."

"Stop it," she admonished, giving him a playful shove.

Their eyes held for a tad too long.

Ooh, there was a definite spark there between my engaged cousin and the sexy football player.

"You two know each other?" I asked, my curiosity running rampant.

"I introduced them months ago," Beth replied.

"And then Baird came into Pennington's looking for a tux for some event or other." Maia shrugged. "We started chatting."

"Then Maia came to see me in the hospital."

"She did?" Beth frowned. "You did?"

Maia nodded. "Of course. Why wouldn't I?"

"So, you're friends?" Beth's gaze darted between them. "Since when?"

Baird shrugged. "A while. Shouldn't we be?"

"Does Will know?"

Frowning, Maia sighed. "I'm allowed to have male friends."

"Callan would not be amused if I had a friend who looked like Baird."

Baird scowled. "Eh, you do have a friend who looks like me."

"You know what I mean. You're more like a brother than a 'male friend.'"

"Och, well ... now I'm equally offended and honored."

"What's the chat?" Callan said as he and Sebastian approached our group.

Sebastian wound his arms around my waist, pulling me back against his chest where I went happily.

Callan slid his arm around Beth as she peered at him with drawn eyebrows. "Did you know Maia and Baird are *buddies*?"

Her fiancé shrugged. "Didn't I tell you that?"

"Nope."

"Why are you being weird about this?" Maia crossed her arms over her chest. "Is it because I'm older than you guys?"

"Oh, aye, you're ancient, gorgeous," Baird teased.

"I'm not being weird. I'm ... surprised. Usually I know these things."

Luckily, Beth was saved from having to explain her awkward reaction to Baird and Maia's newly developed friendship because our pseudo-cousin Sara arrived.

Mum, Dad, Uncle Cam, Aunt Jo, and Belle reached her first as the rest of us crowded around, waiting to greet her. Sara blushed at the exuberant welcome, her eyes misty with grateful tears. As we waited our turn, I explained to Sebastian who Sara was, that after her parents died our own parents had made sure she never felt as if she was without family.

Sebastian processed this and then replied, "Now I understand why you're so amazing."

I couldn't hold back my giddy smile. "Oh?"

He nodded solemnly. "This room is filled with very good people."

Emotion clogged my throat. "It is. I'm lucky."

"Thanks for bringing me here, Sawyer."

"You're not overwhelmed?" I teased.

"Oh, absolutely." He bent his head to press a quick kiss to my lips. "But only in the best way possible."

CHAPTER FORTY-SIX
SEBASTIAN

Two Months Later

My small suitcase sat open on the bedroom floor, clothes and toiletries piled on and near it, readying to be packed. Lily sat at my desk, her laptop open as she edited her dissertation. She'd gotten some feedback from her advisor and had given herself the impossible task of attempting to execute the changes before we left for spring vacation. Even though my parents were in the middle of reconciliation, they hadn't taken back their invitation for me to use our family villa in the south of France.

Miraculously, I'd already submitted my dissertation. Classes had finished and we had three weeks before final exams started. Lily had agreed to accompany me and my friends to the villa, so long as I didn't tease her mercilessly for studying while we were there. I promised I wouldn't as I would also be studying. Sometimes. However, I had villainous plans to distract Lily a little so she had some *fun* before her exams.

I'd invited Sierra and Maddie along because I knew Lily was sad about her friendship group breaking up. As much as I wanted Lily all to myself, *I* wasn't going anywhere. Sierra and Maddie were leaving at the end of May, and the girls should have what time they could together.

Two months, I thought staring at my gorgeous girlfriend as she frowned at her laptop. We'd been dating for two months. It was public knowledge now. When I'd posted a photo of us on social media, I got a call from my family's PR department. Apparently, the press was asking for a comment about the status of my relationship. I didn't think anyone cared. However, I was strangely elated at the idea of the world knowing Lily was mine. I told them to confirm the relationship and warned Lily there might be some articles published about us.

Sure enough, a few tabloids, clearly in want of better stories, tried to contact us both for comment. We ignored it and the articles that were published. Most of the public weren't interested in who I was dating when there were so many people between me and the throne.

Mercifully.

Lily addressed our relationship on the podcast, but she refused to make it an anecdote. She offered advice to other people and couples as per usual, but my girlfriend was very determined that our relationship remain private.

I would have done whatever made her happy. But I liked the fact that what happened between us was, well, just between us. It made her mine and only mine in a way that soothed my inner caveman. I didn't even know that bloke existed inside me until Sawyer.

"I can feel you staring at me," she murmured.

I grinned. "I can't help myself."

"Try. It's very distracting."

"How distracting?"

Hearing the invitation in my tone, Lily gave me the side-eye. "There will be plenty of time for sexy shenanigans at the villa. Right now, I'm trying to concentrate."

"Sexy shenanigans? Beautiful alliteration, my love."

She gave a huff of laughter. "Read your book."

"The book is the problem." I waved the fourth tome in the romantasy series she'd gotten me into. "This one is the filthiest so far."

Lily's head whipped toward me. "Uh, excuse me, there is also a ton of character development in that book."

My lips strained against a smile. "True. There is also an awful lot of cunnilingus and exuberant cock thrusting."

She laughed even as her eyes darkened in a way that made my blood hot. "You should listen to the dramatized audio edition."

"Oh really? Would that be something you'd be interested in doing together during our holiday?"

Her thighs squeezed together. "Sebastian," she whined adorably.

Arousal flooded through me. "That good, is it? Did it make you wet listening to it? Because just reading about it is making me hard."

"You are so mean."

I threw the book aside and swung off the bed. "Let me make it up to you."

"I'm trying to work," Lily murmured unconvincingly, her resolve visibly weakened.

"You were the one who got me into these damn romance books."

She let out a squeal of delight as I hauled her off the

desk chair and carried her over to the bed. I practically threw her on it, making her laugh in surprise as she bounced against my mattress. "I suppose it is my fault, then," Lily agreed breathlessly.

"And I know just how to punish you," I teased, my voice hoarse with need as I reached for the waistband of her leggings.

Minutes later, Lily was moaning and shuddering against my mouth, her thighs tightening around my shoulders as she came.

It thrilled me how responsive she was to me. She'd told me sex hadn't been like this for her before. And while I didn't want to think about her with other men, it filled me with dark satisfaction that I was the best she'd had. I assured Lily she was the best I'd ever had too.

I kissed my way up her soft belly as I crawled over her body, my cock throbbing against the zipper of my jeans. When I reached Lily's mouth, my kiss was deep as I let her taste herself on my tongue. She fumbled with my zipper and I grew impossibly harder at the thought of her focused attention in that area.

Quite abruptly, she broke the kiss to push me onto my back.

Lust-dazed, it took me a second to recognize the tension on her face. Alarmed, I asked what was wrong. Lily swallowed nervously, which had me even more on alert. "Sawyer?"

"I haven't …" She squeezed her eyes closed briefly and then announced through gritted teeth, "I haven't gone down on you yet."

My eyebrows almost hit my hairline. It had not escaped my observations that Lily hadn't returned that particular favor. I took it to mean she didn't like performing the act.

Some girls didn't, like some guys didn't. It didn't bother me. I wanted *Lily* more than I wanted her mouth on my cock.

"I don't want you to think I'm a selfish lover."

I reached up to caress her cheek. "You know I don't think that. We only do things you're comfortable with. Okay? Do you think I could possibly get pleasure out of something if I know you're hating every minute of it?"

Her expression softened ever so slightly. "I love you. And ... I want to return the favor. It's only that ..."

"Lily, I love you too and you can tell me anything."

"I have ... and I know this isn't very sexy ... but I have a sensitive gag reflex."

Amusement tugged at my mouth, but I forced myself not to laugh because I didn't want her to be embarrassed. But she was so adorable. "That's okay."

Her brows furrowed. "Like, it's really sensitive. I can't even brush the back of my tongue without gagging."

The struggle to hold back laughter was growing. "Okay."

"You're laughing at me." She slapped my chest.

A chuckle escaped before I could stop it. "I'm not. You're just so cute, I can't help it."

When her countenance turned tight with hurt, I immediately stopped laughing. "Lil—"

"I've had boyfriends make me feel shit about it, okay. Like, trying to force me through it when it's obvious I'm not enjoying it. So ... I ... never mind." She moved to get off me and I grabbed her hips, stopping her. Possessiveness I hadn't quite gotten used to yet thrummed through me at the mention of her giving blow jobs to other men. However, anger at them abusing her overtook all emotion.

"They're arseholes," I snapped. "And they should be

shot. My father has a hunting rifle that would do the trick. Just give me their names and it's done."

Lily gave me a beleaguered look but stopped trying to get away.

I squeezed her hips again. "We do only what you want to do in this bed. I will survive a life without blow jobs."

She let out a huff of laughter. Although Lily didn't blush, there was always a certain look in her eyes that told me she was mortified. I never wanted her to feel so unsure around me she was embarrassed.

"I mean it, Lily."

She searched my face as she nibbled on her lower lip. I waited patiently, giving her space to make the next move. Finally, she asked, "What if I wanted to try ... but take it slowly?"

The thought of her mouth anywhere near my cock made it salute in answer. "We don't have to."

"I want to. If I can't, we stop. Or would that be torture?"

I grinned, shaking my head on the pillow. "No, it wouldn't be torture."

Nodding with the same determination I'd seen on her face when she was researching, Lily edged backward to tug on my zipper.

I lay perfectly still, amused by her concentration as well as totally turned on by it.

"You won't ... thrust?"

Voice hoarse, I replied, "I'll lie perfectly still, I promise."

Lily freed my cock, her hand a tight fist around it. She gave me a hard tug and I bit out an expletive at the pleasurable sensation. My heart rate picked up as Lily bent her head and took me into her mouth.

"My God." I huffed, the blood rushing in my ears.

Just the sight of her plush lips around the head of my cock was enough to make me want to come.

However, her uncertainty because of past experiences kept me in check. My hands fisted in the duvet beneath me as I tensed against thrusting into her hot, wet mouth. Instead, I lay there, watching and muttering curse word after curse word as Lily sucked what she could of me into her mouth. When she released me, it was to lick my length with such intense exploration—like I was a fucking ice-lolly she was relishing. Bloody hell!

The touch of her mouth suckling on my balls almost sent me flying up off the bed.

"Lily!" I cried out, my hips arching without thought. "Bugger, sorry."

Her sexy, pleased little smile before she took me back in her mouth was almost my undoing.

Anytime a woman had done this for me, it wasn't in this slow, seductive fashion. This torturous exploration created a more intense buildup. As I was begging for release, Lily sucked the head of me while pumping the root with her fist.

"I'm going to come," I gasped out in warning so she could release me.

Lily let go with her mouth but kept her hand around me and my mind blanked as the orgasm *exploded* through me. There was no other descriptor for it.

Shuddering, I melted into the mattress in deep, languid satisfaction. My racing pulse rushed in my ears.

Opening my eyes, I looked down to find Lily sat off to the side, a wide, amused look on her face.

"Bloody hell," I muttered, slightly stunned by the force of my climax.

"I'll say." She snorted. "I had to move out of the way, or

I'd have cum in my hair right now. That was a geyser of a climax, Mr. Thorne."

Laughing, I scrubbed a hand over my face, trying to ease out of my sex daze. Finally, I dropped my hand. "Come here, Sawyer."

Smiling, she moved across the bed. I drew her against me, kissing her softly before she cuddled into my chest. "You liked it?"

Now it was my turn to snort. "Was the geyser not evidence of such? The important question is whether *you* liked it?"

"I did." She turned to look up at me, her dimples appearing with her smile. "It was sexy. I felt good making you feel good."

Such overwhelming adoration flooded me, I momentarily couldn't breathe with it. "Do you even know how much I love you?"

"I'm starting to get the impression it's a lot." Her dimples deepened.

"And these." I reached out, brushing my thumb over the indents in her cheeks. "I'm obsessed with these."

"You are?" Her smile widened with pleasure.

"From the moment you first smiled at me with those dimples, I was a goner for you, Sawyer. I've never believed in love at first sight until I met you."

Her eyes widened. "You didn't love me at first sight."

"I did. I was just too stupid to realize it."

"It was attraction."

"It wasn't," I insisted. "I mean, it was ... but it was more. It was like a sixth sense. Like my instincts recognized you were the one. Maybe even before we met. When I was listening to you on the podcast, I ... I had to meet you. Then I did and I couldn't let you go. Why do you think I carried on that stupid charade? Or why I went to such trouble to get you to be my friend? I know it's bloody cheesy but, my soul knew before my brain did that you're the love of my life."

Emotion brightened Lily's eyes, tears trembling on her lashes. "You're the love of my life too."

I let out a shaky exhale. "It all worked out well for us, then. Thank fuck."

She reached up, her laughter tremoring against my lips as we kissed.

It was the best kiss of my entire damn existence.

CHAPTER FORTY-SEVEN

LILY

Sebastian's family's villa was nestled in the countryside not far from L'Isle-sur-la-Sorgue. It had views of the rugged, green-topped Vaucluse hills and was fifteen miles from Avignon Airport. Sebastian drove me and most of the luggage in a rented SUV, while Harry drove Zac, Sierra, and Maddie in another rented vehicle.

When my boyfriend pulled up to his family's vacation home, it reminded me how vastly different our economic backgrounds were. La Villa Aux Épines (renamed for their family name Thorne) was actually a large, five-bedroom Provençal farmhouse on a plot big enough for ample outdoor living and an impressive pool.

Sebastian took my hand and led me inside, eager as a wee kid to show it off to me. And I could see why. It was all flagstone floors, wooden beams, and impressive stone fireplaces merged beautifully with modern styling. The farmhouse kitchen was like something out of a magazine and all the bedrooms were generously sized.

"This is ours for the week." He tugged me into the

primary suite. There was a modern four-poster bed and a generous en suite with marble tiles and an enormous claw-footed tub. A set of sliding doors led straight out to the pool from the bedroom.

"It's a dream."

"You like?"

"I love," I assured him.

Sebastian kissed me, the kiss turning hungry quickly, and he began leading me over to the bed.

The abrupt cacophony of our friends' arrival broke us apart.

"Later," my boyfriend promised with a growl before guiding me out of the room to greet his guests.

————

The Thornes' French housekeeper had stocked the kitchen with food and alcohol. However, a wee bit weary from our travels, Sebastian drove us to a local restaurant for dinner. Upon our return, we cracked into bottles of chilled beer and lounged around outside all evening, chatting and laughing. It was wonderful. The boys were funny, my girls were relaxed, and I tried not to think about the fact that this was probably one of the last times we'd be together like this.

At night, Sebastian made gentle love to me in a way that brought tears to my eyes, and I fell asleep in his arms with thoughts of gratitude and amazement. There was a small tug of fear in the back of my mind that somehow this, *he*, would go away. But I thought that was normal considering my past relationships, and I was sure over time, that last remaining niggle of uncertainty would fade.

The noise of our friends out at the pool woke us the next day. We grabbed a quick breakfast and showered.

Sebastian was already in his swim shorts before I even left the bathroom, so I told him to go out.

I lingered, staring at my reflection in the large mirror that hung on the bathroom wall. Sebastian clearly loved my body, but there was a huge difference between being naked in bed with someone to walking out into the bright sunshine in a bikini that barely covered your tits and arse.

Especially when Sierra and Maddie were out there to compare me to. Both of my friends were slender in that toned, athletic way I'd never, ever be.

While my thighs and legs were toned from cycling everywhere, my arse still had a jiggle to it. My belly had that curve no amount of tummy crunches in the world could rid, and my boobs were very much hogging all the attention in the bikini top.

Unpleasant butterflies fluttered awake as I tried to force myself out of the bathroom.

This was ridiculous. I hadn't felt this self-conscious in ages. But suddenly, I was Lily from six months ago, covering the rolls of fat on my belly when I sat down.

"What is taking so long?" Sebastian asked, barging into the bathroom without knocking.

I opened my mouth in protest but cut off at the heated look on his face as he ogled my body.

He swallowed comically. "Dear God, am I to spend the entire holiday with a tent in my shorts?"

Instinctually wrapping my arms around my belly, I let out a huff of embarrassment.

Sebastian scowled, coming up behind me but only to unwrap my arms. "Why are you hiding?" His countenance cleared. "Is that what's taking so long? You are *actually* hiding?"

"No," I lied, my eyes wide as they met his in the mirror.

His expression turned chiding as he smoothed his hands down my hips. "You look beautiful. You always look beautiful."

"It's not ... my boobs look ridiculous."

He stared intently at them, his cheeks flushed at the crest. "They look spectacular. Mesmerizing. You should always wear this."

Hearing the sincerity in his voice, I chuckled, relaxing a wee bit. "Even in the height of winter?"

"Yes. We'll get you a fur coat for whenever you have to go outside."

"A fake one."

"Absolutely."

He gave my boobs a playful squeeze that made me squeal. Laughing, he stepped back. "Come on, before I can't leave this room for anatomical reasons."

I was still laughing as he gripped my hand and led me outside.

———

Other than Sierra wolf-whistling at me upon my appearance, I quickly forgot my self-consciousness as I lazed by the pool with my friends. Sebastian said we were lucky the weather was so pleasant. He informed us that sometimes April was very rainy and mild, but we'd stumbled upon a wee spring heat wave.

The boys and Sierra and Maddie fooled around in the pool. I did for a bit until the pull of the sun lounger drew me and I settled on it to study. Studying proved more difficult than I'd foreseen, however, and I ended up switching from my study notes on the iPad to my book app.

"Are you reading those filthy books you've gotten Sebastian into?" Zac called out to me mid pool volleyball.

Irritated, I replied, "They're not filthy just because they have sex in them. Thrillers have sex in them, but people don't call them filthy books."

"She's right," Sebastian agreed. "They are excellent stories. The graphic sex scenes are merely a bonus."

My lips twitched, but I kept reading.

At Zac's snort of disbelief, Harry opined, "I think they're rather good. I finished that one about the true crime podcaster who falls for the local sheriff. So many red herrings. I never would have guessed who the killer was."

"Don't spoil it for me!" Sierra cut him off. "I haven't finished that one yet."

Chuckling to myself, I delighted in my victory of having turned half of our friend group into romance readers.

———

The next day, I got up early to get some studying in while everyone slept. Once my friends were awake, we split as a group. Zac, Harry, and Maddie wanted to explore the village and Sebastian wanted to take me hiking along the river. I invited Sierra along because I knew she loved a good walk. Sebastian once more proved himself to be considerate as he tried not to be overly physically affectionate with me. I knew it was so Sierra didn't feel like a third wheel, and I was grateful to him for it.

It was a lovely morning and as Sebastian guided us back to the villa, his long strides eating up the ground ahead of us, I looped my arm through Sierra's and pulled her close.

"I'm glad we got to do this."

She smiled, a hint of sadness in it. "I am too."

"I'm going to miss you so much."

"Don't," she muttered. "Every time I think about it, I want to cry."

"We'll see each other," I vowed. "My postgrad schedule allows a better part-time job schedule next year. I'm going to save so I can come visit you."

"I'll come visit too." She patted my hand. "I'm so beyond happy to see you this happy, Lil. You deserve someone who treats you like you're precious because you are. And Sebastian treats you that way. He adores you." Sierra grinned. "You brought down the ultimate playboy."

I rolled my eyes. "Don't remind me of his previous wicked ways."

"Oh, come on, you don't need to worry about that. He's over that phase of his life."

"I know." I shrugged.

"But ..."

"No buts," I whispered, not wanting Sebastian to overhear.

"There's a but."

I shot my boyfriend a look to make sure he was out of hearing range. "I didn't miraculously turn into the most confident girl on the planet since dating him."

"Meaning?"

"That maybe there will always be a small part of me that worries he might grow bored with me."

Outrage flashed across my friend's face. "Lily—"

"I know that's my own insecurities talking. Believe me. I'm working on it."

"He *loves* you."

"I know he does," I promised her. "Now, let's talk about your love life. Are you planning on settling down any time soon, Sierra Palmer?"

She wrinkled her nose. "Nope. I have at least six more years before I need to think about taking that part of my life seriously. When I finally settle down, it will be safe in the knowledge that I've had enough sex to (a) not have any regrets, and (b) choose a life partner who knows what he is doing in the bedroom."

I chuckled. "Good plan."

"Does, uh, Mr. Thorne know what he's doing?" she dared to ask.

I understood her hesitation. While I'd always been forthcoming with details of my past relationships or dates, I'd been stubbornly closed mouth about what was between me and Sebastian. "Ohhhh *yes*."

"*Really?*"

"Aye." I stared smugly at Sebastian. "Twice now I've almost blacked out."

"Seriously?"

"Seriously."

"Well done, Mr. Thorne."

"There should be a monetary reward for his achievements. He should teach classes. Men should pay him for those classes."

Sierra giggled loudly and Sebastian glanced over his shoulder, eyebrow raised in questioning amusement.

"Don't tell him that, though," I said hurriedly. "It's good to keep him on his toes. Keeps him eager and *motivated*."

My friend laughed harder.

"What's so funny?" Sebastian called back to us, smiling.

"We're just happy," Sierra called back.

His expression softened as he glanced between us and nodded before turning around.

My friend sighed sappily. "Make a clone of *him* and I might consider settling down."

I grinned, hugging her closer, beyond giddy that Sierra approved of my Sebastian.

———

As beautiful as the day started, unfortunately, it did not end well.

Late afternoon, Sebastian, Sierra, and I made a wee picnic and ate it outside. Then we changed into swimwear to hang out by the pool again. Zac, Harry, and Maddie returned and soon joined us.

"Guess who we bumped into," Zac said as he waded into the water behind Maddie and Harry. He answered before Sebastian could ask who. "Colette." He pronounced it with a French accent.

Sebastian had his arms around me, I was floating against his chest, so I felt his sudden tension. Realization clenched my gut before Zac blithely continued in explanation to the rest of us. "Colette is the daughter of a shop owner in the village. Sebastian hooked up with her two years ago."

Harry cut him an annoyed look before changing the subject. "Who wants a beer? I'll grab them."

"Those French girls know what they're doing." Zac ignored him.

Sebastian's arms tightened around me. "Zac—"

"I swear I can't even look her in the eye now. What was it you called her? The Dyson?" He laughed uproariously.

"The Dyson?" Maddie asked stupidly.

"Zero gag reflex," Sebastian's moronic friend explained.

"Would you shut the fuck up?" Sebastian snapped angrily.

Zac's expression fell. "What?" He looked at me, and he blanched. "Lily, I'm sorry. I forgot."

I gave a brittle shake of my head, waving off his apology. But the reminder that Sebastian had been a manwhore, mixed with my insecurity over my own abilities in that area, plus the idea of him talking about a woman in that way ... I wanted to shrug off his embrace.

"And I never called her that. You did." Sebastian bent his head to my ear. "I promise."

I nodded, shivering at the caress of his breath on my skin.

"Sawyer, I love you," he vowed hoarsely.

Shoving down my own insecurity, I patted his arm. "I know. I love you."

Zac grimaced. "Shit, I really am sorry."

"Probably a bad idea you invited her over here tonight." Maddie glowered at him. "Why would you do that?"

Sebastian pulled me tighter against him. "You did what?"

His friend gaped. "I wasn't thinking. Sorry."

The sound of my phone ringing distracted me from the annoyance burning through my blood and fogging my brain at the thought of having to socialize with one of Sebastian's flings. "I have to get that."

"Sawyer ..."

I tugged out of Sebastian's hold, and he reluctantly released me.

Zac muttered another apology to his friend as I got out of the pool. Grateful for the interruption, I snatched up my phone. It was my mother. "Hey, Mum, what's up?"

Words hurried and shaky, she relayed without preamble, "I don't want you to panic, because she's going to be okay, but January was in a car accident this morning."

Despite her words, panic froze me to the spot. "What? She's okay, though?"

I was vaguely aware of everyone in the pool growing quiet as Mum replied, "She's got a few bumps and bruises ... and a broken wrist. But she's going to be okay."

"A broken wrist?" I cried.

Splashing from behind had me whirling around. Sebastian was wading out of the pool, his features etched with concern.

"January was in a car accident."

"Bugger," he muttered, hurrying out as my friends all followed him.

"She's in the hospital getting checked over, but we're taking her home soon. I wanted you to know," Mum continued.

"I'm coming home."

"No, Jan wouldn't want that."

"I'm not staying here after my sister's been in a car accident. I'm coming home."

"Lily—"

"I'm coming home. I'll let you know when I'm about to board my flight."

"Okay, sweetie. I'll see you soon."

We hung up and Sebastian pulled me into his arms. "She's fine," I mumbled against his chest. "But she's broken her wrist. I need to go home."

"Of course. We'll pack now and grab the next flight."

"No." I jerked away. "I'm not ruining your holiday. Or my friends' holiday."

"Lily, it's fine. We understand." Maddie rested a hand on my shoulder and squeezed it. "We'll all head home."

"No," I insisted. "Please. It'll make me feel worse if you

guys leave too. Just stay and enjoy yourselves and I'll keep you updated."

"I'm not letting you fly alone when you're distressed." My boyfriend's tone brokered no argument.

Yet I argued back. "You come with me, and it'll make me feel really bad."

"Sawyer—"

"Please stay."

He glowered angrily at me. "Fine. But I'm driving you to the airport."

"That I will allow." My hands shook as I ran them through my wet hair. "I'm going to pack."

CHAPTER FORTY-EIGHT
SEBASTIAN

Yesterday 19.46

Lily: I've arrived. Jan's home now so heading straight there.

Sebastian: Let me know when you get there.

L: I will.

S: And let me know how Jan is.

L: I will. Love you.

S: Love you too.

Yesterday 20.31

L: I'm home. Jan is exhausted but okay. Her wrist is in a cast. I feel better seeing her for myself.

S: I'm glad. Tell her I'm asking for her.

L: I did. How are things there?

S: Zac just told me he invited a bunch of people here tomorrow. They're flying in from all over.

L: How do you feel about that?

S: It'll be a distraction from missing you, I suppose.

L: 🤍

Today 09:22

S: Morning, Sawyer. How's Jan?

L: Grumpy but fine. Annoyed at me for leaving you to rush to her side. The gratitude is overwhelming, I tell ya. 😊

S: LOL. Secretly she's pleased. I'm not. I missed waking up with you this morning.

L: Me too. What are the plans for today?

S: Apparently, I have a bunch of guests to welcome, remember. You?

L: I might as well study. Jan's grumpiness is making me long for you and the villa. Remind me I love her.

S: You love your sister.

L: Thanks. Go have fun. We'll talk soon.

S: Love you, Sawyer.

Today 22.23

L: So how did your day go?

S: It has been one long party. The place is packed with people. My parents might kill me if they ever find out.

L: Who are all these people?

S: Uni friends. School friends. People we know from the area.

L: Well, try to have fun. Go enjoy yourself. We'll talk tomorrow.

S: Night, Sawyer.

L: Night, Thorne.

I stared down at the string of texts between me and Lily, wanting her with me for multiple reasons. Truthfully, I was glad January was okay. She reminded me a lot of Juno, so I'd grown rather fond of Lily's younger sister. If Juno had been in an accident, no matter how major or minor, I would have gone home too, so I understood Lily's decision to leave.

But right now, she would have been the perfect buffer. Last night, I'd locked myself in my room, avoiding Colette who came over as per Zac's invitation. Now, however, with all our old friends and acquaintances filling up the place, I didn't feel like I could or should abandon the party. Colette, as it turned out, wasn't a problem. She'd shown up again but was all over Zac.

The problem was Gisele Martin.

Gisele was the daughter of a family friend. Her mother was English, her father French, and we'd run in the same circles for years. We'd slept together casually over those years. Since she was on spring holiday from Oxford at her family's château a mere half an hour from here, she'd taken up Zac's invitation and appeared with three of her friends.

The drunker she'd gotten, the more she attempted to drape herself all over me.

An edge of panic and guilt followed me around the party with her. No matter how many times I told her I had a girlfriend, she merely laughed like I'd said something funny.

"You look like a hunted animal." Sierra appeared at my side, holding out a fresh beer.

"You saw?"

"Oh boy, did I see. Who is she?"

I explained my history with Gisele. "I've told her multiple times about Lily," I promised. "It only seems to make her come-ons worse."

Irritation tightened Sierra's features when she caught sight of Gisele strolling into the kitchen with a drunken sway to her hips. "Leave it to me." Before I could speak, Sierra marched across the room and halted Gisele's travels. I couldn't hear what was being said, but Sierra's body language was aggressive and Gisele's defensive. When Gisele said something with a haughty lift of her chin, Sierra suddenly put her face in hers and said something that made Gisele blanch.

She raised her arms in a surrender gesture, threw Lily's friend a huffy sneer, and whirled around on her six-inch heels, departing the room.

I slumped with relief. "Thanks," I said with genuine gratitude when Sierra returned to my side. "What did you say to her?"

"I told her I'd give her a reason to get another nose job if she didn't back off my friend's boyfriend."

I sniggered. "You didn't?"

"That girl is already an entitled spoiled brat, something I can tell from having only met her for a minute. Add in too much alcohol and she needed some serious incentive to back off. You actually slept with her?" Sierra wrinkled her nose in disgust.

"I didn't really care if she was nice." I shrugged. "I wasn't looking for a relationship."

"Well, no wonder you fell for Lily if all you did before was surround yourself with the Giseles of the world."

"It's not all I did. I've hung around with some very nice women. Smart, sexy, funny women. But none of them felt right. Because they're not Lily."

Sierra clinked her bottle against mine. "That's how I feel about her friendship. Never had a friend like Lily. I'm going to miss the hell out of her."

At the trembling of her mouth, she took a pull from her beer bottle to cover up the emotion. I drew her into my side and pressed a quick kiss to her temple. "She's going to miss the hell out of you. But I promise I'll take care of her."

Lily's friend gave me a grateful nod. "Do you need me to stick around? Play bodyguard some more?"

"No. Go have fun."

"Great. Because I have my eye on your old school pal Brendon."

"Brendon Platt?"

"That's the one."

I grinned. Lucky Brendon. "Don't let him get too drunk, then. He's useless to anyone after four beers."

Her eyes widened comically. "Noted. Bye!"

I waved her away and dug my phone out of my pocket. My fingers hovered over the text conversation between me and Lily. Yet it was late. She might be asleep. And surely, I should be able to enjoy a party with my friends without my girlfriend around.

We would not become one of those sickening codependent couples.

I threw back a swig of beer and ventured through the kitchen to find Harry.

———

For a while I had fun with Harry catching up with old friends. An hour later, however, people were starting to break off into couples (throuples and groups in a few cases too), and the pool looked like the beginning of an orgy. Harry seemed pissed at Sierra for making out with Brendon (I made a note to ask Lily if she knew if something had actually happened between those two) and had buggered off with some random. Zac was hooking up with Colette again. And Maddie had disappeared into her room and locked it ages ago.

Deciding it was time to do the same, I locked the bedroom door on the primary suite and sank down onto the bed with a groan.

I'd turned down the music, but it still played softly

throughout the house because of the wired sound system. There were trickles of laughter and groans coming from the pool area.

My parents would kill me if there was any damage to the house after this blowout. I was going to kill Zac for arranging this without asking.

The plan had been to drag myself up off the bed to change into something to sleep in, but I must have started to drift off because it took me a second to realize there was someone climbing over my body.

My eyes flew open as her face came toward me and her lips crashed down over mine.

The too-sweet perfume couldn't mask the overwhelming smell of rum from the many rum and Cokes she'd downed that evening. Gisele groaned into my mouth, her fingers tugging down the zipper on my jeans.

What the hell!

There was a flash of white behind my closed eyelids and I put it down to the molten anger flooding me. It took everything in me to control it so I wouldn't hurt her as I gripped her arms and shoved her away. Her taste on my tongue made me want to bloody spit all over the bedcovers. "Get off!"

Horror filled me to realize Gisele was straddling me without her shirt or bra on. She laughed, cupping her bare breasts with a ridiculous pout. "Oh, come, Sebby, you know you want to."

"Fucking hell." I pushed her with less gentleness this time and rolled off the bed.

The sliding doors out to the pool were half open, as were the curtains. I'd forgotten to lock them.

Gisele pouted, arching her back as she turned to huff, "You're seriously rejecting *me*?"

Grabbing the throw off the bed, I threw it at her. "Cover yourself up and get out of my room. In fact, find your clothes and get out of my house."

"You can't be serious?"

Rage bubbled beneath my surface. "If I did to you what you just did to me, it would be sexual assault. Do you understand that?"

"No, it wouldn't because I wouldn't have shoved you off!" Gisele pushed away the throw and jumped off the bed, moving past me to grab the top and bra she'd discarded. "I can't believe this!"

"Really? Because I think I made myself clear all bloody night!"

"You don't have to yell at me!"

I grabbed my head in my hands, my fingers tightening into my hair in agitation. "Get out before I say something I will regret."

Gisele frantically pulled on her clothes, anger mottling her pretty face. "You're a prick!"

"And you're an entitled brat." I gestured to the door. "There's your exit."

"Fuck you!" She fumbled with the bedroom door and flew out of it, slamming it so hard I think I heard a crack.

"Wonderful." Shaking from the incident, I moved to close the sliding doors and lock them, pulling the curtains over. I still felt a bit dazed by the whole thing, but an edge of panic rode me at the thought of Lily ever finding out and assuming the worst.

She wouldn't, though.

She trusted me.

I knew she had a history with men that made it hard for her, but she trusted me.

A loud banging on my bedroom door had me growling

in renewed fury. If Gisele was back ... I crossed the room and yanked it open.

Zac stood on the other side, his expression dark and sullen.

"What? What's happened now?"

"I saw Gisele coming out of here."

His accusatory tone had my panic rising to the fore. "It's not what you think."

"Really? Because I think you're Sebastian Thorne, the biggest player I've ever met in my life."

"I didn't cheat on Lily. Gisele broke in here and tried to assault me."

Zac scoffed. "Right. Well, I'm sure that was hard for you."

"Zac—"

"You're going to hurt her." His face twisted with anger. "You don't deserve Lily and eventually you will hurt her. So do us all a favor and break it off now before you mess up her life." My friend turned on his heel and stormed off before I could respond.

My gut twisted with fear and dread.

I knew I hadn't done anything wrong.

And yet, that insidious voice that had kept me away from Lily in the first place reawakened at Zac's words. He was my friend, after all. He knew me well.

What if he was right?

What if I ended up hurting the one person it would kill me to hurt?

CHAPTER FORTY-NINE

LILY

When I woke up, something crinkled beneath my face.

"What the ..." I grumbled, reluctantly lifting my head. Forcing my eyes open, my bleary sleepy vision cleared, and I was suddenly very aware of the ache in my neck.

Oh, bloody hell.

I'd fallen asleep studying last night.

I was still fully dressed. My iPad screen and laptop were black, having probably lost charge, and I'd fallen asleep on an open textbook. Said page was now wrinkled and covered in spots of drool.

"Lovely." I wiped my mouth as I hesitantly arched my neck from side to side to work out an aching kink.

Sounds from downstairs filtered up to my childhood bedroom. My family was awake, and I could smell bacon. My stomach grumbled because I hadn't eaten much in the last thirty-six hours. I'd been too worried about January, even though she assured me she was fine. She'd been in a black cab when a white van ran a red light and smashed into the side of them. Unfortunately, because the cab was going to pull over once it was through the lights, Jan had removed her seat belt. When the van smashed into them, she went flying off the bench seat and broke her wrist upon trying to catch her fall. It could have been way worse.

The thought of anything happening to her had plagued me and my parents. Eventually, assured by her grumpy insistence that she was fine, I tried to get some studying in and spent most of last evening doing just that.

I reached for my phone. It thankfully was charging on my bedside table. I swiped the screen to check the time.

It was after nine in the morning.

Noting a couple of text notifications, I frowned when I saw one of them was from Zac. Since we rarely texted, I clicked on it.

> You need to know who he really is.

The words were attached to an image that caused the room to start spinning wildly.

———

My heart raced in this fluttery panicked way that made me jittery and nauseated. It also made it hard for me to think clearly. I watched my sister study the image on my phone and tried not to hyperventilate as I revisited the photo in my mind. After all, it was burned on my brain now.

It was a photo of a half-naked woman straddling Sebastian while they kissed on the bed *we'd* made love in, in his family's villa.

Poor Jan, with her broken wrist and bruised ribs, had come into my room to wake me up for breakfast only to find me near to passing out at the evidence Zac had sent that the man I loved was cheating on me.

"Did you look at this properly?" Jan asked, expression dead serious for once.

"It's imprinted on my bloody brain," I gritted out, nausea rolling in my gut. "I feel sick."

"Okay, let's take a minute. Before you saw this photo, would you believe Sebastian would cheat on you?"

No! I believed if Sebastian no longer wanted to be in a relationship with me, he'd break things off first. He might have been a player, but he wasn't some horndog, as my mum would say, who couldn't keep it in his pants. The man had self-control and decency. He was more honorable than that!

Oh.

Jan gave me a toothless, grim smile. "That's what I thought. Look at it again. Really look at it."

I shakily and reluctantly took the phone from her. Jan had zoomed in on a portion of the photo. The strange female with her mouth on Sebastian. My pulse increased. Suddenly, the photo told a completely different story. It looked like she was kissing him, and he was screwing his face up, his hands pushing her away, not pulling her close.

"Your boy doesn't look like he's enjoying himself. Your boy looks like he's trying to push her off him."

So many questions roiled in my head. "How did she end up in the room with him half-naked? How did it get that far? Why would Zac send me this?"

"I have no answer for you." Jan gave me a sympathetic pat on the shoulder. "But I wouldn't go jumping to conclusions. If you trust your guy, you should talk it out with him."

I didn't know if I was brave enough to. Having been

cheated on multiple times, it was extremely hard for me to not trust the *obvious* tale the photo told. "Maybe I should call Sierra and Maddie. See if they know anything. Before I call Sebastian."

"Sounds like a plan. I'll be downstairs eating your bacon roll since your appetite is probably gone."

I grimaced. "I'm sorry. I didn't even ask how you are?"

"Eh, forgiven, considering the circumstances. And I'm okay. I promise. Come find me if you need me. I won't tell Mum and Dad what's going on."

"Thanks."

She gave me an awkward one-armed hug because she was still wary of moving her left arm with the cast on. I hugged her back, trying to hold in my panicked tears, and waited until she'd left the room before I shakily called Sierra.

My friend picked up on the tenth ring with a groggy, "Ullo?"

"Sierra, it's me."

"Lil?"

"Aye. Can you wake up, please? It's important."

"Is Jan okay?"

"Jan's fine. It's something else."

"Okay. One sec." I heard rustling and then a male voice lazily demanding, "Come back to bed."

Momentarily distracted from my own drama, I asked, "Is that Harry?"

Instead of answering, I heard her speak to the man. "I need to take this."

"Then come back to bed."

That definitely sounded like Harry. A few seconds later, I heard a door shutting and Sierra spoke. "Sorry. What's up?"

"Did you sleep with Harry?"

"We, uh, we've kind of hooked up a few times. I'll tell you about it later. What's up?"

My heart sped again as I tried to think of the right words to explain the situation. "Did ... did something happen last night, Sierra? Was there ... was there a girl with Sebastian?"

"What?" Sierra's tone was sharp. "What do you mean? How do you ... Look, I don't know who's been talking, but there was this haughty trust fund baby chasing Bastian around the party all night." She sounded breathless with agitation. "He couldn't have been clearer with her if he tried. He told her over and over he had a girlfriend and to back off, and it got so bad I had to threaten the crazy, drunk bunny boiler."

I stood up, my legs shaking as a tentative relief started to flood through me. "When did you last see Sebastian?"

"Lily, what is going on? You know he would never cheat on you, right?"

Guilt riddled me at Sierra's absolute certainty. "Is ... is he around?"

"I don't know. You woke me up. Try his cell. Will you tell me what is going on?"

"I will," I promised. "I need to speak to Sebastian first."

"Okay. Note that I am worried, though. Please call me back when you can."

"I promise."

We hung up and I stared at my phone, trying to catch my breath. Finally, realizing Sierra might go to Sebastian before I could call, I hit his name.

He answered after three rings. "Morning, Sawyer." His voice was raspy like he was either waking up or he hadn't slept. "How's Jan?"

"S-she's ... she's fine."

"What is it?" Sebastian was suddenly alert.

"I ... I ... I'm trying not to jump to conclusions about something." My tears started to come before I could stop them. I had to take a minute to get them under control.

"Okay, you're scaring me," he replied thickly. "Tell me what's going on."

"I ... I'm s-sending you something, okay? It was sent to me this morning." Swiping at my tears, I tapped into my messages and attached the photo Zac sent me. "Okay. I've sent it."

"All right. The suspense is killing me, though. Why are you crying, angel?"

Sniffling, I lied, "I'm not."

"Oh. Well then, you're doing a very good impression of it. Okay ... got it." He went quiet a moment and then suddenly burst into loud, furious cursing. I flinched, switching the volume down on my phone since I had him on speaker. Finally, he began pleading, "Lily, God, Lily, I swear to God, this is not what it looks like. This woman is an old friend, she was harassing me all fucking night, I thought I'd gotten away from her, and I was trying to get to sleep and she crept in through the fucking slider doors while I was sleeping and accosted me. I threw her out, like, seconds after this photo was taken. Who the fuck took the photo? What the ... Lily, God, Lily, please tell me you believe me." His voice caught on a sob. "Please."

I squeezed my eyes closed in utter relief and the tears spilled over. "I believe you."

"Oh hell," he wheezed out and I heard a thud. "Lily ... I'm so sorry this happened. You must have thought ... what ... who sent this? Lily? Sawyer, please talk to me or I might start to think you don't believe me after all."

"I do believe you. I ... for a moment there ... I'm sorry."

He was quiet as he processed what I hadn't said. "I understand, my love. But I would never do that to you."

"I showed Jan the photo and she asked me if I believed you'd cheat. My instinct was no. Even if one day, you grow bored with me, you would end things before you ever betrayed me. You're too honorable not to."

"While I really love most of what you said ... I will never grow bored with you. Is that what you think?" He sounded pissed off.

I flushed, having realized I'd unwittingly shared one of my deeply buried insecurities about our relationship. "No one knows what the future holds."

"I do," he snapped. "You're never getting rid of me. Get used to that."

My lips twitched. "That sounded like a threat."

"Take it however you please."

I laughed at his belligerent response, disbelieving I could laugh right now.

Sebastian did not laugh. "Lily, whoever sent that photo ... they set me up with Gisele. Maybe even sent her to me."

Gisele. I wrinkled my nose at her name. If she was in front of me, I might slap her with my thickest textbook. She'd assaulted my boyfriend!

Yet something else pierced my anger. Something incredibly sad and confusing.

Sebastian's friend had betrayed him. "It was Zac. I'm so sorry, but Zac sent me the photo."

CHAPTER FIFTY
SEBASTIAN

The traitorous bastard was nowhere to be found, though his things were still in the guest room he was using. Striding to Harry's room, I knocked loudly but barged in before he answered, only to halt abruptly at the sight of Sierra sprawled half naked across my friend.

"Bugger, sorry." I whirled around, giving them privacy. Apparently, Brendon had been cast over. But I couldn't think about my friends' drama right now. "Have you seen Zac?"

"No, I haven't left the room," Harry answered groggily. "What's wrong?"

"I'm going to kill him, that's what." I marched out.

"Is this about that call I got from Lily?" Sierra called after me.

I was too busy throwing open the other guest room door to answer. The bed was rumpled and the room was littered with plastic beer cups and food wrappers, but there was no Zac. I rapped my knuckle on Maddie's door, just in case. Lily's friend opened the door as Harry and Sierra caught up with me, dressed in the wrinkled clothing they'd worn the night before.

Maddie frowned. "Everything okay?"

"Is Zac in there?"

She shook her head, wide-eyed at my sharp tone. "No. Is everything all right?"

"Apparently, he's going to kill him," Sierra answered as I moved through the house, cursing the wreckage left by the party.

"Look at this mess!" I threw my arms up as I stood in the kitchen diner.

"We'll help you clean up," Sierra offered calmly. "Do you want to tell us what's going on?"

"What's going on is that arsehole invited all these people here and now has buggered off before I can kill him!"

"You want to kill him for throwing the party?" Maddie asked, confused.

"No!" For ... for trying to break me and Lily up.

For trying to take away the one person who meant everything to me.

Why?

Why would Zac do that?

He was ... he was supposed to be my friend.

I let my rage overtake my hurt because it was easier to deal with the anger.

At least it hadn't worked. At least Lily trusted me. Believed in me.

"Did Zac tell Lily about Gisele?" Sierra guessed.

"Worse. I think he sent Gisele into my room last night while I was sleeping because he sent a photo of the incident to Lily." I tugged out my phone to show the photo to Harry because Zac was his friend too.

Harry's expression slackened as Maddie and Sierra gasped at the photograph of a half-naked Gisele accosting me. I explained to them what had happened.

"And Zac sent this to Lily?" Harry asked in disbelief.

"Yes."

"*That's* why Lily called me." Sierra's pretty expression tightened with rage. "She asked me if something happened last night."

Unease moved through me at the thought of Lily calling Sierra first.

"I told her about Gisele harassing you all night. Then she said she needed to speak to you."

Had Lily decided I could be trusted because of Sierra's account of the evening?

No. I shook that out of my head. She told me she knew when January asked her if she trusted me. There was no way I was letting that little shit mess with us like this.

The sound of the front door opening and slamming shut had me whirling.

Zac sauntered into the kitchen with a paper bag of groceries in his arms. "Great, you're all awake. We ran out of milk, so I thought I'd—" He didn't get a chance to finish the sentence because my fist connected with his face.

Between the surprise of my action and the force of it, Zac stumbled and fell on his arse, the groceries spilling everywhere. My knuckles throbbed as I flexed my hand, preparing to hit him again.

Zac got over the shock quickly, glaring up at me as he wiped at the blood seeping from his now split lower lip. "I take it Lily called."

"Please tell me this isn't true." Harry was suddenly at my side. "What are you playing at?"

Zac got to his feet, kicking the groceries away. He

shrugged insouciantly. "I don't know what you're talking about."

I flew at him again, but Harry bound his arms around me, yanking me back.

"He's not worth it, Bas. Not worth it. And Lily didn't believe him. Remember that. He didn't win."

Harry's calming tone worked, and I shrugged off his hold, letting him know silently I wasn't going to hit Zac again.

Zac, however, glowered. "Don't tell me she's so pathetic as to believe you?"

"Don't be a prat, Zac. If he flies at you again, I won't hold him back and he will kill you," Harry warned.

Sensing my now ex-friend enjoyed watching me out of control, I took a deep breath and exhaled slowly. "Why would Lily believe a lie? One that you apparently orchestrated."

He shrugged, an irritating smirk curling his mouth. "What if I did?"

"So, you did?" Harry stared at him as if he'd never seen him before. "You sent Gisele into his room while he was sleeping and then took that photo?"

"Maybe."

My fists clenched so tightly, one of my knuckles cracked. "Why? What the hell did I do to you?"

He leaned back against the kitchen peninsula, crossing his legs at the ankles in a relaxed pose that made me want to swipe his legs out from under him. "I thought Colette might do the trick, but apparently she fancied me this time around." His eyes were hard with a fury I didn't understand. "Then I saw Gisele following you around like a drunken moron. The girl has never heard no in her life. You pricked her pride, Bas. It was easy enough to convince her to slip into your room. It was nothing personal. Well, maybe a tad personal. My instructions came from a higher order than you. I struck a deal, and I was upholding my end of it."

"Struck a deal?"

Zac grinned, as though he was delighting in what he was about to tell me. "With your grandmother. Princess Mary. She reached out to me. Requested I interfere in your relationship with Lily. Apparently, while she's not as hung up as your mother on the idea of you marrying someone of noble blood, she does take offense to the idea of you being in a relationship with a girl who speaks publicly about her sex life on a dating podcast."

His words had me stumbling back in shock and confusion.

My grandmother had put him up to this?

My grandmother?!

He chuckled. "How can you be so surprised? You're a member of the royal family. Do you really think they'd welcome Lily Sawyer, sex advice podcaster, into their fold?"

Even as my mind whirred with the added betrayal, I focused on my ex-friend. "Why did you agree to do that to me? You know how I feel about Lily."

"Because your grandmother made certain promises about inviting my mother into their circle. It would be quite the coup for her ..." A vulnerable light entered his eyes. "I thought it would ... well, never mind."

He thought it would make his mother give a shit about him?

He'd tried to wreck my relationship because he didn't get enough attention from Mother Dearest?

I was going to kill him!

"That's not just it." Maddie suddenly spoke up, stepping beside me. Her eyes were narrowed with distaste. "He's in love with Lily. I've suspected it for ages."

My head whipped back to Zac. "Are you?"

He glowered at Maddie.

I flew at him, yanking him to me by the shirt as I snarled in his face, "Are you in love with my girlfriend?"

Zac shoved at me, pulling at his shirt to no avail. "Let go of me!"

"Tell me!"

"Yes!"

I released him in abject surprise, not expecting him to admit the real reason for what he'd done.

His eyes were filled with such malice and resentment, I was momentarily stunned. "The golden child," he spat. "Everything comes easily to you. You get everything you want. Even her. Did you know I saw her first? Had been working up the courage to talk to her for ages. Then you swooped in. And the fuck of it all is that you might not have cheated with Gisele last night, but you will one day. You'll hurt her. And I would ... I would never hurt Lily."

"You hurt her this morning," Sierra hissed.

"For her own good!"

"For fuck's sake." Harry turned away, running a shaky hand through his hair. "Who the hell are you?" He whirled back around, staring at Zac in pained confusion. "How could you do this? We've all been friends since first year."

Something flickered across Zac's face, but I didn't give him a chance to respond to Harry because something had occurred to me. "You didn't merely set me up. You went so far as to knock on my door after taking that photo and accuse me of cheating with Gisele when you knew I hadn't. You tried to screw with my head. Do you even realize how messed up that is? There's something seriously wrong with you." I retreated from him in disgust.

"Why not send the photo anonymously?" Maddie asked. "You must have known Lily would tell Sebastian who sent it."

Zac shrugged wearily. "Uni is almost over. We're graduating. What did it matter if Thorne finally found out what I really think of him?"

I stared at him in quiet fury. This bloke *loathed* me, and I'd thought he was my friend. It was difficult to wrap my head around. How quickly he'd made me despise him in return, though. "We're done. If that isn't clear. We are done. You can leave now. And you can kiss any connections to my family for your mother goodbye. My grandmother played you too because she'd never let a snake like you near the family. Even if the two of you apparently have snakelike qualities in common."

His face screwed up in rage until Harry addressed him. "Just to be clear, we're done too. I want you out of my flat by the time we get home."

"It's my flat too," Zac said stupidly.

"Oh, is it? I thought my father paid for it. You were my friend, so I let you live there. You are no longer my friend. Therefore, you no longer live there."

Something like regret tightened Zac's expression, but he pushed past us and gritted out. "I'll get my stuff."

"Oh, and, Zac," Harry called after him.

Our ex-friend reluctantly stopped and turned around.

Harry's face was harder than I'd ever seen it. "Your phone. Now."

"Why would I give you my phone?"

"So I can delete that photograph and make sure you don't have it saved anywhere else. You see, if that photograph ever sees the light of day, I'll not only make sure you're blacklisted, I'll make it my mission to haunt your life, ruining every good opportunity that comes your way. Are we clear?"

Zac swallowed nervously. "*We* were friends."

"You don't do what you did to a friend."

"I didn't do it to you."

"You did it to Bas, so you did it to me too."

Gratitude cut through the chaos of emotion flying around inside me as Zac, face red with indignation, pulled his phone from his pocket and tapped on the screen.

Harry took it from him and spent a few minutes checking it, while we all stood in tense silence.

"Photo is deleted. He had it saved to the cloud, but I've deleted that too." He handed it back to Zac with a look of disgust. "Remember my warning."

Zac snatched it back and stormed off toward the guest rooms without looking any of us in the eyes.

I clamped a hand on Harry's shoulder as Zac disappeared out of sight. "Thanks, mate."

"Always."

"I'm sorry."

Harry cut me a look. "You've nothing to apologize for. I feel like I need a long hot shower. How did we not know what a creep he was? He really hates you. How did he hide that? And why? I mean, other than Lily, why? You've never done anything but be his friend."

"We missed it." I shrugged unhappily. "It happens. Let's not drive ourselves crazy trying to untangle the inner workings of his twisted mind."

"Lily's really okay?" Maddie asked, expression troubled.

Remembering her soft crying on the phone, I had the sudden urge to pull a plane out of the sky so I could get on it and fly back to her. "She is. Once I explained everything. I'm not looking forward to explaining the rest of it to her. Zac's ... *crush* or my bloody grandmother's behavior."

Maddie winced. "Aye, sorry about that."

I'd deal with my grandmother later.

Sierra gestured to the house. "We should clean up and go back to Edinburgh."

"I'm sorry for all the drama and for messing up your holiday."

Her eyes cut flirtatiously to Harry. "Hey, I still had a good time. I'm going to shower first and then I'll help out."

"Just a *good* time?" Harry asked, trailing after her.

"Did they sleep together again?" Maddie asked quietly.

"Again?"

She chuckled. "They've been shagging on and off for the last few months. I think they like each other but are in denial."

"Harry never told me."

"She's Lily's friend. He probably didn't want you getting overprotective."

"I wouldn't. Sierra's a big girl. So, they like *like* each other?"

"You really want to talk about Sierra and Harry's friends-with-benefits situation?"

Dismay and indignation churned in my gut. "If it distracts me from the fact that my friend and grandmother tried to manipulate Lily out of my life, then yes."

Maddie squeezed my arm in sympathy. "You got it. It started the night of our Thanksgiving dinner ..."

CHAPTER FIFTY-ONE

SEBASTIAN

Calling a princess isn't that easy. Even when she's your grandmother. I'd left a message with her staff but so far, the message had gone unreturned. The house was back to normal, the guests all booted out, and Zac had departed.

I'd chatted with Lily again, filling her in on everything.

Now it was after one o'clock and we were getting ready to leave to catch our flight. As Harry helped the girls load their luggage, I called my mother.

I couldn't spend the entirety of the flight worrying if she'd known about this.

"Sebastian, darling, how are you? I checked and the weather is glorious. I must say, I'm a little envious we gave you the villa this time around. We don't usually get such lovely weather in spring, but I know you work hard—"

"Mum, may I speak?"

"Of course. What's wrong? You sound strange."

Without delay, I relayed to her without going into too much graphic detail what had occurred with Zac and Gisele and Zac's confession that my grandmother had put him up to it.

"Mummy?" my mother gasped. "Oh, surely not."

"So, you didn't know about this?"

"Of course not, darling. I'd never do anything so underhanded."

"What's going on?" I heard my father ask in the background and had to wait with growing impatience as Mum told him.

"Dear God, she didn't?" Pa gritted out unhappily. Then his voice was clearer down the line as he asked, "Are you all right, son?"

"Thankfully. But it could have broken me and Lily up."

"Did she say why?" Mum asked, and I realized I was now on speakerphone.

"Oh, Granny hasn't returned my call," I huffed out bitterly. "But Zac said she said it was because of Lily's dating podcast."

"Ah." Mum sighed. "Yes. Mummy did mention she wasn't at all happy about that. It is a little inappropriate."

Instantly irate, I snapped, "Lily could plaster herself naked all over social media and I still wouldn't break up with her for you, for Granny, or for anybody in that bloody stifling institution. All right?"

"I'm not saying it was right. I'm just saying ... you are Princess Mary's grandson, and it isn't entirely appropriate that your girlfriend talks about her sex life to the public."

"Mum—and I'm directing this at you because as someone who worked his way up in life, Pa couldn't give a shit about appropriate behavior and backgrounds—I know you've had a difficult year, so I don't want to be an arse. However, considering the many aristocratic girls you've shoved my way over the course of the last year, I need your promise that you didn't have anything to do with this."

"I already told you I didn't. I *promise*."

"Good. Then I need you to do something for me."

"What would that be?"

"When you meet Lily, and you will meet Lily, you will be kind to her."

"Of course I will." She sounded offended.

"No, I mean it, Mum. No introducing me to women you think are more suitable behind her back or in front of her. Ever."

"Sebastian—"

"Lily isn't going anywhere. Whatever thoughts you might have in your head about the future, let me clarify them for you. One day I am going to marry Lily Sawyer. That's where our relationship is heading, and not you, not Granny, not Queen Anne, or a battalion of Royal Marine commandos are going to stop us. I love you all, but if any member of this family does anything to try to ruin my relationship with Lily again, I will walk away from all of you for good. If you don't want that to happen, I'd start treating Lily like your daughter-in-law *now* because one day she will be."

There was a moment of silence after my impassioned speech and then Pa cleared his throat, "Understood, son. And I'm very happy for you. I'd love to meet Lily if you feel this strongly for her."

"Thanks, Pa. You will. Soon," I promised. "What about you, Mum?"

Mum let out a shaky exhale. "I understand. She must be quite something, then, if you'd throw us over for her?"

I winced at the hurt in Mum's voice. "I love her, Mum. I

love you too, but I won't be made to choose. That was the point I was trying to make."

"You said the same thing to your mother, love, when they didn't like me," Pa reminded Mum.

"I did, didn't I." Mum's tone softened. "Okay, Sebastian. I promise to treat Lily well." Then she repeated dazedly, "She really must be something."

"She is."

"Well, I look forward to meeting her too."

"So that's a promise not to interfere?"

"Believe it or not, my darling, your happiness means more to me than status."

Relief shuddered through me. As honest as I had been in my ultimatum, it would have killed me to walk away from my family. "I love you both."

"We love you too, darling. Well, I best go. Apparently, Mummy and I need to have a serious conversation."

We said our goodbyes and I turned toward my friends whom I hadn't realized were standing behind me, silently listening in.

Maddie started clapping as Harry and Sierra burst into laughter. Lily's roommate grinned affectionately at me. "Bloody hell, do I wish Lily had been here to hear that speech. Should I tell her to start planning the wedding?"

I rolled my eyes. "Shut up."

"I wonder if she'll let us choose our own bridesmaid gowns?" Sierra mused.

"Do I need to wear a tux?" Harry smacked me on the shoulder. "Or with Lil being Scottish, are we talking kilts and flying hairy balls?"

"I hate you all," I lied as I jumped into my SUV with the sound of their good-natured taunts ringing in my ears.

CHAPTER FIFTY-TWO

LILY

With Jan deciding to return to her student accommodation to study for her finals, there was no reason for me to remain at my parents' house. Mum knew something was up, so I'd told her Sebastian had an awful argument with one of his roommates and I'd explain everything later. I'd then returned to the flat to wait for Maddie and Sebastian to return from France.

Sebastian had called me on his drive to the airport and told me what Zac confessed.

It made me sick that one of his best friends had been a snake in the grass. I was also annoyed with myself for not picking up on it, considering what my chosen profession was. From the discussions I'd had with Zac, I'd say his mother's narcissism had affected him more deeply than anyone knew.

And he'd confessed to being in love with me. I shuddered at the thought, suddenly recognizing his affectionate behavior on a new level. I wouldn't usually consider someone falling in love with me creepy. It was flattering and lovely under normal circumstances. But I wondered if Zac had grown to covet whatever it was Sebastian had. That he didn't know me well enough to be in love with me, but he could have developed a twisted infatuation because I was Sebastian's.

I didn't want to think about it.

I didn't want to see Zac ever again after what he'd tried to put us through.

Unfortunately, I would probably at some point have to meet Sebastian's grandmother. Princess Mary. Who hated me so much she enlisted Zac to drive a wedge between me and her grandson, like some dastardly plot from a soap opera.

Bloody hell.

It was an unpleasant realization that your boyfriend's family didn't approve of you. Even worse when that family was one of the most powerful families in the world.

I wouldn't let panic or insecurity drive us apart, though. After I got off the phone with Sebastian, I had a voicemail from Sierra relaying everything Sebastian had said to his parents. It was hard to make out some of it because Harry and Maddie kept interjecting with jokes and teasing.

The gist of it was that I didn't need to worry about my boyfriend's commitment.

Sebastian was all in and apparently not even a battalion of Royal Marine commandos would stand in his way of being with me.

When my flat buzzer sounded, I hurried over, my brow furrowing when Sebastian asked me to let him up. If Maddie was with him, she would have brought him straight up to the flat. I waited at the open door, hearing his footsteps as he took the stairs two at a time.

Then suddenly he was there, looking tired and travel worn but rugged, unshaven, and sexy.

And mine.

Our eyes locked as he bounded up the last flight of stairs. His gleamed with love and determination and something a wee bit desperate.

I understood.

We were both shaken from the drama and the thought of what could have happened if our bond had been weaker than it was. Sebastian swooped me into his arms, kissing me hungrily as he guided me backward into the flat. He slammed the door shut with his foot as I ran my fingers through his hair, deepening the kiss.

When we came up for air, I blurted out, "Where's Maddie?"

Sebastian clasped my face between his palms. "She grabbed a cab and went to Shaun's. I think mostly to give us privacy."

I loved my roommate.

"How are you doing?" he asked, letting out a shaky exhale.

"How am I doing? How are you doing? Zac was your friend."

"He was both our friend." Sebastian scowled. "I can't … I don't want to think about him right now. Lily." He pressed his forehead against mine. "Thank you for believing in me. I know considering what's happened to you in the past that it couldn't have been easy for you."

My eyes burned with tears. "I realized something. Sometimes when we don't believe in people's devotion to us, it's because we don't believe in ourselves. It can be hard for me to believe in myself. But I have to start recognizing that what my past boyfriends did to me was about them and not about me. You've given me so much of my confidence back. I believe in you and maybe I believe in me now too."

"Good," he growled the word against my lips. "I am so glad Olly decided to be a prick and come after your podcast. We would never have met. This tiny campus, and I could have missed out meeting the love of my life."

I pulled him closer, sighing happily. "But thankfully, Olly was a prick."

Sebastian chuckled and then pulled back. "Did you know Harry and Sierra have been sleeping together for months?"

"I had my suspicions." I tugged on my boyfriend's shirt, pulling him toward the bedroom. "We'll discuss our friends' sex lives later. I want to make love to the man who is apparently going to be my husband."

Sebastian rolled his eyes but followed me in. "Those bastards told you."

I laughed, kicking off my slippers. "Every single word."

CHAPTER FIFTY-THREE
SEBASTIAN

Several Months Later

For perhaps a week after we'd graduated, I'd witnessed a weight lift from Lily's shoulders. She was relaxed in a way I hadn't ever seen and seemed determined to enjoy the break from studying before her postgrad started in September.

Now, however, the tension was back. If you didn't know her like I did, you might never notice it. But it rode her shoulders and tightened her lush mouth ever so slightly.

There was reason for it, though, as we were attending the first day of the Royal Ascot. For five days, Queen Anne officially opened the race meet, and Opening Day was one of the biggest deals in the royal calendar. Many royals attended, and it was the one event my mother and father put in an appearance. I think mostly because my mother loved horses, and my father loved the food.

Lily and I stood with my family in the royal enclosure, a

coveted and exclusive area of the racecourse atrium. The
Royal Box sat dead center of it. Queen Anne and her eldest
son, Prince Alexander, were currently seated in it, laughing
together. My cousin Alexander had a rapier wit and was the
only one who seemed to be able to make his mother laugh
like that in public.

We were surrounded by aristocrats, world leaders, a
sheikh or two, and celebrities. Lily spotted the reigning
princess of pop and one of the most famous people on the
planet drinking champagne with her famous actor
boyfriend. I saw the surprise flash across my girlfriend's
face as her head whipped to mine.

My lips trembled with amusement as I watched her
carefully blank her expression once she realized how
obvious she'd been. I slipped my hand discreetly into hers
and squeezed. "Are you all right, my love?"

"Aye," she replied. "Just don't leave me."

"Never. Have I told you how beautiful you look?"

She gave me a grateful smile and squeezed my hand in
return. There *was* a dress code and Juno had helped Lily
pick an outfit. A little blue straw beret with a veil was
pinned into a hairstyle that had taken Lily ages to do this
morning. My girlfriend looked like a 1950s movie star in an
ankle-length retro dress with a conservative neckline and
short sleeves. The skirt poufed out because of the petticoat
underneath it, and the tight bodice accentuated her tiny
waist and curvy chest. It was supposed to be demure, yet I
still wanted to rip it off her in a not-demure-like manner.

Her eyes flashed at whatever she saw on my face. "Stop
looking at me like that," she demanded through gritted
teeth. I barely heard her over the noise of the loudspeaker
and din of the crowd, but I understood her well enough.

I gave her a cocky smirk and sipped at the champagne

from the flute I held in my free hand. I was already planning how to seduce her out of the dress tonight. I might even ask her to keep the hat on. And the shoes. Her shoes were distractingly sexy.

"We're here, we're here!" Juno's loud voice had us both turning to find her and Leona coming down the busy steps of the atrium toward us. Thankfully for my sister, Granny didn't give two hoots about sexuality. She was fine with Juno publicly being in a same-sex relationship. She just didn't want her talking about it on a bloody podcast.

Okay, maybe I was still holding a grudge.

Lily hugged Juno and Leona, some of her tension easing at their appearance. "I'm so glad you're here."

"Terrified, are you?" Juno asked. "Yes, it is all rather intimidating until you remind yourself every single one of these people have to evacuate their bowels every day. They get diarrhea too. Isn't that reassuring?"

Princess Olivia, wife of Prince Frederick, the son of my grandmother's grandfather, turned to glower at Juno in distaste. She stomped her cane down hard before her aide helped her further downstairs.

We waited until she was out of earshot before bursting into laughter.

"Are you all causing trouble?" Mum popped up behind us with Pa in tow. They were dressed in their finest. The sight of Pa's tie made me very aware of the one currently strangling my own throat. I hated a bloody tie. Not to mention the layers of clothing I was currently sweltering in because it was June. Whoever decided men's attire for the Royal Enclosure should include a three-piece morning suit with a top hat in the summer was a sadist.

"Juno is being her charming self."

"Princess Olivia looked like she'd swallowed—"

"Her husband's—"

"Don't you dare finish that sentence," Mum cut off my sister's interjection.

Lily and I had to look away from each other or we'd dissolve into another round of raucous laughter.

I'd introduced my parents to my girlfriend after our final exams. Lily had returned to my childhood home with me for a long weekend. Not only did it give my parents a chance to get to know her, but I got to see for myself that my parents' marriage really was back on track. Pa had stopped drinking too. Clearly scared by his dependency on it during his separation from Mum, Pa was sober. In solidarity, Mum had rid the house of every single drop of alcohol.

Being home, seeing them doing so well, gave me a chance to tell them about my change of career decision. Bolstered by interest from a prestigious art gallery in London, I'd decided to pursue my art career. I didn't take up their offer to sell my artwork because they expected a whopping eighty percent commission, but it gave me the confidence to increase my prices exponentially. Unbelievably, my original pieces were selling for thousands of pounds.

I explained to my parents I was going to use some of my trust fund to buy a proper studio and my own gallery in Edinburgh. They were taken aback but seemed prepared to support me no matter what. Especially once I showed them the art. Mum got misty-eyed at the idea of me hiding my talent from her.

Lily had said goodbye to Sierra and Maddie. It was incredibly emotional for her, but I'd make it my mission to bring the women back together again for visits. Maddie would visit more often because she and Shaun were still together. Harry and Sierra's short-lived friends-with-bene-fits came to an end, and I wondered how attached Harry had gotten there. He'd been in a foul mood since she left.

With the girls gone, Lily and I were looking for our own place in Edinburgh. When I relayed that to my parents, it seemed to really settle on them how serious we were. Pa was generous and welcoming to Lily, and I could tell he liked her immediately. Mum, while welcoming, took a little longer to warm up. I didn't know if it was merely a mother's prerogative to be wary of the woman her son chose to love. However, when Lily and I were leaving, Mum had pulled me aside and said, "She's lovely, darling. Utterly lovely. I understand now."

It was such a relief to have back the parents I'd grown up with and not the crazy people they'd turned into last year.

"It's time." Mum gave Lily a reassuring smile. "My mother, Princess Mary, would like to meet you, Lily."

I tried to keep the scowl off my face. It seemed ridiculous I had to bring Lily before my grandmother to pass some kind of inspection after the shit she'd pulled. Granny hadn't returned my call, but Mum had spoken to her, and she'd agreed to back off. Only because Mum had relayed that Lily was no longer on the podcast and because Granny was apparently appalled by the methods Zac had used to do the job she'd employed him to do.

Mum didn't tell Granny Lily's younger sister January was still on the podcast or that she was outrageous on it in a way Lily had never been.

"We're with you." Juno clapped a hand on my shoulder and gave Lily a nod. "We'll all go together."

Lily tightened her grip on my hand and straightened her shoulders. "All right."

My grandmother was surrounded by the members of my family, including my uncle Michael, Mum's eldest brother, the Earl of Avon, and his wife Pamela. His children, my cousins, were all in attendance, some with their younger brood who were over the permitted age of ten years old.

"Your Highness." My mother gave a small curtsy to her mother since we were in public. "I'd like to introduce you to Sebastian's girlfriend, Lily Sawyer. Lily, this is Sebastian's grandmother, Princess Mary, my brother Lord Michael, and his wife Pamela." She didn't bother introducing the rest of the family as Lily curtsied while I bowed.

"Your Highness," I greeted her with a curt tone.

My grandmother raised an eyebrow, giving me a pointed look before turning to Lily. "Are you enjoying the Royal Enclosure, Ms. Sawyer?"

Lily wet her lips nervously. "I-I am, Your Highness. Thank you for the invitation."

Granny's eyes darted over her, and I couldn't help but slip my arm around Lily's waist protectively. My mother cleared her throat, but I refused to let Lily go. Granny gave me a chiding look before asking, "Your family originally hails from Scotland, then?"

"Yes. My mother grew up in America, but my grandfather is Scottish. As are my paternal grandparents."

"I thought you grew up in Edinburgh," one of my cousins, Grant, interjected. "You sound like a *Scot*."

I'd never liked Grant. Pretentious arsehole. I glowered at him for the way he spat the word *Scot*.

"Michael, perhaps you ought to have provided your children with a better education," Granny retorted haughtily. "If your eldest son is confused by a person sounding like a Scot when they are Scottish."

I heard Juno cover a snort behind me.

Grant huffed. "I only meant that *my* friends from Edinburgh don't sound Scottish."

"Is that what you meant?" Granny cut him a quelling look. "Well, let me educate you. Most people from Scotland have a Scottish accent, and if Barton ever heard you use that tone, you'd never be invited back for Boxing Day shooting ever again."

My lips twitched with laughter. Barton was a stout Highlander and head gamekeeper at the Queen's Scottish estate in the Highlands. Grant practically panted after an invitation every other year.

"I've only been invited once, anyway," he muttered like a spoilt child.

"Grant, do be quiet," Uncle Michael uttered wearily before taking a bored sip of champagne.

"Are we done then, Your Highness?" Juno popped her head over my shoulder. "I'm starving and would like to eat now."

My grandmother peered at Juno. "I heard you said something inappropriate in front of Olivia."

"I might have."

Granny nodded. "Very good." She waved her hand. "Off you go and grab me something to eat too while you're at it."

And just like that the interrogation—I mean, introduction—was over.

———

Hotels were booked to the rafters around the racecourse, so I'd hired a private car and driver to take us to our hotel a whole county over.

We'd been chatting about our day, laughing over Juno's

absolute disregard for royal etiquette and how my grand-mother seemed to love her more for it.

The driver dropped us off at the hotel and Lily and I got into the lift alone. "She seemed to defend me," Lily suddenly said, confusion coloring her tone as I pressed the button for her floor. "Your grandmother. When that man got all snotty about my accent."

"That was my cousin Grant. He is a complete arse and nobody likes him."

"I don't understand your grandmother. She tried to break us up and now she's defending me?"

"Mum says she agreed to keep out of our relationship when she learned how Zac had gone about trying to break us up." I gestured for Lily to get off the lift first as the doors opened on our floor. "Now that she's decided not to be a villainous royal caricature, she won't let you be insulted. She has a strange sense of honor that way."

"You forgive her, then?"

"Not quite. I did enjoy watching her put Grant in his place. Granny might have her own set of standards regarding the institution's public face, but she hates people who act superior to others. And she has a lot of Scottish friends. She didn't like his tone." I let us into the room.

After I shut the door behind us, I stopped Lily, looping my arms around her waist to pull her back to my chest. The thick skirts of her dress rustled with the movement, and I pressed my lips to a spot on her nape that turned her to jelly.

"Oh," she moaned softly, melting into me.

I brushed my mouth over her ear. "You know I love your accent, right?"

Lily sighed happily. "I love yours too."

"And you know I know you hated every single second of this event and I'm so grateful to you for coming with me?"

She turned her head toward mine. "I know."

"We never have to do it again. I am under no obligation now to attend royal events."

"But won't that cause problems with your family?"

"Very doubtful."

"We can go to the events," she replied half-heartedly.

"You were so uncomfortable, which makes me even more uncomfortable than I already was at these things to begin with."

"They're your family."

"We can visit them in private."

"Sebastian—"

"Unless twenty-nine members of the royal family are struck down by some fatal mysterious plague, there is no need for my attendance."

"Well, if that's what you want. But know I can pull up my big-girl knickers and attend one of these things ... once in a blue moon."

I kissed behind her ear, grinning. "Thank you for the generous offer." My hands slid down her poufy skirt. "Now, how do I get underneath all this fabric?"

Lily giggled and the sound made me grin with wicked intent.

"Is this an attempt to challenge my skills?" I teased, pressing a kiss to her bare shoulder. "A kinky version of Where's Wally?"

She let out a cackle of laughter, making me grin harder. I patted down the skirts, pulling at the fabric.

"Seriously? Are we playing a sexy version of Hunt the Thimble?"

"Hunt the What?"

"You've never heard of Hunt the Thimble? Well, in the usual version, there's a thimble or a small object involved. In this version"—I raised my head to whisper hoarsely—"I'm referring to your pussy."

Lily shivered and waved an agitated hand toward her back. "The buttons. Just unbutton it."

"Really? You want to do it the ordinary way?"

"Sebastian!"

Laughing even as my cock throbbed, I started unbuttoning the back of the dress. Lily pulled the sleeves off and then shoved it and the petticoat beneath down and stepped out.

Then I almost came in my trousers. I gaped at her as she turned in her heels to face me. "What are you wearing?" I sounded like I'd been smoking for twenty-four hours straight.

Lily smoothed her hand down her hips. Her black lace-edged bra barely contained her lovely breasts ... but it was the black lace-edged suspender belt, garters, and thigh-high stockings that were making all the blood in my body rush toward the appendage desperately straining for freedom.

Lily recognized the look on my face and smiled sexily as she unpinned her little hat and threw it on the floor. I watched her unpin all that magnificent hair and fisted my hands as it tumbled around her shoulders.

"Don't," I insisted quietly when she went to remove her heels. "Keep those on."

She raised an eyebrow, eyes dancing with mischief. "As you wish, Your Highness."

Impatient heat rioted through me, my words gravelly as I prowled toward her. "Inaccurate, but effective."

"You like that, do you? *Your Highness.*" Her laughter

turned into an excited squeal as I swept her off her feet and carried her over to the bed.

As I tumbled down over Lily, intent on ravishing and loving her until she was replete and warm in my arms, I wished for the first time since I was sixteen, a year I'd stopped wishing for anything because I didn't believe I deserved to.

Now I wished.

I wished for a lifetime of this.

A lifetime of her.

ACKNOWLEDGMENTS

Thank you to everyone who ventured back into this world with me and brightened my day with your beautiful messages of love for these characters. Perhaps, unsurprisingly, I've slipped back into this world as though I never left. Lily and Sebastian's story was a pure joy to write and one I wish I could experience over and over again. The writing journey, however, is always made easier by the support of those around me.

To my friends and family, thank you for always supporting me no matter what. I love you lots.

To my amazing editor Jennifer Sommersby Young who battled the flu to get these edits back to me so I could stay on deadline. And also for saying this was in your top five! You are a superstar warrior and I appreciate you more than I can say.

Thank you to Julie Deaton for proofreading *A Royal Mile,* catching all the things, and for loving on Lily and Sebastian too!

And thank you to my bestie and PA extraordinaire Ashleen Walker for helping to lighten the load and supporting me more than ever these past few years. I really couldn't do this without you.

The life of a writer doesn't stop with the book. Our job expands beyond the written word to marketing, advertising, graphic design, social media management, and more. Help from those in the know goes a long way and I have my very own "social queens"! A huge thank-you to Nina Grinstead, Christine, Kim, Kelley, Sarah, Josette, Meagan and all the team at Valentine PR for your encouragement, support, insight, and advice. You all are amazing!

A huge thank you to Sydney Thisdelle for doing all your techy ad magic to deliver my stories into the hands of new readers. You make my life infinitely easier and I'm so grateful!

Thank you to every single influencer and book lover who has helped spread the word about my books. You all are appreciated so much! On that note, a massive thank-you to the fantastic readers in my private Facebook group, Samantha Young's Clan McBookish. You're truly special. You're a safe space of love and support on the internet and I couldn't be more grateful for you.

A massive thank-you to Hang Le for creating another stunning cover in the world of ODS.

As always, thank you to my agent Lauren Abramo for making it possible for readers all over the world to find my words. You're phenomenal!

Finally, to you, my reader. Thank you for reading. I couldn't do this without you.